RISE OF
TOURNIQUET

DANIEL DORN

Rise of Tourniquet
Copyright 2021 by Daniel Dorn

Cover Artwork by Rose Pokrywka.

Interior sketches by Daniel Dorn.

ISBNs: 978-1-7363899-0-4 (Print)

978-1-7363899-1-1 (Ebook)

CONTENTS

THE PROLOGUE

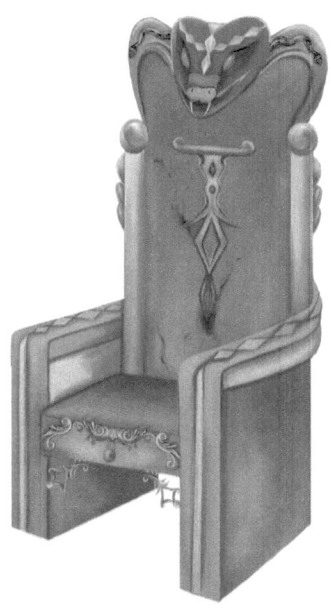

Name: Captain Red Blood

Weapons: Sword Agnomus-holds power of the 7 seas.

Powers: Lifeforce absorption-depletes others' soul energy, causing reverse
aging to user.

Power Type: Elemental

CHAPTER ONE: CAPTAIN RED BLOOD

S anctus Port. We left that place this morning just an hour ago. The ocean was gloomy but the best part of all, no 5X. The 5X is a group of five kids: Jared, Fern, Jak'al, Kat, and Cyclone. We fought several times in the past, but I give my thanks to Neptune for having them out of my hair today. No matter what I do, I can't seem to rid my mind of that one battle on that dark, stormy night; last night.

***

All of us were fighting on the ship I am sailing now. Well, the first one. You see, my ship was called the Hira Conte', "The Lovely Goddess." It was named after the woman that the Brothers of Legend, Eka and Iro, had both fallen madly in love with. Regardless, with the help of my allies, Metsys and Dahnarak, we had the upper hand against the 5X.

Metsys had pale white metallic skin and a black visor arrayed with glowing green digital symbols stretched from the top of her forehead to the bridge of her nose. Unlike most cyborgs, she could change her facial expressions, but she usually wore a devious smile that covered a large portion of her face. Her blue iron dress had several pieces chipped off as a result of fighting. The same could be said for the now-sparking wires that made up her artificial ponytail.

The other valued ally in my three-manned crew was Dahnarak, a demon from the pits of Gavalakia. He sprang out of the invisible world wearing only a yellow clown suit decorated with purple polka-dots; however, his most gruesome feature was his marvelous claws that dragged to the ground with a single extension. About a third of his face was composed of nothing but devilishly sharp fangs, whilst the other two-thirds contained a pair of orange eyes and matching curly hair on top of his head that freakishly contrasted with his gray skin. Together, the three of us made the Second World War look like a simple speed bump.

Metsys' blue energy beam was immediately consumed by Fern's pollen spore counterattack prior to her fist plunging into the cyborg's cheek. Her tough metal leg then smashed downward into her opponent's shoulder with a sickening crack. Metsys turned and eyed Kat. She chuckled wholeheartedly before evading her stealth attack by activating her fusion thrusters. Metsys now hovered above them whilst Fern's eyes glowed an intense shade of green. Unable to stabilize her unique abilities, Fern's hands zapped the same color until her leather gloves melted off completely. The wooden crates aboard the ship simultaneously started to burst open. Fern lifted her hands, and the plants within the crates shot out and wrapped around Metsys' torso. Kat advanced once again, but to her surprise, the vines failed to restrain their opponent. Metsys then backhanded Kat in the jaw as she flew across the deck of the ship.

Meanwhile, Dahnarak fought against Jak'al and Cyclone. Normally, Jak'al's powerful howl would've deafened Dahnarak long enough for Cyclone's wind to knock him off his feet. This time it didn't. Everything went wrong for our opponents and right for us. It made me smile. The demon clown leaped toward Jak'al and plunged his huge claws into his furry chest.

"Jak'al!" Cyclone screamed.

"You're next!" Dahnarak hissed, retracting his claws from the giant half-human before turning to the young man. The red and silver-suited bandit brought his hands together as huge gusts of wind formed from the dismal rainy skies, then assumed the form of two fists. He shoved the whirlwinds straight into the deck as Dahnarak leaped backward before the currents could pummel him and said, "My turn!"

Jared and I fought at the crow's nest. Ice blasted from his fingertips as I deflected the beams away with my sword, Agnomus. The golden handle of my noble blade was shaped like a pair of entwined snakes enclosing a black gem which was crafted to the center of the handle. The gem seeped with a bizarre power that granted the user authority and control of the seven seas. With it, no man, woman, or child could stand in my way. That's why blockading Apex City's docks proved to be so easy—and why this fight wouldn't last much longer.

My saber flanked Jared's left side as he dodged in the nick of time. He leapt off the crow's nest and hovered over the edge, eyes blazing red with hatred. A scalding energy beam trailed from his pupils. I fell face first and lost my black feathered hat to the winds of the storm. Bringing his palms together, he shot an icy beam which instantly hindered my attempt to run once the ice glued my feet to the boards of our fighting area.

"Metsys!" I cried aloud, fixing my eyes on my ally as she freed herself from the grasp of the young women.

CHAPTER ONE

"You see, Captain," Jared spoke over the chilling winds. "You are a coward, taking people's life forces for your own control!"

I heard a thud and turned to see the cyborg squatting on the rail of the crow's nest. "And you see, Jared," her synthetic voice was somber, yet fierce. "You and your friends were foolish for coming here. And now you shall suffer the consequences." She jetted toward him and flipped while pressing the temple of her visor. A helix of electricity coiled around my shins and knees, thus enabling me to lower myself to the main deck.

Jak'al let out a harsh grunt and continued to stifle the pain while Cyclone hooked his foot around Dahnarak's ankle. Then Cyclone flew low and fast enough to make the clown's head continuously bounce into the deck. His nails angrily pierced the mast as Cyclone involuntarily changed his flight trajectory. Now heading toward the sky, the aerial manipulator flung Dahnarak even higher before delivering a harsh series of jabs and then finishing him with a crushing heel stomp to the spine. The unconscious demon spiraled to the deck, only landing after Jak'al snatched his neck, slammed him, and left him with a stomp.

Long colorful streaks circling the ship indicated that Metsys had not yet defeated Jared. After bringing myself to the main deck, Kat tried to disarm me as I punched her away. She rolled back to her feet, shooting strings of non-lethal bullets at me through her double-barreled silver pistols. They fell like flies against Agnomus, but she kept running. In one fluid movement she reloaded her guns and popped the magazines using the flat of my saber. Her bullets ricocheted upward, catching Metsys' unsuspecting fusion thrusters and causing her to stagger uncontrollably until she crashed through the ship.

The impact sent me falling through the huge burning gap of the ship and onto an antique table in the center of the galley. The legs collapsed as I felt something trickle down my side. I lifted my fancy white shirt just enough to see the mark behind the partially tattered cloth. I winced, immediately grabbing for my bleeding side.

"I can take—others' blood—why not my own?" I cursed at my abilities. To make matters worse, my friend the wrecking ball made a hole in the ship. My eyes filled with fear as the galley became overwhelmed with ocean water and weighed down the ship.

"Here!" A voice said from above. I looked up to see Fern. Her forest green suit was tattered and her cheek was slightly purple with bruises. She lowered a vine thick enough to lift me from the filling galley. "Take it!" Would the five of them not just arrest me if I gave in to her demand? Suddenly, I had a plan and took the vine. She helped me to my feet, but that didn't stop the Hira Conte' from taking on more water. "Alright," she began, "let's get you to—"

"Let's not," I murmured, spinning her and placing Agnomus against her throat.

"Fern!" Jared cried aloud.

"Jared," I started in, "perhaps this will teach you a lesson in why not to meddle in my affairs."

"You came to Apex," Jared protested. "You answer to the 5X!"

"I answer to no one, not even Neptune." I chortled, then winced from pulling a muscle at my damaged side as Fern glanced with her peripheral vision. "Regardless, we'll all be dead in a matter of seconds."

CHAPTER ONE

"We can still escape," Kat insisted, steadying her guns on me as the water continued to rise.

"Don't you know; the captain always goes down with his ship." I laughed as lightning struck the peak of the mast. We all turned toward it as it caught ablaze. "Death by fire or water?"

"Neither!" Fern cried, thrusting her elbow into my side. I went down, but not before grazing her elbow with my special touch. Instead of breaking into a run, her body immediately drained itself of all energy. She lifelessly slumped over as her eyes filled with an unfamiliar green aura. Frighteningly, her skin grew frail and thin as my physical age dropped about two decades.

I sneered at the remainder of the 5X through the face of one their age. I charged at them, parrying Jak'al's forceful move with Agnomus before stomping the stab wounds Dahnarak had delivered so viciously. Cyclone's gray eyes were locked onto me as Kat rubbed her purple feline necklace and assumed her panther form. We battled while Jared aided Fern. Her eyes continued to glow brightly.

"What?" Jared questioned once a bed of vegetation formed beneath her. Her hands raised automatically. "Fern are you— AHH!" Jared flew back due to an electric mass of colorful pollen spores shielding her. Black marks appeared on his palms and forearms. Vines the size of trucks suddenly thrashed about, quickening the vessel's sinking process.

"NO!" I screamed, watching my beautiful boat fall to pieces. "Stop! Stop!"

Not long after, we all resorted to hanging onto a structural object of the boat as it capsized. It was too late to run and too late to fly. Fern was no longer in the picture, but plenty of her plants swiped toward me. I had foolishly latched myself onto the wheel and swiped at the flying vegetation with my saber.

However, a twig-like vine snatched Agnomus from my grasp, crushed the handle, and bent the blade. Both my heart and eyes filled with wrath. I released the wheel and fell straight into the raging sea below.

Underneath the waves, a powerful entity was forming. It didn't take much to deduce that it was Fern unconsciously creating a large plant specimen. How was any of it possible? I swam toward her, screaming as I did, our conflict completely invisible to anyone above the water. The creaking of my ship falling apart echoed behind me. None of the other 5X members seemed to be conscious now, which meant they would awaken to a dead plant, if they themselves were still alive.

Fern's floating red hair formed the nucleus of the plant mass, making her much easier to spot. Not even once did I resurface for air. Adrenaline coursed through my veins as I finally reached the girl. I lunged at her, but she shot me with a purple sleep spore. My anger. My frustration and wrath. Had it truly been bottled so quickly? She sent out a vine which forced me all the way back to the ship's hull. My neck bones cracked. I managed to slip into unconsciousness before enduring the dreadful pain of another blow.

The following second everything went black.

***

The only thing I cared to remember the next day was losing Agnomus. After several years of fighting, I realized no other earthly possession could defeat it. Before now, nothing could separate my blade and I. It was like we were connected in some higher fashion—more than a mere man and sword; rather like an old pirate and the sea. When I was holding Agnomus it was like the entire ocean was centered in the palms of my hands, and now it was twisted as if it were an infant's spoon.

CHAPTER ONE

My mind was blank upon awakening. I opened my eyes to see a small blurry fishing crew wearing heavy, dull ocean-waders. The men surrounded me, eyeing me awkwardly as if they had fished me out of the sea. Above them were masts with netting that webbed between each post.

"Where are we heading?" I asked weakly.

"Um, nowhere," one of them replied while offering his hand to help me up.

I immediately recalled Fern outstretching her vine to me and lightly pushed his hand out of the way before standing myself upright.

"You okay?" he asked as I peered over the man's shoulder and toward the ocean.

"Where is the Hira Conte'?" Looking back at the men, they all bore the same confused expression at my inquiry.

"The what?" another man finally asked. My hand slithered down my side and I jumped at an odd texture. Noticing my reaction he added, "You got a pretty nasty gash there, but we managed to fix it up for you."

I lunged at him and twisted his shirt collar. "Take me to her!" I demanded, pulling him closer. "Now!"

"I...don't know...what...you're...talking about!" he choked out.

"Hey, put him down!" one of his buddies ordered, coming at me.

"Landlubber," I spat as I tossed the one I had into the bed of the fishing boat.

"What is your deal?" the first man asked while assisting the other. "Come on."

Their conversation muffled as they headed for a different boat and sped off into the blue. Dozens of boats were docked along a pier leading to a stone wall and asphalt walkway. After examining my surroundings, I stepped off the fishing boat and onto the pier only inches away.

A rumbling in the water caught my attention. I walked to the end of the pier and looked off into the area of which it came. Medium-sized fish fearfully swam out of the way of the rising object.

"What are they afraid of?" I asked myself.

"Me," a voice rumbled from below. I leaped back, falling to the pier as a man who looked to be in his forties appeared. He had neatly combed dark brown hair atop a muscular, squarish head to compliment his penetrating masculine build. A heavy black cape draped behind blood-red armor, and water spilled off his suit as our eyes met. "Hello, Captain." He spoke with a voice of authority.

"Captain?" I repeated. "Do I know you?"

"Not at all. But I know you are still weak from yesterday."

I questioned the stranger's reply and saw an empty scabbard strapped to his left hip. "What do you know about yesterday?" I asked cautiously.

"More than you." He tossed an item onto the pier in front of me. I looked closer and discovered it was my feathered hat. I grabbed for it, but he yanked it away with a green telepathic cloud. My attention was his once more. He cleared his throat. "All have lost at least one material possession within their life." He stated. "If not, then they have not yet experienced life."

"Aren't we all ephemeral?" I asked impatiently as another telepathic burst dried his dripping cape.

15

CHAPTER ONE

"What about your sword, Agnomus? I can give you that again."

"At what cost?" I asked after slight consideration. "My soul?"

"I'm not one to deal with the spirits." He explained with a stern look. "All I want you to do is join me in a series of competitions."

"What about the 5X?" I demanded. "I want to see them fall."

"If you join me, I will make sure that you get to squash Jared all by yourself." He continued. "I will assure you then; I shall return the favor of your victory by presenting Agnomus before you once more."

"You speak well," I said with satisfaction.

"As I ever have." The mysterious man smiled. "However, I must test your strength." His stance then stiffened into a fighting position.

"Fighting is a language in which I am quite fluent," I stated. "If you wish to fight, I shall grant your request!"

Luckily, I made the first few hits. He was a little faster than me, but not too much to handle. I placed him in a headlock once his thick elbow stabbed my bandaged side. Seriously, that was getting old. Seconds later, his eyes shined like fire as he flipped me over himself. He stomped a plank loose from the pier and it slammed my nostrils. Now with my nose burning I pushed myself back on my feet. I reached for Agnomus, but quickly remembered again.

"Looking for your trusty sword?" he chuckled, raising a brown eyebrow at me.

My heart burned as my fist flew at him. Just as I attacked, he leaped back, landing onto a nearby boat. Deciding to mock his movements prolonged our battle, only on not-so-solid ground. My arm swung his way as he pulled a nearby rope from the mast above. He brought the rope around my neck and then choked me against the mast. I felt my face turn purple from loss of air before yanking the rope forward, causing his head to knock into the metal post.

Before he could recover, I grabbed his head, and shoved it between the dock and the hull of the fishing boat. His head submerged under the watery crevice as I pulled another rope connecting the boat and the dock. The boat's edge shut against the pier, locking the man's head in between them.

"How's this for strength?" I growled as water flooded into his lungs. He kicked me away as my sight blurred again. The minute I stood back up, he was out of my sight. A war cry caught my attention.

Upon turning, the man's blood-red boot swung angrily into me. He apparently found another rope connected to the mast, swung toward me, and then knocked me back onto the pier. He blasted smoke spheres as I scooted away with my forearms.

"No hat, no sword, and no ship," the man began. "Not much of a pirate now, are you?"

I charged at him one last time, but he easily knocked me the other direction. I rolled to a kneeling position. I had been defeated.

"You are strong."

"You mock me?" I growled lowly.

"Not at all. I'm actually quite impressed." He replied. "Not many people last after fighting with me. Perhaps I went too easy, but I brought this fight upon you. Now for accepting my request and entertaining me this long, what can I give you in return?"

CHAPTER ONE

After that fight? Had I even accepted his request? Would he grant me Agnomus sooner than anticipated? But the promise to squash Jared was a more soothing thought. How was he to do this, and what were these competitions he spoke of?

"The one thing I need the most would be another ship, please," I finally answered, figuring I would learn these things along the way.

The man smiled, walking to the end of the pier. "Good thing I took the liberty of dragging your old one all the way over here." His hand waved over the rolling swells of the ocean surface. The sound of old structural material seeped underwater as bubbles rose to the top. Then a mountainous ship climbed above the shallow waves before us. How could this have happened without the presence of magic? The soaking ship was decorated with seaweed and a few flopping fish along the sides. I gaped in awe as my mouth stretched into a smile, seeing the golden engraving on the ship's side hull: *"Hira Conte' the Second."*

"Now," he started again, "you keep your promise, or I will take this down just as easily as I got it up." He tossed my hat at my feet.

As soon as I picked it up I turned to thank him, but the Good Samaritan had vanished.

"There you are!" a synthetic voice spoke. I turned to see Metsys walking, slightly faster with every step. "Where've you been?" she asked. "There are no reports on the 5X. Do you know what that means?"

I still couldn't get my head out of the clouds and couldn't reply.

"Captain! Do you know what this means?" she repeated, shaking my arms forcefully.

"What?"

"There is no sign of the 5X, which means—"

"Apex City is vulnerable," I said, returning to reality. "Come, we must go now!"

"But your ship—"

"This one?" I asked, motioning to the new beauty.

"That's yours?" she asked, jaw dropping. "Where did you find that?"

"I'll tell you once we board." I returned my hat to its proper place.

***

Later I recounted to Metsys everything that had happened to me earlier that day, while she provided me with an extremely detailed description of all that had occurred the night before. Once we were caught to speed on things, she paced back and forth on the deck, while I kept my hands firmly mounted on the wheel.

"I don't know about this," she spoke up cautiously. She placed a finger on her chin then turned my way. "Did he say what this contest was about, or for?"

"Not really. He could have been busy; regardless, I have to keep my word."

"I'll go with you," she blurted. "We still have no sign of Dahnarak, and you're practically defenseless without Agnomus."

"Thank you," I grumbled.

"So we have the ship, and he wants you there." She paused in thought before speaking again. "How can we trust him? Why not sail to the other side of the globe?"

CHAPTER ONE

"I'm not sure how he found me in the first place," I reminded her. "Besides, I'm not giving up on Agnomus."

"Then why take this vessel over that weapon?"

"I can't sail with a sword. We need to reach Apex City while the 5X are lost at sea."

"Perhaps they're dead." She smiled. "When do the contests begin?"

"He didn't say," I replied. "But who are we to turn down an invitation?"

"That is also correct," she admitted as the symbols on her visor flashed a different message. Her metal skin glowed when the blue moonlight swam over it.

My eyes widened having just noticed a minor detail. "Metsys."

"Yes?" she asked, gazing upon the skyline of the main city as the cool breeze reanimated me.

"How did you find me?"

She remained silent, before answering. "My signal readings." We both knew one's signal could only be read if some sort of tracking device was attached. I pushed that thought in the back of my mind. Then she suddenly said, "Let's go wake this city up!" and then she leapt over the edge of the ship.

"Metsys!" But it was too late.

Openings appeared on her hands. Seconds before she hit the water her jets activated, spewing fire from her feet and palms. Water splashed into the air as she took off for the city.

"Wait!" She couldn't hear me, but that didn't stop me from chasing after her.

CAPTAIN RED BLOOD

The 5X headquarters came into view, a normal apartment building with huge cracks flowing up the sides, cradling two figures that caught my eye. One seemed to move faster than the other. Was it being chased? I whipped out my telescope to get a closer look and sure enough, it was a pair of millennials in full sprint, one after the other. That was typical in a city filled with so much young blood. I made out that the figure being chased was a young, dark-skinned girl wearing a light amount of spiked armor.

Oddly enough, her pursuer was a boy, but purely black with what looked like a glowing red spiderweb on his body. It was unlike anything I'd ever seen before. The pair had an odd sense about them. A strange air lingering within the caverns of my mind informed me that these people would not be seen only once by Metsys, Dahnarak, or I. That new voice in my head told me that one day—somehow—our fates were bound to align.

Name: Settris, AKA Connie Sett
Weapons: None
Powers: Telepathy, Puppeteering, Perception Tampering
Power Type: Cosmictry

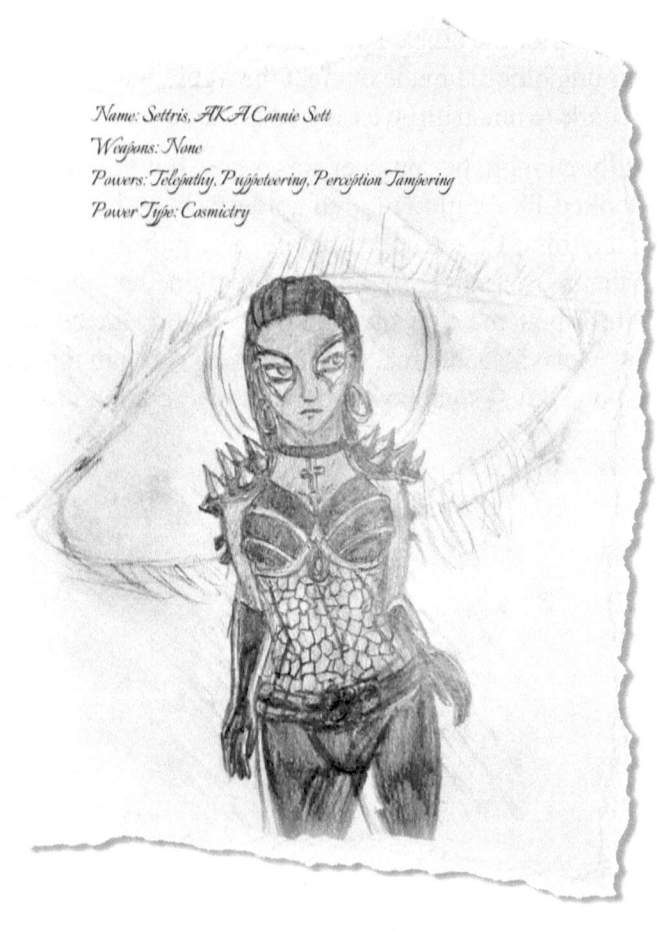

CHAPTER TWO:
SETTRIS

N one of Apex City's citizens seemed interested in answering my questions about my cousin upon her disappearance. She and her friends had left on a small trip she promised wouldn't take too long. I prayed to God that she was alright. Unlike most of her other friends, only I knew her secret—and how desperately that secret needed to be kept.

***

While leaving third period today at Apex High, I passed by a teacher breaking up two rebellious-looking students from a fight before escorting them to the principal's office. One of the young men looked straight into me. Our school was a moderate size of about three-hundred pupils, but oddly enough, I had never seen him before. Wisdom brings resolution while petty fighting prolongs war.

"What was that about?" Katherine said, speeding up from behind.

"I'm not entirely sure," I admitted under my breath.

"What?" she cried out, spinning me around. "I've never heard that coming from you. Normally you can just...read on the spot, can't you?"

"It's not as easy as you think it is," I briefly explained. "It depends on the maturity of the mind."

"Not to mention the willingness."

"Yeah," I began again, "it's hard to snoop around in someone else's conscience without them getting a bit suspicious. But there are those few exceptions."

"You've got to show me how to do that." The two of us laughed identically. Due to our same brown skin, sparkling smiles, and almost matching eyes, people usually mistook us for being sisters. Our relationship promoted our sisterhood, but we were just identical cousins.

"Speaking of things I need to show you how to do," I spoke as Katherine's smile faded. "Maybe I should teach you how to talk to your parents? I can tell by the look on your face that you still haven't told them yet."

"No, I never got the chance to." That was an excuse.

"Look, Kitty," I said, my eyes shooting at hers. "This is selfish of you! Your parents need to know these things. You can't just push them away. Look, I know you all are in a bad time, but you still need to tell them."

"Get out of my head!" she cried as I shushed her upon entering the library.

My voice automatically lowered to a whisper. "Look, girl, you can't keep sneaking out of the house, your folks worrying about you like crazy!" I glanced at her purple cat necklace. "What's your excuse anyways?"

"That's none of your bus—" She was interrupted by a constant bleeping on her group's wrist communication device.

"Looks like you have your own business."

"Connie," she sighed. I crossed my arms and placed my book bag onto the table. Katherine and I continued glaring each other down until she left the library undetected.

"So much for gaining a decent education," I mumbled, removing several books from my bag and snatching it before it could slide off the wooden table.

"Nice reflexes," a boy sitting behind me whispered. Although I hadn't turned to face him right away I already envisioned his smooth, mocha-colored skin and dark, curly hair. He was quite handsome, despite the swelling bruise covering one of his pale-green eyes.

"Who gave you that little beauty mark?" I asked, turning to him.

"I didn't catch his name. Only his fist." He chuckled as I smiled. "He started it though." I lifted my eyebrows with brief aggravation and returned to my books. "Today's my first day."

"Welcome," I said, flashing him a smile.

"What book is that?" he started up again after a few seconds of awkward silence. I showed him the cover of the slim book. It had a rose, a strip of ivy, and a gavel, and could easily be converted into a script.

"And yours?" His achromatic cover pictured a young woman in a black hat partially hidden behind a pillar of billowing smoke with the title written in an elegant red cursive font. "So, you went to the principal's office, and you're now in the library why?"

CHAPTER TWO

"In-school suspension." I should have known. "Luckily, I can get caught up on my work."

"Black eye and homework. Not a great first day, huh?"

"Something tells me it'll get better before it's up."

Until this day, I had never seen him before. More importantly, an odd power seemed to block my telepathic wavelengths. For the first time in my life, I was asking someone stupid questions that I would have easily obtained answers to upon my first sight of them. Lately, I wouldn't even have to make eye-contact with a stranger before knowing half of their life story. Throughout the rest of the day, I watched him carefully. Could he be one of the criminals that Kat had faced in the past? Criminal or not, of one thing I was certain—he was trouble.

***

"Back so soon, Kitty?" I chirped as Katherine took her seat beside of me during lunch.

"Yeah, it was just a burglary."

"A Kat-burglar?"

She returned a dark glare my way.

"People die in burglaries too," I muttered. Her thought feed suddenly streamed into my own. Life was stressing her out, so much that she desperately wished for someone to take her place for one day. Kat was always committed to her other friends, but felt unappreciated at times. She knew she was a single part in a much larger plan, but occasionally questioned what exactly that plan was. After all, she wasn't born into the other group, neither was she their property. Perhaps all she really craved was a normal life.

"Take mine."

"What?" she looked over in astonishment.

"You practically let me in," I replied, tapping my temple with my index finger. "There's nothing you can keep from a mind reader."

"No, there's nothing that I can keep from you," she breathed heavily. "I know I won't ever get a break anyways."

"As if you have a choice."

She raised an eyebrow at me.

"I may not know where the key to your house is."

"What does my house key have to do with—"

"Found it!" I laughed.

"Wow, Connie, I really should've seen that one coming," Kat replied, shaking her head in the sudden realization that she had left her thought patterns still opened to me. "There's no sense in arguing with you about it now, but we'll have to meet at your house."

"Why mine?" I asked.

"My comrades are very strict, and I'm never going to let my parents see me wielding double-barreled pistols in their house."

"As long as I have the location of your 'business,' and you're at your home, then I'm fine."

"Thanks, Cuz," she said as we hugged.

"So who's your friend?" Keisha asked me, happily strolling toward the table, armed with her food tray.

"Who?" I asked.

"You know, Stalker Boy!" she laughed.

"How did you find out about him?" I asked, blushing as Kat smirked. "What did you do?"

"Nothing, I just saw how he was looking at you after the fight," Kat playfully shot back.

"Harsh little bugger, isn't he?" Carmelita commented, making her way to the table too. "Nearly killed the other one."

"I'd say it was fairly matched," Keisha said. "Besides, we all have our bad days. Give it some time, Connie Sett. You have nothing to worry about."

"I know that," I muttered, cradling my head. "Just drop it."

"Just ask him out," Carmelita suggested, casually making a heart with her hands. "He could be your prince."

"Knock it off!" I growled, knocking her arms down.

"Ooh, she's smilin'!" she said, walking away for a moment.

"Okay, maybe in some strange way he is kind of cute," I admitted as they all leaned in. "But he's so not my type." Kat and Keisha groaned and rolled their eyes. I turned to Carmelita who was a few yards away speaking to the boy and waving at us. "Seriously?" The boy faced our table, confidently readjusted himself, and walked toward us. I sluggishly shrank under the table. "Can this day get any worse?"

"I sure hope not," I looked up to see the boy.

"Get rid of him!" I hissed at Kat who simply shook her head, grinning.

"Is that how people sit at tables nowadays?" He smiled.

"Who says 'nowadays' nowadays?" Keisha whispered to Carmelita as she shrugged her shoulders. The boy helped me off the floor as I noticed a device mounted to his wrist.

28

"Hey what's that?" I asked. He dropped my hand and grabbed for the device.

"Wh—what?" He said with shifty eyes. "You've never seen a watch before?" Evidently, Kat wasn't the only one at Apex High with a secret. "Sorry, I uh—gotta go—class." He rushed out of the cafeteria, nearly tripping as he did.

"Perfect couple," Keisha smirked, high-fiving Carmelita as Kat and I relayed the same thoughts.

***

That evening an orange sun sank softly below the horizon. The surrounding streaks of pink clouds matched nearly every object in my room, including the fuzzy pillows that sat neatly atop the pink bedsheets. Besides Kat's white fluffy-hooded jumpsuits, the only other not-pink thing was a cream-colored antique dresser that was once our grandmother's.

"I remember that," Kat reminisced. "It has a lot less dolls on it though."

"Grandma Alba loved dolls. She had to have at least one of every kind."

"And country," Kat added. "She was such an inspiration."

"Silly, she still is." I laughed a bit, holding back tears. "She was so excited to show me it for the first time. I hated it." I bit my lip in remorse. "She had planned on giving it to me, but then I was only a child. You couldn't play with a dresser. Looking back on it, I assume we were all once children who wanted childish things."

CHAPTER TWO

Kat put her arm around me, pulling me into a hug before humorously suggesting, "If you still don't like it, I'll be more than happy to take it off your hands."

"I've grown used to it now," I said, wiping my eyes. "It's as if Grandma Alba still lives on through it." Kat thought the same, but we would never forget our precious memories of her. "Enough tears," I stated as Kat handed me one of her jumpsuits. I changed in the small bathroom connected to my bedroom.

Afterwards, Kat spiked my hair and worked on my makeup to mimic her normal crime-fighting attire.

"Okay, now," she said after applying my eye makeup. We were definitely sisters now.

"Oh my gosh! This calls for a picture!" I grabbed my hot-pink digital camera, and we posed in front of my mirror to snap a good one. "That's a keeper, and I am so putting that online!"

"No!" she protested.

"Why not?"

"My secret!"

"You're right. Sorry, I got carried away. We've never had this much fun together. I mean, I have friends, but you're my closest, Cuz." I apologized, forgetting all about her secret life as an American superhero.

"Yeah, this was pretty fun." She admitted. Suddenly we both jumped at a beeping noise. "You'll need that. *Mi* commu-tracker *es su* commu-tracker." She handed it to me, and we left the house, but not before taking one last glance at Grandma Alba's old dresser.

***

SETTRIS

"What've we got, Jared?" the redheaded girl asked solemnly as she entered the 5X headquarters. Her forest green eyes matched her short-sleeved denim top, and scattered along her cheeks were soft brown freckles. The creature sporting a pair of tattered shorts walking next to her resembled an Egyptian god. He had piercing golden eyes and his entire body was covered in thick gray fur, except for his muscular human-like arms.

"Two of our usual suspects," Jared replied from the opposite side of the room. The torso design of his uniform created an X along the chest with two leather sashes. The blue sash trailed from his right shoulder to his left side, overlapping the red one underneath that was stretched opposite the other. Blue metallic guards were mounted onto his shins and forearms.

Jared continued giving the layout of how his group would successfully take down the duo harassing Apex as a gray-eyed boy with a lightning bolt striking a C on his torso stepped beside me. During this encounter with the hero group, I decided it was best not to pry into their personal lives, so I was clueless as to who the new boy was.

"Kat," I jumped as he whispered. "You look a little…" he paused. "Different."

"Different," I replied, casually tucking a lock of newly spiked hair behind my ear. "How?"

"I can't put my finger on it, but something feels off." He explained. "I can't feel our connection."

Before he could say another word, I quickly linked our minds. They were clearly in sync with the missing feeling. I discovered that this other 5X member was Cyclone, and how, evidently, he, too, shared a secret with Kat. My mind was instantly invaded with memories from his perspective of he and Katherine holding hands and kissing. I backed away after the

31

small dream wondering why she hadn't mentioned Cyclone to me in the past. We stared at each other for a few seconds until the jackal-man spoke up.

"You two coming?" Jak'al asked as Cyclone rubbed his eyelids.

"I'll be there in a minute." No he wouldn't. "Don't wait up." The hybrid creature made his way out the door as Cyclone summoned a controlled whirlwind. He managed to keep the gales inside the apartment complex and rendered the electronic sliding doors locked while his gray eyes morphed black. "She hates you. That's why you can't feel anything."

"Cyclone, what are you doing?" the jackal-man yelled on the other side of the door.

"Cyclone, stop!" I ordered as his strong winds shattered surrounding glass objects. The glass shards immediately entered the swirling gusts in front of him as he slowly hovered toward it. The rapidly spinning shards relentlessly shredded the furniture as some impaled the walls. The other two 5X members charged back to their headquarters upon hearing the ruckus, and Jak'al and me pleading for Cyclone to stop.

"Cyclone is dead," the boy said with an echoing voice. "Only Hurricane remains." I had no choice but to look into Cyclone's head again. In order to fully incapacitate him, I would have to humanely disconnect his brainwaves from the strange power that possessed him now. Hopefully I could link myself to whatever this "Hurricane" was. I had to act fast. He continued to advance into the tornadic blender of glass shards that would have easily shaved the flesh from our bleeding bodies as I took a leap of faith. His army of glass shards all stopped swirling in midair, then turned their sharpest points toward me. With a mere flick of his hands the particles swarmed. With a huge burst of sudden power, I tackled him to the ground, pressing my palms firmly against his head.

I saw flashes of light, scenes of Cyclone's life. His entire life up to this point ran through my head as I emerged into his. Strangely, I couldn't find any remnants of Cyclone's memory. It was as if I had been sucked into another dimension forged from pure energy.

"What is this place?" I asked myself, deeply studying the environment.

"Help me!" I peered across the odd land to see an elderly man muttering behind a cocoon of black cloth. "I—I'm so cold," he muttered, his eyes wide with fear. "I don't know where I am. Darkness. So—so much." My heart pitied him, and I felt urged to walk his way. "Who are you?"

"A friend," I murmured after slight hesitation. I assisted the bony man to his feet and examined him further. He was as thin as a skeleton and his robe was ripped beyond repair, with gashes revealing scant filthy rags he wore underneath.

"Y—you're so kind," he gasped heavily. "What can I do for you in return?"

I thought for a moment, cautiously weighing my options. "Just moments ago," I began, informing him of the predicament I found myself in. "I was reading a boy's mind. We—I know him as Cyclone."

"Ah, yes," he cooed. "I know of him."

"Would you happen to know of an entity called 'Hurricane'?"

"Hurricane is much more than a demon or ghost," the elder continued. "He is an alter ego of your comrade hailing from the future."

CHAPTER TWO

"How do you know that?" I asked, intrigued and a bit surprised at the sudden change of the tone of the atmosphere.

"You and I share a similar ability, only my reach is greater." He waved his hand as some sort of sphere manifested before us. "Far greater." A scene formed within the sphere. Fiercely ripping a parchment in front of a fireplace was Cyclone. He looked only a few years older, and a sickly woman in a lacey dress spoke modestly to him.

"Yes, Hurricane," she began, lustfully caressing his back as he collapsed to his knees, facing the warm flames. "The Cyclone you once were is dead. Along with your friends. It won't be long now."

The vision ended, and I snapped back to reality, still subduing an unconscious Cyclone and still hearing the old man's voice in the back of my mind. Finally, the other members burst into the room.

"You've got some serious explaining to do!" an Australian man barked at me, restraining Kat by the wrist.

Since the entire group had their hands full with Cyclone, Jared was forced to call in three of the Extended-X members. Any time the 5X connected with another sect, they would provide them commu-trackers that would enable the teams to call for backup.

"You're not Kat!" Fern yelled at me.

"I had the assistance of Lance and Amethyst, and we still couldn't take 'em!" Gaako, the Australian, growled as the young man, Lance, entered the room walking Amethyst over to the couch. "Mind the glass."

Lance occasionally winced at the ugly gash upon his own chest, but chose to ignore it and continue to treat his partner.

"It's okay. I'm here," he whispered to her, lightly stroking her paling cheek.

Nervously, Kat and I took turns explaining my involvement with recent events to the rest of the group. Neither of us cared for the outcome, only that the truth was told. Kat's comrades were disappointed but somewhat sympathetic. After all, leading a double life had never been associated with a happy ending. That thought is what prompted me to let Cyclone tell of our encounter with Hurricane to the others when he was ready.

***

The next day, Kat and her friends went missing. I don't know what happened to Gaako, Lance, or Amethyst. That night I returned to their headquarters, praying to find answers, but I managed to find something else instead.

Now lacking Kat's signature jumpsuit, I successfully hid my identity by braiding my hair and painting my face. Red paint lined with yellow surrounded my hazel eyes while my neck supported a choker with a silver cross. Hopefully the charm would keep me out of trouble. Mounted on my shoulders were spiked, lightweight guards, and a flexible, yet protective carbon fiber plate hugged my core region. On my legs was a pair of vinyl pants and beneath were inch-thick elevator heels.

As I came across the 5X headquarters, I became witness to a robbery. "Hey, stop!" I cried as the thug turned my way. I caught a glimpse of his face and shuddered. His skin was as black as night. The only hint of color was in the glowing marks decorating his face and the bit of matching glow found in his mostly black eyes. I couldn't quite put my finger on it, but he seemed vaguely familiar. His mugging victim shoved him away and attempted to run; but she was too late.

CHAPTER TWO

A single mark on his forearm forcefully protruded from beneath the sleeve of his dark hoodie and morphed into a blade that plunged through the girl's chest. My mouth dropped open as blood sputtered out of her mouth like a motor rejecting oil. Once the streetlight hit her, even more emptiness filled my body.

"K—K," I struggled to get out as the young woman's body slumped into my arms. "Keisha!" I jumped, shrieking in horror as marks of the thug's glowing red energy streamed across the ground toward me in separate bands.

"Don't scream," he hissed. "Or that," he pointed to my friend's cold, lifeless body with his blood-red saber, "will be you."

I closed Keisha's eyes, and faced him. "Murderer," I snarled. "Respect the dead, you soon will be!" I threw the first series of hits as he knocked my arms out of the way before sending a crushing blow with his foot into my chest.

"Now that's more like it," he said with an edge of satisfaction.

I kicked his legs out from under him, and pinned him to the ground. My fists knocked into his face multiple times until his glowing marks grew brighter. I leapt back as his hoodie caught fire, revealing a continuous web of the sizzling red streaks. Did his bones carry this bizarre feature? I stomped at him as he kicked up into the air and landed to his feet. I blocked his next move, grabbed his leg, then punched the area behind his knee.

He stumbled backward, but caught himself. He glared at me angrily before rushing for another attack. I blocked his forearm, and punched his throat after my arm rubbed against a device latched to his wrist. In a second, my opponent's face changed to a lighter tint and his eyes into an alluring green.

My mouth hung open. "You?" I asked, backing away. "How? Th—this can't be real."

"I assure you," he rasped. "This is very real." His hair became as a collection of sharp black bones as before once he touched his watch, becoming the demon again. Horrified, I charged in the opposite direction as he chased close behind. He threw smaller red knives past my face as my body began to catch up to the events surrounding me. In a sudden fatigue, I turned down an alleyway and kneeled, trying to catch my breath.

The dark man's chuckle echoed within the alley walls. "Bad move. Now you have nowhere to run."

"What do you want?" I gasped heavily.

"In your current position, I'd suggest a kiss," he cackled.

"That would be poison, coming from you!" I barked.

He leaned in tauntingly. "Wanna taste?"

Unable to view his thoughts, I forced myself out of the alley by leaping off a dumpster and heading up a nearby fire escape. I proceeded to climb it until I reached the rooftop. As soon as I looked up, I noticed a figure standing in front of me.

"Hello," he smiled casually, teeth glowing from the blue moonlight. "Again."

We ran across the buildings, back to the main road, then planted our feet onto another rooftop when a huge pirate ship docked itself at the edge of Apex City. Suddenly something splashed just above the water and flew toward us fast. I caught a glimpse of it, and it resembled a humanoid missile. The object's jet-force impact of entering the city sent the boy and I falling flat against the building's roof. I grunted painfully as the young man growled in annoyance.

I used this to my advantage and stomped my right elevator heel into his pointed nose. He painfully pressed his head against the building and bit his lip at the throbbing discomfort.

CHAPTER TWO

"Bravo, bravo." The two of us looked up to see a certain old man clapping his thin hands.

"What are you doing here?" I asked, lowering my voice and distancing myself from the killer. "Isn't it a little dangerous for an elderly man such as yourself to be wandering around on rooftops at night—or any time of day, for that matter?"

"You call me elderly, yet you do not know," he began in a raspy voice, "how old I really am." Suddenly his withered body changed into a middle-aged one as he finished his sentence. He was rather tall with a heavy, muscular build, thick chin, and strange armor.

"Are you not the man I saw yesterday?"

"Are you not the Pacifist, Connie Sett?" he stated, asking for my identity.

"I only fight within reason."

"Such as this?" he asked, motioning to the dark boy behind me. "Would one consider war to be within reason?"

"War?" I questioned.

"My home world is near being invaded." He looked away for a moment and then turned back. "I am hosting a series of competitions on Eka's Island to create an army suitable enough to take on the dark forces advancing on my planet."

The boy and I eyed each other in a daze. That proved we couldn't have imagined the same thing.

"But what about school?" I asked. "What about our families?"

"I'll handle that," he said. "All you two have to do," he pointed off in the distance, "is be on that ship in two days."

I thought about it for a while. Something kept me from reading his mind, but he did give me valuable information about

Hurricane. This man needed my help with his planet. Obviously, he was far from ordinary. Maybe this is how I was to repay him? I finally made up my mind and nodded in agreement. "Okay."

"I'm going too," the boy muttered as the man eyed him. The way the man looked at him was as if he also had a debt to pay. But my heart still burned with fury. I would never forget the way Keisha looked me in the eyes as the lights faded in hers. Could my participation in these contests enable me to avenge my fallen friend? Would it allow me to find my dear cousin?

"Thank you," the man smiled. "You don't know how much I appreciate your decision." He turned to look at the boy's wrist device. "Nice watch. Wherever did you get it?"

The boy glared back at him.

Name: BlackByrd, AKA Austin Byrd
Weapons: None
Powers: Forcefields, Astral Projection-soul exits body
Power Type: Shadowsty

CHAPTER THREE:
BLACKBYRD

The padded cell in Apex City Asylum was my only sanctuary. I admitted myself there about two months ago to keep away from my father. In my asylum, by myself, all alone, stood nothing but peace and quiet. Unlike some of the more mentally unhinged patients here, I could leave whenever I pleased. Sometimes without even physically heading out the door. These abilities of mine allowed me to travel anywhere out-of-body at fast speeds.

There were three major classifications of super-abilities: elemental, cosmictry, and shadowstry. *Elemental* refers to any power of or relating to earthly elements. *Cosmictry* is associated with abilities pertaining to celestial or astrological energy, while *shadowstry* is linked to the usage of black or white magic, but does not require a malevolent manipulator. My abilities were, by far, classified as shadowstry.

I've been to thousands of famous landmarks without even having to pay my way in. I was completely invisible to other tourists or festivalgoers. It may not be the most fascinating ability, but it is the rarest. However, there are downsides to spirit-traveling, like the fact that there's no efficient way to defend your physical body. Spirit-traveling is only gifted to those responsible enough not to kill themselves accidentally. Monitoring your body is always important, I recall an inmate, Samuel Pine, breaking out of his room. He, too, had a strange ability. I know this because we'd got in a fight the night before.

***

I was on my way back to my cell after visiting the Taj Mahal. Upon my arrival, I heard the asylum workers freaking out over Pine escaping his cell. Apex City Asylum was a facility conjoining both a jail and an asylum, and Pine was crossing over from the detention wing. My soul safely reentered my body. My eyes shot open to the sound of his footsteps, but couldn't determine why he would be coming down this way.

I heard the electronic beeping of the security keypad before Pine slid a cardkey through the tiny slot connected to it. Pine stepped into my cell unit wearing a vicious sneer. "Hello Austin," he began as the door slid shut behind him.

"How do you know my name?" I asked.

"I know more than you think." His wild, animalistic stare matched his uneasily shaking hands. A single pistol was gripped tightly in his left hand.

"Not that I'm really concerned, but aren't you right handed?" He ignored my comment. "Where'd you get the gun?"

"A guard, obviously."

"I didn't know firearms were allowed."

"They are with a handful of Franklins."

"I didn't think you were strong enough to actually take one down," I replied sarcastically. "What brings you here?"

"You're coming with me!"

"I'm not going anywhere."

"Then I shall take you by force!" A bullet flew at me. I jumped out of the way and tackled into him as he dropped the gun onto the padded floor. He grabbed my shoulders and headbutted me. I stumbled backward, nearly knocking my head against the metal bedframe. I leaped back up, and shook off the pain.

"Well, okay then," I murmured before blocking his following attack.

The side of his closed fist bashed my abdomen before thrusting toward my face. He stood proudly as an unearthly feeling spread across my forehead. It was as if he knocked it with a handful of needles.

"You," he started, "are not the only one with super-abilities, Mr. Byrd."

"What did you do to me?" I asked, my sight fuzzing a bit.

Suddenly, lengthy quills jutted out from beneath his skin. "I lessened your existence to mere seconds." He stepped forward and shot his foot into my throat as I fell against the wall. While using it for support, I felt Pine grip my neck as a thousand needles scraped against my skin. He shoved my face into the wall. The wind was knocked out of me as I continued to suffer from brief asphyxiation before being thrown across the room.

My energy drained as the quills disappeared into my skin. What was I to do? Just as he was walking toward me, he began to multiply. He snarled as a long needle jutted out the middle of his throat.

"Are you feeling dead yet?" he taunted as the long pin neared my eye. I slammed an open palm into his ribs. He then cracked my arm over his knee before I exited my body. My body slumped to the ground. Suddenly, everything was quiet. Pine stepped over to me, tapping me with his foot. After a moment of believing I was dead, he headed for the sliding door. "The Master will be so pleased!" he grinned, prying the door open with a spike.

Just as he stepped into the door frame, I smacked the controls. The thick metal door shot at him from the side as he stopped it with his palms. In his attempt to hinder the door from cutting his spiked body in half, I flew back into mine. I rushed to him and kicked the door as the rest of him fell out the on other side.

"And stay out!" I cried as he was detained by guards. I looked down and cringed at seeing his severed leg twitching within the crack of the sliding door.

***

The following day something was clouding my memories. It was like my encounter with Samuel Pine was all a dream, but I knew that was far from the truth.

I sat in the waiting room watching Candice Misty Luda, the receptionist. She was about my age and the best thing about the asylum. She had dark hair, lime eyes, and a smile bright enough to act as a second sun if the world were to ever black out. Sitting on her desk was her daily paper version of Mount Everest, and at the basin were pictures of kittens. On the wall behind her was a cat poster that read: "Hang in there." Pretty ironic seeing that the picture was held up by a single tack.

A big man wearing a MacIver plaid shirt and a red hat with fading yellow words of a towing advertisement came inside.

"Morning," he cooed politely to Candice.

"Hi there, how may I help you?" she asked sweetly.

BLACKBYRD

"I'm here to see Byrd. Austin Byrd," he said. "I'm his father."

She's heard of my dad through the stories I've told her. She bit her lower lip and tapped her temple with the end of her pen. "S—sure," she replied hesitantly. "I'll go see if he's awake."

My dad laughed. "Yeah that's how he is. Lazy."

"I don't understand," she turned as they headed down the hallway.

"What? Laziness?" he replied, stopping before reaching the door as I flew back into my body.

"No," she answered. "How does Austin have you for a dad, but stays here?"

He pondered that thought for a moment, then shrugged. "How does a pretty girl like you work in an asylum?" She fell silent. "I can give you more."

"You can?" she asked, clearly interested. He nodded his head. "Here's his room." She said, quickly changing the subject. She tapped the keypad, and the door slid open.

"We'll talk soon," the man told Candice as he fearlessly strode into my room. "Hello, Austin."

"Get out." I neither faced him nor opened my eyes.

"Good to see you too," he said. "Look, you're not crazy. Come home."

"Get out!" I growled with more temperament.

"Look, how about you—"

I ignored him.

"I know you hate me so, but why do we bother with it? I can take you somewhere. Somewhere we can fight. Somewhere we can settle this world and save mine."

CHAPTER THREE

"Shut up!"

He sighed heavily.

"Get out, now!"

"Fine. I will. But don't say I haven't done anything for you."

"The only thing you've done for me is turn me into what I am today," I explained. "You made me, Frankenstein."

"Frankenstein's creation was his son." He placed a hand on my shoulder. In my fury, I discovered a new ability. His hand flew off me and he slid across the floor. He managed to catch himself on the rim of the door. "Goodbye, then." He sulked, heading back to the waiting room as my spirit followed.

"How was your talk?" Candice asked from behind her desk.

"Good," he replied with a weak smile.

"So," her tone changed, "about what you were saying before."

"Oh. Yes." He began. "I want you to help me."

"Sure. Help with what?" she said, inching closer. I shouted at her, but she didn't seem to hear me.

"My wor—no, you'll think I should be locked up in here."

"No I won't," she put her hand over his. "Please tell me."

"Oh, alright," he continued, "So my world is being destroyed and I want to go out and find special people to help me regain it. And if I don't, then my world will be absorbed by an evil source." Candice's smile faded. "You don't believe me—do you?"

"Sorry, but no. In fact, I think it's very rude of you to come in here and say such hurtful things while standing amidst an asylum." He tossed a few photographs onto her desk. She grabbed them. "What is this?" she asked, holding up a picture of a clown who seriously needed a dermatologist.

"That'd be one of the evil forces attempting to take my home-world. Jexter."

"Jexter the Jester?" She raised a brow. He nodded and pulled out a few more photos.

"Torch, Camille, Ari, just a few of the forces eating away at my world." she looked away uncomfortably. "Won't you help me?"

"Look, why don't you call the army?" she whispered. "Or the C.O.R.E.?"

"It took me long enough to make you believe," he cried. "I don't even know if you do."

"If by 'special people' you mean 'powers,' I don't have any."

"I have a laboratory. I create heroes to help me win this war."

"Okay, whatever. But I still don't—" she fell face first to her desk, unconscious.

"Candice!" I cried.

"Nice job, Viper," he said. The purple-suited assassin peeled her body off the seat and dragged her before my father. Dad turned to face me and our eyes met.

"What?"

"By the way, Austin," he spoke. "You're grounded." With a flick of his hand, my spirit immediately rushed through the hall and returned to my body. My lungs burned from gasping for air just before I lost consciousness.

***

The next day was even weirder. I couldn't spirit-travel and the door was locked. I attempted to use my powers on it, but it wouldn't budge. Candice was the only thing on my mind for the past night. Was she still out there? It was vital to my existence to find out. Suddenly a piercing scream echoed within the waiting room.

"Candice!" I heard breaking glass and footsteps coming toward my room. My first assumption was Samuel Pine again, but there was a certain air that told me otherwise. Other inmates were going belligerent, some mistaking the intruder as a demon from their nightmares. After an eerie silence, someone was banging on my door. I took cover to the back wall.

"You leave me no choice, door!" a muffled voice said from the other side. I clasped my ears as a loud siren shot through me like a sonic boom.

"AHHHHHHHHHHHHHHHHHHHHHHHHHHHHHHHHHHH!"

The metal sliding door fell to the ground as a young woman stepped onto it, looking around.

She had peculiar boots, tight black pants, and fishnet sleeves connected to her small, unzipped leather jacket. Underneath the jacket was a shirt with a flaming pink skull that matched three colored spikes in her otherwise-jet-black hair. Around her neck was a strange necklace shaped as a heart mixed with a butterfly. She also wore several rings and a pair of lacey fingerless gloves.

"Come out, come out wherever you are, Austin." She had an accent from the land down under. "Peekaboo, I see you."

My eyes widened, but I kept quiet.

"Well you're no fun. I didn't actually see you anyways," she said.

What was it with people coming into my room unannounced? It defiled personal space, not to mention rude.

"Show yourself. Now."

She sounded irritated, and I couldn't help but to feel a bit sorry for her so I stood up from behind the bed. "Who are you?"

"I'll tell you that later," she said hurriedly. "Right now we need to go."

"No, I like it here, I'm safe!" I said as she pulled my arms.

"Oh yeah? Not for long. Let me give you a slight decoration to shake things up in here, yeah?" She threw her head back and let out the loudest wail so far.

"AHHHHHHHHHHHHHHHHHHHHHHHHHHHHHHHH!"

Shimmering waves circled the air surrounding her high-pitched screech. I grabbed my ears and fell to the floor. She wiped the sweat off her brow once everything fell under a blanket of silence as it had before, then turned, helping me back to my feet. Huge holes gaped in the walls. The sunlight blinded me from the other side as my ears continued to ring and a brisk wind made me shake slightly as the sounds of cars and street life reawakened me.

"Acid screaming," she said. It was doubtless that the young woman was out of place, but, admittedly, some fresh air wouldn't be much of a sin either.

***

We were walking down the streets of Apex City. It felt weird actually walking to places instead of spirit-traveling. It was nice.

"Alright, first things first," the girl said as we stopped in the middle of the sidewalk. "You need some new threads."

"What?" I replied, tugging lightly on the bottom of my current attire. "These are fine."

"Look, people are going to notice you escaped an asylum—"

"With your help," I interrupted.

"Those scrubs would make it more obvious!"

"Scrubs? And you call *that* clothes?" I replied, motioning to her outfit. "You look like a Gothic hooker."

"At least I don't look like a painted bandage!"

"A painted bandage?"

"Did I stutter?" She rolled her eyes before starting to walk again. "Come, I need to finish packing."

"Packing?"

"I'll explain it to you later," she said, grabbing my hand.

Eventually we reached an apartment complex at West Street. She led the way as we entered the building, but I fell behind, feeling as though we were being watched. I looked everywhere examining our surroundings to ensure the coast was clear.

"What are you doing?" the girl broke in as I snapped back to reality. "Stop goofing off and get in here!" she yanked me up the apartment stairs and escorted me to a door leading to a room packed with cardboard boxes. Styrofoam beads crushed under our steps as we settled in. She pulled the door shut and leaned against it, sighing deeply.

"What, no candlelight dinner first?" I began coyly.

"Ha, ha, ha," she growled between her teeth.

"Are you at least ready to explain what the heck this is all about?"

"I'm still trying to figure that one out," she replied. "Let's just say I'm going somewhere for a little while."

"So do you normally pick up random strangers from an asylum to accompany you?"

"Not until today," she said with a sad expression. "You're just going to have to trust me."

"We just met!" I reminded. "You took me away from my home against my will—which is practically kidnapping—and brought me to some apartment that it seems you yourself have never been to before. I know nothing about you...I don't even know your name."

"Josie?" We were interrupted by the door creaking open. I looked down to see a tiny gray-haired woman with thin, circular glasses. "Who's this?" she asked, motioning to me.

"Uh," she was at a loss for words as I made a face at her, revealing to her my discomfort toward the situation. "Mom, this is my new friend who I busted out of an asylum by screaming at the door." Like that made any sense.

"I can live with that."

Immediately, I jumped in. "Hi, I'm Austin." I smiled, shaking her hand. "Austin Byrd."

"Hello Austin." The woman replied sweetly. "Why, aren't you quite a handsome fella. Josie never told me about you before."

"Well, that's how she is!" I laughed just before realizing how much I sounded like my father.

"I know—"

"Mom!"

"What?" she smiled. "Oh, I must be embarrassing you two. If you need anything, I'll be downstairs."

"Well, that's the thing," Josie said. "We were just leaving."

"Leaving?" she asked, looking at both of us. "Where to?"

I shrugged and allowed Josie to take the lead. "I'm going to find my friend. I had a dream the other day that he was in danger."

she explained. "Archangel was the last place I saw him. That was years ago, and I've never seen him since. I have to find him."

"Who?"

"That doesn't matter, I need to save him," she said, suddenly serious. "This feeling keeps growing stronger and stronger every minute!"

Missing someone and having a growing drive to find them. That was a feeling we both shared.

"Okay, okay, calm down," her mother replied. "If you need to go, then go." She went up to her daughter and wrapped her arms around her legs as Josie bent over to her. She then backed off and looked into her eyes. "Just promise me you'll be safe."

"I will be. I promise."

"You will always be my little girl."

Tears streamed down their faces. "And you will always be my little Mom."

She sniffed hard as her mother left the room. Then she turned, fumbled through a box of clothes, and handed them to me. "These were my brother's. You remind me a lot of him."

"I would hate to see the way you two argued."

She let out a small grin. "Well, now you know why I have to go."

"But you said 'your friend.'"

"The man I'm referring to is my friend; my brother died in Archangel."

"That explains the moving," I deduced.

"Exactly," she replied. "And now that I know where my friend is, we have to get going. I'm not losing him again."

"I don't mind helping you with this at all," I spoke up. "But next time, would it kill you to ask?"

Solemnly, she turned back and said, "One may never know."

***

Josie remained in her normal attire, carrying a medium-sized suitcase as I walked by her side wearing her brother's old clothes. I wore a comfortable black hoodie over a dark T-shirt, jeans, and combat boots. The focal point of my new look was a circular medallion with a red jewel in the middle of a five-pointed star. When the light hit it a certain way, the gem's beams resembled a bird.

Once we came across Apex City's docks, Josie chirped at a young man. "Ah, a visitor!"

"Visitor?" the tan-skinned boy who was wearing a gray hoodie and jeans exclaimed. Unlike Josie, I was cautious. I couldn't explain it, but he seeped with an immense power. "I'm not visiting, I'm here to fight!"

"So am I!" a girl with braided hair answered, walking up to the scene.

"I was hoping to see you here," he replied.

"I'm guessing you two know each other?" I asked.

"Yes," the young woman replied. "And definitely not on good terms."

"Might we ask why?" Josie commented.

"You'll find out soon enough," the boy hissed.

"If words are too much, you could always give us a demonstration," she tempted.

"My thoughts exactly." The short-tempered boy thrust his arm out as I put myself between the two. "Watch yourself, punk!" he barked at me.

"Leave the lady alone!" I shot back as he threw a punch at me. I dodged, but unintentionally fixed myself for his following blow. My face slung sideways as he attempted another. I ducked and grabbed his hand. Then I yanked him forward into a spin and bent his head back before thrusting my elbow into his throat. He toppled over as I proceeded, pressing all my weight in one foot onto his chest while simultaneously pulling his arms upward.

His bones cracked and popped like a heavy string of fireworks. My hand knocked against his watch as a scalding beam of light made it retract unwillingly. Evidently, the glowing lines trailed all over his now pitch-colored flesh.

I stumbled back, staring at him. "You're one of them?"

"I'm one of nothing." His voice morphed into a chilling growl. He came at me with a sweeping kick just before plunging his foot into my chest and forcing it harder into me. "Let's see how *you* like it!"

"So which one are you betting on?" Josie asked, striking up conversation with the baffled-looking girl merely yards away from our fight.

I finally gained enough strength to cast a force field to knock him out of the way and entered a powerful state of meditation.

"What's he doing?" the girl asked Josie as the two stared in awe.

Everything turned black as all my mental senses heightened to their capacity. Now, while out of my body, my opponent would be unable to damage it unless he attacked the shadowy field as well. That would only do more damage to him due to the shell's magic coating.

My spirit kicked him from behind as he searched for an invisible attacker. After a long while of having my fun with him, his tattoos started to glow brighter than when our fight began.

"This is why they call me *Enrage!*" Immediately, the marks unleashed a blood-red burst of energy. I tried to protect my physical shell, but the force field shattered like glass. The surge of energy then sent my spirit flying back into myself as the rest of me crashed into a nearby brick building.

***

"Austin!" Josie said. "Austin, wake up!" I slowly woke to the sound of her voice. "There you are!"

"Is he alright?" I heard from the crowd of people around us. "What happened?"

"Quiet people, quiet down," Josie ordered. "He's fine."

"What happened, Jos—" she shushed me.

"Call me Garika," she whispered.

"Why?" I asked. "I just got to know your real name."

"We have codenames now," she said, pulling me up. I was weak but didn't require assistance to stand upright. "I'm Garika now. Here's some more people." She motioned to the figures behind her. My vision was still a bit blurry but I managed to make out who was standing before me. "This is Enrage."

"Yeah…we've met," I said. "Thanks for the greeting, by the way."

CHAPTER THREE

"No problem," His smile revealed two vampire-like fangs. He still hadn't changed back to his human form.

"Continuing," Garika said. "This is Settris." Settris gave a mild smirk.

We all turned to the voice of an announcer coming from a man dressed as a pirate who was standing beside a feminine cyborg.

"Greetings, ladies and gents," he spoke boldly. "I pray you are all ready to depart for Eka's Island?" Several nodded, others cheering in response. "Good then!" he cried before waving his hands over the shallow ocean water near the docks. A swirling crimson aura filled the small area and without warning, the whirling portal began to consume the docks. Boats were ripped off the posts to which they were previously tied as the ground shook harshly. I could barely breathe due to what was going on around me, and because Garika was fearfully squeezing my sides.

We were all caught off guard by a huge spike emitting from the sea. As we continued watching it, more of the structure appeared. Eventually the rest of the seaweed-coated ship became visible.

"Welcome aboard *Hira Conte' the Second*," the pirate continued. "No pushing, shoving, biting, clawing, scratching, kicking, hitting, or blowing things up until we reach the island."

My final thoughts prior to departing Apex City was, *How on earth was this safer than my asylum?*

THE
COMPETITIONS

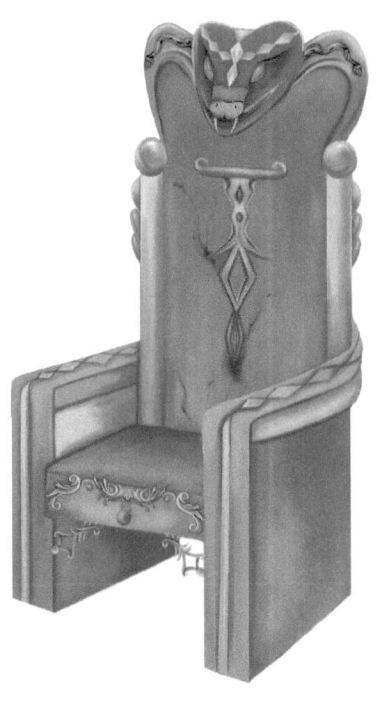

Name: Felinis

Weapons: Claws

Powers: Self Enhancement-morphs her stripes into lava and turns fur into metal

Power Type: Elemental

CHAPTER FOUR:
FELINIS

T he sun soaked through my fur as warm sand stirred between my toes. Sea foam lined the edge of the sandy shores and my whiskers tingled against the cool ocean breeze. Eka's Island had unique topography, and equally intriguing contenders for this year's competitions. Tourniquet dedicated these contests to Eka, the Brother of Darkness. Coming from someone who had heard the legend, I found that a bit unsettling, but for a very long time, in the beginning of time, darkness wasn't all evil. Not until after Eka's fall.

"Felinis," a familiar voice called.

"Master." I bowed to Tourniquet respectfully as he made his way toward me in his gold-plated and leather armor.

"Of all my Angels of Anarchy, you are the only one I can completely trust," the Master replied. "There is something I must tell you."

"What is it, my lord?"

"The Inigmus C.O.R.E.," Tourniquet continued. "They failed to meet my demands regarding the Cyborg Centurions."

"What about the Krow Specters?"

CHAPTER FOUR

"Likewise."

"So your plan finally commences?"

"Yes." He stared intently across the horizon. "The war will begin shortly." He turned back to me. "They also gave me another valuable asset. Unintentionally, that is."

"Excellent." I smiled. "Perhaps I'll have another sister soon."

"This is what happens when people attempt to track this location. Which reminds me," he began. "I understand your loyalty to me is unquestionable, and I pray it remains as such."

"Anything, Master," I answered.

"A ship will be arriving soon. Ensure all passengers have exited the vessel, and then destroy it."

"But Master, if this vessel is the one you told me about, did you not consider it as one of your most frightening creations?" I spat. "It mustn't be destroyed!"

"Unquestionable loyalty," he reminded. "On this island there will be absolutely no contact with the outside world."

"Thy will be done," I said seconds later.

"As always." He smiled proudly. "And don't forget," he paused once more. "Stay out of sight." He turned, vanishing into a thick cloud of smoke.

***

Moments later I left the comfortable scene and stood, awaiting the ship's arrival on a miniature rocky bank jutting out of the sand a small distance away from my previous position. The oceanic green vessel was draped in heavy chains and ascended approximately fifteen stories high. The enormous skull planted to the ship's front plowed through the water as it continued sailing toward the island. Not long after, the boat anchored itself to our shores and released the drop bridge at the mouth of the skull.

The black stripes on my fur began to glow orange like lava as I watched the passengers make their way out of the vessel. Once the coast was clear, I unleashed a magma stream onto the ship. The impact sent debris flying in every direction as panicked civilians threw themselves to the beach front. After dealing enough damage, I attempted to pacify my fire, but something kept me from doing so. I struggled, accidentally flailing my beams as I did, causing even more devastation before my feet finally slipped out from under me. I landed hard on the ground as a dark boy with red markings rushed to my aid.

"Are you alright?" he screamed.

"I'm fine." I coughed, swatting him away. A concoction of dust and sand filled my lungs, causing me to breathe uneasily.

"We've got to get out of here! BlackByrd, Garika, where are you?" he cried frantically without receiving an answer.

"Maybe your friends are already to safety!"

"They're not my friends! I just want to make sure they're not dead yet!" he blurted, heavily examining his surroundings.

"What's the difference? We must leave or *we* will die!" As soon as the words escaped me, a cry for help came from within the sinking ship. My fur stood on end from fear as a dark-skinned woman in lightweight armor waved, pleading for assistance. Her back arched into harsh coughing as the dark man charged after her.

"NOOOO!" A long scream caught my attention from my left. "MY LADY!" he raised his arms toward the vessel rather than toward the woman.

CHAPTER FOUR

As I wondered about this, my attention was snagged by the other boy, who now had the unconscious victim flung over his shoulder.

"Come on!" he yelled as another explosion rocked the beach front. We stifled our shaking, then started to move. I was so tempted to look back, but I clamped my eyes shut and kept running. Once we were out of the line of fire, a couple of Gothic-dressed humans appeared, standing on a bank. The dark man came to a halt and laid the woman down.

"What did you do?" the young man wearing a black hoodie and medallion asked, steadying his breath.

"What?" the dark one hissed.

"What did you do to her?" He attempted to grab him, but he instantly shoved his attacker backward into the other girl.

"Nothing!" he cried out. "I didn't do anything!"

"He speaks the truth," I began. "I was there. He saved her." My words calmed them down long enough to hold a decent conversation. "Are you alright?" I asked, glancing at each of them.

"I am; she's not," the woman with the miniature Mohawk exclaimed, tending to her unconscious friend.

The boy with the medallion faced the area with all the excitement and asked with concern, "Was there a bomb hidden inside the boat?"

"No," the dark one hissed, peering back at the woman he saved. "Not likely."

"Something had to cause it."

"Felinis, what are you doing?" Tourniquet asked, appearing from the dust behind us.

"Oh, I was just—"

"Leading our contestants to the palace for our ceremonial feast?" he replied.

"Yes," I answered uneasily. "That is exactly what I was about to do."

"Excellent." He turned to the rest of the group and looked down at the armored girl lying on the ground. "Settris, arise." She awoke suddenly, rubbing the back of her head. The other girl stumbled back.

"What happened?" Settris asked groggily.

"You don't want to know," the hooded one started up as other boy glared at him.

"I was just explaining that the feast will begin shortly."

"Feast?"

"Great, I'm starving!" the Gothic girl exclaimed.

"Then you've come to the right place," the Master replied. "I suggest finding a seat. Our current contests will be packed."

"Contests?" the armored one asked, mentally recounting her whereabouts. "This is the island. Who will we be facing?"

"Not who," he paused. "What. You shall face the most fearsome of creatures, deadliest of assassins, and maybe even those closest to you." He finished, eyeing the boy with the pendant. The two of them glared darkly at each other until another man hobbled toward us, assisted by an android. His face was flushed and his veins pressed tightly against his skin. Rage forced his body to shudder against his will as he locked eyes with my Master.

"Did you see," his rugged voice began. "What happened back there?"

"Yes, I did." The Master said with a calm demeanor.

"When I find the landlubber who did this to my ship, I'll kill 'im!"

"Don't fret, Captain. *He* may be closer than you think."

I let out an amused grin as the Captain's robotic helper looked straight through me.

***

After climbing the wide concrete steps leading up to the temple, the long cream-colored veils hanging at the entrance blew open, revealing its interior. Golden pillars lining the halls protruded from the marble floors, and the humans I escorted murmured in awe.

"Wow!" the Gothic one cried.

"So that's what you've been up to for all these years," the hooded boy whispered, nearly losing himself in the ceiling fresco of previous contenders, with my Master placed in the center of the painting.

A pair of immense wooden doors opened by themselves, revealing another room. Inside was the feasting hall, holding at least a thousand hungry combatants who would soon be fighting for the same title. I may have been Tourniquet's servant, but even I was participating in his competitions. The humans settled at one of the numerous tables stretching nearly the entire length of the room as I stood beside a comrade of mine.

"Greetings, Mantis," I said with a smile.

"Greetings," he retorted. Mantis was another member of Tourniquet's elite group, the Angels of Anarchy, but he once dedicated himself to the Assassin's Guild, that is, until they presumed him dead after his disappearance. "Are you alright, Felinis?"

"I'm fine, just a little…" I paused for a moment and saw Tourniquet peering over toward us from his golden snake throne. Flames flickered in his glare, an ability he used only if he were extremely upset. Thank goodness looks don't kill. I still wondered why he ordered me to destroy the Captain's ship. I was well-aware that he despised the thought of communication with the outside world, but wasn't it a bit extreme?

"A little what?" Mantis' robotic voice spoke, bringing me back to reality.

"Never mind," I whispered, ending our short conversation.

"Welcome one and welcome all," Tourniquet stood and announced as everyone finished entering the room. "I am sure you all have plenty of questions for me, but first, let me introduce myself. My name is Tourniquet, and this is Eka's Island." Applause filled the hall for a few seconds. "This year's competitions are held in favor of Eka, the Brother of Darkness."

As he continued speaking, I noticed a former opponent of mine staring at the girl in lightweight armor whom I had brought in. My formidable rival was Korax. He was one of Tourniquet's many cyborgs, and had nearly killed me in our last encounter. I would have been dead if it weren't for the heroic efforts of Mantis. My heart was always bitter toward the idea of humanoid machines, but Mantis and Tourniquet's army proved rather exceptional.

"The victor," the Master was saying as I redirected my focus back to him, "will become the savior of my home planet, and the individual responsible for this task will be granted their heart's desire. Although our current competitors are many, there can only be one savior. May the strongest prevail."

CHAPTER FOUR

"Your savior has arrived!" someone spoke from the back. I turned to see a bony-faced young woman sporting a silver cape over a sleek metal battle suit with fishnets trailing her upper thighs. Smaller fishnet patterns rested in her gloves while a head of short, blazing magenta hair bounced in perfect rhythm with every step she took toward the Master's throne. She slid into a halt and placed her hands on her hips, reading my Master up and down. "Hell—o, Daddy!"

"And who might you be?" I asked, taking a step forward.

"Princess Quazar," Tourniquet spoke as I turned to him. "Heir to the throne of her uncle, Leonis Kyu."

"In the flesh!" she chirped.

"You believe you are capable," Tourniquet started back, "of saving my world?"

"I wouldn't have shown my face in your challenges if I didn't," she retorted.

"Then I assume the contests are over." He smiled placidly, resting against the backrest of his throne. The hall filled with astonished whispers. My fur tingled uneasily. The woman grinned. Her pink topaz irises seemed to bore a hole through me until I suddenly blurted out.

"This contest is just beginning!" As soon as the words escaped me, hundreds of people began to cheer.

"It seems you two have just commenced it," Tourniquet said, adjusting his seating. "Felinis versus Princess Quazar."

"I do admire the sound of that," the princess replied, examining me. "I've never faced a freak like you before."

"I've never seen a princess without a crown."

"I'll wear your head."

"I am the more superior specimen," I purred, stepping down from my previous position.

"Superior?" she scoffed. "Compared to a scratching post."

"Let us see!"

My stripes became like lava yet again as I leaped on top of her, shoving my claws into her shoulders. She let out a painful yelp as I rode her to the marble floor. She wrapped her legs around my waist, lifted herself off the ground, and managed to throw me to the opposite side of her. My claws left white streaks in the ground as I half stood, looking up in time to snatch the woman's foot. I flung her away and she bounced across the floor before rolling to a stop.

Still conscious of her current state of agony, the woman mechanically peeled herself off the ground. She turned to face me yet again and tossed her short cape aside. My mouth dropped open, along with many others' as four pink-trimmed hornet wings protruded from behind. I took a single step back from intimidation. The following second she charged, wings buzzing loudly. She shot her knuckles into my gut and then followed her attack with a blast of hot-pink energy that sent me flying backward into a pillar. The impact caused my arms to stretch around it as Princess Quazar plowed into me with the speed of a missile.

Huge chunks of rubble rained from above as onlookers below scattered out of the way. Now freefalling toward the temple steps, I burned my nails white hot, and pressed them deep into Quazar's forearms. She instantly kicked me away with both feet, while concurrently hovering in the air. As I entered a downward spiral, my glance shifted between my attacker and the steps as I wondered how to cheat death yet again.

CHAPTER FOUR

Suddenly, I energized enough lava to coat most of my being, then hardened it. The now-metal covering of my body was heavy enough to send ripples throughout the steps upon my landing. Quazar stared at me in sheer terror as the metal swam off my body and knocked her out of the sky. Just before she could land, I caught her fragile wrist and swung her onto the concrete steps. Her arm shot out and she flipped back up, sending the stiletto heel of her boot slicing a patch of fur off my cheek. I shot a dripping magma stream toward her as she wrapped her wings around herself in a defensive shell.

"Now I have you." If she dared to open her wings for even a second, my power would surely vaporize her pathetic existence, thus making my victory inevitable.

"Stop!" she protested, her wings chipping off into singeing particles of ash. "You win! You win!"

"All of my battles end to the death!" I snapped, forcing the hot beam forward with each step I took.

"Not this one," a voice rang as the world itself melted away. Our fighting immediately ceased as my Master glared at me. I looked around and, to my surprise, we were back inside the feasting hall. All the damage remained quite visual. The pink-haired princess collapsed before me, and I knew victory was mine.

***

"I had her right where I wanted," I began in hushed conversation with my Master while others feasted. "But you took away my chance to relieve her of her puny life."

"That puny life is an important piece of my plan, Felinis," he retorted. "I don't understand how you fail to see that."

"You know just as well as I, that I've never showed mercy to my opponents."

"But do you win every battle?" he asked with an empty expression. "I am your Master. You are the servant."

"Which is why I can serve in Quazar's place," I spat. "Why would you consider her value beyond that of your humble servant's?"

"Her wasp-like abilities and strength in mind proves a huge advantage for my army," he lowered his voice to a whisper as a few people started glancing in our general direction.

"And you find me lacking?" I asked.

"Not at all," he answered. "Just a servant."

Why was Princess Quazar's presence in the competition so important? What was Tourniquet hiding, and would the world have a way to stop the chaos he could potentially unleash? Suddenly, I thought of a close friend.

Name: Chaos

Weapons: Chaos Sword-a cruel, jagged blade

Powers: Chaos Wind, Critical Endangerment-morphs areas into immediate
hazard zones

Power Type: Elemental

CHAPTER FIVE:
CHAOS

I walked back to my cabin for the night after the brilliant battle my ally brawled. The wondrous warrior, Felinis, allowed no one to stand in her way, and pledged more allegiance to Tourniquet than anyone I've ever known, including myself. I lost myself in that thought before sliding open my cabin door and stepping in front of the mirror adjacent a wooden chest of drawers. I began to remove my armor, starting with my helmet. Looking in the mirror, I stared at length at the scar upon the left side of my face.

**

Several years ago I was ordered to patrol the forest district located miles away from my cabin. It was much like your typical scary woods; however, yours probably lacked an enchanted barrier that prevented lost souls from interfering with the living. Some souls had gotten lost, others were abandoned or had even fallen victim to the contests. But their fates remained the same; stuck in the woods until Judgement Day.

CHAPTER FIVE

Paranoia invaded my mind as I cautiously traversed the path. Every so often a soul would scream off in the distance. As terrifying as the woods were, the Master still worried about intruders. They certainly wouldn't be foolish enough to come to the island intentionally. Any pair of feet that touched Eka's Island were bound to find themselves running for their lives at some point within the competitions. It was clear that the humans who came to the island willingly were destined to die first. They have no clue as to what they're up against.

Just prior to reaching the intended area, I looked up to see a snowy figure overhead. It was an owl perched on a thick tree branch. Was it a spirit? I continued, but to my surprise it vanished. I then jumped slightly as a mist zipped behind me. Leaves of bushes and trees rustled harshly as more spirits moaned. I pulled out my uniquely shaped Chaos Sword and gripped the handle tightly.

"Who's there?" I asked. "Show yourself immediately."

"Where's the fun in that?" a silky voice whispered in my ear. I whipped around and was completely overwhelmed by a swarm of ghost bats, their bodies lit like candles, and then disappeared into a black sky. I leaped back up as a woman ascended from a shadow cast on the ground. My heart dropped into my stomach. She had sparkling green eyes and wavy white hair the same color as her leather suit that was trimmed with black flames. A sheer cape clung to her sharp shoulder pads.

"Corona?" I asked.

"Corona isn't here anymore," she hissed between her teeth. "But I'll be more than happy to deliver a message." Several craggy blades slid out the sides of her wrists as she ran at me, yelling. I blocked her first move before catching her other wrist. The knives retracted and then speared out of her palms. The single, wire-thin blade extended in length until I thrusted my knee into her side.

I swung my saber at her numerous times as our melee weapons clashed, sending piercing metal shrieks throughout the forest. When I found an opening, I plunged my sword at her. She spun around, missing my attack by nanoseconds, and closed my arm in her leg. I pulled back immediately as a blade shot out of the sole of her high-heeled boot and swiped past my face. Quickly, she stabbed her other foot blade at me.

I locked her ankle with my sword, and headbutted her.

She stumbled to the ground. "Whatever happened to not hitting girls?"

"Whatever happened to you, Corona?" In my attempt to reason with her, she returned with a sharp attack. Was my old friend still intact? How did she gain these new abilities? We danced a deadly game until I sent a gust of Chaos Wind in her direction. The magic burst caused a nearby tree to explode and send shrapnel at her. Her slim body cartwheeled back multiple times to avoid the splinters before she gracefully performed a hand stand.

Instead of flinching from my charge, she whipped her legs around, simultaneously crashing her blades with my sword as she did. Skill did not begin to describe what sort of bodily coordination she had mysteriously gained. She suddenly slipped out of my sight, and I turned to see her emitting from a shadow painted on the ground. As I reached out for her, she slithered around my arm and jutted her blades out of her feet as a new pain settled its way near my heart.

"You see, Chaos," she began as I dropped my sword. "I'm faster—" she vanished, and reappeared through a wispy white portal above. "And stronger than you." She placed her palms into my skull shoulder pads, then shot her blades down the length of my arms.

My nerves shuddered within me as her knives tapped against my bones. She spun herself around, wrenching the blades deeper inside me. She followed this move by slipping my helmet off as she dismounted my shoulders. I fell flat against the ground as my helmet rolled off in the other direction. The woman stood over my weakening body. I reached for my sword, but her knives flashed out, pinning my palms to the forest floor.

I pressed my teeth together viciously as my fingers writhed at the young woman now slithering beside me. "You claim to have remembered the old me." Her green eyes sparkled at mine like a charm and her fingers gently stroked up my left side. "Perhaps this is something you won't forget about the new me." Her palm rubbed my cheek just before a blade struck my eye.

After that night, I failed to remember much. However, I was quite aware that the woman I once knew was now a stranger.

***

The following moment, there was a knock at my door, along with a muffled voice. "Chaos, are you home?"

I recognized it, and opened the door. "Felinis?" I asked. "I was not expecting you. Is something wrong?"

"I require your assistance," she replied earnestly.

"How formal. Sit." I motioned her into a seat and handed her a cup of herbal tea concocted from Vagura Root. I would have died that dreadful night without discovering that remarkable healing remedy. Ironically, I was thankful to have been attacked in the forest district rather than a different part of the island. "First, congratulations on your victory."

"You attended?" When I nodded my head she said, "I fail to see it as a victory, but that's why I came to speak with you this evening."

"Oh?"

"You guard the temple, don't you?"

"I do now," I affirmed. "The outer perimeters. Why do you ask this?"

"I need to get inside."

"What for?"

"Nothing, I'm just curious."

"In your case, Felinis, curiosity would not be good." She shot an evil glare at me. "Forgive me, but I cannot simply take you inside the temple against the Master's orders, and without a valid reason."

"I have a feeling," she started, "that Tourniquet could be hiding something from us."

"How can you be sure?" I asked.

"I am not, but I believe my opponent may play a large role in his potential operation."

"You're his servant, aren't you?" I began. "Can you not ask him yourself?"

"Not without raising his suspicions," She reminded. "He did briefly update me of his association with the Inigmus C.O.R.E."

I was all ears now. The Tah'leet Soldiers' scanners, located at their Central Officer Recruitment Environment, had obtained readings of electronic transmissions emitting from the island at the exact time when hundreds of their people went missing. Tourniquet was ill-tempered, but far from disorganized. If he were devising something against the C.O.R.E. he must plan it in secret first.

"If you are to infiltrate the temple," I said, standing up and walking over to my equipment. "You need a guide. Mantis is best suitable for the job. Tourniquet has programmed the schematics of the entire island into his databases. We can find him at the main courtyard and infiltrate the temple from there." I only despised having lost my fellow assassin to a machine, but he would've died if it weren't for the Master's haste actions. "Shall we begin?"

"Not so quickly," she spat. "What happens if we get caught?"

"By the twins?" she nodded. "They're strong together, so we separate them."

"From each other, or down the middle?"

"Whichever proves the fastest," I said with a grin before pulling my helmet back on.

***

Gargoyles were lined across the rooftop surrounding the back courtyard leading to the temple as Felinis and I cautiously closed in on Mantis' location. Together, we had narrowed our search to a single wall of doors on the lower walkway without running into trouble, but I still decided to play the watchdog anyway while Felinis advanced to our ally's living quarters. As I was waiting for possible threats, a flash of white lightning clouded my vision.

White suit. White hair. Green eyes. The young woman sat perfectly atop one of the gargoyles, her face gleaming from the delicate moonlight.

CHAOS

"Beautiful night," she cooed, staring off into the moon.

"You!" I yelled.

"Two brothers," she began, "created by God, and promised wives if they could master their dominions of light and dark. Iro, the Brother of Light, was presented with Hira Conte', but Eka, the Brother of Darkness, would never attempt to gain his. In his jealousy, Eka stole her innocence, forging a bloodline of pure evil. When Iro discovered his treachery, he split the world into the continents we have today."

"Why are you telling me this?"

"The moon, so…" she paused, changing the subject and facing me solemnly, "…damaged."

I continued to look up at her as she turned away and spoke.

"Two-sided, like a coin. Having both a frontward, haunting splendor and an equal, yet opposite dark malignance that hardly any see."

"Where is Corona? Where is the woman I know?" I asked her, raising my voice as she continued her soliloquy.

"Evil? The dark side of the moon?" she chuckled. "Darkness has never been evil. Instead, it has renewed us through sleep— sleep that heals us. Even enabling the sun to sleep, thus protecting us," she paused before faced me once again. "From the light we all know." Puzzled over the riddle, I waited for her to make her point, but another flash tore at the scene, sending me back to reality.

"What happened to you, Corona?" I wondered to myself.

"Chaos!" I whipped around to see a bony-faced man wearing royal purple assassin attire guarded by a leather breastplate. Two thin pieces of metal poked out from underneath his hood that resembled fangs, hinting at his codename.

"Viper," I said slowly.

"What are you doing out of your cabin?" he hissed suspiciously while taking several steps toward me.

"Guarding the temple," I answered.

"This is my area," he shot back.

"And I apologize. To answer you truthfully, I forgot tonight was my night to patrol the inner halls. I was actually heading there now."

Viper was the cleverest and wisest of all competing assassins, but I only hoped he was foolish enough to accept my words as genuine.

"Very well," he retorted hesitantly. "You may pass." He turned and continued where he hed been going. I breathed a sigh of relief and quietly made way down a different path. However, as soon as I did, a single snake-shaped arrow wisped past my face. In one fluid movement, I circled around, snatched it out of the air, and flung it back at the assassin wielding a matching purple bow forged from his own soul.

"Tourniquet has a new guard for the temple," Viper stated, having caught me in a lie.

"Who, your brother?"

"No," he replied, straightening himself into a fighting stance. "He's on his way here."

"How quaint of Rust to look after his younger sibling." I smiled behind my war helmet.

"He is my flesh and blood," Viper continued. "You disregard family and bring shame to yourself."

CHAOS

"A warrior relying on another's aid?" I suggested. "Apparently, I'm not the only one."

Now I had slithered under the snake's skin. The bladed ends of Viper's energized bow struck my Chaos Sword, sending purplish-white sparks trailing around our movements. I landed a successful slice against his abdomen before he managed to jump off my sword in my second swing. While in midair, the fangs of another arrow dug into the stone walkway. Viper then yanked himself forward with the purple energy linked to the back of the projectile, sending his feet pounding into the center of my chest.

I stumbled back before unleashing several bursts of Chaos Wind. A trio of arrows intercepted the cloud and created a blast large enough to shake the whole courtyard. The door leading to my intended destination was replaced by a gaping hole. Felinis and Mantis stared at Viper and I from the other side as I cried out to them.

"Rust is coming!" I warned. "Go now!"

The pair made haste for the temple as my battle progressed. The assassin's fingers stabbed the air beside my head multiple times until our forearms met. I locked my fingers around his and pulled him into a headbutt. My right fist then pulverized his gut before I knocked him sideways with my left. He entered a short-lived daze that granted me the opportunity to thrust into his back with both feet. A loud crack emitted from his veiny hand as it hit the ground, but that didn't hinder him from sending more arrows soaring my way. I knocked them down with a single swipe of my Chaos Sword and looked up to see Viper pressing his bow against it.

"I will not let you pass!" he hissed.

"I no longer need to," I spat.

CHAPTER FIVE

His serpent soul manifested and slithered behind me. I spun around to take defense against the lunging snake, but fell victim to another trap. Viper had struck an arrow into me. The fangs pierced my shoulder and collarbone. Despite my dense armor, his toxins had entered my bloodstream. I had been induced with his venom. Death was near; but not for me. I had reached my last resort.

"Chaos," Viper began, coming closer. "Do you feel my power? Infecting your veins? Withering each cell in that soon corpse of yours?" I smirked at the gargoyle mounted on the wall above him. "Clearly, you do, or else you wouldn't be lying there, decaying in front of me."

He grimly summoned another arrow. He pulled back the string, readying to fire. My sight glowed orange-red as my hand hovered over the stone walkway. Viper shot his arrow. The statue fell out of place. Viper partially rolled out of the way before he let out a scream in pain. His arrow stopped in front of me and vanished into thin air.

The snake squirmed, grunting in his useless attempt to crawl out of the statue's hold. "I'm going to rip out your heart!" he threatened.

"From there?" I mocked, standing up. "The medics will cure me of your stain, but I cannot guarantee your survival." I hurried to find the other two, but, unbeknownst to me, Rust had appeared to aid his brother.

***

"Brother!" The figure wore similar attire as Viper, only an amber-brown color.

"Get this off me!" Viper snapped without hesitation.

CHAOS

Rust reached under the gargoyle and pushed it off his twin's weakening body with extraordinary strength.

"You are severely damaged, but I can heal you."

"Then be silent and do it!"

A blotchy energy sphere formed between Rust's palms. Viper screamed in agony as he was slowly imprisoned in a healing crystal.

"Tourniquet cannot know that you fought outside of the contests! It is a violation of his rules."

"Like you ever followed the rules," Viper said before Rust closed the crystal imprisonment.

"I will leave, but will arrive again to take you home." With a snap of his fingers, the barrier became transparent and he left the scene.

Not long after his departure, the Master exited the shadows and strolled toward the crystal. He placed his hand against it as Viper screamed worse than before. Tourniquet smiled.

Name: Mantis AKA Subject 7Z-421
Weapons: Curved Hook Blades
Powers: None
Power Type: Elemental

CHAPTER SIX: MANTIS

SYSTEM: ONLINE

STREAMING DATA: 100% COMPLETE

---SUBJECT 7Z-421---

CURRENT MEMORY:

THE CENTRAL OFFICER RECRUITMENT ENVIRONMENT

Tourniquet looked like a shady character too, with an expression so intimidating that he decided to change it. Under a new guise, he spoke greatly to the massive array of Tah'leet Soldiers wearing their signature metal and leather uniforms who were standing about an auditorium.

"Imagine," he began, "a world in which war cannot exist." He paused, then slowly began to pace. "My creation allows such a world to prosper. As you see, I have brought a friend. Originally known as Subject 3B-306, Locust was a warrior, much like you all, but a tragic fall struck him half-dead. But that was no hindrance to the restoration of his old mind into a new vessel. Say hello to Subject 7Z-421. Say hello to Mantis."

CHAPTER SIX

Instantly, my curved-hook blades shot from the compartments on my forearms. The onlookers murmured in awe as four elite warlords looked from behind their tinted glass enclosed balcony. My "restoration" was far from anything I wanted, but it had been the only way to save my life.

My ideal reality would have to wait. Nothing was worse than having your humanity stripped away and being left in a body that wasn't even yours. My free will had been removed. By merely flipping a switch, I could be turned off, reset, reformatted, and forget everything this portion of hell brought me. This was my reward. I lost my life for saving another.

Tourniquet continued, "With my Cyborg Centurions and Krow Specters, never again will human lives be put on the line for matters of war."

"Wait," one of the elites spoke. "You want to destroy war with an army of robots?"

"Precisely." Several murmurs arose from the audience. "These robotic sects, the Centurions, guard as sentinels, and the Specters hunt and eliminate potential threats. With these in your grasp, no nation would dare rise against you or any other nation. You would become all powerful and have fleets to patrol your cities at your disposal."

"So this would also eliminate jobs for our people who have worked and trained to become soldiers?"

"With my Android Factor Venture, training would no longer be necessary, and as far as jobs go, I would hire your soldiers as repairmen."

"Correction," another voice spoke. "We would hire them as repairmen."

"Does that mean I have your approval?" The audience froze quietly. "You do value the safety of the C.O.R.E.'s inhabitants, don't you? They may be soldiers, but are their lives of any less value than ours? You have the power to commence the change of a lifetime. My Android Factor Venture allows you to bend machines to your will rather than your brothers and sisters. Isn't that better than throwing the lives of your citizens away into endless chaos? Every day, innocents put their lives on the line for the freedom of others." Tourniquet explained. "Our young people—dying before they've lived. Why would anyone want that? Never to dream, never to succeed, or become parents."

Some soldiers began staring at their feet, others wiping away tears. Other than his insult toward machines lacking free will, he even had me convinced at his performance. What would the elites say? The anticipation was overwhelming.

"Unlike many presentations we've seen in the past," a new voice spoke, "yours has certainly taken us by surprise."

If they only knew, I thought to myself as the voice continued.

"You have a sound argument and a clear passion for your work. However, we will stand by our current armed forces. Thank you and leave safely."

* * *

The two of us exited the auditorium and started down a corridor when a black-haired woman bumped into Tourniquet.

"Oh, I'm so sorry!" She cried, nervously passing by him. "I have a meeting I'm already late for, and it's my meeting! Please forgive me!" We turned, watching her walk away as a small rectangular slip of laminated paper lying on the floor caught my eye.

CHAPTER SIX

On it was the woman's picture along with her name. *Candice M. Luda: Receptionist, Apex City Asylum.* Tourniquet smiled darkly as he morphed back into his true form. Blood-red armor decked his body as a black cape hung about his broad shoulders.

"I'll be seeing you again shortly."

I created a portal and we returned to the island.

***

The scene was replaced by a static blizzard. Chaos joined us once more. I removed my circuitry from the computer.

"So that's why he wants to wage war with them?" Felinis began.

"What are you talking about?" Chaos asked.

"Tourniquet spoke to me about attacking the C.O.R.E. and how Quazar's role was necessary for creating his army."

"Attacking the C.O.R.E?" Chaos replied. "Why would he do that?"

"Clearly, because of the A.F.V.'s rejection," I said, motioning to the screen before us.

"Wouldn't it make more since if he launched an attack for the C.O.R.E. nearly finding the island?"

Felinis and I stared at him. "Now, what are *you* talking about?"

"Mantis once told me that some of the spectators and competitors Tourniquet brought were Tah'leet Soldiers. You also mentioned that around the same time, the C.O.R.E. had obtained strong signal readings coming from the island's general location. Not long after that, you departed to the C.O.R.E. with the Master."

"So there were dealings with the C.O.R.E. prior to the Android Factor Venture being rejected," Felinis stated with wide eyes. "What if it wasn't an offer, but a diversion?"

"What do you mean?" I asked.

"If Tourniquet was attacking out of anger with the rejection of the A.F.V., then he would've attacked by now. So why the wait?"

Chaos turned to me. "If what you told me was true, then what is the possibility that the Tah'leets dispatched a team to retrieve their lost citizens?"

"Quite likely," I retorted.

"If that's the case, the attack is to punish them for nearly reaching the island," Felinis spoke.

"And send those search parties back home," Chaos sighed, finishing her statement. "In addition to your diversion theory, the A.F.V. must have been a threat. In other words, Tourniquet showed them the very weapon he'd be attacking with."

"Weapon?" I asked. "You mean me?"

"Maybe, or maybe you aren't alone," Felinis said.

"Do you think Tourniquet could be using contestants from the C.O.R.E. to destroy their own city?"

"I don't know, but something tells me we're about to find out," Felinis stated. "He did inform me of two types of machines he intended to use."

"May we proceed to the temple?" I suggested. "Perhaps we could find more answers there."

Felinis and Chaos looked hard at each other until he spoke. "We will proceed at dawn that we may keep this matter hidden but from our eyes."

CHAPTER SIX

"Where can we go?" Felinis asked worriedly. "Viper has seen us."

"But Tourniquet has not," Chaos pointed out. "And Rust is still on the lookout."

"And we departed before his arrival. He doesn't even know who he's looking for," I observed.

"He was probably too busy tending to Viper's wounds." Chaos smiled. "And Viper must have cried agonizingly through it all rather than telling him who left him that way."

We all laughed.

"We'll keep this between us. Safe travels," Felinis concluded.

***

I was kneeling on the ground, my head weighed by an unexplainable pressure. I stared emptily into a rocky ground coated with a layer of cold powder. My fingers grazed the powder and I turned the tips toward me, watching the white particles vanish from my touch. Then I ran my fingertips down the hills of my palms and slowly slid them to my forearms. Something was wrong; instead of metal, I felt a strange jelly-like coating.

"What?" I exhaled, my breath visible. My hand reached for the hood of my cape, but it grazed something else instead. Abnormal small fuzzy needles poked from my head. I pressed my hands on them and yanked hard as signals rushed through my nervous system. My hands forcefully dropped in front of me as I laughed wholeheartedly. A rush of energy brought me to my feet as tears formed in my eyes.

I had it again. Felt it again. Was again.

MANTIS

I opened wide my arms and let the snow fall against my face, feeling every drop sink into my pores. This was a luxury I have long missed. Once a victim of the cold, I was now its companion. My facial muscles stretched into a smile as the warm sun embraced me, as if overseeing from its cloudy fortress and outlining the shadow of mountains with a flawless orange glow.

A faint noise released me from nature's deep allure. I turned and flicked my wrists to extract my claws, but nothing happened. I ignored the thought and saw a snow-covered creature with dark locks apparently losing battle to a machine.

"No!" I cried, running toward the pair. The machine stepped closer to the creature, pulling back its arm with the intention of delivering a final blow. The surrounding air shone brightly, almost mimicking the sun. I pressed myself to move on—hook blades or not, I was a weapon.

Now only feet away, I tackled the metal heap with his arm still charging his final shot. The landscape stretched into the sky until I realized we were falling. We traded kicks and blows until he released the shot into one of the rock walls. Then he vanished into a portal as rocks pummeled me from above and crashed into the raging waters below.

Two men cried out, "Locust!"

Before I met my fate, an immense shadowy mask opened its mouth and shut behind me.

***

I jumped up back inside the palace. "That should do it!" I awoke to two other allies of mine. Their names appeared on my internal visor.

89

CHAPTER SIX

The one tagged "ANIMAL" had brown, fingerless gloves that were a few shades darker than the hair covering his body and the lion tail protruding from behind him. His compelling orange eyes could induce fear into his victims and, despite his name, he was a very talented technician.

"You just had a few bugs," he said. I wondered if he fixed them or ate them. "How did you get all the way out here?"

Apparently I had been kneeling here too. I examined my surroundings and discovered I was in a tall-windowed pearl corridor.

"I—" I stuttered. "I can't remember."

"A few more minutes from now and you would have reached the temple's main room," Animal replied.

"Which is where we're going now." Her high-heeled boots clomped past us as her sheer cape shifted in the wind behind her walk. "Come now, we're going to be late," moaned the white-haired, green-eyed, "LIGHT."

"Alright, we're coming," he said, giving me a helping hand.

"I applaud you for assisting me, Animal," I began.

"No problem," he spoke as we walked to the main room.

I thought for a moment, "Wasn't her name Corona before?"

"Wasn't yours Locust before?" he replied. "Can't really say, but I'm sure this 'Corona' is far from perfect."

"What makes you say that?"

"Evolution," he explained. "If she was Corona, then she is Light now. And, like you, she has since evolved and is no longer part of that insignificant human race."

"Humanity is the direct opposite of perfection," I stated.

MANTIS

"Which is why it must be eliminated," Light stated from afar.

"But I was a human upon conception," I said. "Someone like myself cannot fully evolve from their past. I was and will always be human."

"But, Mantis," Animal said, "you aren't. That was then. This is now."

Clearly, they misunderstood my point. I glanced at the floor and witnessed an inky centipede crawling into a crack.

***

"You called us, Master?" Light said with Animal and I entering by her sides. Tourniquet sat at one of his golden snake thrones, this one located a few steps above the row of tables in the main room. Atop his throne sat a cobra with red-jeweled eyes that seeped power and stared directly into our souls. Good thing I no longer had one.

I noticed that no damage remained from Felinis' encounter with the princess. Tourniquet must have cast a reversal spell to fix the premises. I observed other Angels of Anarchy seated around a long table. My system schematics uploaded several names: CAPTAIN RED BLOOD. METSYS. PRINCESS QUAZAR. ENRAGE. TESLA.

Nine of us total, with a suspicious few missing.

"Subject 7Z-421, Mantis," Tourniquet began. "This is Cap—"

"I know who they are," I snapped, cutting him off.

Enrage was as dark as the night itself, aside from the red markings lining his body. His hair was made of sharp bones and he had black and red eyes. He didn't look too happy to be at this meeting—or any other for that matter.

91

CHAPTER SIX

Tesla was a beautiful Hispanic with a blue undercut hairstyle and a silky swath of hair thrown over her shoulder. She wore a black trenchcoat, coal gray pants, and high-heeled boots with buckles on the side. Her eyes were like Tourniquet's. His occasionally flickered small wildfires, but Tesla's constantly flashed miniature storms like those seen on summer nights.

"I added that effect myself," Tourniquet spoke up, sparking conversation. "How do you like it?"

"Not a bit unsettling," I lied as another zap trailed from one iris to the other.

"Cheers," Captain Red Blood said, raising a glass. "We are here," the pirate continued after clearing his throat, "to settle a little dispute between us and the C.O.R.E."

"What do you mean by 'little dispute'?" Animal asked suspiciously.

"The Inigmus C.O.R.E. has denied Tourniquet's offer." Princess Quazar said.

"The A.F.V.? Turned down?" Light repeated, testing her hearing.

"Yes. And your Master has a plan that will overrule their decision." The webbed man spoke, his tattoos glowing brighter after every word.

"That's right," Tourniquet said, turning to the boy. "Our *New Hope*."

The boy ground his fangs together.

"And what do you mean by overrule?" I asked.

"Destroying it," he answered.

"Who?" Animal asked.

Tesla replied, "All of us. From the inside out."

"Tourniquet, you can't be serious," I said, still surprised how right Felinis and Chaos were. "Could you imagine the hate and war you will stir up?"

He scratched his chin and said, "What were you expecting?"

Unfortunately, I could find no answer.

"Besides, the weapons have already been made," Metsys spoke.

"Everything is going according to plan," Princess Quazar chirped.

Light turned to Tourniquet. "You wanted them to reject it?"

"Yes."

"Why?"

"To divert them away from the island and allow these contests to continue."

How right they were.

"So," I continued, "you willingly brought soldiers from the Inigmus C.O.R.E., knowing they would call for help, only to return to their home, threaten them with *me*, and plan to attack just to hinder them from finding the island?"

Tourniquet simply smiled and said, "Contact with the outside world is not prohibited. This is their punishment."

"Why are you so determined to keep these contests?"

"To allow the victor to save my home world."

"Why have a sole winner to save your world when you could use the army intended to destroy the C.O.R.E. to save it instead?"

CHAPTER SIX

"That army consists only of powerless bodies and mindless vessels."

"Such as myself? You formed me; am I a mindless vessel?" I cried out.

"Yes, you are," Captain Red Blood reminded me. "And don't let humanity get in the way of that."

I tackled him and pinned him to the floor, pressing the dull end of my blade against his throat.

"Mantis, heel!" Princess Quazar ordered.

"I am not a dog!" I yelled at her before turning back to the pirate. "I have had enough disrespectful banter about humanity's flaws coming from humans! In fact, I used to be one, but you know absolutely nothing of that!"

"Don't just stand there; do something!" the captain choked.

Quazar jumped into a hover and sent a magenta sphere smacking into my back before landing next to Tourniquet. I tumbled forward and recovered fast enough to block an incoming attack from Enrage.

Tesla threw off her trenchcoat, revealing a blue leather suit and two electric, claw-shaped katars. Her veins glowed from the electricity running beneath her skin. Thankfully, my system had already downloaded data from her and Enrage. With the right buttons pushed, Tesla could overload herself, and Enrage could unleash supersonic waves of pure hatred. I was dealing with a walking power plant and a demon brat with a temper tantrum.

"We've got your back," Animal said with Light, running up to my side. "I'll take care of him!" Animal growled at Enrage, clenching his fists.

"Lights out!" Tesla taunted Light, charging her claws.

Light was as fast as her name and was already inches from the other woman's face, her knives jutting out of her wrists. The pirate and robot advanced toward me.

Animal fought Enrage and Light battled Tesla, which left me with the Captain and his assistant. I ejected my curved blades and charged furiously at them. Metsys blasted a red beam that hit my chest and sent me sprawling backward into the pirate's meaty hand. A green-and-red aura emitted from his palm as my body writhed painfully. When he tossed me away, I looked back and saw that he suddenly looked ten years younger.

"But how?" I asked myself.

"There's just enough humanity left in you to allow me to kill you," he chuckled.

"Deep inside your circuitry," Metsys added. "You're still alive. You were human once. I, on the other hand, never was." She sent another red beam at me.

I stopped it with my blades. "You say that like it's a good thing!" The beam pushed me, but not enough to make me lose footing. Suddenly the pirate absorbed her blast and became even younger and stronger. He then slashed at me with his ruby-encrusted cutlass. I parried his attack, but he knocked the side of my face with his boot. I winced as an obnoxious ringing deafened me from the impact.

He came at me again. I spun around, and to my surprise, it was Metsys' foot. Her fusion thrusters burned my metal face. She walked with her hands while kicking me, both thrusters on full blast. Seconds later I caught her, but then realized it was the captain. He punched me and crashed his cutlass against one of my curved blades. Upon turning again, Metsys struck me from above.

CHAPTER SIX

The others were enjoying their fights. At least that's what Light said while deflecting a blue bolt from Tesla's claw while keeping their fight balanced on a table. Light performed a handstand and swiped her legs merely inches away from Tesla's throat. Tesla stuck out her electric claw and flanked Light. The bolt sent her flying onto the far side of the table. Light rolled back to her feet, vanished, then arose from Tesla's shadow.

Tesla's knee crashed immediately into her rising opponent's neck before her electric claws stabbed her core region. Light flew into the wall opposite the room. Her back cracked harshly.

"Is that the best you can do?" Light groaned, standing back up.

"It's all I have to do!" Tesla sent a bolt trailing directly at one of Light's craggy blades. Electricity made her shutter, as she gritted her teeth. In a blink, the woman in white appeared to the woman in blue and kicked her until Tesla's blood coated her blades. The same bolt changed paths and struck Tesla as Light flipped out of the way.

Meanwhile, Animal and Enrage continued exchanging brutalities. He had never seen such an astounding competitor such as his newfound rival.

"You're good," Animal admitted, spitting blood onto the ground. "But not as good as me!" His inner beasts roared from deep inside.

Animal swiped at the glowing man multiple times before his tail snatched Enrage's throat in mid-roundhouse kick. Then he yanked Enrage's face into his left heel before slamming him to the ground with his other foot.

Enrage growled, then became a blur. Enrage spun in the air and landed the back of his heel against Animal's defensive arms. Murder was written in their eyes, though both were equally matched. Animal flung Enrage sideways. Enrage recovered with two energized blades swinging uncontrollably.

Animal was cut several times, but finally managed to crouch and grab Enrage's neck as before. He pushed himself up as his tail yanked Enrage into a headbutt. The blades vanished, and so did Enrage. Suddenly, he revealed his position by chopping between Animal's bruised shoulder blades. Partially stunned, Animal fell to his left knee and winced in pain.

Enrage's hands met his opponent's shoulders as his tattoos moved onto Animal, burning at their peak. Animal howled as his flesh sizzled under the markings. His tail whipped Enrage's legs and his tattoos retracted. Then Animal pinned him and punched his face repeatedly until Enrage's face glowed with fury.

Metsys placed my right arm in a lock, attempting to pierce my neck with my own claw and shoving it closer and closer. I retracted my blades, but that didn't stop the cracking of whatever was left from the bones in my arms. I could have tripped her if it wasn't for the pirate swiping my legs out from under me. He chuckled and pressed his cutlass against my throat.

Suddenly, as if given an extra burst of power, I shoved Metsys off me and kicked her square in the chest. She stumbled as I tackled her.

"You know the good thing about being part human?" I asked with the flailing cyborg beneath me. "It keeps someone from doing this!" I found her active chip, ejected my claw, and cut it out of her system. She dropped immediately.

"Metsys," I said, standing up. "Desynchronized."

Enough lightning spewed from Tesla's weapons to provide power to cities for months. As the two women fought, Light noticed how focused Tesla was on aiming at her wrist blades.

CHAPTER SIX

Light ran up to her and leapt up into the air. Tesla shielded herself, expecting a landing, but nothing came down. Tesla looked about the premises. A wisp of diamond-like white lights appeared from behind her as Light lodged two blades within her opponent's back. Tesla screamed as Light lifted her into the air, electricity trailing in every direction.

Tesla's bolts left the sky and redirected toward Light's blades. Light endured the shock, but Tesla convulsed uncontrollably. Blue lights burst out of her broken body and her skin soon glowed white with pure electricity while smoke was emitted from her pores. Light backed off as Tesla remained suspended in the air.

Just as I suspected, Tesla overloaded. Her searing corpse burst apart as lighting pierced the air about the room. One bolt planted itself into Enrage as his eyes and markings flashed blue momentarily. Now it was his turn.

"Animal, get back!" I cried out. He took cover from the glowing man as his skin became red. His breathing increased, along with his heart rate and blood pressure. He lifted his arms in front of his face and curled himself almost into a ball before he quickly reopened himself. His limbs stretched out, along with his back. His head pointed straight toward the ceiling as he screamed his heart out.

Thick waves of hatred emitted from him in all directions. We all took cover behind a table that had been flipped earlier. Captain Red Blood stepped in front of Metsys. He opened his arms as his colored aura appeared once again to absorb the energy. He gritted his teeth, unaware he shielded us all, until the power was his.

Moments later, Enrage collapsed to the battlefield. He had been defeated along with Metsys. Tesla was dead. Animal,

Light, and I were fine. Tourniquet looked down from his throne with Princess Quazar next to him. Captain Red Blood turned and smiled darkly, his eyes sparking red.

Apparently, he was just getting started. The three of us exited our hiding spot and stepped up to finish the battle. We all charged. The pirate struck Light, then shoved her away. Then he rammed his cutlass into Animal's stomach and started coming toward me. Was it because I defeated his assistant? Could I progress? Could I defeat him?

Before I knew it, I was looking up at the Captain with his boot pinning me to the ground.

"Kill him," Tourniquet said.

"I can't!" I cried out as his boot continued to press down on me. "H-he's too…strong."

Tourniquet chuckled slightly. "Who said I was talking to you?"

The world was ripped out from under me. The pirate opened his hand as a light emitted from his palm. Funny. My last word was *strong* and the one thing I lacked was strength.

"Subject 7Z-421, Mantis," Tourniquet's voice echoed. I watched as Captain Red Blood's palm continued to glow. My life flashed before my eyes. Would I become human again? What would become of Chaos, Felinis, Animal, or Light? I hated my new life—but at least I had one. "Desynchronized."

Name: Jared
Weapons: None
Powers: Heat Vision, Icy Spheres, Flying
Power Type: Elemental

CHAPTER SEVEN: JARED

M
y face scraped against a sandy surface. Water rushed into my face, making me cough and thrash harshly. I shook and pushed myself up with my forearms to briefly survey the area. My drenched suit weighed me back into the water. I pushed up again, this time scooting out of the ebbing tide.

Upon moving halfway up the shore, I collapsed facing the stars, my chest heaving painfully. The air's intensity enticed me as my sight stretched into further darkness. My eyelids grew heavier by the second, soon encasing the throbbing eyes. It was like my entire body was anchoring itself to the shore with no intention of detaching.

"The team!" I cried, lifting and grasping my side before lying down again. I peered back into the blue, desperate to find any trace of my fellow comrades. Then I saw a redheaded girl floating face-first in the water.

"Fern!" I rushed to her, sloshing through the thick waves as I did. I flipped her over and pulled her to safety then placed my ear against her heart, and fingers to her wrist. "Fern! Fern, wake up!" I cried, shaking her.

Suddenly, she awoke with normal eyes unlike the glowing ones from our fight aboard the captain's ship where we had last seen each other conscious. She coughed up sand and water while I helped her sit up.

"Jared," She moaned once she had calmed a bit.

"Are you alright?"

She didn't answer; simply pointed off in the distance.

I quickly turned to see Jak'al carrying an unconscious Kat in one arm and Cyclone in the other. The hybrid slumped to the ground. Fern and I struggled his way.

"How are you holding up?" Fern asked, viewing the deep cut on Jak'al's torso that Dahnarak had left during our previous encounter.

"Better now," Jak'al replied. "The salt burned, but healed it for the most part."

"Then a little Vagura Root should do the rest," she said, pulling some from her pocket and handing it to him. He nodded in thanks and took the healing agent before peering at the other two. Despite their unconscious state, Kat and Cyclone were still holding hands.

"Thanks for getting them, Jak'al," I said.

"Isn't that our job?" he chuckled. "It wasn't easy."

"It rarely is," Cyclone stated, lifting himself off the ground. He groggily turned to Kat. "Kat. Time to get up."

"Five more minutes," she groaned. We all smirked.

Cyclone turned back to us. "Yeah, she'll be fine."

I smiled. But after just a moment I noticed that Fern was gone. I glanced at a new trail of footprints and felt an irresistible urge to follow. I walked away from the others, hoping there were no plants nearby other than the dead grass sprouting from the sand bank. Fern sat, cradling her head, arms crossed and mind drifting in the watery horizon. Her orange-red hair wisped in the night's breeze.

"Beautiful night, huh?" I stated rather awkwardly, trying to start a conversation.

She sighed heavily. "Only if crashing pirate ships are beautiful."

I ignored her remark and sat beside her.

"Why couldn't I control myself?" she continued. "Time after time lately I've been losing control, and there's nothing I can do to stop it." Her emerald eyes locked onto me behind warm tears while I nearly lost myself in her peppery-freckled complexion. "I'm not strong enough."

"Don't say that." I wrapped my arms around her as she buried her face into my chest. "That's a lie and you know it. You are strong. In fact, you proved you're the strongest on the team."

She pushed away and snapped. "Don't you get it? I lost control. I brought down an entire ship! If I proved anything to this team, then I proved what a danger I am."

I sighed as well. "Maybe you're dangerous, but that's temporal. Give it time. Just because you lose control doesn't mean you're incapable of trying to keep it."

"Are you implying that I've not been trying?" Fern growled, sharpening her tone.

"No, I mean—"

CHAPTER SEVEN

"For your information, I've been doing more than trying, but every time I have control, it doesn't take long before I lose it again!"

Instead of arguing, I kept my peace and walked away.

Cyclone and Kat listened to Fern and mine's conversation from afar.

"Can you believe him?" Cyclone asked.

"Can you blame him? At least he's trying to talk to her, unlike some people."

Cyclone took her words like a knife. "What am I supposed to say?" he barked. "I don't understand how she lost control of her powers."

"And here I'd be, guessing that you, of all people, would be an expert on that," Kat said, glaring at him from the side.

"Excuse me?" Cyclone frowned. "Where is this coming from?"

"I don't know, the future perhaps?" she said, raising a brow.

Jak'al walked up to them. "Is something wrong?"

"No," Cyclone mumbled, eyeing Kat angrily. I stomped past the trio as Jak'al's eyes met me.

"Where are you going?"

"Out!" I stated, before shooting up into the air and landing hard elsewhere.

***

My chest burned with fury. That was all I felt when leaving the scene. Why were they all acting like that after everything that had just happened? We were literally fighting for our lives against vicious waves, and now it seemed we were on the verge of taking each other's. It didn't make any sense. I refused to think of it and tried to calm myself. The water looked different now—as if it were friend rather than foe. It made me think of the docks back home. It wasn't the best landmark, but it was home nonetheless.

Home—the place I longed for. I originally thought we would all return after our battle on the Hira Conte'. No matter what became of Captain Red Blood and his companions, they've either met their fate or are bound to be brought to justice. As soon as the 5X is ready, we'll be on the lookout for them.

Suddenly, a faint illuminating light hovered over the distant water. Was it an apparition or an enemy's device? Then it floated toward the shore, away from my position. To avoid leaving footprints with the potential of being tracked by natives of the unfamiliar place, I followed the fire by hovering. The light was a flame, like the precious head of a lit candle. Then the flame stretched into a pillar and disappeared into an opening on the bank side.

I landed and walked the rest of the way. The light was so soothing. As if I could sleep from where I was standing and still be warm. Although it was fire, it still gave me cold chills. It felt familiar. Like an old friend whispering to me that everything would be alright though my team and I were on a strange land.

To my surprise, the fiery pillar took on a human-like shape. Sparks shot at me. I yelped, startling the figure as it turned, revealing the side of a woman's face. She turned her head slightly to reveal pale eyes with small pupils. Hurriedly, I flew away in the distance until thunder rolled in the sky.

"Oh no." I speedily flew back to the group.

CHAPTER SEVEN

***

Lightning struck the sand at my next step, turning it into glass just before it shattered around me. I froze and looked up to my attacker. Hurricane sent another bolt my way, as I blocked it with an icy sphere.

"Where'd you come from, new Hurricane?" Hurricane asked.

"New Hurricane?" I enquired. "Haven't you seen a mirror lately?"

"I am not Hurricane!" He spiraled down and torpedoed my chest. I fumbled onto the sand and turned to Fern.

"What's going on? Where's Cyclone?"

"We don't know," Fern answered. "He just up and vanished."

"Then Hurricane appeared," Kat said, pausing from shooting her pistols. "Claiming that *we're* all *him*!"

"Oh no," I groaned, just before Jak'al caught Hurricane and slammed him to the ground. "Jak'al, stop!"

"Why? He's the enemy!"

"No he's not!" I cried out.

Hurricane chuckled and blasted a bright bolt from the center of the swirling cloud in front of him.

"Think about it," I told the girls. "Cyclone disappeared while Hurricane appeared."

"Are you saying that he's actually Cyclone?" Kat questioned as Hurricane landed between us.

"I've been Cyclone, Hurricanes!"

Fern released several spores at him. Just as he was launching his next attack, I sped into her. My eyes widened to see a small blinking light attached to her shoulder. I removed it, and she immediately transformed into Hurricane before our eyes.

"Whoa!" Jak'al exclaimed.

"Now there's two of them?" Kat spat.

"Fern?" the Hurricane who had been attacking us cried out, making his way to her.

"Don't you touch her!" Kat yelled defensively as Hurricane shoved her out of the way, making another device fall off her.

"Kat!" He cried apologetically in realization as she also transformed in our eyes.

"Cyclone!" she said, embracing him.

"I'm so sorry."

"Same."

"Apparently these were making us view each other as Cyclone's future self," I deduced, removing them from Jak'al and I.

"Then how could I see Hurricane too?" Cyclone asked. "Nothing hinted at you all, not even your powers. I just saw him with every move you made."

"Don't you have one too?"

"I didn't find one," he answered.

"With these devices attached we saw ourselves normally, but it caused us to see Cyclone as Hurricane because he didn't have one. When the girls' were removed, from our perspective, they also turned into Hurricane, while *you* saw them normally."

"So they must have been altering our perception of each other somehow," Jak'al proposed. "While those without a device looked like Hurricane to the ones who were wearing them."

"In short, can everybody see each other the right way now?" Kat groaned tiredly. We all agreed.

"So, the real Hurricane must be responsible for this," I concluded, crushing the last device.

***

A disgusting red claw with a network of pulsating external veins pierced the central staticky monitor. "They found them!" The sickly woman spat with bloodshot eyes as the other smaller monitors began to lose signal also.

"They found what?"

"Oh, um," she retorted innocently, turning to the masculine man entering the room, "nothing."

"I know that's a lie." His suit was red with a jagged "H" trailing down the middle. Behind him was a tattered black cape, and atop his head was slicked, spiky hair. A storm raged in his eyes. "You've been down here all day and accomplished nothing?"

The skin of the sickly woman's arm peeled forward, covering up her red claw. "Ugh, fine. Let me ruin my brilliant surprise!" she complained. "Okay, so you see these small blinkies?"

"*Blinkies*? Is that even a word?"

She shrugged her shoulders, "It's probably somewhere in the dictionary. Anyways, Captain Red Blood's minion, Metsys, she and I just so happen to be great friends, so I asked her for a favor," she explained. "I gave her blinkies to attach to the 5X's suits. Once she applied them, I was able to track…" she plopped down in a nearby chair and wheeled back to her fuzzy screens before finishing, "their every move."

JARED

"Well, well, well, Fever! What a wonderful idea."

"Excellent, isn't it?" she asked. "Thanks to Metsys, the five of them will go insane and I would've destroyed them from the inside out!"

"So…what were you yelling at earlier?"

"Oh nothing," she sighed heavily. "Just that they discovered my brilliant babies."

The man walked closer as the storm in his eyes intensified. "Prepare the portal. We have a delivery to make."

***

After our most complicated battle amongst one another, we decided it best to search for a place to stay the night. We had no intention of staying for a prolonged period, so we avoided the temple and headed straight to the infirmary nearby. We were greeted by a handful of doctors who were happy to provide us a place to stay while remaining undetected by the island's other inhabitants. Or so we thought.

The girls were fast asleep whilst Jak'al stood outside, deep in thought, occasionally glancing up into the nighttime sky. My aching head rested on my fist as I sat in the waiting room before Cyclone stepped in.

"Are you alright?"

"Yeah, you seemed worse than I did. How are you holding up?"

"Better than before," he admitted. "I'm just glad you found those chips when you did."

"Me too," I said. "Actually, that's not the only thing I found."

CHAPTER SEVEN

"What's up?"

"Fern and I had a small misunderstanding, so I left to cool off for a bit, and saw a woman."

"This is an island, so you're bound to see somebody," Cyclone chuckled.

"Well, she didn't seem like she belonged here," I continued. "But at the same time, it was like I knew her."

"Was she someone we've fought back in Apex?"

I considered that for a moment, "No. I don't know, maybe I was seeing things. After all, all this ocean water we've been under might still be in my system."

"Well, we're definitely in the right place for you to get checked out," he replied. "Should we ask people about the island to get a better understanding about the predicament we're in?"

"Maybe, but not right away," I said. "We need to devise a better strategy. There's no telling who we can trust around here. This is nothing like home." I caught myself staring down the hallway as a small spark caught my attention. I paused, believing it to be the woman again, and ignored it. But when it happened again I murmured, "But observing doesn't require strategies."

"Well, I guess I'll rest up for a bit if that's everything," Cyclone said.

"You do that," I stated. "You'll need to get some sleep after everything that's happened today." I made sure he left before making my move.

I walked around the room, studying the equipment, when the aura I sensed suddenly felt *wrong*. Along the walls and shelves of the medical facility were syringes filled with a strange green plasma that reminded me of a criminal we once fought.

JARED

Come and see, a voice whispered temptingly in my head. Though it seemed concrete, it felt as if it were coming from another room. It was my duty to find its origin. The whisper continued to chant the phrase.

Come and see, come and see. Then I came upon a door that read "RESTRICTED" in bold letters as it easily slid itself open. A counter in the corner held a smiling harlequin mask that stared back at me with empty eye sockets. A charred body lay on the examination table in the middle of the room underneath a thin, blue, papery sheet.

Come and see, the voice tempted for the last time as I made my way to the mask. The door shut and locked automatically as a long, awkward moan arose. In the corner of my eye, I could've sworn that the body was standing inches from me.

My heart leaped into my throat as I whipped around. The body was still covered, but I had no method of opening the door without blasting it and being detected. I turned back from examining the door when a laugh made my skin crawl.

"Heh, heh, heh, heh, he, he, he, he."

Peering back at me was the ugliest thing I've ever seen in my entire life. Whatever was left of its face was freakishly scarred and its irises were a green-yellow color with black rings around them. The whites of the monstrosity's bulging eyes were an oily black, and devilishly pointy ears were mounted on either side of its head. It greeted me with an abnormally large smile with sharp teeth.

"What the heck?"

The thing laughed creepily again and leaped into the air before locking his legs around the light fixture, causing them to flicker. It wore a jester suit with a black-and-red diamond pattern with a partially shredded golden neckpiece.

I grabbed a nearby syringe and held it above me. "Stay back!" The demon growled at me playfully. I stabbed the syringe at him, but he merely smacked it away.

"You shouldn't play with such sharp objects!" he giggled as I braced myself for battle. In a flash, he pinned my neck against the wall with his foot. "Now, now, you're not playing fair!" He glanced at the mask and snatched it with his freakishly long tongue, pulling it tight against his face. Then he placed a belled hat from his pant pocket that matched the peculiar attire on his head. "I'm ready now!" he proclaimed, tossing up a ball with a neon-green smiley face. It made a slight ticking noise before bursting into flames. The demon laughed and pointed at me.

"You must be dying of laughter!" I said. "Let me put you out of your misery!"

"Oh," he hissed back. "I thought you were a hero! Don't worry, blood makes me happy too!" he slapped his knee and continued with an evil, rolling laugh. "Okay, time to get serious now, I guess!" he balled his fists and charged at me.

"Bring it on, clown."

"Name's Jexter!" It sounded like he said "Jextah" with his strange accent. Was he a relative of Dahnarak's? He threw a hit then spun around to kick my chest. I fell to the ground, my head just inches from hitting the examination table. I gritted my teeth and leapt back up.

I blasted him straight on the chest with my heat vision and sent him flying to the opposite side of the room. Various potions and medicinal aids spilled onto the floor as more of his bombs went off. Smoke clouded our lines of sight. I seared the smoke to unmask his presence, but lost track of his movements. He couldn't have just disappeared; it would've been too good to be true.

"Hey!" I heard from above. Jexter had somehow pinned his claws to the top of the ceiling. Behind my back, I charged two ice-spheres. He bent close enough where our faces were leveled, this time without his mask. "What's up?"

His forked tongue darted out of his mouth. I quickly sidestepped and froze it with an icy grip before ripping him off the ceiling. Before he could recover I struck the other sphere between his shoulder blades and smiled as the blue shrouds entered his bloodstream, freezing him in place. As his gruesome body continued to crystallize, I flung him down.

"Now you," I said as he backed cowardly against the wall, "TALK!"

Name: Jexter
Weapons: Smoke Bombs, Prehensile Tongue
Powers: Inhuman Flexibility
Power Type: Shadowstry

CHAPTER EIGHT:
JEXTER

T alk now!" I'm guessing the kid was getting tired of playing. He was so angry that his eyes were even glowing red while I was freezing like an Eskimo. He stomped on my half-frozen back. We both heard more than just the ice cracking.

"What ya' want?" I asked, annoyed. He stood there expecting me to have the answer. "Look dummy, don't take 'til tomorrow, I gotta pee."

"Get up!" he yanked me off the floor. "Who do you work for?"

"Jexter works for no one!" I replied. "Not even Tourniquet." I didn't care if he owned this stupid island, no one expects me to fight, or do anything for that matter! I'm a big kid now and surprisingly smart enough to pick my own battles!

"How do you know him?"

I raised an eyebrow.

"Tourniquet!" he reminded, shaking me.

"Quit it!" I pushed him away. "You're going to make me puke!" He slung me down, causing me to knock my noggin. "You want to hear my story, do you?"

CHAPTER EIGHT

"I just want answers."

"But do you truly know your question?" Confused, he stood straight and glared down at me. "I'll answer all your questions, *after* you hear my story. 'Kay punkin?"

"Fine," He replied with a stern look on his face.

I smiled back, not that he could tell, for I was putting on my brilliant mask. "It all started like this in the Kingdom of Reyes. This place, this castle, Reyes, was ruled by King uh...whatever. He was a very nice dude. Any-who, I met this lovely lady..."

***

I was walking about the market street, looking for someone to spook. The night was calm and the moon was a sweet, beautiful blue. But I *hated* quiet moments and, for me, scaring people was an addiction. Fear was my drug, and a pure sickness to others. I was always told that scaring people made their skin crawl, and I intended to watch that happen.

So I was creeping about, minding my own business, when my eyes had finally locked onto my next victim. She donned a fancy white gown and was sniffing a glowing bushel of forget-me-somethings. I can never seem to remember their names. Then I realized she was picking the perfectly pretty flowers and putting them in the bun of her hair.

Sneakily, I tiptoed toward her and only looked down when a twig snapped under my step. Wide-eyed, I peered back up at her. She was still picking those dang flowers! She didn't even bother turning around! To make sure I didn't make another mistake, I made one huge step and planted myself next to her. Perhaps I would die from her beauty. I tapped her shoulder, and she jumped slightly at the sight of me.

"Oh, you scared me."

Clearly, I did not. I expected a much better reaction; if only it weren't for that stupid stick.

"You don't need flowers to make you beautiful," I said, politely smacking one of the flowers out of her smooth hand.

She smiled. "That's not what my husband thinks,"

My heart sunk. "Your, husband?" I asked, nervously running a hand through my thick brown hair before resting it on my neck. "How could a lucky man such as he say something like that?"

"Oh, I don't know," she replied. "I wish I had the chance to take it back."

Then I had a lovely idea. "Anytime you want a do over—"

"Isabelle!" a distant roar interrupted me.

I glanced back and forth before leaping into a nearby bush. It was surprisingly uncomfortable.

"Please don't go," She called out as a large bearded man in an aged leather apron appeared behind her.

My heart pounded with excitement. Whatever was to become of her?

His meaty hand snatched her forearm and he leveled his face to hers. His breath must have smelled like cow dung based on her disgusted expression from the moment he opened his mouth. "What in Eka's name are you doing out this late?" he demanded, yanking the glowing forget-me-somethings out of her hair. She smacked him away.

"I do not need your protection or permission. I can and will venture out of my own volition!"

CHAPTER EIGHT

Oh cool, she rhymed! Suddenly I heard a loud smack and leaped out of the bush. Her face flustered a bright red and the large man turned to me.

"Who is this?" he bellowed as I waltzed to the couple. Her tears choked her voice as the man just raised his own. "HUH?"

Once the moonlight illuminated his brute-face, I recognized him—Malacus Olrello, the blacksmith. For years we hated each other, and this scene wasn't really helping. I kneeled next to Isabelle and put her arm over my shoulder.

"Put my wife down!" he demanded.

"Your wife?" I carried her now and looked into her eyes. A pure, sweet, innocent gray peered back at me, though her right cheek was still red from her abuser. "Try, er—victim!"

She motioned to me that I could put her down, and the moment I did, she vanished into the night.

"You dare challenge me, you insolent swine?"

"I happen to like bacon," he swung at me, but I moved fast enough to jump out of the way.

Unbeknownst to us, the king and his men were exiting the castle. Using my deceitful talents, I quickly developed a plan, and couldn't help smiling about it. I grabbed Olrello's hands and clamped them around my own neck. Giggles. The knights readied their crossbows and swords as the king ordered my release. Thanks to my plan, Malacus Olrello became furious, leading to his inevitable arrest and escort to the castle dungeon.

"Thank you so much, that crazy dude wouldn't stop for anything!" I informed the king.

"You're welcome."

He replied weakly with his old self.

"How can I repay this generosity?" I hoped he'd ask me to become a knight. It was my dream to become a knight. That's all I cared for, other than scaring the living Beelzebub out of people.

The king scratched his gray beard. "How would you like to be my jester?" he offered.

"I would be honored!" I snapped back to reality. "Wait, what?"

"I wish for you to be my new jester."

Hmmm, I thought, *the last one was brutally mauled by a wolf. I can't wait.*

"If you worked for me, you would never have to worry about this kind of situation again."

I considered it for a bit. "Okay, I accept your offer," I said. "Now, how much are we talking here?"

"Hmm?" asked the king.

"Like bi-weekly, part-time, minimum wage, volunteer?" I scoffed, rolling my eyes. "Cuz honestly, I hate both."

"Both?"

"Eh, no thanks," I continued. "We can talk more about pay later."

***

"Now that you are a part of the high society," the maid accompanying me up the stone staircase conversed. "You can have the last jester's old room." Torches were mounted on posts on either side of the stone hall. Fancy wooden doors were just yards apart from each other, each leading to separate rooms.

"Alright, so which is his room?" I asked curiously.

"Here." We came upon a door, slightly different from the others. It was so disgusting it looked as if the entrance were made of cobwebs.

"Not to sound rude, but has this door ever been cleaned?"

"It's the strangest thing," she answered, "but every time I used to clean off the cobwebs, later on the same broom I used would be outside my door and broken in half. I don't understand how it happened or why!"

"Really? How peculiar."

"Very. So…now I just let it go,"

She opened the door and the inside of the room was completely empty except a single sheetless bed and chamber pot. Let's not confuse those two!

"You never added anything to this?"

"We never thought we needed to," the maid answered. "Not every day does the king ask for someone to be his jester."

"Good point." Not every day do they become dog food either.

"If you need me, just call."

"So what's your number?" I asked.

"You should definitely practice the jokes." She left with a rather confused expression.

"Service sucks here anyways," I moaned, pulling out my cellular device to simply toss it aside. I spread my limbs and soared to the bed, and soon discovered the kingdom must have been too lazy to get a mattress as well. I laid flat on the thick wooden board. "Ow. I'm in heaven."

Upon the sheetless bed was my new red-and-black diamond-patterned attire, folded neatly, along with a pair of belled shoes and matching hat. Well, you know, until I landed on it.

I picked up the suit, blew off the dust and spiders, and made a face. I removed my filthy garments and pulled the costume over me. It was slightly tight, but fit just right. Ooh cool, another rhyme! Anyways, I pulled the pants on and fastened the belt before slipping on the shoes. Now I liked scary things, and this room was a bit too boring for me to handle, so I decided to explore the castle.

I slid the stone hallways and down the railing of the coiling stairway. To my surprise, an old maid was coming up the stairs with supplies. It was too late to move, and I slammed into her.

"Gotta go!" I cackled. She glowered and helplessly got back to her feet. She was at least eighty-something, so she had plenty experience with standing back up on her own. I didn't need her attitude.

I sprinted down the last hall when a torch caught my attention. The fire sizzled and poofed! I landed into the wall to shield myself as my pulse heightened excitedly. Then the fire took on the shape of a fine lady, even her hair was made of towering flames.

"Hey, Hot Stuff," I said, exiting my hiding spot. She turned to me. Her eyes were tiny white pupils and she was impressively stunning. "How's a hug sound?" I asked her.

"Dreadful," she responded. "Touch me and you will get burned."

"Where did you come from? Are you a knight also? I've never seen you before."

"I am not a knight, but a warrior all the same," she said. "You are not a knight either."

"Well, of course I am!" I said proudly.

121

CHAPTER EIGHT

"Avoid the blacksmith," she warned.

"Excuse me?"

"Avoid the blacksmith at all costs. He seeks something more precious than your life."

"That fat fool is deep in the dungeon."

She evaporated moments later, and I continued my adventure. I found the king standing by a couple of knights.

"Well, look at you," he said to me. "Now it's time to test your worth as my jester."

"You mean jokes?" I replied.

"That is what a jester does around here. They're harlequins, comedians," he said.

"Yeah, I just don't know any." Let's just say I had a much better sense of humor than your average Joe. "Fine. Uh…Got it!" I thought for a moment. "What is the name of the man who can catch the moon?"

The king and the knights were puzzled. They looked at each other funnily. They were trapped. Right where I wanted them— confused. "What?" a knight asked.

"A *knight*," I said, laughing. They joined in too.

"Get it?" One of the knights laughted, "He catches the moon because—Wait I don't get it."

"Shh! Give us another." The king ordered.

"Thousands of these tiny things work together to create the big picture," I said.

Stunned again; they had no idea!

"Could you give us a hint?"

"The things are colorful and tiny that create a big picture." One knight whispered the riddle to himself. I was beginning to get annoyed. It was so easy! "Just so you know, you can't give up on this one."

"Mosaic tiles!" the king cried.

"Yes!" I replied, pointing. "Alright, here's the last for now. The man who makes it, doesn't want it, the man who wants it, doesn't use it, and the man using it, doesn't know he has it!" They were completely stumped on this one. Surprise, surprise. Then I heard a low, deep growl behind me mumbling the correct answer.

"A coffin."

I turned to see Malacus Olrello's brute face looking back at me.

"Of a dead man," he finished.

"Correct!" I replied.

"How did you escape the dungeon?" the king asked as the two knights unsheathed their sabers.

"Because you forgot to shut the door!" I cried out, causing the two knights to laugh hysterically.

"Now that's funny!" one cried as the king glared at him.

"It wasn't too hard," Malacus Olrello growled as the three started to back away cautiously. "Your so-called knights were easy to kill. By the way, their puny swords," he reached his huge fingers and bent one of their blades. "Make wonderful tooth-picks!"

"That's enough!" I said, running up to him. The giant knocked me over and my body went limp.

***

CHAPTER EIGHT

The stench of fire lingered in the atmosphere. I was restrained by leather straps on the armrests of the seat when a sinister chortle arose. "You fly. For too long, you've bothered me."

I recognized it was the blacksmith. This must have been his workshop. The floor shook every time he took a step. "What do you want?" I asked. "Please, I'll give you anything!"

"Actually, I was planning on giving *you* a gift instead." He tore off my blindfold and I suddenly saw a burning white item. "I forged this from an amber housing poisonous yarators. Little demon-scorpions capable of intoxicating beasts as tall as towers. They are known for exactly that reason."

He used a metal picker and brought the hot thing to my sight. The object was a highly heated and nicely constructed mask. Funny how the mask was the same exact proportions of my face, huh? He brought the white-hot metal toward me.

"STOP! STOP! YOU DON'T KNOW WHAT YOU ARE DOING!"

But Malacus Olrello didn't care. He advanced—slowly, ever so slowly inching the thin mask onto my now-sizzling face. I howled in pain, my body twitching, legs jerking, body convulsing! It burned— oh, how it burned! My flesh popped and seared as it melted, fusing with the hot mask. The pressure erased my breath, my hands and fingers played an invisible piano that only orchestrated despair. Even the mask's indentions of eyelids stuck to my own.

Suddenly the amber mask was now completely stuck on me and refused to budge—until Malacus mercilessly yanked it off!

The air singed my naked face as I looked closer at the mask. Hanging off the side was a floppy thing. It looked like skin. Malacus Olrello tore it off and tossed it in my lap. To my fear, I discovered exactly what the slab of skin was. I stared back at me, screaming. It was my face.

"Now you suffer."

***

Dead…silence filled the area. The blacksmith was nowhere to be seen. The fire was out. My shackles were loosened. Only the stench of burning flesh remained. My face felt weird. Oh, well, you know. Not hurting anymore—just numb. A numbness I couldn't explain.

I let out a scream that would curdle anybody's blood. I immediately hit the ground and forced myself to crawl over to the fleshy slab of skin that used to coat my face. My face. Yarators that had been freed from the amber crawled between the strings of my facial muscles. In my attempt to rid them, they would only burrow deeper inside my tissue.

My hand shook as I picked up the slab and attempted to put it back on. When I saw failure in my actions, I stuck my finger through the eye socket and held it.

Then it hit me like something that hits. I frowned and threw the face away. I was free! I didn't need it! I was so enlightened! How did I not see it? This whole time my face was just weighing me down! I would be so much more powerfuller without my skin. I wanted it gone. ALL GONE! I was so excited. I could scare whoever I wanted now—and with more than enough disgusted feedback! At least more than just a miniature jump. I looked forward to smothering my face in EVERYTHING! No rainfall, pillow, or bag of needles would ever feel the same against my skin.

Everything was different now, and I loved it. And without eyelids? I wouldn't even have to worry about not scaring people. My eyes would always be open; I wouldn't miss anything.

CHAPTER EIGHT

"Jester," said a voice that made me jump.

"Please, come forward!" I retorted. "Help me."

A hand touched my shoulder. I turned around and laughed eerily, though the man was not fazed. "Do you enjoy *frightening* people, or frightening *people*?"

"Yes."

"We don't know each other." He paused. "Not yet anyways."

I thought for a second, wondering what he could possibly want from me, and then he waved his arm around as a strange fog formed. A dream perhaps? I couldn't put my finger on it, but I liked what I saw. The mist floated in front of us.

"Your talent for sneaking up on people is no ordinary gift," he said, gesturing to a figment of me in the smoke wearing the strange mask, tiptoeing behind Olrello.

"Your enemy." I smiled as he died at my hands before the vision morphed to a new picture. "And the girl of your dreams..." he trailed off.

I saw Isabelle hugging my neck as I kissed her, the me with my own face, that is. Her smile nearly brought gator-size tears to my eyes. "I can grant you your heart's desire."

"How do I get this strength?"

"The poisonous yarators," he explained, pacing. "They keep you from dying and give you massive speed and strength, at least for now. Unfortunately, their poison will eventually kill you after altering your mind."

"Too late for that!" I squealed. The man looked at me, annoyed, before speaking again.

"Luckily, I have a way to prevent that."

I had so many mixed emotions and my mind was filled to the brim with questions. How long would it have taken for the poison to kill me? And when? Is this what Hot Stuff had warned me about earlier? "How do I live forever?"

"I'll tell you once you finish Malacus Olrello."

***

I left Malacus' workshop long enough to devise a scheme before heading back. Outside it, I waited to finish him once and for all. I smelled the heat of the furnace as hammering noises filled my ears. I poked my head through the window with caution and gasped at the sight. Isabelle was standing there, hammering a mallet against a thinning metal. The handle of her creation resembled a pair of intertwined snakes.

I peered over to the corner. Strangely, Malacus Olrello was bound in chains against a post. I believed that brute deserved so much more than that. I leaped into the window and tiptoed to Malacus Olrello. His face was bruised and he pleaded for help through a muffled mouth. I smiled, showing my new fangs at him, shaking my head.

"You took my face; I'll take your life and live forever!" As I raised my claw at him I turned to Isabelle, who stared back at me coldly.

"Who are you?" she asked.

"Hello, darling, it's me! We met earlier, remember?" I chirped as she made a disgusted face. "I had a little work done. Hubby here gave me QUITE the facelift!"

"State your reason for being here."

"A mysterious man came to me, showing me a vision," I explained. "It showed that he was dead," I indicated to Malacus, "and we were together. He also told me that once I killed him, he'd tell me how to live forever."

"The vision was only half true." She picked up the blade she'd forged and walked up to Malacus and I. "He died." She stabbed the saber through the column and his spine.

"NO!" I screamed as Malacus choked out his last breath.

"But I shall never love you."

I was so full of anger and frustration. She'd stolen my immortality! "You vile woman!" I jumped and tackled her. My hands finally managed to wrap around her throat, but soon lost their grip due to a hard kick. Then she jumped on top of my shoulders and wrapped her legs around my neck, causing us to topple to the floor. I flicked my tongue at her and it wrapped around her arm, which was going for another blow. Then I flipped backward and flung her into the column. What exciting powers came along with this new curse of mine!

Her fragile back cracked against the pillar before she collapsed like a ragdoll. She weakly stood upright as I leaped over to her. I grabbed her right shoulder and smiled at her evilly before flinging my wet tongue in her ear. She jerked away in disgust and kicked my chest. I landed into the main worktable as several spherical devices fell, rolling along the ground. The impact shook the wall and made a bear's head land in front of me.

Malacus Olrello could so use an extreme makeover, workshop edition. Running up to me, her eyes red with anger and smoke billowing from her flaring nostrils, Isabelle attempted another hit. I tossed the bear head at her while kicking the spheres. They exploded, making smoke arise. How fancy!

Isabelle coughed and I dropped from the ceiling and on top of her—obviously a blind spot. She struggled. I laughed. Her back arched as she flung me off.

"I'm sick of playing games!" she cried out.

"I'm not!" I retorted, leaping and kicking her with both feet and perfect hang time. Isabelle flew backward into the wall as it collapsed on impact. The dust covering her mixed in with the foggy night air. Her eyes widened in terror as my fists planted on top of her skull.

She fell onto her back. "Now time to finish you off!" I screamed in her ear. I snatched her limp ankles and dragged her over to the edge of the cliffside across from the workshop. I flipped the woman over and looked her dead in the eyes. "This was for tricking, ME!" I stomped on her shins and flung my tongue around her neck and held her over the cliffside as she cried relentless pleas and reasons why I shouldn't commit a crime like that.

"You're not a killer!"

"I'm not; you are! You took my chance for immortality! You killed me!" I yelled, slipping my grip. She squealed in fear as my tongue caught her small, but able wrists again. Waves crashed the island side below.

"What do you mean? How was I supposed to know?"

I released my grasp completely and smiled, watching her fall to the jagged rocks below.

"That's going to hurt in the morning." Something caught my attention on the ground. It was the sword she'd been fighting with. My foot knocked it down to join her in the sea. "Maybe it'll hit her, if we're lucky." I waved goodbye to both her and the sword before walking away.

CHAPTER EIGHT

I returned to Malacus Olrello's office, tiptoeing through the fallen wall, and stared at his corpse for a good five minutes. He seemed to be more immortal than I did. Then my attention turned to something else.

"Death mask," I said, picking up the relic. "Thanks," I told Malacus' still form. "I don't think you'll need it anymore, so I'll keep it. Besides, you made it just for me."

I pulled it on and returned to my room in the castle.

***

"You fool!" the man barked.

"I thought you'd be pleased," I said back.

"I said I would tell you how to gain eternal life if you killed Malacus Olrello!"

"I know. Isabelle got in the way!" We looked at each other for a few seconds. It was quite relaxing.

"Fine," he replied. "But you will have to wait."

"Wait?" I screamed as he nodded. "I'm dying here!"

"I know that, but you can wait."

There was no point arguing. If this man could give me life, then I must obey his commands. I accepted the fact and moved on.

***

"And that's my life!" I finished my long, eccentric monologue. "Next time you can take a part, or…or I can use voices!"

"So you actually saw a fiery woman?"

"Oh yes!" I cooed dreamily.

"Do you know anything else about her other than what you told me?"

"No sir-ee! Why did she stick out to you of all things?"

"That's none of your concern," the boy replied. "How did you come back from the dead?"

"Excusi?"

"You never gained immortal life. The yarators kept you living, but poisoned, and, from the sound of it, that was centuries ago; so how are you still alive?"

"Wishful thinking?" I suggested. I couldn't tell him. A girl's gotta keep her secrets, ya' know? "As you should know, Tourniquet rewards the winner of his competitions with whatever the heck they want. At least that's what I've heard. So good luck, Biscuit!"

"What? No...I'm not in the competitions."

I laughed evilly. "Silly! Anyone on the island *is* a competitor— with or without consent—which probably means this will be our first and last chat."

"What do you mean?"

"Didn't you and your buddies wash up here the other day?" I asked him.

"How do you know about that?" he asked me.

"Stuff goes around. You five washing up here was your ticket to Hell! Welcome to Hell!" I wondered how badly he was freaking out inside. I could tell by his facial expressions that he was getting mixed emotions too.

Suddenly there was an indifferent freezing noise at the wall. I looked over there so quick that my neck popped painfully. I ignored the funny feeling and looked back up to the wall before pulling the teenager beside me as the amber-ice flew toward us.

I peered around the table behind which we hid as a rusty voice boomed, "Where is Jared?"

Name: Rust
Weapons: Rusty Hammer
Powers: Teleportation
Power Type: Elemental

CHAPTER NINE: RUST

S how yourself!" I ordered. A young man stood up from behind the examination table. "Make haste! We are scheduled for a fight in the main palace!"

"How do you know my name?" he asked.

"Tourniquet told me about you and your team. He's teleported them to the palace already. Failure to comply will result in their demise."

"Wait a second!" he exclaimed, scanning the room as if he were expecting someone to follow.

"Do you jest? Cause me to delay and you'll be dealing with the Master on your own." I granted myself a head start out of my makeshift entrance without waiting on him.

***

The walk back to the palace felt much longer than the one leaving it. Jared and I were greeted by the giant doors at the temple's front, already opened like the mouth of a predator ready to devour. An inanimate Tourniquet glared at us as idle contestants lining the room groaned, peering back at us through stone eyes. Though I showed no sign of it, part of me felt as if they would tear us apart like wild dogs upon Tourniquet's command.

"Well, it took ya' long enough!" said a weird Australian girl.

"*You* didn't have to look for him," I snapped.

"This is Rust and Jared's first battle, but it could very well be their last." Tourniquet spoke as we centered ourselves before his throne.

"Thanks for the pep talk," Jared mumbled.

"He made us late."

"No matter," Master Tourniquet replied. "You two shall fight Talon," he began, motioning at a pale-blue woman with pitch black hair who stood on his right. She unfurled her wings, which had been covering up her body, and flashed her claws. Talon was the eldest of the five Siren Sisters. The other sirens were Cathydra, Qeera, and the twins, Torre and Lorre. Talon's party was unable to attend the competitions, however, she was indeed a formidable opponent, given the rumors were true. "And Lance."

"And who?" Jared asked me.

"Be quiet."

"Who did he say?"

"J-Jared?" Lance stuttered, recognizing his friend. He turned to the throne, "I-I can't fight him."

"Then you will die," Tourniquet responded. "Rust and Jared versus Lance and Talon."

"I won't fight you," Jared told Lance.

"Didn't you hear?" I began. "He's not meant for you." Jared stood directly in my way, shielding his ally.

"You won't fight him either."

"Then you will also die." I stepped forward, bumping his shoulder. "I accept the challenge." I eyed Jared. "Although I prefer to work alone."

"What do we do?" Lance mouthed to Jared as he shrugged.

"FIGHT!" Tourniquet roared.

I summoned a rusted battle hammer and blocked the bird-woman's first blow before slamming into her.

"I thought she was mine," Jared whined.

"I was blocking her attack!" Immediately after, Lance struck me over the head with his electric double-ended staff. I fell, then rolled back before throwing Lance into Jared. Several members of the audience murmured, "What is he doing? Wasn't that his partner?"

"What do you say we take these guys on together?" Lance asked Jared.

"Doing so would result in me killing the lot of you," Tourniquet said. "But nice try."

Lance stared at him blankly before turning back. "Guess we have no choice then. You would do the same for Fern, right?"

"What?" Jared said. "You can't be serious. We don't have to fight."

"Fighting and killing are two different things." Lance replied as a new wildness settled in him, almost mimicking that of Talon's. "But I'm not losing to you!"

Jared yelped as Lance jabbed his electric staff into his knee and shot a thousand volts through it. He screamed, reaching for the weapon, but I froze it with a rusty aura before tackling him.

CHAPTER NINE

I punched him multiple times, then formed another hammer over my head as Talon's thick wing draped over me. A sudden whirlwind of slashing claws overcame me as my stomach churned. She ascended quickly and once she released me, my eyes shot open to see the arena floor. The palace room filled with shrieks. A second before my head would have cracked open, I transformed myself into an amber wind and reappeared in a stance.

The onlookers cheered as I continued. Lance's staff came down to strike again as a force pushed me out of the way. I gasped to see Jared shoot an ice ball at Talon, freezing her as she screeched. Then he flew up, tackling the anti-angel into the air as volts swiped back and forth in front of me. I backflipped into a handstand as the spear's end missed me by inches before I jabbed Lance's abdomen. My leg slammed into him as I spun, forming another hammer, and smashed him to the ground.

I teleported into the air, grabbed Lance's arms, and headbutted him while freezing him in amber ice. Then I flipped off his back, flung him, and watched his carcass shatter into a million pieces before an awestruck audience.

"NO!" Jared and his comrades screamed. Time stood still. I looked at Jared and his countenance was stricken, as though his stomach had leapt into his throat.He couldn't move. A woman, perhaps the one Lance loved, stood out among the rest. She was a plain-faced, red-haired woman in a purple huntress uniform. Tears streamed down her face. She cried his name. Obviously the scene tormented her.

"Rust, restrain yourself," Tourniquet ordered, relieving me of daze.

"But this fight is not finished!"

"You had your kill," He paused and looked toward my partner. "Now it is time for Jared's."

All eyes were on Talon and Jared. If he failed to kill her, then he was dead ever since the battle commenced. Now was the time for either of them to be finished. Talon flew toward Jared and blocked almost every one of his attacks. She then flipped, kicked his back, and dug her nine-inch claws into him. The audience gasped and covered their eyes as she tore through his flesh like thinning latex. Saliva spilled onto his back as a ravaging madness consumed her. It was quite disgusting, yet strangely satisfying. He laid there helplessly as she continued torturing him. She definitely lived up to her name.

Tourniquet flexed his index finger, and suddenly Jared flew straight up, forcing Talon off him. Where did he get that burst of energy? He slammed her multiple times before freezing her in place with his icy spheres. She was stuck—caught in a pillar of ice.

"Excellent," Tourniquet began as the crowd grew silent. "Now detach her soul from her body. It doesn't matter how you do it. Remember your friend; let her feel what he felt."

His heart pounded so hard, I swear even I could hear it. Rage filled his being as he stared into the creature's white-ringed eyes. And yet he remained steady, still—emotionless. Here I was thinking Lance was dead. Jared could be mistaken for a corpse; all he needed was a sarcophagus. The demon peered back at him, smiling and drooling horridly. She started to laugh, a laugh that angered him more and more. People in the crowd forced themselves to look away from the audacity—until Jared finally had his answer.

He whispered, "I spare her."

"What?" Tourniquet asked, standing up in a fury. "What did you say?"

CHAPTER NINE

"I spare her!" He dizzied himself, staring into the pattern of the tiled floor, tears clouding his vision. The demon continued to laugh uncontrollably. "I spare her!"

"You have got to be kidding!" one person cried.

I slid Lance's head with my foot and crushed it with my large hammer as Tourniquet scowled. Shadows loomed around his flaming glare. I could find a much better trophy.

"So, Master," I whispered proudly to the man who barely deserved to look in my eyes. "Who wins?" It killed him to say that the team of a human had won. Not me, but Jared. He may not have been entirely normal, but Tourniquet despised all who supported humans. I, on the other hand, was an assassin, and had no room left for humanity.

He looked about the broken pieces of Lance, then to the unhinged Talon, and sighed bitterly. "Rust and Jared wins." he finally announced. The crowd cheered as Tourniquet rubbed his strained eyes.

***

"That was so hot how you killed him!" Light said at our small fire. What could I say? I was the life of any party, and a playboy at that. Women fell for me, especially when they were my opponent. That took the expression "hitting on" to a whole new level.

"Ah, but he was rather handsome," Ari replied, "while he lasted." A chorus of cackles arose.

"He was taken anyway."

"That's just sick," said one of the four young women standing a few feet away. Some of Jared's companions, I presumed. The purple huntress still seemed rather distraught. It's all just a game. How did some people not understand that? A game filled with winners who lived and losers who died. Anyone would have to despise themselves to allow themselves to fall victim here. I continued peering over my shoulder at them until another spoke.

"Maybe you can kill Talon and the rest of her sisters sometime?"

"I intend to. It still surprised me that Jared did not," I replied. "He will learn." Again. It was part of the game.

"Especially here!" Princess Quazar chirped with a devilish smile.

"Can you believe them?" the dark-skinned woman wearing only a small amount of armor whispered to her friend in white.

I averted my attention from them yet again and spoke to the girls at the fire, "Did you all count how many weapons I used?"

"Two?" the weird Australian from earlier asked.

"Nope."

The orange-haired girl in the forest-green suit left her small group, "Three?" she asked, walking up with her hands placed subtly behind her.

"Yes."

"How? I only saw your hammer," Quazar replied, knocking a lock of short pink hair out of her face.

"One," I summoned the hammer before tossing it into a cloud of dust and flexed my arms. "Two and three!"

We all laughed and smiled.

"Don't forget the legs!" Light cackled.

"That's all I needed," the orange-haired girl mumbled, walking away as Quazar eyed her suspiciously.

***

CHAPTER NINE

An enormous open-ceiling platform was buffeted by leviathans underneath a disheartening gray sea. Lance slowly lifted his head and examined the imprisonment. He attempted to sit up, but found his stiffening body impaled by craggy blades jutting out of a wall. He couldn't move. His nerves shuddered beneath his half-rotted flesh and he screamed harshly after trying to ignore the pain.

"No, no, no!" He winced. The world shifted upward, causing gravity to unpleasantly yank him off the blades. Once he realized the ground was stable for the time being, he took a few steps forward before stumbling back down. *Is this a ship?* he thought as a figure ran up from behind and latched to his damaged body, shaking him violently.

"Where were you, Lance?" she cried.

"Amethyst?" he whispered in awe.

"You were supposed to be mine!" she spat. "We were supposed to be together! Make a family! But you quit! You gave up on us! How could you? How could you?" Her face distorted, growing scales, her eyes swelling as she spoke until her beauty had become a mere memory. Then a faded purple vapor appeared through her head; an arrow.

Lance looked up to the figure standing a short distance away. "Mirages," he spoke with vicious tone. Then Lance dropped the young woman's body as it evaporated into the nothingness it had previously formed out of. "Killing them is the only method of keeping them away, and every time you do, a new soul is beckoned to this realm."

"This realm?" Lance asked.

"Traeustristya," the rugged killer replied.

"No. You don't mean?"

140

"Yes," he replied. "Surrounding you is the very section of Hell itself, Traeustristya; the Caged Seas. Here, monsters of the deep keep this prison thrashing about as it does. Each time someone falls into the waters, they are consumed and enter another torment."

"Who are you, and how do I know you're not just another illusion?" he asked.

"I am Viper and have survived much harsher things than this realm can offer. Whether I am a mirage or not depends on how you would feel about speaking with one." A tremor caused the prison to shift again as the two braced themselves. A black serpent from the depths craned its head over the prison and peered down at us. Viper summoned a misty snake that lunged over us at the monstrosity, piercing it with its fangs. Moments later, both retracted.

The man gripped his heart. "My serpent soul can only take so much."

"How did you die?" Lance asked, catching his breath.

"My own brother, Rust," he said.

"Rust?" Lance repeated. "You mean from the contests?"

"Yes, how do you know?"

"A man named Rust killed me as well."

Viper's eyes lit up as he focused on the black sun of Hell. "Where is your body?"

"He shattered it."

"And mine has been corrupted by his amber-ice crystal," Viper began. "Although your body remains in pieces, I know an incantation to bring those together once more."

"Are you talking about bringing me back to life?" he asked, eyes flickering with whatever minuscule amount of hope that remained.

CHAPTER NINE

"That I cannot do," he began. "My soul existed in my vessel, as did you in yours. However, I could trick the very powers of Hell by allowing myself entry to your old vessel. I will then traverse the human world and smite Rust wholeheartedly and bask in my resplendent vengeance."

"Hold on," Lance interrupted, "why exactly do you need my body to get there?"

"I can undo broken bodies, but not purge poisons. Even if I am poison," he explained.

"Would you be able to bring me back in yours or his body, and switch us back?" Lance said. "Do what you must; all I want is to be with my jewel, Amethyst."

"When Rust dies, I will then forge your soul into his body," Viper sneered. "Not only will you gain his powers, but you will be reunited with your beloved Amethyst."

"But wouldn't I look like the man who broke me?"

"How priceless is your jewel?"

Viper opened his mouth as a glowing snake slithered out of his throat. Its eyes opened as it stared into Lance's neck. Lance's pulse quickened sharply as he gritted his teeth and fists hoping to ease the incoming pain. His eyes clamped shut as the viper lunged, planting its fangs forcefully into its prey.

***

I leaped out of bed in a cold sweat. My room felt strangely unsafe. I got up, counted three swords on my rack, and lightly splashed water in my face while in the adjacent bathroom. Then I stared into the mirror to inspect a bubbling wound on the side of my neck. Before I could touch it, the mark distorted into a hideous smiling face. I looked up and stumbled back as a charcoal-colored creature with bloody eyes reached out of the mirror.

I jumped and found myself back in my bed. Apparently, I had never moved. I stood to inspect the scene, whirled around to my sword rack, and counted two of three.

"Wake up call!" a happy voice shouted, placing my sword against my throat. I snatched the blade and corroded it before seeing a man in a decorated mask and aged jester's garb.

I snatched his neck, freezing it in rust, lifting his body higher and higher. "That's *my* sword! And this is *my* room. And I *hate* mornings!" Finally, I kicked him across the room. His stout legs allowed him to perform a perfect split in the threshold of the door.

He pointed and hissed, "I'll see you at Hanara!"

"Get out!" I shouted as he flipped backward. Once I knew he was gone, something else gained my attention. An inky black centipede crawled along the floor before melting into a mass of ooze. I kneeled next to it and saw the substance was unlike anything I had ever seen before. "Why, Hanara?"

***

"I have work elsewhere," Tourniquet began, sitting on his throne as the palace room filled with whispers. "Since I am unable to attend, Isabelle will take charge. She has chosen the following arena to be the Hanara Amphitheatre."

"Am I still in the competition?" I murmured from his right.

"Yes. But the next time you have a partner," he turned, his eyes blazing into mine. "You will work together, or you will forfeit." He returned his attention to the crowd. "This will occur tonight; however, I suggest you all leave as early as possible. The theatre will be packed." He dismissed the mass, and they went about their business.

Tourniquet stopped Chaos and motioned him forward.

"Yes?" he asked.

"Speak to Rust," he said back. "See what you can do to sway him."

"He will not listen to me." Chaos paused, shaking nervously. "Not after Viper's incident."

"Viper's incident? Did he share the same fate as Mantis?" He smiled, circling him. "Viper, who was killed by Rust. Mantis, who was also killed by Rust. He seems to crave blood all for himself, thus disregarding the very competitions in which he fights."

"But Master," Chaos growled, "you know exactly who committed those crimes. Rust is innocent."

"Tell that to Lance," Tourniquet whispered. "Besides, if you know the truth, then you should also know better than to test me. You and Felinis, stalking the night like mice." He inched closer to him. "Mind you, I *let* you live, and if you fail to bring Rust to me, I'll happily change that."

***

I had progressed halfway down the path to the amphitheater when the leaves on the trees rustled. I jumped a little and summoned my hammer in case it was the jester again. Looking up, a silver figure disappeared behind a part of the tree trunk on which it stood.

"You've been spotted. Come out of hiding now." The figure fell to the ground with a thud and gazed up at me before standing and removing its helmet. A white scar trailed down his left eye.

"Chaos?" I asked. "I'm surprised to see you in the forests."

"I didn't mean to frighten you," He replied.

"What brings you here?"

"I'm on my way to the theatre."

"Afraid of walking alone?" I jested. "Where's your cyber-friend?"

"Dead."

We both stopped in our tracks, the air suddenly thick with seriousness.

"And he's not the only one," he said, raising his voice. "Mantis… Lance…your own brother!"

"Are you accusing me?" I asked, astounded. "Viper's not dead. I sealed him in a healing crystal," I paused in thought. "From the statue you collapsed!"

"Do not blame me, the Master has told me everything."

"Not enough." I scoffed.

"What is it like, killing so many in so few days?"

"Lance was my only kill. Why are you suddenly supporting the Master? Or have you forgotten how you received that scar?"

"The Master was testing my strength. He knew nothing of Light's presence."

"Or he ordered her to attack." He paused at my words. "Just a theory."

Chaos became silent and glanced over his shoulders. "We rebelled."

"We?"

"Me, Felinis, and Mantis."

I was all ears now.

CHAPTER NINE

"Now Mantis is dead at Tourniquet's hands. He plans to attack the Inigmus C.O.R.E."

"It is awfully suspicious of him to disappear during his own contests all of a sudden," I noted.

"What action must be taken?"

"Win."

"There's but one title for becoming his home-world savior."

"Then have faith," I replied sternly, understanding how serious the situation was. "He will pay for his sins. For the time being, we must keep this matter to ourselves and give pretense to our knowledge of it."

***

The theatre surged with life. Lining either side of the entrance were goddess-sized statues of Hanara, overseeing the hundreds of audience members sitting on curved limestone seats that disappeared into the floor. Hanara was a previous victor of the competitions who was granted something different than being crowned savior of Tourniquet's home planet. Those monuments were the soul of her final victory. It was a place so sacred that it felt as though any new fight would not only be a violation, but an insult.

A sorceress with a black-and-white mane stood at the blood-filled hearth in the center of the amphitheater, conjuring incantations. As she continued to chant the words, Animal and I cautiously took our places. We all stood in awe as the blood began to raise out of the hearth. Shortly after, the red mass melted into a feminine shape. The thick liquid melted over her body, forming into ancient armor and leather battle skirt. The blood slithered into her grasp and became her spear and shield. The leftover blood that did not turn into armor flowed behind her as a live cape, leaving drops upon the ground as it waved.

"I am Isabelle," she said, raising her hand to the audience. "Tourniquet could not be here this evening, as you have heard." She paused and looked over to Animal and I. "I hear you are tonight's fighters?"

I almost lost myself in the bloody woman's pool of magnificence. "Uh—yes."

"Very well," she said. "Audience, welcome the brave Animal and Rust to the arena." The crowd immediately roared with cheers. "Your opponent will be—"

"ME, please!" an evil voice squealed. I turned to see the jester from earlier. Maybe he *wanted* his butt kicked. He flipped down the stairs from the top of the amphitheater. I wondered how it was possible for something so annoying to be so coordinated.

"You!" she barked in remembrance.

"Thanks, doll!"

"Fool, I'm not calling on you," she yelled. "What are you doing here?"

"I told him I would see him at Hanara," he explained. "It's only fitting that we should face each other now."

"Would you like me to escort him out, Hostess?" the sorceress asked.

"No, I shall let him compete and be plagued by his presence no longer." Isabelle turned back to us. "I don't care which of you perform the task."

We moved and took our stances and listened for the word.

"Begin."

Name: Viper
Weapons: Dual-Bladed Energy Bow with Snake Head Arrows
Powers: Serpent Soul-can manifest a soul as form of a snake
Power Type: Elemental

CHAPTER TEN: VIPER

A three-way match. My twin brother, Rust, versus Animal versus the strange new opponent, who was apparently named Jexter. At least that's what he kept squalling during their battle. Jexter's legs swooped over Rust's head as he leaned back. Then he grabbed his ankle, froze it with his amber-ice, and flung him to the ground.

"Ow!" the clown cried out. Rust's hammer formed from the air and came down onto his torso. "Ow again!"

Animal's tail wrapped around Rust's neck as he yanked him backward. He screamed as his heel soared at his face. Rust shielded himself and blasted an intense burst of energy that sent his opponent flying. My twin was soon greeted by a bomb with a green smiley face painted on it. Jexter hoisted himself to a tree limb using his lengthy tongue as a harness and snatched the disoriented Rust from above. Rust struggled as the demon's nails stabbed his face. Once he managed to release his limbs from Jexter's lock, he formed a rusted blade and sliced the clown's tongue.

CHAPTER TEN

"AGHHHHHHHHHHH!" he squealed in agony. It whipped everywhere except for back in his mouth, spraying blood as it did. He managed to finally suppress it underneath his mask.

"This is absolutely repulsive," the sorceress who had summoned the current hostess whispered to her.

"That's the point. Let him suffer," Isabelle replied. "You may return to your desert if you like." They shrugged and continued to spectate.

Animal reappeared, leaping off a higher limb and swiping his claws at Jexter. "Why is everyone picking on me today?" he cried as Animal sliced his claws up his side, flipped, and thrust both legs into a kick that forced him to land on his elbow.

Rust charged at Animal while he was down, but his hammer soon met Animal's spinning legs as he performed a handstand, his tail latching onto the hammer as he pulled himself on top of it and swiped at Rust then jumped off as Rust retracted it.

Rust summoned another hammer soon enough to block Animal as he charged again. "Chaos told me about Mantis," Rust began in a whisper. "You two were close. Tell me what became of that situation."

"Even if I wanted to, now is not the time!"

"Is it true you all now serve the Master out of fear of Mantis' fate?" he fell silent. "Because he wanted to launch an attack on the C.O.R.E.?"

Before they knew it they were both on the ground. The jester lifted his mask for his slobbery, bleeding tongue to zip back into his mouth.

"Now, now, don't leave me out of any juicy gossip!"

Animal leapt up and ran at him from behind, but was met by Jexter's boot before Rust kicked his other leg, making him fall. Rust stood and stomped the clown's face into the ground. Blood trickled from under Jexter's mask as shock blanketed him. After just a second, Rust dropped his huge hammer on the middle of his body. Just as the men thought the clown was down for good, he laughed like a hyena, boiling their blood. As he stood back up, his mask shattered and his gruesome eyes shot open.

"You…broke…*my*…*MASK*!" He screamed.

Rust raised his fist to conjure a final blow when Animal's tail coiled his forearm and Jexter's forked and bleeding tongue wrapped around his leg. Both pulled, but he wouldn't budge. Rust spun forcefully, spinning them around and making them slam into each other. Jexter stopped laughing, having been knocked out. Isabelle smirked, hoping it was a good sign.

Now it was just Rust and Animal. He leaped at Rust as he kicked his chest, causing him to stumble backward. Pain scorched through Rust, but he persisted. He never retreated from a fight, and there was no reason to start now. Animal flipped backward as Rust flung energy at him. Rust jumped back in place and held out his hands. Huge gusts of amber-ice wind flooded around him. He yelled as he immediately froze in place. Rust ran up to his opponent and kicked his chest.

At this, I began to laugh and several audience members stood in awe, covering their mouths in disbelief. Including me; my laughter cut short and I stared blankly at the scene through Lance's face as Rust's eyes locked onto mine.

Animal kicked the dazed Rust and grabbed his hair. "I forever serve the one who brings peace to the world through difference. Justice will rise from his ashes; fear and pride shall be his horse." That was the pledge to Tourniquet. It meant that he would bring peace to the world by having over taken it. Anyone who got in his way would be purged, and the conqueror would have no remorse—just like the C.O.R.E.

"You don't have to be afraid, Animal!" Rust started. "We can work together. Fight Tourniquet together."

"Hostess," the sorceress said. "Look."

Isabelle stood and raised her hands. "Halt!" her voice rang across the amphitheater. "Jexter loses. Rust and Animal neutrallis."

"What?" Animal cried. "How am I neutrallis?"

"Neither of you claimed full victory over besting two opponents," the sorceress explained. "You are neutrallis because you defeated Rust, but couldn't claim full victory since Rust beat Jexter. Rust is neutrallis simply because he beat Jexter and lost to you."

"Now bring forth the next competitor," she ordered.

Animal objected. "I'm not finished yet!"

"Yes, you are," she said. "The fight ends at my command. Now Rust must battle a familiar face."

"Oh yeah?" asked Animal rudely. "Who?"

Suddenly, a small portion of a nearby tree rotted away as I shot a snake-shaped arrow at it. Their gazes traced the trajectory point straight to me as I stepped out from behind another tree where I witnessed it all.

"Me!" I said through Lance's body.

"Lance?" Rust questioned dumbfoundedly.

"Lance?" a young woman in purple shouted within the audience.

The urge was too great to resist. I had blown my cover and hardly even cared. My brother would pay for his transgressions along with that condemned Chaos! As soon as this brotherly feud ended, so would Chaos' breath! He would pay for crushing and rendering my previous vessel useless. Soon the two of them would know how it feels to be broken.

"Looks can always be deceiving," I replied. Apparently he hadn't noticed my venomous arrow stabbed into the tree.

"What's going on here?" Animal cried angrily. "You can't fight him!" his blood boiled, morphing his face into a sweaty red countenance. "I was just getting started!"

"Why don't you go back to Inigmus C.O.R.E. and fight your counterpart, Jason Porter, instead?" I suggested. "Funny how the original always wins."

I was referring to the fact he was a clone of the Tah'leet Soldier, Jason Porter. Animal, AKA, Oliver Fox, was one of Tourniquet's experiments who was fused with animalistic DNA mixed with Jason Porter's original strands. In his attempts to destroy the Tah'leet Soldiers, all of Oliver Fox's trials resulted in nothing but error.

Clearly offended, Animal gritted his teeth and cut his orange eyes at me. "You always failed at simple tasks. Perhaps that's why Tourniquet's been bringing me to the mainland lately, and why he's had to resort to other means regarding the Tah'leets." He became more and more irritated with every word I spoke.

As I said this to Animal, the audience couldn't help but support me. The sorceress gently placed her hand on his tensing shoulder.

"He's not worth it," she whispered in Animal's ear. Seconds later, his breathing paced itself and he unclenched his fists. The two stepped out of the way as I spoke to my brother.

"You will pay for what you did to me!" I cried to Rust, who still had no idea of my real identity.

"You knew one of us had to go," he replied. "It's the rules of the contest."

"No, maybe Lance knew that."

"Wait, what Chaos said—" Rust mumbled. I think it was then when his vision cleared. "Brother! Who did this to you?"

"You did!" I struck an arrow at him as he moved aside. "Your crystal didn't heal me, it killed me! Poisoned me into a comatose state before stealing my life completely. You never even came back!"

"I swear I intended to, but the interlopers needed to be taken care of."

"More than your dear brother?" I swung the bladed end of my bow at him as he dodged.

"You know what I mean!" he cried. "We were guarding the area, and now you're so cowardly to face me in another man's body?"

"Cowardly or clever?" I questioned. "Lance consented, and now we can both get our vengeance."

"You cannot attain vengeance for something that never happened!" Rust said, throwing a sphere that I easily dismissed and formed into an arrow. "I placed you in that crystal, but my powers aren't even capable of toxicity. You of all assassins should have known that." I shot the arrow and yanked myself with the spirit link connecting it. Then I forced my weight down on my brother, pressing my bow into his arms.

"Then, pray tell, who did?" He bore a confused look. "Answer me!" His calves shot straight, the impact sending me upward.

"Riddle me this, brother," he stated, leaping up and punching my side and face. "Why would I transgress against you so? And what have you done against me that would cause you to believe such a thing?"

His body whirled while still airborne and he kicked me into the limestone seats as onlookers dashed away. The seating area became severely damaged and Rust flew at me with his hammer. It landed right where I was just standing. He continued chasing me on different parts of the amphitheater seats as I slithered and leapt past frantic audience members.

"You are the smart one, right? Prove it!"

With that remark, I shot a poisonous arrow that struck its fangs into his shin. I yanked my bow and he fell to the ground.

Turning on the ground, his hands shot out blasts of amber-ice and I instinctively flipped back just as a newly formed hammer slammed into me, causing me to stumble. In return, I jumped up and shot a toxic spear at my infamous brother, which hit the center of his throbbing chest. I wondered what the audience thought of Lance's new powers, or how he managed to come back to life. His head almost cracked open on the stone edge surrounding the blood hearth from which Isabelle was formed.

"You're right, I did inherit the brains." I landed behind him as our clashing weapons sparked a fire in the blood hearth. I yanked off his hood and inched him toward it. "A shame you only inherited charm." He stared into the flames. A single strand of hair singed, making him yell. That tiny sound would never amount to my agony in the unseen realm. This moment reminded me how I refused to come back to the living, only to find myself unable to feast my revenge on my foolish brother. From out of nowhere, Rust gained a full burst of energy.

"That's right, and everyone will see those brains splattered across this battlefield!" His strong legs swiftly choked my torso. Seconds later I was thrown to the other side of the fire. We both exchanged hateful glances. In that position, how had he even done that? He flipped away from the fire before regaining his former stance, his eyes beginning to glow a bright copper color.

"Two can play at that game!" I said, performing a similar stance. My eyes blazed a bright purple, and our powers instantaneously locked against each other as our energies released. When the toxic and rust bolts swam through the fire, the resulting flames shot up about twenty feet into the air. The still-seated audience members all leaped and cheered. I charged at Rust, jumping over the pillar of fire, then landing with one hand on the ground. Rust came close to hammering my spine. I threw my leg up, locked his elbow in tight, and kicked him across the face. While still in the lock, I ripped a small dart from the pouch mounted on my side and struck it under his chin.

That Rust disappeared. A decoy. I should have known. Somehow he'd managed to cross over to my side of the hearth before I landed on the opposite. Perhaps he was more clever than I gave him credit for. Scary thought. The edge of Rust's boot scraped my cheekbone as I fell backward.

He leaped, then stood over me, his rusted hammer, one downward swing from sending me right back to the grave. The audience chanted, "Kill him; kill him; kill him!" The color in my eyes faded as we turned toward the current hostess. Rust could not kill me unless she allowed it. She shook her head. Then Rust absorbed the hammer.

"Be thankful she said no," he whispered.

***

Once everyone had dispersed from the amphitheater, I was well on my way to a meeting by way of a path in the woods. Along the path I noticed a girl. She had bright eyes, light skin, and orange-red hair. She wore a well decorated fur collar with a purple jewel in the middle along with a shimmery, matching uniform underneath.

"How long have you been my shadow?"

"For as long as you've been my guide," she admitted, coming out of her hiding spot. She trotted up to me and immediately embraced me. Her tears streamed down my chest. Our hearts pounded in unison, but I had no idea why. She lifted her head, and stared deeply into my eyes, speaking in a modest whimper. "How did it happen? How did you come back to me?"

"Come back?" She must have been referring to Lance.

"Your face and body," she continued, placing her hand against it. "It was frozen, crushed by that assassin, and now you're all here. It-it's a miracle!"

"Rust," I murmured. "You are that assassin in disguise!"

"Honey, no, it's me," she smiled. "Your gem. Your Amethyst."

That name. That unmistakable name. I heard it in the unseen realm, and like a wayward spirit, it returned to haunt me.

CHAPTER TEN

"Remove yourself." I tried to walk past her, but she stopped me again.

"Where are you going?"

"I have been summoned."

"Take me with you!" she pleaded. "Or better yet, let's leave this place. We can get Jared and the others later. We'll send a rescue team."

"I don't have time for this," I whispered. "You're not keeping me from my destiny." Her eyes met the ground as she collapsed in tears and wailed. See, Lance, I told you I'd keep my promise to you. To reunite you both.

***

The pathway of the woods stopped in front of a mountainside. The princess stood there casually, her abnormal pink hair glistening in the night. Was she waiting for me? She had to be.

I walked up to her. As soon as her eyes met mine she opened her hand, turned back to the mountainside, and stabbed her neat fingernails into it. Vertically and downward she slid them as a slight shaking of the rock revealed a doorway leading to a hidden area. The glowing room marred my eyes a bit before they fully adjusted to the light.

"The Master will see you now."

THE HALF-TRUTHS

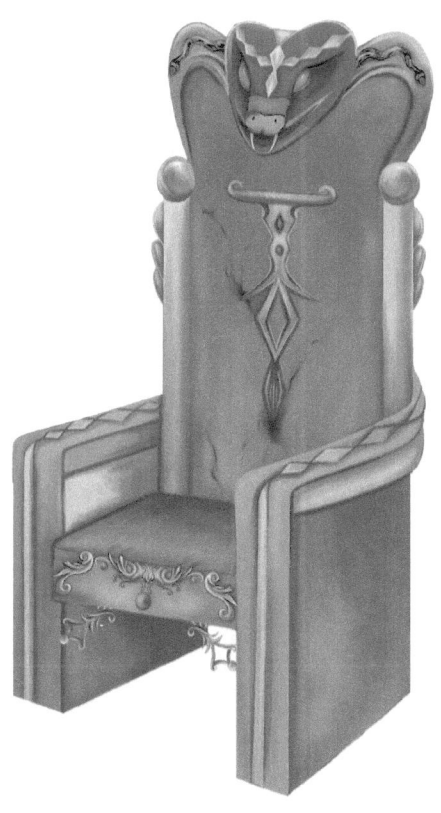

Name: Garika AKA Josie
Weapons: None
Powers: Acid Screaming-acidic waves are produced when she screeches
Power Type: Elemental

CHAPTER ELEVEN: GARIKA

D ang!" Jak'al cried out. "Signal's lost." Kat sighed and backed away slowly.

"Don't worry," Fern said comfortingly, putting a hand on her friend's shoulder. "She'll be back soon."

"I don't know, Fern," Kat replied. "Why would Amethyst just have run off like that? This place is just so—"

"Sadistic and weird," Jared commented from the other side of their room with his back facing them. His teammates stared at him in shock. "We all know it's true."

"Speaking of sadistic and weird," Cyclone started off, breaking the ice. "Why didn't you slay that demon?"

"Cyclone—" Jak'al moaned.

"Honestly," he continued, cutting him off. "It doesn't make sense! That guy killed Lance! He wasn't saved!"

"I'm not killing anyone," Jared said, silencing his comrades. "I-I'm not going to lose my soul and turn into something like that. That's insane. And that's exactly what Tourniquet wants." The others backed up in realization. "We

161

get angry, we get furious, and the next thing you know we're willing to kill anyone and anything just to stop the pain, only to satisfy us until the next fight; and then, we make more. I refuse to kill, and these contests are not an exception."

"But can't it be? Just this once?" Cyclone said. "We are in a death-match after all."

"Cyclone, you're starting to sound like Hurricane," Jak'al spoke. "What would you have done?"

"Probably let the adrenaline do the work."

"That's not right," Kat said, grabbing his hands tightly. "Look at me." His eyes met hers. "We don't kill; my guns aren't even lethal."

"But our powers are," Fern chimed in.

"Well," Jak'al began as he pulled his hands away from Kat and focused intently on his notes about different competitors. "These contestants won't seem as lethal by the time we're through putting all this together. Fern obtained a voice recognition on Rust."

"I did," she agreed, tossing a device.

"Rust," I repeated as the moniker entered my headset while remaining perched in a tree outside their room. "So that's his name." I jotted that down in my Pretty Kitty notepad. I could gain all my intel by letting them do all the work.

The teamwork this particular group had shown was quite impressive. We'd had a few fist-fights back in Apex, but that didn't stop me from keeping an eye out for their leader. I wouldn't want such hotness to go to waste. Ah, but his male companions weren't too bad either. I'm not a sore-desperate housewife waiting for some hero to sweep her off her feet, but I'm willing to make an exception. Usually I kept all those thoughts aside. I've had my eyes on another boy. Austin Byrd. The only problem with him was a girl named Candice… something. But I could take her.

I leaped down from my perch and landed onto the cold stone walkway.

"Garika?"

"Settris!" I smiled, turning and sliding my headset into my leather coat pocket. "What are you up to?"

"Oh, nothing really," she replied. "Have you seen BlackByrd lately?"

"Now that you mention it, no; I haven't."

"I know we're supposed to be in our rooms right now," Settris sighed. "But I'm just so worried about him. I think he might be in trouble. Would you mind helping me look for him?"

"Sure, what direction?"

"I don't know," she looked around aimlessly. "I cannot communicate with his psyche."

"English," I groaned, annoyed.

"I can't see his brain," she said. "I can't read his whereabouts or his thought processes."

"Some mind reader you turned out to be."

"It's pretty tough."

***

We were heading down a dirt path through the woods after Settris told me of her relations with Enrage. "So you want revenge on Enrage for killing you and Kat's friend?" I asked Settris during our search for BlackByrd.

CHAPTER ELEVEN

"Not necessarily," she replied. "To be honest, I'm not sure what I want. After all, I did find my cousin, and clearly we're in a much larger situation right now."

"But isn't there something else?" We stopped in our tracks. "Anything? Tourniquet promised us our heart's desire."

"Only if you win the contests."

"That's what I'm saying," I continued. "What if you win that title of becoming his homeworld savior? Isn't there anything you want?"

Settris looked me dead in the eye. "What could I possibly request, Garika?" I paused in thought and found no answer. "I can't bring Keisha back or stop Enrage from taking her from me in the first place. All I can hope for is that we all leave here safely."

"In other words," I began. "You don't know what you're fighting for?"

"I fight for peace."

"That's an oxymoron."

"I'm surprised you know that term."

"Very funny."

"Since you asked me," Settris continued, "what are you fighting for?"

"Don't you know that already?" I asked. "You're right next to me, haven't you been reading my mind?"

"No," she vaguely replied. "I don't want to."

"Because of my vivid imagination?" I cooed, rubbing shoulders with her, smiling.

"I don't have to read your mind for that. You put the 'pro' in profanity."

"Thanks." I smiled, cocking my head.

"I didn't read your mind because I trust you. I can tell after meeting you that you've never had the chance to make real friends besides a few people. So feel free to tell me anything. My psyche is off."

I kept silent. Could I tell her about it? She said she hadn't been reading my mind. Would she believe that Enrage had saved her from the pirate's ship before it exploded? I was filled with thoughts I craved to share, but I couldn't gain too much of her trust; we might end up having to kill each other someday.

Settris grabbed her head uneasily.

"What is it, Settris?" I asked.

"Sadness. Large quantities. Just above our—"

We heard a heavy gasp along with a snap. Feet dangled directly in front of our next step.

"Heads," she finished as we looked up at a fresh suicide. I covered my mouth in horror and moaned with tears. "Th-that's," Settris stuttered. "Amethyst!"

A chain wrapped around a large tree branch squeezed at the poor woman's neck while her arms swayed with her empty body.

"We need to get her down," Settris said. She jabbed at a device she earlier explained to me as being a commu-tracker to contact the 5X. Suddenly, nearby bushes rustled and she put it away as I gasped sharply.

CHAPTER ELEVEN

"Who goes there?" A formal voice ordered, making its way closer. Settris and I rushed for cover as a woman with stunning composure gripping a majestic iron spear tightly stepped into the area. Red droplets were the only guarantee one could ever trace her path due to her cape of blood. Her attention turned to the fallen. She steadied her hand over the ground and cast a spell. "Reaver; Devour."

"What does that mean?" I asked Settris quietly as we hid.

Her eyes flashed and she cringed. "You don't want to know."

The reaver crawled out of the symbol cast on the forest floor and writhed toward Amethyst, its bones cracking and enabling its body to lengthen. The extended arms wrapped around Amethyst as a jagged trench grew from the nose to the stomach. Hands with the texture of tongues coiled around her and slowly pulled her in, tightening the chain.

"Settris, why aren't we doing anything?" I asked frantically.

"Gotcha." Settris clenched her fist, then quickly faced her palm toward the reaver. A faint wind encompassed us for a moment. The reaver stopped after dropping Amethyst.

"What are you doing?" the armor-clad woman exclaimed. "Devour her at once! I order you to do so!"

Settris grabbed my arm and I felt weary for a second before she fearlessly strode out of place.

"Isabelle Diaurma!" Settris addressed the woman, using an Australian accent.

"I thought I smelled a telepath!"

"Settris, what are you doing?" I asked, realizing she was acting odd.

"Oh nothing," she replied. "Just taking dear Reavy here for a walk." Isabelle and I bore confused expressions. "Allow me to show you." She thrust her closed fist downward as the reaver mocked her movements and slammed its face to the ground, then into a tree. Settris concentrated even more. Was she inside the beast's mind or puppeteering it somehow?

The reaver sped up to Settris, and swiped its arms as I cried after her. She threw her body backward and clasped her limbs around it, then rode it until landing in front of Isabelle.

"You take her, I've got the reaver," I told Settris.

She looked at me and scoffed cockily, "I've got both."

Isabelle jabbed her spear furiously at Settris countless times as she nonchalantly dodged every attack, making her deadlier by the minute.

"You know," she started, "the definition of insanity is doing the same thing over and over and expecting a different outcome."

Isabelle gripped her spear with the backbend of her neck, spun around, and struck at Settris with her left arm. Settris' left hand snatched Isabelle's before she spun right and thrust her elbow into Isabelle's nose. After disarming her, Settris stabbed the ground with the spear, swung around it, and kicked Isabelle multiple times with her elevator heels. Once she landed a great distance from her, a furious and rather embarrassed Isabelle angrily reclaimed her spear and stomped toward the dark-skinned girl. And here I was thinking Settris didn't fight!

The reaver came at me, swiping its arms. I danced around them and performed a quick stance before throwing all my right side's weight at it. Both my legs crashed into it before it pinned me against the high part of a tree trunk with the little amount of hair I had.

"Aahh—" I started just as the tongue-hands coiled my throat, some entering my mouth. I did all in my power to kick them, but they only trapped my limbs. I did the only thing left. I bit them, and luckily, they retracted. I dropped to the ground and tried again. "Now as I was saying; AHHHHHHHHHHHHHHHHHHHHHHHHHHHHHHHHHHHH!"

The beast quickly crawled away as my first pulsating shriek ripped limbs off trees and corroded rocks from the acid. Isabelle's cape waved uncontrollably. Settris fell to the pathway, begging me to stop, but I continued as I walked up to the creature.

"AHHHHHHHHHHHHHHHHHHHHHHHHHHHHHHHHH!"

Once my screaming came to an end, all our ears rang, even the monster's. It stunned it long enough for me to launch a fist between the reaver's white eyes. Now it was Isabelle's turn.

Settris lunged at Isabelle as she summoned a shield from her bloody cape. Settris kicked off it just as her opponent's spear sliced down her midsection whilst airborne. She flung her spear to her side as Settris flew past me. The spear cut the air around me, shooting sparks near my face. I hurriedly escaped the close encounter and tripped the warrior. She flipped backward, using her weapon like a crutch, and spoke.

"You must not want your friend *that* badly, do you?"

"Of course; I like being friends with *Settris*. How dare you talk about her like that!" I said defensively, both of us knowing she wasn't talking about her.

The visor of Isabelle's helmet came down and sent a blast of heat vision. Settris entered my mind and threw me to the ground. I shot a dark glare her way until I realized what she was doing. The beam melted a hole through the reaver.

"No!" Isabelle cried as the ground swallowed her pet.

"You should really use your head more," Settris suggested. She charged for another attack, but we simply tossed her aside. Her hands shook violently, her head dosed with sweat. What a twit!

"That Austin dude came through here earlier, so tell me where he is if you still want your eardrums intact," I threatened.

"I'll never tell."

"I knew you'd say something like that," Settris smiled.

***

Her makeup was sweat, dirt, and a pair of violently quivering lips. Tears seeped from her closed eyelids and fell onto the bruises on her arms. Even parts of her scalp were bloody, indicative of someone tearing out her black locks of hair. Two mechanical guards stood in front of her. One silver and the other bronze, which shot a spike into the ground, causing her to scurry away like a tormented animal.

"Stay in that corner or Korax will have his fun with you." A pillar of light stretched from between a pair of iron doors on the opposite side of the room. It was the big buff dude in shiny gold armor and shabby cape that we saw when we came to the island. It was Tourniquet.

The guards lifted her as Tourniquet kneeled with open arms. "Candice Luda. What a pleasure it is to—"

CHAPTER ELEVEN

"What do you want from me?" she interrupted. "Are you going to turn me into one of them? A monster? A freak? Huh? Brainwash me? *What?*" Her innocent lime eyes looked up at him pleading, no—clinging to mercy.

He rested her chin in his hand. "You're much too beautiful to destroy completely." She gulped. "Besides, you of all people should know I can perfect you. Tell me, are you not the slightest bit intrigued by my creations?"

"You mean your abominations?" That comment earned her a harsh blow from Korax.

"Please show some restraint," the big man whined. "She is still a canvas," he continued. "Do my abominations frighten you?"

"Y-you kidnapped them!" she spat. "Turned them into slaves. The people from the C.O.R.E., my friends..." She broke into tears.

"What makes you believe you had any relationship with them at all?" he bellowed. "You are invaluable; an asset only I can truly appreciate. All I must do is perfect you, and you will be complete."

Just outside of the mountain, Settris and I made our way to the scene, still unaware of BlackByrd's location.

"Who's out there?" asked the pink-haired princess.

"What's your plan, Settris?" I asked her.

"Be quiet," she whispered as we continued.

"What are you doing back here?" she asked. Now I was confused again. "I thought you said you were meeting someone."

"It is none of your concern, Princess Quazar," Settris spoke.

I looked in front of her. A holographic shroud shaped like Isabelle veiled Settris as the princess' spellbound eyes glowed. Settris, how clever she is!

"What are you waiting for, your Daddy? Open this door!"

She scowled and opened it.

While the door still opened, someone's cold, sweaty hands blanketed my mouth. Settris spun around, dropping her shroud, as we were relieved to see BlackByrd. But suddenly—

"Intruders!" Princess Quazar spat.

"Good timing, BlackByrd," Settris groaned.

He laughed nervously, "Yeah, I guess I could've waited until we were on the other side."

"Oh well, looks like we've got a new problem on our hands," I stated as we all turned to the princess.

"Daddy doesn't like surprises!"

She flew up in the air with her wasp wings and shot pink plasma balls at us. Definitely not the hospitable type! I dodged each one, but there were a few close calls. She buzzed over to the entrance point as Settris caught her in a psychic pull.

"Get through before it closes!" Settris yelled, restraining Princess Quazar as they started fighting. BlackByrd and I tumbled inside the mountain moments prior to the opening locking shut.

"Garika, BlackByrd," Tourniquet addressed us. "It's so nice to see you two again." I clenched my fists as the woman behind him gasped at the sight of Austin. He looked down at her.

"Candice!" he cried, running toward her. He knelt beside her, peered into her eyes as she coughed blood. "Are you alright?"

Her lip quivered. "Better now," she whispered hopefully.

"What've you done?" Austin asked, looking up at Tourniquet darkly. The shadows around his eyes made him look just like his father.

"Nothing yet," he replied with a mirrored expression. "I am merely preparing to perfect this woman." He said, motioning to Candice.

"I don't think so!" I threw an openhanded chop toward him, which he easily countered. He pulled my body toward his and flung me around with his huge arm. How romantic, but now was not the time! He then put me in a ground lock, while I looked up at Austin. Tourniquet then tossed me up and slammed his boot into the center of my back.

I flew toward the "lovebyrds" as Tourniquet pulled out his sword. BlackByrd assisted me back to my feet and hurled streaks of blackness toward his father.

"I haven't the time for this. Korax, Porcupine, kill them!" Tourniquet ordered the robots before they were consumed in a column of smoke and ashes from BlackByrd. That didn't seem to do much good. The two mechanical beings simply walked out of it and up to us aggressively, assuming a battle stance.

"We will crush you!" the bronze one told me.

"That's what you think."

"Garika, no!" BlackByrd left Candice to run over to me. He loves me. "We'll take them on together!" Hmm, together eh? He said it, not me.

GARIKA

He took Korax, which left me with Porcupine. He hissed at me as I cartwheeled toward him. After recovering, I grabbed his neck with my legs and threw him onto the opposite side of me. He was dizzy, but still manageable. I turned around as he was getting up.

"Come here!" His forearm compartments emitted two long spikes. He thrusted his right arm by my face and I cooed, passing by him and leaping. I wrapped him into a lock again and rode him to the ground.

"You're not very smart, are you?" I taunted.

He stabbed my leg with a spike, causing me to fall to a knee. Then he kicked upward, landing back into a perfect stance before hurricane-kicking me to the ground and pinning the palms of my hands with spikes. I screamed—good.

"AHHHHHHHHHHHHHHHHHHHHHHHHHHHHHHHHH!"

The spikes melted away, and so did parts of Porcupine's armor, specifically one of his rather interesting legs. Well, part of it anyways. He shot more spikes. The first flew through a piece of my hair and the second ricocheted near my foot as I cartwheeled away. The last managed to lodge into my shoulder. My body hit the ground again as my arm bled once I pulled the spike out.

I dizzily forced myself up and kicked Porcupine in the gut as Korax came up to bat. He swung his metal raptor claws at me as I leaped up into the air. The weapons struck against the side of Porcupine's metal helmet.

"What was that for?" he hissed angrily.

"She moved!" he spat in his defense. I flipped between the arguers. My body spun horizontally as I grabbed Porcupine with my hands and Korax with my legs. I had practiced that move my entire life and finally got it right. The weaklings landed next to Austin, where he finished them off.

He crushed Korax's armor by making black ink flow through his helmet. I eventually grabbed Porcupine once more and screeched directly into his visor until he collapsed.

BlackByrd clapped as he slowly walked toward me. I took a bow. "You're a better fighter than I thought you'd be."

"Thanks, but you should know how well I take care of myself," I said, wiping black ooze from my face. Apparently, that's the juice that kept the robots going. "Now where and why did you scurry off to?"

"Actually, I've found some pretty important—" He then grunted painfully and grabbed at his stomach. My eyes widened and traveled to his wound.

A bloody, purple sword was being pulled out and the culprit stood behind him, sneering. He kicked Austin's body away as Candice and I screamed.

"No, no, no, no, no, no, no, no!"

"He had to go, Garika. That's the rules of the competitions."

"No one has to die!" I protested, my tears smearing my makeup.

"Have you forgotten why you brought him here in the first place?" he hissed. Candice's eyes widened in horror.

"I almost didn't recognize you without your old body," I responded. "Viper." Everything quieted.

"Well, Garika, if I didn't know any better, I'd say that you actually loved this boy." He walked up to Candice, restraining her. "You can thank her for bringing you here as well." I refused to see her grief-stricken face and averted my eyes as

GARIKA

Viper turned back to me. "The princess will clean this mess up once she destroys the telepath. You know the next phase."

I lay down on the floor and closed my eyes as Candice wailed.

Name: Jak'al
Weapons: Black Iron Claws
Powers: Deafening Howl, Enhanced Senses
Power Type: Elemental

CHAPTER TWELVE:
JAK'AL

S creams were coming from within the forest, so my team decided to investigate. Luckily, Settris had earlier activated her commu-tracker, and a mixture of clues and scents led us straight to the side of a mountain near the forest's edge.

"Connie!"

"Kat!" the cousins embraced.

"Are you alright?" Kat asked, grasping her arms.

"Yeah," she responded. "Unfortunately, I lost to the princess when she was guarding the door."

"What door?" Jared asked. Settris pointed to the mountainside, and Jared drew a shape in the rocks with a concentrated beam of heat vision, revealing a metal door. "Jak'al, tell us what you hear."

I pressed my ear against it. "It's hollow."

"Figures," Cyclone stated.

"Not the room. A heart." I turned to Settris. "Did you see how it opened?"

CHAPTER TWELVE

She waved her hands and formed a rather impressive duplicate of Princess Quazar, who stabbed her nails into the door, opening it immediately. "Something like that," Settris concluded.

"Nice," Cyclone commented. "I honestly couldn't tell the difference."

"This one's smarter," Settris stated matter-of-factly.

"This could be a trap. Proceed with caution," Fern warned as the door echoed behind. She sent glowing pollen spores floating about the room like miniature stars. Kat's eyes lit up. "Chandeliers," she observed, looking up at the ever-stretching royal ceiling.

"That aren't lit?" I finished. More spores revealed that the chandeliers were draped with cobwebs before they ignited the candles sitting in the holders and lighting up the rest of the room. The strangest part was the layout. It was nothing like a mountain at all. In fact, it was more like a laboratory. The room was full of computers and blinking boxes of technology, and lining sections of the walls were tanks filled with green plasma.

"Careful everyone," Jared whispered under his breath. "That's an order." He looked at one of the containers. "Wait, I've seen this before."

"What is it?" I asked.

"In my encounter with that *thing*, there were syringes filled with this green ooze. Do you and Cyclone mind retrieving a sample of this? We need to figure out what it is."

Cyclone and I were in the process of examining the material when Settris exclaimed, "Garika!" She rushed up to a woman lying on the ground with a punctured right shoulder. "Kat, help me!" she ordered, seeing her gaping expression.

"I will...I am, it's just...she's," Kat began.

"An enemy," Fern said, walking up to them. "You shouldn't be so surprised."

Settris looked back at Garika solemnly. "Without my powers, I trust her and I'm willing to give her the benefit of the doubt. Right now, we need to help her."

"Already on it," Fern said, holding some Vagura Root and kneeling to her. "We can trust her for now, given the circumstances."

Her eyes were still adjusting to the light when she leaped up and screamed out: "BlackByrd!" We all looked at each other, confused, as she kept analyzing the room in a panicked state. "Where is he; have you seen 'em?"

"Seen who?" Cyclone asked.

"Austin…he goes by BlackByrd," Settris explained. "Garika and I came here looking for him, but that's when Princess Quazar attacked. Perhaps she could have taken off with him, being the only one who could open the door from the outside. Didn't I hear another woman from this side?"

"Yes, BlackByrd and I found Candice and were attacked by robots," Garika said.

"Robots?" Kat cried out.

"Yes, they were called Porcupine and Korax. We defeated them, so they couldn't have relocated Candice."

"Maybe those were the hollow hearts I sensed." I said. "The emptiness inside was loud enough. If he was trying to find her, then it would make sense to keep them apart."

"So, if the robots didn't take her, who did?" Cyclone asked as I sniffed the air.

CHAPTER TWELVE

"Poison. Do you remember seeing anything toxic?" Being half jackal, I had heightened senses. The silence indicated she was either trying to recall what happened or choosing what details to share.

She looked up at me and said, "Not that I can think of." Was she leaving something out, protecting someone—and if so, why? "That's not all," Garika continued. "Tourniquet was acting pretty rushed, and was also talking about perfecting Candice, maybe through experiments?"

"Maybe that's what this green stuff is for. But there's something strange about the readings."

"What is that?" Jared asked.

"There aren't any," I replied. "Apparently, this material doesn't exist."

"Evidently it does."

"Not yet," Cyclone replied. "But I bet I know *when* it comes from. Let's just say I apologize for my future behavior."

"Again?" Kat cried as he shrugged. "We'll get back to that."

"Settris, do you consent?" Fern asked.

"I do; however, I fell unconscious during my encounter with the princess," she reminded. "I'm afraid a strange force has been affecting my abilities lately." Settris read Garika's mind and everything agreed. Everything but one detail.

"What do we do now?" Cyclone asked. "We've got two missing victims, several unconscious people, and a madman running about."

"We'll look for the madman," Garika said. "He's the only one who could've possibly ordered Candice to be relocated. We can at least interrogate him to then find her."

"Interrogate Tourniquet?" I wondered. "That should be interesting."

"Alright," Jared began. "Fern and Cyclone, you take Garika to look for Tourniquet and find leads on Candice. Settris, Kat, Jak'al, and I will look for BlackByrd."

"This may be a rather large assumption to make, but where there are prisoners, there are dungeons," I said.

"Actually, Jexter gave me an entire history lesson about this place. A blacksmith he once knew was placed in a dungeon, so there should be one around."

"But we can be sure." I tapped the end of my nose with my index finger. "Come on." We walked away.

"You!" We turned to see another criminal from Apex City and his companion. Captain Red Blood and Metsys.

"Ready for round two, Captain?" I barked, stepping toward them.

"You are no Mantis, Jak'al." Metsys spoke. "I have since evolved from my last battle. This will prove no challenge."

"Personally, I would love to see your little flower girl lose control, since I don't have another ship for you," Captain Red Blood said to Fern.

"At least this little flower girl destroyed that vessel. Besides, is that really something to brag about?" Fern asked. "Kat, Settris, take care of Garika. This time I may just lose control willingly."

Metsys leaped at Fern, and I tackled into the pirate. Fern spun around furiously and shot pollen spores at her. Then they switched places. The captain lifted Fern by her throat as she kicked his. Metsys flipped over and over, missing all my hits.

CHAPTER TWELVE

Captain Red Blood knocked Fern aside and ran up to me. I clapped his sword between my hands.

"What happened to your old sword, Captain?" I asked, noticing he wasn't fighting with Agnomus.

"I can kill you with any weapon I wield."

"Just not Agnomus?"

"Jak'al!" Fern cried as Metsys flipped up from behind. I couldn't stop her. She hit me in random spots, paralyzing me. Then Metsys leaped, ran across my chest, and left with a hard stomp after activating her jets before landing.

I howled, causing her system to freeze for a second. I spotted Fern raising her hand over the ground as the whites of her eyes glowed green. A tiny sprout appeared a second before forming into a vine whip. She grabbed the vine and cracked it over the pirate's face. Seconds later, he grabbed for his eyes as a fresh searing wound ran past them.

"All pirates wear their scars proudly."

"And all weeds must be plucked!"

They charged again. Fern struck out her hand as the vine whip shifted into a swirl of thorny roots and wrapped around them. Then she shot her other hand upward as the roots gripped the ceiling, hanging the pair upside down.

"This is war!" Captain Red Blood yelled with a red face. "You hear me? This is the last time! I will kill you all! Don't you walk away from me!" From underneath, another sprout grew into a large, flowery Venus fly trap and clamped its jaws tight with the fiends in between. It wasn't fatal, just amusing. Maybe someone would come to their aid.

***

The 5X broke into two groups. Garika had a hunch about discovering Candice's location, starting with investigating a spot she claimed acted as another hideaway for Tourniquet, leaving with Fern and Cyclone. That left Settris, Kat, Jared, and I tracing the same underground path that Captain Red Blood and Metsys had appeared from. Hopefully it led to BlackByrd. I followed whatever scents I could pick up; unfortunately, the trail was also mixed with dirt and stone from the walled pathway.

"This area was definitely man-made," Jared stated.

"Unlike the place I had earlier found," Settris added.

"You mean the library?" Kat asked as Settris nodded. Jared and I paused and looked at them oddly. "We never told you?"

"Told us what?" we asked.

Settris began, "Back when Kat, Fern, and I were collecting information from contenders, I came across a small rainforest where the plants grew books."

"Books?" I asked, amused.

"I'm serious!" she continued. "Fern would love it, by the way. It's near the training grounds, and I was trying to do some research about the island."

"Any luck?" I asked.

"A bit," she replied. "I was able to learn some of the history. But, more importantly, someone had been trying to hide experiment logs, like files and documents."

"Were any of those about Candice?" Jared asked. "When Garika mentioned Tourniquet performing experiments on her?"

"I didn't have time to read them because someone was coming," she replied. "Although I read her mind, I can't help but feel as if she's keeping something from me. Why did you mention poison?"

"My nose never lies," I explained. "A person with toxicity entered that room before we arrived." Maybe that's what she was leaving out. But why?

"Stop," Jared ordered. It was Talon. Thankfully, her back faced us, but she had appeared without warning, like a ghost.

Settris waved her hand, creating an invisible haze that allowed us to follow her. The creature's head twitched like a spastic bird as she sharpened her claws along the walls. She laughed hideously as we cringed with disgust.

"That boy!" she squawked, facing a torch along the wall. She looked at her reflection in her magnificent claws before poking the torch and bursting into flames. We gasped, but tried to stay hidden. Then the flames leveled into armor and a wide pair of wings sticking out of a woman's back. Even her hair was fire! She had a strong formal accent. "He doesn't know what he faces. This is unlike anything they have ever known."

"Can you read her mind?" Jared asked Settris, knowing very well it could be our only chance. Settris closed her eyes and entered the mind of the mysterious woman.

"She's," Settris answered, "an angel."

"Danger," the angel looked around before turning directly to us. "You shouldn't be here; let me warn you that—" The fire was mashed out by a pit wolf with rattling bug-like spikes on its back. Kat touched her purple feline necklace as it glowed and morphed her into a panther with three jewels perfectly aligned on her forehead. The cunning wolf glowed black.

"What?" we gasped as it altered into a familiar face.

***

Garika, Fern, and Cyclone were all walking toward the beachfront on the edge of the bank. "Are you sure he's out here?" Cyclone asked.

"I've got a good feeling," Garika replied.

"But why all the way out here?"

"I'm not sure, I mean…Tourniquet did have a secret hideout in a mountain." They looked up to a flame hovering over the tides and toward a cave on a nearby bank. "Should we follow that?"

"Carefully, but yes," Fern said. She dialed a pattern into her commu-tracker. In case of emergencies, it would shoot out an intangible high-proton beacon, alerting the rest of the team. I've only used it twice. The first time was an accident. They entered the cave, following the fire as it turned into a winged woman.

"Wait a minute," Cyclone began. "She must be who Jared had seen the other day. He told me at the infirmary, but said it could've been an illusion."

"Then we can't all be hallucinating?" Garika asked.

Fern tapped her commu-tracker again, calling Jared as a green hologram of him shot up from the device. "We've found someone who fits the description of the woman you were telling Cyclone about the other day."

"Now is not a good time!" He informed. "How did you see her anyway? She was just here."

"I'm not sure, but is this really new for us?" she replied. "Just thought I'd notify you. We're heading into a cave at the beachfront now."

CHAPTER TWELVE

"That's where I saw her the first time. Stay safe. Over and out."

They advanced once again, heading deep under the sand. The fiery woman's body lit the way as she took gradual steps. Did she know they were there like she did with us? It did seem as if she knew the place. She led the way until fizzling into sparks.

"Can someone turn the lights back on?" Garika echoed through the cave as the other two shushed her.

Suddenly a bluish-black light appeared from a distance. "Get down!" whispered Fern as they shielded themselves behind rocks. Two silhouettes kneeled to Tourniquet, who stood in front of the portal emitting strict blue currents—the only light left within the underground cave.

"Evening, my lord." The woman's hair was orange, eyes yellow, and skin nearly the same shade of green as her dress.

"I have lured the 5X here," Tourniquet told the pair.

"Cyclone too?" the man asked, raising his eyes to Tourniquet. They were gray and had wind formations blowing in them.

"Of course," Tourniquet replied. "One of my agents is working on that right now."

Through their conversation, they discovered that it was Hurricane and Fever Vyrus. Two criminals the 5X had faced many times, only they were different from the others. Not only were they from the future, but Hurricane was the future version of Cyclone. With Fever's high intellect regarding time travel, she could take Hurricane to the past and constantly attempt to persuade Cyclone to villainy, so that Hurricane would someday exist.

"Here's what you requested," Hurricane said, handing a canister full of green liquid and a rare-looking rock to Tourniquet. Upon taking the items, he smirked.

"He still resists," Fever began. "I've even tried sickening the 5X, causing Cyclone to fight his allies by seeing four Hurricanes."

Stupidly, Cyclone leaped out from behind the rock. "I won't fight them!" his voice was surprisingly louder than normal. He gritted his teeth as the other three smiled at one another.

"Speak of the devil," Fever said. "We were jus—"

"Shut up!" Cyclone interrupted.

Fever's eyes shone a terrible red as she flew up to him and caressed his face. Upon this action his veins poked out from under his skin and his gray eyes held a disgusting yellow tint.

"Watch your mouth," she warned in a somber whisper, glaring down her nose. She jabbed him in the neck and side with two fingers. As she strode away, he shook on the ground, his skin much paler than usual. "I might not kill you, but I can infect you all the same."

Now the girls leapt from their hiding positions and rushed to him. Garika put Cyclone's limp right arm over her neck and Fern did the same with his opposite.

"Be careful, that's contagious."

"Pick on someone your own size!" Garika screamed.

Fever studied them. "You two look about my size."

***

Kat shifted back to her human form. "Gaako, what are you doing here? And what happened to your suit?"

Jared and I gaped, noticing something terribly wrong with our ally.

187

CHAPTER TWELVE

The suit wasn't his signature green-and-brown leather one with his bandana; instead, it was black leather tactical gear with metal plates. His face supported an eye patch on the left side that covered a fresh scar than ran all the way down to his lip.

"Oh, you like it, do you?" His accent was much rougher than Garika's. "I've been perfected by Tourniquet's splendid work. Now I have all kinds of new powers. Super-strength, shape-shifting, just to name a few."

"This isn't you!" Kat cried out.

"You're quite right, Kitty," he said. "This is the new me."

A majestic tiger-woman ran up from behind him, placing her hands firmly on her hips. "What are you all doing here?"

"I can handle them alone, Felinis," Gaako said, pulling out Lance's staff. How did he get that?

"This area is strictly forbidden," Felinis demanded. "Trespassing results in your defeat. Now is your only opportunity to depart honorably."

"We're part of the 5X, we never back down!" I said.

"I found him!" Settris said, picking up BlackByrd's psyche.

"Great!" Jared cried. "Jak'al, Kat, see what you can do about changing Gaako's mind. We'll get BlackByrd."

"No, you won't," Felinis hissed as I stopped her, allowing Jared and Settris to pass. "Why do you assist humans? They fear you."

"No, they don't," I replied.

"They should," she hissed, lunging.

***

"Ooh, fate's brought us together, BlackByrd," said the wasp-woman from within the cell, wrapping her arms around him. He was chained to the wall by his wrists and bandages wrapped his midsection. "You were meant to stay here with me, forever!"

"Get off me you stupid bug!" he protested as she ran her fingers through his black hair.

"Hey!" Jared called as they turned to him and Settris. "Let him go!"

"Why don't you join us instead?" she tempted vexingly, stretching her arms and walking to the bars. "I'm sure we have plenty room for two more, don't we, BlackByrd?" He spat on her and she left a red hand print on his cheek. "I give you hospitality and my love and care and this is how you respect your future queen?" Her screaming was much louder than what I'd heard about Garika's.

"Leave him alone!" Settris yelled, kicking the bars.

She looked back in disgusted remembrance, "You won't fool me again!"

"Ah, but you make it so easy."

She made the bars intangible long enough to pull Settris and Jared into the cell. "I'm the warden of this cell," she explained as they stood back up. "And you will do exactly as I command!" Her hands opened, forming pink plasma spheres.

Jared and Settris eyed each other and smirked at her folly.

***

Gaako refused to listen to reason, leading to our battle. Kat pulled out her double-barreled silver pistols and relentlessly fired at him. Gaako easily blocked them by spinning the electric spear before sticking an end inside one of Kat's barrels, making it explode. He swung the spear so fast that she could feel the wind as it moved past her cheek. The electric tip stung her gut, and she began convulsing. I caught her, but received a few shocks as well.

She flashed me a quick smile as Felinis' claws came at me. She planted herself beside me and delivered a decisive roundhouse-kick to my back. I was flat on the stone walkway when her claws flayed my face. Flesh and fur flew off me and I raised my legs and to grab her waist. With her trapped in a perfect lock, I threw her over me. Her palm arched gracefully against the ground as she flipped further away before staring viciously and charging once more.

Gaako morphed into a pit wolf again and pounced on Kat. She tumbled before assuming her panther form and fought back.

"The Kat versus the dog? Say it isn't so."

"It is, and you'll always be a gecko to me," She bit back, referring to his old abilities.

I lunged at Felinis as she flipped, kicking my head upward. I steadied myself and swiped my claws at her crossed arms while her stripes stretched into an iron coating. Sparks flew until I finally managed to scratch through. She yelped. I could see in her eyes that she now saw me as her equal. But who would finish this fight? Next she shot a magma stream that obliterated the walls.

The two other beasts somehow managed to dodge the burning beam until I released a howl that made Felinis' eardrums shudder. She cupped them, which gave me the perfect opening. I ran toward her, leaped, ran sideways across the wall, stabbed my claws into her shoulders, and flung her over me and to the ground. She decided to take a cat nap. Face first. Kat turned human again after defeating Gaako.

"Y-you okay?" she rasped, wiping the sweat off her forehead.

"Yeah," I panted, chuckling a bit. "Let's go find the others."

***

Fern blocked Fever's veiny red claw with her forearm while Garika kicked up at her. Fever snatched her leg and yanked her into a split as Fern rolled across her back to kick Fever. The girls recovered, performing a stance as Fever thrusted her red claw at Fern.

Fern cartwheeled to the side, but upon standing, a string of hair singed to ash. She always kept dogwood petals in her gloves, making it possible to use her abilities when no plants were around. She shot her hands forward, tripping Fever with roots that coiled her ankles. Then Fern and Garika switched place, and Garika tossed dust into the air before spiraling a shriek aimed at Fever.

"AHHHHHHHHHHHHHHHHHHHHHHHHHHHHHHHHH!"

The swarm of particles seeped into the pores of Fever's skin, making splotches of blood appear on her face. Seizing the opportunity, Garika stabbed her with the heel of her boot, making her fall back and eventually land on a stalagmite.

Tourniquet smiled.

"Fever!" Hurricane yelled, pausing from fighting Cyclone and rushing to her. He lifted her off the stalagmite and shook her. Blood gushed from her body as it twitched wretchedly, the acid also beginning to take effect. "No, no!" he laid her down as the air intensified. The air pressure shifted in the cave, making it hard to breathe. "You'll pay for that!" he yelled at Garika, making two gusty spheres.

As he flew up to them, I grabbed his tattered cape and yanked him back. He stumbled and glared at me and the others entering the cave. Jared had earlier frozen the "warden" against the wall, and we traced Fern's location here with the commu-tracker, and arrived using another underground pathway.

Now it was the 5X, Garika, Settris, and BlackByrd facing Hurricane and Tourniquet who simply watched the battle unfold. Scratches and dirt created our masks. Our muscles had melted into gum, and none of us could stand without shaking violently, but still we persisted. The day was not saved yet. Sweat beaded our temples like raindrops as we rasped heavily.

Hurricane charged our way with dual wind swords. He slashed one across Cyclone's chest then jabbed the second through me. It didn't stab like a regular sword, just shot wind through us, but the pressure was all the same. He was truly dangerous. Garika's screams didn't seem to affect him anymore, and Fern was running out of plant material and trapping strategies. They grew weaker as they were thrown about the cave like ragdolls. Physical attacks were just suicide compared to the physique of the monumental man.

BlackByrd used smoke magic to cloud Hurricane's vision. Hurricane's cape whipped away the clouds of black smoke and, to his surprise, Settris stood behind him. She puppeteered him to continuously slam his back into the cave wall. Although it throbbed in pain, he snatched her and Kat as Jared tackled into him.

"GET OFF ME!" Cyclone flung three wind spheres at him as Garika shrieked acid yet again. After that, Fern wrapped the last of her vines around him while Kat shot him six times with her functioning pistol.

JAK'AL

I shoved him onto the ground and punched his face before shooting my claws through his skin. As I flipped away, Jared finished him off with a blast of heat vision and ice that froze him solid. Seconds after Hurricane's frosty defeat, we all turned to a slow clapping noise.

"What an excellent performance. And what extraordinary coordination with your powers." Tourniquet's voice boomed.

"I held up my end of the bargain. Now it's your turn," Garika sighed.

"Do you think you are in any position to give me orders?"

"Yes, I do, because I did what you asked me to do," she explained. "I can take them back if you like."

"What?" I asked. "What are you two talking about?"

"You tricked us!" Fern spat at Garika. "I should've known."

She fell silent. She never did that. "I had my reasons," Garika modestly spoke in her defense. "Besides, it's not like a massive fight won't sprawl out between all of you, so you have somewhat of a chance."

"That we will, no thanks to you!" Fern muttered.

"My pleasure."

"Do you realize what you've done?" Cyclone shouted. "What could possibly be so important that you would turn us in to them?"

Tourniquet snapped his fingers as someone appeared.

"Gaako!"

"Garika!"

"What?" I exclaimed as they embraced. "You two knew each other?"

CHAPTER TWELVE

"I'm sorry, Austin," Garika said.

"Wait," he began. "This is your missing friend? He's the reason you brought me here! It was all a trick. You've been working for him all along!"

"That she has," Tourniquet stated. "Some people crave power, others fortune, but these two simply wanted love. I ordered him to bring Lance and Amethyst—which he was more than willing to do—and for her to bring you, my dear son."

"Does that mean you were never our real friend, Gaako?" I asked. Neither of them made eye contact. Not even to each other. "I hope you two are worth it."

"Even if they aren't for each other, they are truly useful to me," Tourniquet said. "They have lured the most contenders here, besides myself."

"Don't you know that people are going to die?" Cyclone cried out. "Look at your handiwork, Garika!" he motioned to Fever. "She may have been bad, but none of us would have done that to you. You killed her all by yourself!" I'm glad his opinion was different from earlier.

"I will only say this once," Tourniquet replied. "Join me, and I shall grant you your heart's desires as well." He stretched out an open hand.

"Isn't that what the contests are for?" I asked. "To win, then gain whatever you want?"

"Yes; however, how many will fall by the wayside? Only one will win the entire competition, and are there not thousands of contenders here?" Tourniquet smiled. "Why wait until the end? Wouldn't you rather indulge in your pleasures while you're alive now? All you must do is serve me."

"Why?" Fern hissed through her teeth. "Why?"

JAK'AL

The others were too weak to say anything. To *do* anything. Garika glanced to BlackByrd before turning her eyes back to the floor. Jared and Cyclone exchanged glances. Kat's mouth dropped open and Settris' did the exact opposite. We had been betrayed enough times in the very short span of being on this island. Finally, I snapped and ran up to him, my teammates calling my name.

Tourniquet blasted me with a screeching bolt of black lightning. I landed on my back, my fur smoldering from the intense power as I grabbed at the pain. It felt like my ribs were changing positions. Jared and Fern ran up to me.

"Well, now that that's all settled," Tourniquet started back with Garika and Gaako on either side. "You all have a fight to prepare for." The three turned and vanished from the scene.

"UGH!" I growled. "That one really hurt."

"Yeah," Fern said. "That was reckless, why'd you do that?"

"So we can add that little detail to our notes," I grunted. "Maybe his power and the ooze are connected."

"You're a genius," Jared commented. "Or incredibly stupid, but let's hope for the best." We all laughed a bit, trying to stay ever-optimistic, given our new situation.

Name: Blood

Weapons: Sickles

Powers: Teleportation, Summoning, Matter Manipulation- can alter state
of his body

Power Type: Elemental

CHAPTER THIRTEEN: BLOOD

The sun mutilated the earth beneath my steps. Upon my side was an empty canister I only wished to fill with the droplets of sweat across my forehead to transform into a potable substance. The day was miserable—and I deserved every bit of it. Everyone returns: that was the code I inadvertently broke after leaving my brothers-in-arms behind on a mission. The leader of our Assassin's Guild, Jahil Kambhu—the Silver Cheetah—had exiled me until I brought Locust and Chaos back alive.

My quest had led me to Dove Island, which neighbored the place of Tourniquet's competitions. Given that, all that remained of my path was to simply cross the Rurra Inlet, provided I survive the blaze of wasteland in between. I stepped onto a cliff edge and peered across the miles of sandy horizon through my binoculars. My scarf wisped in the wind as two women appeared. One had a golden bull tiara pushed against a black-and-white mane. Silk strands from her dress connected to the rings on her fingers. The other wore ancient armor and a cape of blood. I laid flat against the ledge as I watched their interaction.

CHAPTER THIRTEEN

The armored one kneeled and greeted the other.

"Hail, Modos."

"Isabelle," she replied.

"It is always grand speaking to you, but what has caused this particular occasion?"

"You were quite a great hostess at the Hanara Amphitheatre."

"Why thank you, and I give you my gratitude for resurrecting me." She spoke powerfully. "But what has caused you to do so?"

Modos paced and then said, "Do you know who killed you those centuries ago?"

"Yes, the harlequin of course. After I destroyed the blacksmith."

"You mean your husband?"

"That man was no lover of mine," her voice grew deep as Modos' white eyes lifted in smirk. "Why the sudden interest?"

"Before Tourniquet ordered your resurrection," she continued, "he was well-aware of your death."

"What do you mean? He knew?"

"Jexter isn't your only enemy." The warrior's eyes widened. "Malacus Olrello ripped off the jester's face. After that, the Master offered him eternal life if he could but kill the blacksmith. However, when he returned to his shop, he saw you had already performed that task."

"So I just got in the way," Isabelle stated, clenching her fists.

"No, you were Jexter's replacement," Modos continued. "At least that's what Jexter hoped for. Unfortunately, Tourniquet would not grant him eternal life for killing you as he had previously hoped."

"You're telling me that Tourniquet knew about this and never told me?"

"That is not his only contradiction."

"Surely he wants me alive now. Doesn't that make up for everything?"

"Perhaps he wishes to kill you again. Technically, you were just born yesterday. So I can't see why you're too surprised."

"Why are you telling me this?"

"Just thought you could use a friend."

"That can't be all. What are you planning?"

She turned and waved her hand over the ground. Within seconds, the surrounding sand climbed into four pillars. Between them, more sand morphed into a cylindrical shape before catching fire and becoming a flaming hourglass.

"What is that?" the warrior asked.

"Like the master," Modos began, "I have wandered this world for many years. Once I got what I wanted, I came to this island and became the sentinel of this relic. Here, from Dove Island, I have been able to monitor Eka's Island and have seen boundless secrecies unfold. Many from Tourniquet himself."

"Does the Master know about this?"

Modos faced her with a tilt of her head, smiling. "That I do not know."

CHAPTER THIRTEEN

The warrior grasped her spear and pointed it at the other woman. "This is a direct violation! I cannot allow this. If the Master were to find out—"

"Which he will not," Modos interrupted. "It should be evident to you that he can no longer be trusted. Additionally, if it were not for my power, you would not be standing before me. Although, it is unlike me to fashion threats; I can take lives much easier than giving them."

"I'm guessing you want me to be your servant?"

"If that is how you view it."

"I thought you had everything you wanted."

"However, you do not," she began. "I can help you achieve that."

"Now you're starting to sound like the Master."

"You have much to learn. For example," she motioned to me as the sand shifted under me, pulling me closer. Before I knew it, I was looking up at the women and was greeted by Isabelle's spear. "The eavesdropper."

"Who are you? Why are you here?" Isabelle spat, embarrassed.

"I'm looking for two men," I replied.

"Given his attire and direction, they must be brethren assassins," Modos said, first looking at Isabelle.

"They are my brothers whom I abandoned months ago."

"Months ago?" The sand beneath her shifted closer to me. "What makes you think they're still alive?"

"Faith and proof."

"Two entirely opposing factors," Modos said.

BLOOD

"I know they're alive!" I cried. "I heard one of them had damaged another competitor. He goes by the name Chaos."

"The only chaos you will find is the one growing inside you when I alert the Master of your arrival!" Isabelle yelled before taking off.

"Really hope you got through to her," I scoffed, standing up.

"She'll come to the light eventually. Until then, she'll remain a pawn in my game."

"I care not for that. Only to bring them back," I said. "Have you seen them?"

"Modos sees all," she said, motioning to the hourglass.

"Then allow me to use your magic device."

"First," she said, sand sliding toward the bottom of her dress, "Prove your worth."

"Sounds fair," I replied, clenching my fists.

"In the words of Eliot, the human poet, I will show you fear in a handful of dust." She thrusted her hands, making dirt and sand fly into my eyes. I shielded them as her foot stomped my chest.

She conjured more spells and before I knew it an enormous crevice opened, pulling me closer and closer to a growing sand pit. I stabbed my dagger into the ground in a rather futile attempt to stop sliding, but my tiring body surrendered anyway and slipped into the widening fissure. Sand filled my lungs, but I refused to give up. My body liquidized into a puddle of blood prior to teleporting out the elder witch's trap.

Soon enough the entire scene started to mix as though she were controlling the weather. Before I knew it, we were brawling in a sandstorm. Huge columns of sand gusted toward me with each of her movements. Leaping over me, she kicked my back. I blood-ported and grabbed her from behind as she flung me to the moving ground, stamping her boot into my neck. Rolling, I missed her next attack, blood-ported, and kicked her. She disappeared beneath the sand, but the fight was far from over. The witch summoned five pillars which enclosed themselves around me.

I slipped and this time sand trapped my limbs. The pillars opened to reveal a four-eyed monstrosity that the witch controlled from the inside. Apparently, I was in the palm of its hand.

"This is going to hurt," she said, sending her fist down forcefully. I dreaded the next moment. The monster pushed me to the ground. The pressure oddly hindered my teleportation.

I was forced to crawl to the surface of the sand pile. My vision was speckled with grains, and sand had also violated my ears and mouth. I had to defeat her—it was the only way to save my brothers, whom I owed immensely.

Before realizing what I was doing, I flung oceans of solidifying blood onto the base of the sands in multiple spots, hardening them into stone. Now Modos could no longer manipulate the sand at the bottom of her creation, making our feud lean in my favor. She continued her attack from within the beast, hurling gusts of particles at me as I solidified them and dodged their trajectory. At the first opportunity, I shot a blood blast directly at her that flew through one of the eyes and landed on the bull artifact on her tiara.

Moments later, the head of her monster hardened into a stone imprisonment that collapsed.

She moaned weakly and crawled out of one of the eye openings. I stepped to her, looking down. "Now, let's see through your looking-glass."

***

Modos' flaming hourglass revealed the last known whereabouts of Chaos and Locust. In order to find them, I would have to get very close to Tourniquet. Although I now knew where they were, I still lacked a specific plan to retrieve them, not to mention what trouble Isabelle would stir as soon as she reported me.

I was in no position to join the contests. Just save them and get out, undetected if possible.

Last I saw Locust, he had fallen down a ravine trying to save a tigress creature who was being attacked by a cyborg. Chaos and I tried to save him, but the two fell, and neither of us were sure if they'd survived. I had retreated to get help, but upon my return, none remained at the scene. Thankfully, a robotic source of mine from the inside informed me of their presence on Eka's Island. That is what ignited my journey.

She also warned me that the island's leader planned to attack the Inigmus C.O.R.E. I wondered why; his competitions had no gain, but the C.O.R.E. had everything to lose—the daily violence and fight for survival they were forced to endure to keep peace within their countries was hard enough in itself.

My source also informed me that the "Master," claimed that the purpose of his competitions were to find people who would save his home planet, but apparently he only sought one champion. So why not have all the participants work together?

I cared not, but at least it put something besides the remembrance of failing my comrades in my mind.

Before me were the ancient ruins of Reyes, where I beheld a knight armored in bronze with skull shoulder pads and a red feather poking out of his helmet.

"Blood? What are you doing here?"

"Chaos?" I asked as a spirit of desperation overcame me. "It's been months since I've seen you! Now let us retrieve Locust and return home."

"Locust is dead," Chaos sighed grievingly.

"What? How? The hourglass revealed his location!" I protested. "I know where he is; we can retrieve him together."

"When Locust fell," Chaos began, "Tourniquet was the only one who could put him back together. I had first reached his body and begged the Master to repair him. He performed the task, forging a specialized mechanic vessel which he called 'Mantis.'"

"He's not even human anymore?" My source had neglected to discuss that with me.

"He's not even *alive* anymore," Chaos emphasized.

I shuddered as fear altered my once hope-filled expression.

"Tourniquet killed him," he stated bitterly.

"Why would he grant him new life to simply take it away?" I was reminded of the conversation between Modos and Isabelle. The island's owner was indeed a fearful man, but his motives didn't quite make sense. But were they ours to know? Any mastermind has methods to their madness. But why did he do this to multiple people?

"The tigress," Chaos continued. "The three of us became allies, and went against Tourniquet when discovering his plan to attack the Tah'leet Soldiers. Mantis fell victim to our rebellion. Felinis and I found out afterwards."

"But the hourglass!" I said again. "He is alive! The witch of Dove Island has made it known to me!"

"You shouldn't have come back," Chaos said. "You may fall victim as well. No one is safe here."

"I left Eka's Island before—unscathed."

"It is good to have you back," a voice roared as the scene changed before us. Chaos and I suddenly found ourselves standing in a brick courtyard with walkways overhead, supporting a muscled man in golden armor.

"There he is, Master Tourniquet," Isabelle said. Both she and a pirate accompanied the master.

"Thank you for informing me. It is rare for someone to come here once, but to come willingly for a second visit— my, my. Why don't you three give him a proper greeting?"

"Three?" Chaos and I turned to a whirring sound as a blue-and-white cyborg plowed into him, taking him into the air.

"What are you doing?" I asked the female cyborg. "I thought we had a deal!" The symbols on her visor changed as her smile widened.

"Our contract has expired." The jets on the bottom of her feet blasted as she and Chaos fought.

CHAPTER THIRTEEN

"And I thought I was the one without honor," I mumbled as Isabelle and the pirate landed to the courtyard in a kneel. Isabelle's blood cape sparked, emitting her spear and shield.

"What honor do you deserve, assassin?" asked the pirate.

"No more than you, sea bandit."

"You say that like it's a bad thing. Besides," he pointed with his ruby-encrusted cutlass, "she's the only partner I have left."

"Then prepare to lose this one as well."

I summoned my daggers then enhanced them with blood as they curved into sickle shapes. My arms swung in a circular motion as the sickles clashed with the pirate's sword. But I was blasted back by a cloud of green, feeling drained instantly. Surprisingly, the pirate looked about a decade younger. I peered at my own skin to see that it became slightly aged. Did he suck away part of my soul? My sickles hooked his shoulders and I smacked his neck with my ankles before running up his body, and kicking him away. Upon landing, Isabelle's spear pierced the ground beside me. With impeccable timing, my leg swept backward, latched to the spear, allowing myself to spin up it and kick her.

She stumbled as her helmet's visor came down. She stomped toward me, screaming as heat vision blazed from between the slits of her helmet before she ripped her javelin out of the walkway. I blood-ported and was caught in an odd telepathic cloud. My energy was drained once more as I re-formed around the pirate's sword. I grunted loudly as he chuckled.

"Time for you to leave," he said, lifting his sword. "Let me help you with that!" He then bound me in a hovering spell, draining more energy, and punched me away. As I flew toward Isabelle, I blood-ported around her beams and flashed human, kicking her in midair. She rolled to her feet as my sickles left several white scratches across her shield prior to her bashing me with it.

She spun, her spear sweeping just under my feet as I jumped and blood-ported, wrapping myself around her body as I solidified. I laid straight on her shoulders and clamped my thighs around her neck before overpowering her, flipping to the ground. While still in my lock, I jumped up quickly and gave the warrior a harsh stomp to the face.

Meanwhile, the cyborg gripped Chaos like a bird of prey as they flew around the courtyard.

"Feel the sweet release of death that I cannot," she said calmly with a large grin plastered to her metallic face.

Chaos nicked her shins with his strange sword before yelling, "Chaos Wind!" The robot's legs were forced forward as the gusts sent them flying uncontrollably. Chaos used that to his advantage. He dropped, caught her arms and used them to swing to her back. Upon raising his sword, she barrel-rolled into the wall.

He caught the gaping mouth of a gargoyle as she flew, her damaged jets making her attacks unpredictable for both. He climbed the gargoyle and sent more gusts of Chaos Wind in her direction. White hot fuel from her palms and feet singed his armor. The fire and the wind collided, exploding the surrounding area. My ally fell with a weighted thud while the robot lowered herself gracefully. Rubble rained on us before she took off with him again, this time flying toward the Master.

"NO!" I yelled, reaching out.

CHAPTER THIRTEEN

"Blood." He winced. My heart raced. Whatever blood was left in me raced through my swelling veins. I was literally one rescue away from returning home and regaining my lost authoritative positions. It couldn't end here. I blood-ported to the walkway. The robot stomped at my fingers as I leaped up, hooking the edge with my sickles and climbing.

"Give him back!" I yelled, swiping my weapons at her mercilessly. She tossed him to Tourniquet. He caught him in a mass of dark energy that slowly consumed him before shoving me back onto the courtyard below.

Isabelle punched me directly over my heart as I fell, grabbing at the wound. The pirate's cutlass sliced me several times until large droplets of my own blood painted the courtyard. The two stepped my way intimidatingly as I chanted under my breath. My eyes shot open as my droplets formed into ravenous white-eyed yipping beasts called sevims. The snarling blood wolves overcame my opponents, pinning them to the ground.

While my sevims attacked, I caught myself on the fountain and shoved my hand into it as it boiled, turning red. The blood wolves' bodies bubbled and smoked. Swirls of blood flared from them, dripping scorching liquid around my struggling opponents as they chomped their weaponry. The pirate pressed his hand into the sevim above him, attempting to drain its life force. He gritted his teeth, and succeeded, despite the pain, and formed into an even younger frame. Eventually, the warrior was able to incapacitate hers as well. The sevims exploded, splattering blood onto their faces and the courtyard.

Finally, after all the fighting and searching, my journey had reached its end. Had I really failed again? Did I waste my time? Was I foolish for coming back and unintentionally entrapping myself here once more?

Tourniquet and the cyborg peered down from the walkway as he spoke. "Blood."

I glared at him, barely able to hold my head up, exhaling forcefully. I had given it all I possibly could—and was still unable to save them. I had failed Locust and Chaos twice now. Isabelle and the man restrained my arms. It was over.

"Welcome to Eka's Island—again," he said as I stared hollowly into our blood bathed surroundings and the ever-reddening fountain.

Name: Luda
Weapons: Electric Crescent-Shaper Daggers
Powers: None
Power Type: Shadowstry

CHAPTER FOURTEEN:
LUDA

Hundreds of guests had gathered to the main palace to watch Light and I fight. It seemed we were fighting throughout the entire day, without the slightest of interruptions. We persevered, both hoping the Master would allow us to kill the other. He had plenty disciples of his Angels of Anarchy, and her death would prove no loss—especially not to me. At least she was an interesting rival.

I headbutted her nose while she pinned me to the floor. Blood gushed down her face and my foot thrusted her abdomen. Her torso slumped forward as I mounted her shoulders and threw my arms diagonally, flipping her, mid-cartwheel. A wire-thin craggy blade exited the palm of her hand, shooting into the floor as she stopped herself. The knives slid out of her feet as they bent forward, allowing her to stand.

I popped my neck and we flew. Her right foot diced the air beside me as I dodged and electrocuted it with my dagger. She ignored the stab wound and absorbed the shock to the blade jutting out of her other wrist that she soon swatted at me. I almost forgot she was practically a human lightning conductor. She spun, my lighting still sparking off her curved blade. Upon summoning both wrist blades, they sliced upward, passing over my forehead by inches. Distracted, I received a generous cut to my right arm vein just before she whirled around to provide another.

"My bad," Light chirped, hurling herself at me.

I danced around her craggy blades until an opening appeared. I smacked her chin upward.

"Now it's my bad!"

I blocked the girl's calf leg as the crowds chanted our names.

"Light! Light! Light! Light!"

"Lu-da! Lu-da! Lu-da!"

I watched as her body vanished through her shadow. I surveyed the area, waiting for her to pop up again. Her feet jutted out, and would've been the death of me if I hadn't reacted in time. Her killer feet whirled around multiple times while she simultaneously performed a perfect walking handstand. She continued this rather bothersome feat about three more times, disappearing, then popping back up out of nowhere with hopes of landing a hit. It's no doubt that she was fast—but so was I.

Unfortunately, I realized that the only way to keep her still was to force her hand and take damage. Nothing would hinder her from making that mistake. When that rare moment happened, I needed to be strong enough to stun her and then finish her— once and for all. In my daze, she managed to kick the bend of my knee. I returned the favor with a quick jolt from my daggers just before slicing some flesh off her face. Light disappeared into the floor and flashed behind me, sending her abnormal wrist blades piercing through my shoulders. I stomped her away as she flipped numerous times, then landing perfectly enough for my lighting to strike her.

More green lightning zapped out the crescents, it trailed above the audience's heads and then turned to her. Light used her gruesome blades to deflect and absorb their power. A shroud of light manifested itself in her aura, strengthening her, but I endured. While I was waiting for her next move, Light teleported to me, continuously shooting huge blasts of ultraviolet rays. I barricaded myself in a cage of bolts so her lights would pass me. Eventually, I countered one using my electric daggers.

The now-black beam darkened the face of the dumbfounded Light. I scoffed and spat blood upon the floor. She soon recovered, but we couldn't fight much longer. We had one another's flesh under our nails and blood soaked our knives, yet our deaths set our priorities. The crowd roared.

I ran up to her as she still held the same expression. I leaped, kicking the uppermost part of her back as she turned, allowing my daggers to plant themselves firmly into her neck. Light's sparking body twitched and jolted uncontrollably for at least a full minute. Tourniquet couldn't help but smirk sadistically. The palace hushed as I lifted my leg over my head. Within that quiet second, my heel swiftly dropped, crushing her shoulder as she crumbled to her knees. We both turned to Tourniquet, who nodded at me. Light gaped in amazed betrayal over the privilege he gave. It was that signal—that simple nod—that sealed one's fate. Light didn't look so good.

Her green eyes stabbed each section of my soul.

"Thanks for entertaining us," I said, tossing the tiny amount of flesh I had sliced off her face earlier. "I think I'll keep you alive so you can live with this defeat."

Tourniquet arose from his golden snake throne and made his way to me. His rough hand clasped my wrist tightly as he lifted it. Victory was mine.

CHAPTER FOURTEEN

"Luda wins!" his voice boomed throughout the room. I looked over to Light. Miraculously, she stood, glaring at the audience chanting my name, and then at me. I heard a whisper in my ear.

"I will get my revenge." It was Light, but she was so far away. A person passed my line of sight before she disappeared for the last time. Or so I thought.

***

I was making decent progress for Baron's Pointe. It was a mountain named after the notorious air explorer, Barone`, who discovered it in the 1600s. Strangely, flying machines were created approximately three-hundred years later. Perhaps Orville and Wilbur were not the first humans to create a successful flyer? My thoughts were interrupted by an explosion on the forest floor behind me. The impact sent me flying to my face. I struggled to stand while a previous contender was back for another beating.

"Too slow!" She was perched on a thick tree branch, her white corseted suit still tattered from earlier. "I would've preferred that you killed me."

"That's a bit extreme, isn't it?"

Light leaped down, gracefully walking up. In the blink of an eye, her knives slid disgustingly out of the sides of her wrists. It looked like she just zipped by me, but in reality, I was covered in gashes from head to toe, kneeling and grasping my heart.

"Controlling light allows me to move faster than the speed of light."

"That explains why I could hear you so closely earlier when you didn't even move," I summarized weakly.

She laughed, looking at me over her shoulder. "And that's just the beginning."

About five white Light clones rushed up to me and attacked as she simply watched. They could hurt me, but not even my lightning could affect them. If anything, the bolts just strengthened Light's attacks. Soon I was laid flat again. The only movement the original Light made was when she breathed. How was I to figure out this puzzle? *Could those things travel faster than light?* I thought to myself, gazing into the sunset.

"Send your lights out again!" I provoked as I stood, getting an idea. I hadn't planned that far ahead, but hopefully I could make it to the shadows of the trees before the duplicates did.

"If you insist." Light opened her hand, re-summoning the five clones. Their speed was quite impressive, but I had to stay focused. I pushed myself, the clones nearly stepping on my heels, as my forehead glazed with sweat. My foot met the shadow's edge and her clones immediately vanished. I scoffed at Light, who stumbled back in astonishment.

"You're only forgetting one tiny detail, Luda," she said, holding her thumb and index finger close together to demonstrate.

"And what would that be?"

She teleported and landed onto the tree limb above me.

"Me." She disarmed the tree of one of its limbs and hurled it my way. It would've knocked me over if I didn't move in time. Her wrist blades clanked against my crescent daggers, giving off a high-pitched ring. Light grabbed me and teleported us back onto the leafy forest floor. Then she rammed my head into another tree.

215

CHAPTER FOURTEEN

I turned and she pushed me against it, our arms pressing together. A blade jutted out her palm and she enhanced its power and inched it toward my throat. She stroked the glowing tip of the knife down my neck, sending chills down my spine.

"Good riddance," she hissed as my eyes clamped shut. Then suddenly her blades retreated into her flesh and froze. Her emerald eyes shrank, her skin paling as a dark power wrapped around her core, keeping her from killing me. Then she slumped over.

I looked over to a young man with black hair, who I assumed had come to my rescue.

"I could have taken her myself."

"That's not what it looked like from here," he replied. "And a 'thank you' would've sufficed."

"Thank you."

He bowed slightly. "It's so good to see you're safe," he said, hugging me.

"Unhand me!" I exclaimed, backing away. He stared at me, confused.

"S-sorry," he stammered. "I know it's been a while…since the asylum and all."

"Excuse me?" I questioned. "Asylum?"

"Yeah," he said, as if I were supposed to know what he meant. "The asylum. Back in Apex? I know things have been weird, but surely you haven't forgotten?"

"Correct," I stated. "You can't forget what you were never told."

He stared at me once more, this time his mouth dropping.

"Baron's Pointe!" I cried, leaving the scene. "I'm running late to a fight, and it's *my* fight. My thanks for the save though."

He grabbed my hand as I walked by him. I turned. Pain filled his eyes, and I flashed him a dark glare. It was like he was in a trance. I tried to pull my hand out of his grip, but he wouldn't budge until I finally yanked it forcefully away.

"What's wrong with you?" I asked, walking faster and faster, peering over my shoulder to ensure he didn't follow.

He just stood there, staring blankly off into the woods. "I was thinking the same thing," he stated.

***

My new opponent was a Krow Spector cyborg with a gas mask and bland goggles—Porcupine. Finally, someone different than Light. I'd had enough of her. I analyzed my opponent more closely. His armor was a dun-brown color with an array of spikes arrayed covering it. One of his legs seemed different from the other. A malleable material wrapped around his joints and lower core region. Possible vulnerable points? If I aimed my attacks there, then I literally just won the battle. The audience was stunned. I think it was the first time they had seen a robot on the battlefield. Something told me that it wouldn't be the last.

We looked over to Tourniquet, who was just now lowering himself into the golden snake throne in the new arena. So far it seemed that every area had one. Porcupine and I impatiently waited for the starting call.

"Begin!"

We charged at each other as thunder rolled in the gray skies above us.

CHAPTER FOURTEEN

Porcupine shot hundreds of toxic pins at me. Several slid under my skin. My eyes widened fearfully as I proved unable to pull them out. Their poison entered my bloodstream as three cyborgs spun within my blurring vision. I scanned them, trying to evaluate which was the actual just before allowing his metal boot to stomp me. A massive bolt of lightning temporarily blinded everyone, including Tourniquet.

Once I could see again, I scooted away from the giant divide the blast had left in the ground between us as the audience gasped.

Porcupine dove toward me while in the air, aiming a thick quill at me. I rolled sideways, and he stabbed it into the ground. I flipped onto my feet as he went ballistic. His metallic fingers gripped my arm and his spiked knuckles plowed into my chin. I stumbled a bit, but slammed my knee against his head. My leg closed around his neck and I shoved my sparking daggers into the goggles of his mask. He let out a muffled scream, clawing for his damaged eyes. Blood mixed with an oozing, tar-like substance excreting from the gas mask as he scowled.

I gasped in disbelief. The mechanical helmet gave off gray smoke as two coffee-colored eyes peered back from behind the shattered glass circlets. He was human. His eyes shrank as if he had been freed of hypnosis. Frantically, he grabbed the base of the helmet and pulled, but it was locked tight. His back arched as he stepped dizzily.

"No, no!" he coughed woefully, blood and black ooze flowing out of his mask. "I never wanted this! I change my mind!"

I used that to my advantage and ran up to him, kicking him with both legs. To my surprise, he caught and threw me on his opposite side. I flipped back up, charging my daggers, and shot more bolts his way. As they trailed toward him, he dodged them before kicking me. My body flung sideways as more pins slithered under my flesh, blurring my vision again.

I knew his weaknesses—all except the one I needed the most. How was I to attack flawlessly? Regardless of his distance, whether he was close or far, his needles would injure me. Maybe craving a new enemy was a bad thing. I had Light figured out; but this man was different, especially now that I knew he wasn't just a machine.

His spikes rained from above as lighting from my daggers bounced between each of them. Once he landed, I snatched his wrist and elbowed his gas mask before using his body as a shield. To my surprise, hundreds of needles stabbed the ground around us. He pushed me away angrily, and I tripped, landing on a bed of needles. The needles stuck out of my arms like reverse acupuncture. My blood rushed, but adrenaline didn't seem to kick in—I was paralyzed. Froth sputtered out of my mouth as a dozen hazy Porcupines landed on me. I let out a hard grunt as he simply cocked his head and hovered over me like a cybernetic ghost. I stretched my neck to look at the Master, waiting for him to release me. Finally, he looked at Porcupine and nodded. The kill signal. I was not going to die! Even if I did die through the contests, I refused to be killed by this competitor.

Forcing myself off the pins, I gritted my teeth as the many miniature punctures bled. He looked at me, bewildered, as the audience chanted my name.

"Now, now," I began tiredly. "You don't want to disappoint my adoring fans, would you?" We charged for the last time. I danced, avoiding his movements until leaping off his lunged knee. My crescent daggers left gashes in the areas covering his joints, leaving him paralyzed. "Now let's see how *you* like it!"

A coiling trail of lightning snaked out of the gray, thundering clouds above and met my mechanized opponent. The blast created another pit, sending his body more than six feet under. Tourniquet jumped out of his seat and stared at the scene. Once the blinding light had ceased, a single, fully mechanical leg remained, falling lifelessly. The audience roared in amusement. The Master should've known better than to nod at anyone else but me. I was destined to be his victor, one way or another.

***

I returned to my room located in a private sect of the temple where nobody could bother me. At least until I heard a knock at my door. I placed my daggers down on the bedsheets and peeked through the crack.

"Who's there?"

"Hurry, you've got to let me in!" the black-haired boy cried.

I retreated, standing straight as he pushed the door open, surprised by his energetic entrance.

"Who sent you, and what gives you the right to—" His hand cupped over my mouth as he slammed the door shut. He motioned for me to be quiet then slowly removed his hand.

"Listen," he whispered sternly. "that was the first day you have ever been in a fight. It took me a while to put it together, but I finally figured it out."

Who was he? He seemed vaguely familiar.

He continued, "Each second that you're here, you're—you're forgetting who you are!"

"Who *I* am?" I said, raising my voice. "What about *you*? Barging in here like some lunatic, telling me about *me*. I don't need your help, and I haven't forgotten anything."

"What's your name?" he asked.

"My name is Luda," I answered. "I was born to serve the Master, and I am a vicious cold-blooded killer."

"Yeah, you really killed that woman out there," he said sarcastically. "And I meant your first name. What's your first name?"

"My name is Luda," I repeated. "I was born to serve the Master, and I am a vicious cold-blooded killer."

Tears formed in his eyes. He put his hands on his waist before wiping his exhausted countenance. His tone lowered, almost inaudible. "First," he cried, biting back tears. Why was he behaving like that? "Name."

"There," I enunciated, "is no such thing as a first name." His eyes widened. "People have but one name. I don't know where you're from, but that's how things have been since the beginning of time." I stepped to the door. "Now please," I said, opening it. "Leave."

He handed me a laminated slip with writing in tiny font that was full of information about a woman who had a striking resemblance to me. She had a dark head of hair like mine. Sparkling lime eyes like mine.

"What is this?" I asked.

"You," he breathed.

"Excuse me? *Candice* Luda?" I scoffed. "That's not me; so unless you're looking for a fight, then I suggest you leave."

CHAPTER FOURTEEN

"Tourniquet is my father; he's been experimenting on you and he wants you to forget everything about your past!" he said. "That's why you're forgetting everything."

"Get out."

"You need to know the truth."

"Get out—now!" I screamed.

"You've got to believe me!" he pleaded, shaking my arms. "Please, you have to—come back! This isn't where you're meant to be! Your memory, it's fading!"

"Guards—" I started, raising my voice even louder.

He continued to yell, desperately trying to get me to listen to his whimsical ideologies. Shaking. Shaking my already weakened body.

"GUARDS!"

"Y-you have to remember! Just listen to me! Please! He's been erasing your mind! You don't know who you are!"

"GUARDS!" I howled as a group of Tourniquet's elites burst into the room, detaining him.

He reached out to me, still spitting out random things. "Please!" he screamed over the noise of them yelling and picking him up. He clawed his way past them as if his life depended on it. As if *my* life depended on it. "Candice!" He cried, reaching out to me as they pulled him back again. "I—"

The last thing he said made my blood run cold.

"I can't do this…alone."

Then there was silence.

***

Tourniquet was removing his armor and cape when I came into his bed quarters. I didn't bother knocking on the door.

"Who let you in?" He made no acknowledgement of my presence.

"You didn't even look at me."

He turned, removing his other shoulder pad. "I didn't need to. Your heavy breathing was a dead giveaway."

"You know what I mean!" I cried. "You gave Porcupine the death signal."

"I did not. I nodded toward you."

"No, you didn't!" I raised my voice. "Admit it—you wanted him to kill me, didn't you!?"

He sighed heavily and fully turned to me. "My son was telling the truth." I was all ears. "Once Porcupine failed to bring him to me, I hired another to perform the task; but you were a witness, and I couldn't just leave you with everything you knew." His square face gently inched closer to mine, his hot breath fuming into my cheek. "But none of that matters now, does it?"

"Of course, it matters," I said defensively. "That's my past!" I yelped as he grabbed my shoulders and pushed me against the wall.

"That's not what you were saying mere hours ago," he reminded me, backing off.

"So what do you want from me?"

"Everyone and everything must be perfected."

"Perfected for what?"

"The competitions."

CHAPTER FOURTEEN

"To save your home world?"

"Yes."

"Then why aren't you making an army?" He fell silent. "Wouldn't that make more sense? Instead of making everyone fight to the death, and if you have acquired the means to do so, then make an army to save your—"

Then it hit me. He watched intently as I put the pieces together. If that was the main point for hosting the competitions and bringing all those people together, he would have been doing that already. That's what BlackByrd was trying to tell me—not to trust his father.

"There is no home world. You're from earth," I stated flatly.

He nodded. "Actually, you're much closer than you think. However, I must say, I am quite impressed by your skills of deduction. Whatever gave me away?"

"Because if you had any interest in saving any planet, you would have been creating an army already." My mind flashed to a scene of a laboratory. My memories were coming back, but it almost made me sick. "The cyborgs…those were once people. You've been experimenting on them. You gave them powers, but not to fight a war—to fight each other!"

"Very good," he said as I tearfully backed away from him. "Go on. Tell me, where did the powers come from? What was the exact process of how they obtained those perfections?"

My mind raced. I wasn't sure. I didn't know anyone who would have crossed that information. He just stood, smiling, challenging me to unveil his master plan. I then thought further. The rebellious-looking girl who fought with Austin. She wiped off a black ooze material off her face after their fight. Maybe that played in to his ultimate scheme.

LUDA

I murmured the only thing on my mind at the time. "You're evil!"

"You know what else is evil?"

"What?"

He snapped his fingers.

"What am I doing here?" I asked.

"Your name is Luda," he spoke. "You are born only to serve me, and you are a vicious cold-blooded killer. Just like me."

Name: Enrage
Weapons: Blood Sabers-arsenal manifesting from his tattoos
Powers: Blazing Marks, Hatewave unleashes gigantic waves of pure hatred
Power Type: Shadowstry

CHAPTER FIFTEEN:
ENRAGE

T hat guy didn't stand a chance," I laughed from our table at the tavern near Baron's Pointe.

The stuffed head of a bear was mounted on a thick wooden post near light fixtures made of antlers. Along the medieval walls were several portraits of a helmeted pilot with goggles, a scarf, and a bushy mustache that curled up on either end. Below one picture was a glistening gold plaque engraved with: *Barone` Morel, the Great Pilot.*

I didn't care whose name was on it. Gold's gold. I smiled at it as a voice called me out.

"Don't even think about it."

"Well, if it isn't Little Miss Perfect," I hissed at Settris. "Who's your friend?"

"No concern of yours," said the armor-clad, dark-skinned woman.

I eyed her up and down. "Did she tell you what happened to the last one? She really fell for me. Especially after I stabbed her."

"Why you—"

CHAPTER FIFTEEN

"Settris, stop." The girl in white put a hand on her shoulder as I chuckled, entertained. "You really don't remember me, 'Katherine of the 5X,' do you, Enrage?"

"Sorry, doesn't ring a bell," I responded.

"I find you rather hard to forget. A man darker than night, despite the blood-colored webs covering his body," Kat replied.

"Guilty as charged," I admitted, cradling my head and propping my feet on the closest chair. "What brings ya' 'round here anyways? Haven't you figured out I'm dangerous?"

"I've seen worse," Settris stated.

"We're keeping an eye on our infamous criminals," Kat answered.

"That's a waste of time. You should be worried about yourself. You could die here you know."

"True, but so can you."

"Death or staying alive to be arrested," I said, gesturing. The others at my table laughed, including a harlequin who was being nosy and arched backward in his seat, his head now upside-down to enter our conversation.

"What are you all laughing at?" the clown asked.

"Mind your own business, freak," I snapped.

He laughed then mumbled. "You're one to talk."

"What did you say?"

Recognition flashed in his eyes. "Wait, you're the one Master met at the—"

"Quiet," I warned in a hiss.

"To have her—" he continued, pointing at Settris and laughing hysterically. "This must be really exciting for you!"

"That's it!" The red beams on my body blazed brightly as I punched his masked face. Everyone around moved just in time as I tackled him, breaking the table in half.

"Gotta love a good bar fight!" he cackled just as my incoming attack was interrupted.

"Halt!"

The whole tavern turned and faced an armored woman with brown hair and gray eyes who stood at the wooden door.

"How umbelliferous!" the freak said, slipping out of my grasp and through the opening of my legs. "First you stole my life, then you almost refused to let me fight, and now you steal this one from me?"

"I have no concern of you or for you, Jexter," she replied then looked up to the groups of people. "I was ordered by Tourniquet to inform you all of the intensity of the upcoming battle. It will include nine competitors."

"Nine?" Some people whispered. "That's the most there's been in a single fight."

"I suggest you all start practicing as those who will be competing still remain unknown. All except—you," she said, turning to me.

"Me?"

Her armor rattled as she stepped my way. "That's not a problem, is it?"

"I don't think you're supposed to name specifics, darlin'," Jexter said.

"I gave but one detail, and if you speak back to me about it, the only thing the audience will see of you is your head on the end of my spear."

CHAPTER FIFTEEN

"Mmm, shish-kabobs!"

"So…that's eight remaining," Settris stated. "Are Kat or I in this round?"

"I was not made aware, but based on your appearances, I'd say you would be the first to fall."

"And join your reaver?" the warrior frowned. Settris' eyes glowed lightly. "She's telling the truth. She only knows the one."

"No," I answered, regaining their attention. "That won't be a problem at all. In fact," I turned toward the girls. "I'm looking forward to it."

"Excellent," the warrior's formal voice cooed. "The following contest is where the real fun begins."

***

"Is everything alright?" Kat asked Settris, blocking her hit and landing an unexpected grab. Her hand smooshed her cheek. "You seem a little off."

"Me…a little off?" Settris said. "You're the one losing."

"Yeah, still." She broke her lock and threw her sideways. Settris' thick elevator heels clomped against the training grounds as she landed. The two stood still for a bit. "What's up?"

Settris let out a heavy sigh before answering. "It's Enrage."

"That's not surprising. You mean how you still can't read his psyche?"

"Yeah," she replied. "I've never had this much trouble with anyone. He knows something important, but there's no telling what that could be without a direct interrogation."

"I'm glad that's an option." The two laughed then turned to a grumbling sound.

"Tourniquet has insulted me for the last time!" I mumbled angrily, conveniently out of earshot. I was stomping toward the Library of Plants clutching a manila envelope. Inside it was me. My file on how I obtained my abilities. My secrets that I planned to erase. "I'm my own man. I don't need anyone, nor do I want anyone. I just want to come back to you."

Settris turned to her friend as they watched closely. "And maybe that's our answer."

Vines dangled from the overhead canopy and diverse foliage decorated the paths below. I swatted a wide leaf out of my face as I headed deeper into the multi-tiered jungle. Unbeknownst to me, the young women tailed me from a safe distance. I stopped at a carnivorous plant that emitted a random piece of literature.

"Interesting." Kat whispered while she and Settris remained hidden from my sight. "He's the one who's been leaving files here." Settris nodded.

I yanked the book and angrily swept through its contents. I glanced over my shoulder before shredding the envelope with my fangs and watching its remnants snow onto the pages. I clamped the book shut and shoved it back into the plant, watching it disappear through the length of the stem and return to the invisible collection underground. I exhaled, overcome with an immediate calm, feeling my burden of anguish was coming to an end. Finally knowing I could stand up straight. Knowing that dozens of books were filled with secrets no longer accessible to Tourniquet—or so I hoped.

"Enrage." A synthetic voice said behind me as I spun around, stress invading my mind again.

CHAPTER FIFTEEN

"Metsys; Animal," I gasped in a sad attempt to act casual. "What are you doing here?"

"We just believed it kind to update you on current events."

"I'm listening." I snapped.

"Tourniquet has attacked the Inigmus C.O.R.E.," Animal informed.

"As he planned. And wasn't that what you fought alongside Mantis to prevent?" Animal looked down, ignoring me as I clapped. "Well done." He was reminded of Tourniquet's renewed influence over him after Mantis had been killed. He had cowardly restored his faith in him, choosing to serve him once more, only this time out of fear rather than reverence.

"The war with the Tah'leet Soldiers has begun." Metsys continued. "Due to this, Tourniquet intends to dispatch the last of his machines which brings us to Isabelle's earlier remark."

"About the next round being where the real fun begins?" They nodded. "It sounded like she was referring to something big."

"Like an elimination round."

"Exactly." I agreed.

"No, I'm telling you," Animal replied. "It is an elimination round."

Kat and Settris gaped at each other while I shuddered.

"Unfortunately, it seems our truce has come to an end," Metsys stated.

"That was rather short-lived."

"As will we be in the following fight," Animal continued. "Apparently, there's all kinds of surprises."

"Why is he planning this?"

"He's attacked the C.O.R.E., and with that being his priority motive, I infer that the competitions are coming to a close," Metsys said.

"But how does a war on the mainlands relate to the competitions here?" Animal asked. "Are they not mutually exclusive?"

"Yeah, didn't Tourniquet claim that he wanted his home world saved or something?" I asked. "Something's missing."

"That's what he told me." Settris whispered to Kat. "And I sensed he was telling the truth."

"Is there a possibility that he wasn't?" Kat asked her.

Settris considered the thought. "But why would he lie about that?"

"Given that he was telling the truth, maybe Tourniquet did want to attack the Tah'leets, but that doesn't mean that was his only motive. Otherwise, what's the point of having the competitions in the first place?" Kat inquired.

"Good idea, Cuz. We need to figure that out, but right now, we need to warn the others about this." The bushes rustled as they stood.

"What was that?" Metsys asked, turning toward the sound.

"I'll go check it out." Animal said, thrusting his arms and breaking into a run as I took to the opposite direction.

Moments later, I ran to the end of an upper branch of the miniature multi-tiered jungle. Then I looked up to Kat swinging toward me from a higher vine, her feet knocking my chest as I rolled backward. Settris appeared from behind as my tattoos swam onto the veins on the giant leaf we stood on. It burned them as I alerted the others.

CHAPTER FIFTEEN

"Metsys, Ani—AHHH!"

Settris closed her fist with an outstretched arm as my marks zapped and slithered back onto me, my head pulsing brutally.

"Let us pass, Enrage," Settris demanded. "We know why you're here."

"Oh yeah? And why's that?" I asked, leaning forward.

"Those files you dropped off," she answered. "They must have been some sort of experiment logs. Only now we've caught you in the act and know you've left others too."

"Who told you that? It's not like you can read my mind."

"True, but we do know about Candice Luda," Kat broke in. "Tourniquet's been conducting experiments on her, and she may not be the only one."

"Not to mention, this area houses a special hivemind; a central processing point for all data collected. Like a natural computer. All I had to do was connect to its mind to find the most interesting reads," Settris explained.

"I'm not telling either of you anything." I hissed.

"You don't have to. In fact, we're telling you to keep quiet."

"What?"

"You wouldn't want the ones who warned you about the elimination round to find that their information was being dropped off into plants that anyone can access, do you?" Settris said. "That's where your plan was flawed. You never expected anyone to find those parchments and put them back together, did you?"

This feeling was all too familiar.

"Really, Settris?" I growled. "You dare blackmail me? Tell about my life being jeopardized? After what happened back at the ship?"

Her eyes widened. "What are you talking about?"

"You fell unconscious just prior to the pirate's ship blowing up, remember?" I explained. "And just who do you think brought you through that?" She looked down in sheer realization. "You only remember waking up, don't you? But you never considered who psychically moved you."

"What do you want?" She yelled defensively. "First you killed our friend, then you saved me? It should've been me instead of her."

"That's noble, but stupid." I spat. "She saw I was one of Tourniquet's experiments, so I panicked."

"You didn't have to kill her!" Kat cried.

"That's some pretty ironic words, coming from you. We're in a fight to the death on an island in the middle of nowhere, or have you forgotten?"

"If that's the case, why are you here?" Kat yelled.

"I have my reasons. You two don't know the dark like I do."

"And what's that supposed to mean?" Settris asked.

I laughed devilishly, "Why don't you read my mind and find out?"

"Enrage!" Animal yelled from a distance, interrupting our conversation. "You see anything?" We fell silent.

"Remember, you saved me," Settris began in a harsh whisper. "For that, we'll keep your secret safe, but you must agree to let us leave in peace. Fail to do so, and our next encounter might not result in the most beneficial outcome toward you. Especially if we meet in the elimination round. That's just something to consider."

They stared back at me through fearless eyes. Ready to face whatever I chose their fate to be. I've only seen that determination in one other individual. A person headstrong, brave, and far better than me. That look was only one I could recognize. No matter how quick or problematic their next challenge would be, they certainly proved to be strong enough to face it together. I looked down, gritting my fangs, reminiscing that certain soul, wondering if they were even alive and if I left for the right reasons. I had specific orders to follow.

"Animal!" I yelled.

"Yeah?" He answered.

Their hearts stopped for a second, their expressions turning to stone.

"There's nothing here!" I continued. "Whatever it was must have escaped. I'm heading your way now."

They both exhaled quietly. "We are forever in your debt." Settris said solemnly as Kat attempted to study whatever secret plan she had tucked away in that cunning mind of hers. For a telepath who couldn't read me, I could undoubtedly admit she was truly extraordinary.

***

All were gathered at a tall gate leading to a narrow path that stretched to a craggy plateau. Tourniquet was already seated at his golden snake throne between Princess Quazar, who sat in a silver throne, and Isabelle, who winked at me from her bronze one. As soon as the spectators took their places, Tourniquet announced, "Today's the day!"

236

ENRAGE

The day we all dreaded.

I remembered Isabelle's haunting words of what was soon to befall. Only I and a few others knew what this arena represented—the result of Tourniquet's plan reaching its conclusion. His apparent attack on the mainlands and how he no longer needed all of us—only one; whomever fate allowed that victor to be. It could be any of us, yet no one at all. The competitors in the Mammon Grave denoted nine of thousands. How many were bound to meet their end? The participants were still unknown. Tourniquet's voice echoed throughout the melancholy skies of the mountainous arena.

"Welcome all to Mammon Grave, a site renowned for its spontaneous and habitual collapsing of itself just to alter its shape."

"So, technically speaking," Isabelle spoke. "Not only will you not be on level ground, you won't be fighting on the *same* ground as you did previously."

"This, like many of you, is deadly and ever-evolving," Tourniquet continued, watching me. "Additionally, each competitor has a device inserted in the nape of their neck set to detonate if that person has failed to move within fifteen seconds, killing them instantly."

The audience gasped, some screaming, as my hands snapped back, noticing an odd feeling protruding under my skin on the back of my neck. I knew I was competing, but how did that get there without my knowing it? It was pointless to ask. The worst was yet to come.

Princess Quazar stretched and whispered in his ear.

"Oh yes, we've yet to name our participants," Tourniquet said. "Rust, Captain Red Blood, and Metsys."

CHAPTER FIFTEEN

Upon hearing their names, they stepped out of the audience and into the center of the arena.

"You are not going to like this," Settris whispered to Kat.

"What, why?" she whimpered.

"Animal, Talon, Enrage."

I took my place.

"Why, Settris?" she snatched her wrist. "Why are you standing?" She tapped Cyclone and motioned him to join her.

"What?" All the 5X exchanged looks.

"No, he doesn't have to do this, and neither do you," Jared said. "We can find a way out."

"This is the way out," Settris spoke.

"No!" Kat said. "I'm not—I can't have you two go out like this!"

"Cyclone and Settris," Tourniquet named.

Kat shrieked from the audience as they attempted to calm her. I ignored it. I had my orders.

"And Princess Quazar," The pink-haired princess' smile vanished as she turned to him, gaping. "Don't act like you won't enjoy it. Go have some fun." He smirked.

She cut her eyes at those competing and lifted off her silver throne before breaking flight and landing with us.

"This should be good," Animal murmured as we dispersed to the sides to initiate the fight.

"We've got this," Cyclone told Settris, who let out a modest smile.

Settris whispered from an ancient scripture, "Blessed be the Lord my strength, which teacheth my hands to war, and my fingers to fight."

I watched her carefully.

"At least three must die before the end call. Some will fall to their opponents; others will simply fall to the grave itself," Tourniquet explained. "GO!"

We ran madly, wondering who to fight first; who would fall first. Nine competitors in an all-out brawl, and three had to die. Our strengths, the other's weaknesses; our weaknesses, the others' strengths. Our feet had barely even grazed the ground and it had already started to fissure. Tourniquet raised his arms as the audience's seats and connected thrones shook out of place and hovered into the air. Stalactites hung underneath it. The surrounding gates lifted and circulated the arena like a rotating shield, as the spectators were placed just above it.

I staggered before looking ahead to Talon, who braced herself on all fours, walking toward me like a rabid dog. Her feathers were clearly ruffled. I kept my sight locked on her as she pounced, reaching her claws out at me. Instinctively, a tattoo shot out of my hand and manifested into a blood saber that I sliced multiple times before eventually hitting her. She stumbled, salivating vehemently, her stare nearly bulging out of her head. She roared then lunged, swiping her claws until I slammed my palm into her side and knee to her face. I turned to agitated screams from Cyclone and Settris as Talon's head whipped around to see them.

"The children!" she hissed before we both caught ourselves standing still and quickly exited our dazed state. Fifteen seconds was all we had. To think we could be penalized—killed—simply for standing still was crazy. Anxiously, Talon glanced between me and the other direction as I lowered, missing a hammer that knocked her backward.

I peered up to see the assassin Rust then heard the buzzing wings of Princess Quazar.

"Daddy knows about your secrets!" she yelled at him.

"Whatever do you mean, Princess?"

"You can't hide the theater events from us!" She blasted swarms of energy spheres at us as the ground creviced. I tripped, grabbing the edge of the rising shaft that Rust stood upon as he instinctively pulled me to safety.

"I could've saved myself," I informed.

"And I don't require your assistance with her," he began, motioning to Princess Quazar. "But a swift end would prove advantageous for us both."

"I get your point," I said, stepping beside him. "After all, we do need at least three, right?"

"That goes for me as well," The princess reminded, blowing up the surrounding area. Pillars of dirt shot up as we ran. Rust's hammer evaporated as he shot blotches of his unique amber-ice. She maneuvered past his attacks, growing faster and angrier by the minute. As a larger blast made its way toward her, she stopped, catching it in a portal and opened another in front of us, Rust's projectiles recoiling on us.

Rust's aura froze me in place as his body rolled across the jagged landscape. Princess Quazar's feet stamped on the ground making it shift again before stepping toward me predatorily.

"An insurgent and a demon," she uttered.

"I think you're confusing those with you," I said, attempting to distract her while readying my free hand.

"What pitiful last words!" she squealed, her spheres resembling magenta flames as onlookers exclaimed.

"Stay back!" I warned, as my marks started to blaze underneath the crystal. "Stay back!" The crystal immediately exploded, sending shards toward her along with random heat flares. I examined my palms quickly and yelled, blasting countless beams from my pointer fingers her direction. Princess Quazar opened another portal, then accidentally released the blast between Talon's shoulders as she headed toward the 5X allies. Talon snarled and chased after the frightened, retreating princess.

I made my way to the edge and looked down to Rust, who was slowly recovering, while being reminded of my main objective.

Meanwhile, Cyclone and Settris battled Captain Red Blood and his pet cyborg. Metsys blasted at Settris, who lunged forward, her warm beams passing just above her before she flipped backward, missing another. The machine froze for a second as the green icons on her visor burned red and her smile morphed into a frown. Metsys' fusion thrusters pushed far beyond their capacity as she went haywire, performing an airborne roundhouse kick toward the psychic who simply evaded the kick. Once an opening appeared, Settris swung her foot into the cyborg's neck.

"Are you prepared to die?" the pirate asked Cyclone.

"Funny, I was about to ask you the same thing." Captain Red Blood's forearms swooped down at his opponent, who stopped them with his wind before swinging his body and kicking him. Cyclone rebalanced himself in a stance as the pirate made a second attempt, this time successfully managing to grab his neck and drain a portion of his lifeforce. His body altered as he punched him away. Cyclone caught himself on a wind current and charged as Metsys flew toward him, apparently having

241

given up on Settris. While airborne, she locked her legs around his neck, rammed him to the ground, stomping the back of his head numerous times before turning to Animal, who was yelling her name.

He balanced on his tail and kicked her into the air with both feet before flipping away. I launched off his back while summoning two blood sabers, severing her circuitry, and rammed my head into her visor, making it crack. Her companion cried after her, as her backup jets allowed her to regain her former position. Metsys evaluated her current situation through the busted cracks of her damaged visor, analyzing each of our faces and how she planned to escape her impending doom. Once she believed the puzzle was solved, she brought her arm back, ready to strike as a repetitive beeping noise arose.

SHING!

Oil spewed from her once-smooth white metal face. Settris looked away disgustedly as the pirate screamed himself red. Spikes protruded out of her facial orifices, shattering what was left of her visor and the varying symbols that would never shine through it again. Had it truly been fifteen seconds? It was like she'd only stood still long enough to blink. Honestly, I couldn't tell which was more sickening. The method by which she died, or the fact that witnesses took pride in seeing the filth as entertainment. We looked at one another, shocked, as more beeping noises erupted from our devices. Immediately, we forced what little savage movements we could conjure until they made a chorus of approving beeps.

"You all will pay for that!" the Captain yelled. "She was irreplaceable. A treasure more priceless than your lives!" Settris and Cyclone stepped before him, ready for whatever was bound to come, while the princess and winged demon clashed endlessly.

"One down, eight to go," Animal growled, blocking my path intimidatingly.

"Wait," I began. "You're picking a fight against me?" He rolled his shoulders, popped his neck, and boasted.

"Sorry, Enrage, but someone's going to live—and that will be me."

"I highly doubt that," he snarled and stomped hard as the land moved, making me stumble. He soared off the higher cliff with his arms over his head as I blocked, summoning a dagger. My marks burned him, causing him to back off.

"What a cute blade!"

"It'll carve your flesh!"

He shoved his fist at me as I stepped back. Our arms struck multiple times as I shoved my knee into his stomach. He slumped forward then climbed me before placing me in a lock and using his tail to force my own weapon toward my eye. I slammed my head into his face and flung him over before cracking his arm.

Rust lifted and rubbed his head, surprised he hadn't fallen to the depths, and made his way to Animal and me as the platform holding the others fell, smashing against ours. A crevice appeared, swallowing several of us. The wind boy flew out, grasping Settris, and was knocked away by Princess Quazar's sphere while she fought Talon and simultaneously avoiding the rotating rings of the gate. Talon's claws scratched the length of the princess' back, chipping one of her four wings. She spun around, correcting her flight pattern before charging toward her multiple times, striking the bird-woman with her stinger-like heels.

Sparks scattered over our heads as Captain Red Blood's sword struck into the heightening pillar. I dug my claws, attempting to stop until my marks connected to it. My hands took turns absorbing and attaching my marks, allowing me to ascend the pillar. Animal's tail coiled around a piece of rock jutting out and he hurled himself toward the captain, summoning his inner beasts. The shafts started to collapse, meet, and reform. Adrenaline pulsed through our bodies, pushing us past our limits. Animal viciously kicked the pirate downward. He fell, grabbed his lion tail, and drained some of his stamina to reach the top.

Just as I was about to climb out of the collapsing pit, the orange-eyed Animal snatched my neck with his tail.

"I'm *not* dying alone!" he growled, scaling the rock wall with the help of his tail while the shaft slammed shut behind his steps. I pushed forward, whether he was attached or not, I had to get out. Dirt fell into my mouth, clogging my already-difficult breathing, but I persevered. He was much faster than I anticipated. Laugher mixed with nervousness, and pain inadvertently escaped me as my fingernails hooked into the ledge. Yet I was still weighed down by the ferocious and unwelcome excess mass.

"Looks...like," I choked. "You...just...did."

"What?" he barked, sweat pouring.

The shaft enclosed his shin. He howled agonizingly. I grabbed his tail as he struggled to free himself and sent sizzling rage marks flowing down it as it retracted. My eyes glowed blood red as my colors reversed prior to unleashing a blast from the very pores of my skin. I screamed as the red-hot energy entered my opponent. Smoke pillared out the crevice and into skies as the surrounding ground burst into flames, leaving glowing cracks on Mammon Grave and crumbling more platforms.

A persistent and annoying beeping noise echoed as the charred Animal howled and screamed, frantic sweat and tears flooding from his face like a fountain. I became entranced. Five. Four. Three. Two. One.

SHING!

Blood splattered everywhere. Spikes emitted from his burnt skin before the ever-moving shafts slid against each other, grinding his still-warm corpse beneath the eternal blackness which housed it now. When my aching body finally stood on level ground, I stared emptily into the new floor. Flat, flawless, brilliant. The exact opposite of the fight. It was so surreal, as if it were impossible to ruin. It reminded me of how things used to be before all this. How I used to be.

I turned and was instantly grasped by the throat. It was the pirate.

"I kill you, and this nightmare is over!" he cried as Talon came spiraling down, gripping Princess Quazar. We fell back as the last contestants regrouped.

I shot more blasts from the marks on my fingers toward the wild Talon and Princess Quazar while Rust did the same with his aura. Captain Red Blood's sneak attack was intercepted by Settris and Cyclone just before the entire area tilted vertically, causing many to slide onto the next closest shaft of ground. Settris and I landed, rolling to the middle of the shaft before realizing everyone else was on an already-taller pillar.

CHAPTER FIFTEEN

"Settris!" Cyclone screamed, looking down as a ring caught his arm, taking him off the shaft. He had fifteen seconds. Finally. I had reached my target. I watched her, slowly extending a mark that formed into a saber and keeping it hidden by my side. As soon as she turned to me, rubble and debris shot up around her.

"NO!" I cried, reaching out for her. She let out a sincere smile as the ground fell out from under her. I dove, my tattoos latching to the edge, and the other around Settris' wrist. Below her was nothing but a fiery, endless abyss that shone in the reflection of my eyes. Her hand grazed my watch as I transformed to human. She continued smiling and our eyes glowed.

***

"So, Anton, will you do it?" The man's cape was thick and dark, much like his voice. His armor, a collection of forest green dragon scales.

I turned to my father's bed. Still asleep. I, however, could not. All medical personnel and I assured him that he needed to rest, that it was the only proper way to heal from his condition. But he was an older man, and one minute rest may result in his last. So I forfeited my sleep in hopes of easing us both. Death was all too prevalent at New Hope. No wonder they had a sanctuary. I wiped some tears and said, "Just don't hurt him."

The man released a deep, hearty chortle. "If you fight to save my home world, your old man will be as good as new. Furthermore, I will grant you abilities to become a true contender of mine."

I looked up at him with sodden eyes. His expression stayed as solid as his stature.

He continued, "With this, you will have uncapped power." He handed me an interesting device resembling a watch. He was joking, right?

I swatted the item out of his grasp. "How stupid do you think I am?" The man scowled. "Do you honestly think I am so desperate to believe a man dressed in some weird costume and—" Fire appeared in his irises as my father winced, spitting up blood, and his hands tightening the sheets. The heart monitors hastened hysterically as alarming notifications popped onto their screens. "Stop! Stop!" I pleaded. The man smirked. I choked up and rushed into the halls. "Nurse! Someone, help!"

To my surprise, they were all frozen by an unexplainable force.

"One who refuses to believe in God, and yet fears the afterlife," the man stated, "for others."

"How do you know about that?"

"I've existed for centuries," he began. "And I am insisting you to take but a portion of my direct power, yet you refuse? A power ensuing ceaseless wars—that I sought you out for specifically—of which I believe you are capable of wielding. How did I manage that, you wonder. You, Mr. Bearce, are not desperate, or at your last resort. Young man, you have no options left."

I considered that thought for a moment. "What do you want me to do?"

"Even the Devil believes in God, thus the Devil will you become." He snapped his fingers.

CHAPTER FIFTEEN

My veins widened, my eyes bled red. My knees surrendered before the armored man as my teeth shed out of bleeding gums, soon replaced with razor-like fangs. I screamed painfully as my blood boiled. The curly hair my family always picked on me about was now sharp fragments of my own outstretched skull. I felt my muscles swell as I was consumed with wrath and fear. When this odd and excruciating transition was complete, I clawed at the ground, leaving white marks upon the speckled tiles. The man squatted and spoke. "Feel better?"

My new black-and-red eyes automatically shot at him before I snapped, shoving him against the wall.

"What did you do to me?" Even my voice had changed. It became a raspy hiss that echoed throughout my being. I breathed heavily, still clutching his bulging neck. He revealed the watch and stuck it onto my wrist, activated the disguise setting, and all the pain disappeared. I was myself once more.

"They'll—" he coughed. "Suspect nothing."

"Who?"

"Anyone."

So many questions filled my mind as I released him.

He rubbed his neck as he continued, "When Iro discovered the unforgivable actions of his brother, wrath entered the world. When Eka discovered his brother's bloodlust for him, he hid, causing fear to enter the world."

"Don't you speak to me about fairytales."

"Why, Son? You're in one."

***

Another scene flashed. The man and I had set up a rendezvous atop a random building in Apex City.

"You will enter a contest to see if you are worthy enough to save my home," he spoke. "Tonight, you will meet a young woman named Connie Sett, self-given codename, Settris. That device will keep her out of your head."

"What is she, a psychic or something?"

"Yes, but nothing too impressive," he continued. "You will chase her, leading her here. Once she is convinced to join my contests, she will become your target. Eliminate her during any part of the competition, and your father will be spared from his disease."

"It's incurable," I reminded.

"Not for me."

"So…I kill this girl, and my father lives?"

The man nodded.

"What happens if I don't win? Or if someone else kills her instead?"

He put his hand on my shoulder. "Then it would be better if you hadn't been conceived at all." He smiled but a dark aura rolled off it. "But don't fret. I will allow you a clear window of opportunity, my son."

My head felt funny. The man disappeared, and when I returned from my daze, only a single detail stood out to me. That unforgettable name: Tourniquet.

***

CHAPTER FIFTEEN

As our minds returned to the present, it was as if time was slowing. What was I to do? Pull her up, let her live, and let my father die? Or let her go, and pray Tourniquet was a man of his word?

"Do it. For him." I looked at her intently. "Do it, and all of this will be over." She glanced down, bit her lip to suppress the tears, then peered into my soul. "It's alright, I've made my dues. I have my peace with this world. I couldn't see it earlier, but you were the soul I was meant to touch. All I had to do was get to know you."

I couldn't possibly do it; but if I failed, would she suffer a much more gruesome fate? She didn't deserve that.

"Connie," I whispered in defeat. Everyone continued fighting on the platforms above us, completely oblivious to our dialogue. Cyclone had only a few seconds left before his device activated. In fact, it was already beginning to sound.

"I can't hold on much longer," she winced, her arm twisting tiredly.

"I'm sorry," I told her. "I never meant for any of this to happen. Please forgive me."

"Sweet Anton," she spoke, breathing her final breath. "I already have."

"For father," I released her as she closed her eyes, embracing the flames of her fate. The whole audience stood, gasping, including Isabelle and Tourniquet. My weak body fell flat against the rock floor as I clung to it.

She didn't scream. Not a sound. No exclamation. She knew it would happen. It was so unfair. It should have been me. It should have been me. A whoosh of fire engulfed her body, along with my heart. It was a cardinal sin to cage my tears any longer. Steam rolled off my marks as the tears landed on them.

"W-what've I done?" My first true failure. My forehead pressed against the rocky cliff and I sobbed harshly.

"Well done," Tourniquet smiled as Katherine screamed.

"CONNIE!"

Name: Kat AKA Katherine
Weapons: Non-Lethal Double-Barreled Silver Pistols
Powers: Shapeshifting
Power Type: Elemental

CHAPTER SIXTEEN: KAT

Once the seats reconnected to the rocky layers of new ground along the Mammon Grave, I stormed to the survivors walking across the narrow path leading out the arena.

"She's dead!" I yelled. "Dead!" The man I confronted turned just before I punched him in the face, leaving a mark almost the same shade as his tattoos. I shook off the burning sensation and screamed, "Because of you! You didn't know her!"

"Stop this, Kat!" Fern warned, snatching my wrist with a vine.

"Don't tell me what to do!" I turned to Enrage, who was still wiping blood off his face. "Tell them!" His unforgiving eyes targeted me like missiles. "Tell them how you killed Connie in cold blood."

"He doesn't need to," Jared informed, tearing up. "We were there. We know how you feel."

"No! No! No, you don't!" I screamed, my tears drawing lines of mascara down my cheeks. "We weren't cousins; we were sisters—and it's my fault for her coming here."

CHAPTER SIXTEEN

"She was worried about you," I turned around, my heart filled with disgust. "She came here to find you, and succeeded."

"You've taken enough from me!" I tackled Enrage off the narrow path as we soared toward the smoky abyss below.

"KAT!" my team cried as Fern snatched us with a collection of vines. I quickly assumed my panther form and swung over to him, clamping my teeth into his thick, red-webbed neck as he screamed agonizingly. Once they pulled us up, I flashed human and was restrained by my comrades who scolded me for damaging him. He collapsed to his knees, steam rolling off his marks as he cried.

"The pain you felt in that small amount of time is nothing compared to what we've endured upon arriving," I screamed as Cyclone pulled me close. "For the pain I'm going to feel every day I live, knowing she's no longer alive. Waking up, realizing I could have saved her—saved her from you! What were you thinking?" We started to head back to our quarters. "What were you thinking?" I repeated.

Something broke inside me. Something I could no longer contain.

***

I must have cried myself to sleep. I didn't remember coming back to our room, only that my greatest asset had been taken away. My cousin. My friend. My Connie. Dead. Though I refused to believe it, we were all witnesses. Everyone at Mammon Grave was. I never even knew about Keisha's death until reaching the island, and now Connie fell to the very competitions she'd spoken to me about. I cried a tear for every memory shared and every moment that would be lost. Every secret held between us and every whispered prayer. I was sick; rotting, the remnants of my core. Had she died, or was it me?

***

I was walking deep into the forest, sensing an unusual feeling of déjà vu just before coming across the mountainside where Settris and Garika had searched for BlackByrd. In front of me was the exact door we had passed earlier when looking for them. I examined my surroundings, and my hand mysteriously went through the otherwise tangible object.

Once I fully stepped through, I realized it, too, was the same room from earlier. A faint glow came from the containers housing a green substance as I felt urged to walk to a new part of the wall nobody had previously investigated. I rubbed my necklace and turned into a panther to better survey the darkness while remaining undetected. Something pulsed on the other side. Although it didn't feel alive like flesh and bone, a strange energy surged. I passed it also.

Stretching further into the depths of the mountain was a flimsy, grated stairway that seemed impossible to hold Tourniquet himself from his massive physique.

"Again," I heard Tourniquet bellow from the bottom. It resembled a miniature factory. Someone let out a tortured scream as I noticed inanimate robotic vessels hanging about the walls. I leaned in for a closer look when a shadow cast on the walkway slithered, stood up, and kicked the center of my back. The dark mass encompassed the entire scene until I splashed into it like flood waters. I scratched the thick black currents attempting to stay above them before flashing human and coughing up some of the liquid.

CHAPTER SIXTEEN

The blackness stretched into a pillar before leaning over me and forming a face that resembled a black version of Jexter.

"You shouldn't have come here," It hissed as a two large rows of fangs sprouted from its mouth. I braced myself, screaming as it swallowed me whole.

***

I shot up, still coughing uncontrollably, as the rest of my team rushed to my bedside. They tried to calm me, but my body was thrust forward as the thick, black liquid slugged out of my throat, along with—centipedes.

Everyone froze, staring with concern. Cyclone fainted.

"We're going to the infirmary," Fern commented, grabbing our equipment.

***

The medical area was practically barren. Perfect for a potential ambush. Only a handful of workers and patients were inside while Fern monitored the outer perimeter.

"Ahh," I moaned as the medic pressed a small wooden stick against my tongue.

"Hmm," she thought out loud.

"Hmm, what?"

"Nothing," her voice scratched. "I see nothing out of the ordinary. Just a nightmare, you say?"

"But it seemed quite realistic," I answered. "It wasn't like anything I've experienced before, and to have circumstances that passed into the real world."

"That's interesting."

"Yeah," I said. "By the way, how do I know I can trust you?"

"Modos has seen all," she replied. "I concern myself not with idle matters; therefore, I remain neutral. Occasionally speaking truth to whomever it concerns."

"Right," I continued, accepting the fact. It wasn't like many other options were available. "So I came to a mountainside,"

"One you had previously discovered," she added. Perhaps Modos had seen all.

"Yeah," I replied cautiously. "Inside were these green containers, but this time I found another room hidden behind a wall. It was like a factory."

"How does she know about that?" a strange voice exclaimed. I watched, but Modos stayed still.

"Did I say something?"

"I thought so," I replied.

Jared despised any of us traveling alone. If Modos was not trustworthy, at least Fern was still listening outside.

***

Fern's arms were crossed as she leaned, staring deeply into the entrance of the woods. A bit of rustling interrupted her focus when a blue lightning bolt trailed out of it, striking the ground next to her. Thankfully, she had moved just in time. Someone was coming.

A tan-skinned assassin whose battle suit matched her bluish undercut hairstyle exited the forest, flipping a pair of golden claws in her hands. She stopped upon seeing Fern.

CHAPTER SIXTEEN

"Nice earrings," Fern complimented, admiring her bolt-shaped jewelry.

"Nice freckles," She replied, lightning flickering in her irises.

***

"Anyways," I continued speaking with Modos, "The following moment I was attacked by a shadow that resembled Jexter. Whatever it was made the whole world blacken and caused that stuff to drown me. And then I awoke and came here."

"And the centipedes," she said. "Can you tell me more about those?"

"I was hoping you knew."

"I do, silly girl," It was the voice again.

"Then say it." I demanded. She looked surprised. "I don't know or care who you are, but I order you to show yourself immediately."

"Kat!" Fern cried from outside. "We've got company!"

My gaze set to Modos as I walked to the door. Just before I could leave, her outstretched arm morphed into a thick, inky centipede and blocked my path.

"And just where do you think you're going?" Her voice had changed to match the other. I whipped out my guns, both aimed and ready.

"Fern, I'll be out there as soon as I can!"

Modos' arm detached, hindering my escape as her face oozed, distorting into the harlequin's mask. The thing's back twisted awkwardly as a ghost-like mist billowed off it. I shot multiple times, my bullets splashing into its thick, liquid body.

Its midsection opened for a second, revealing the swarm of bullets I had released just before they all flew back toward me. My eyes shrank fearfully as they miraculously passed, all except for one that rehoused itself in one of my pistol's barrels. It exploded, making me flinch involuntarily. The entity zipped in front of me, grabbed my neck, and threw me into some medical paraphernalia on the other side of the infirmary.

I swiped a syringe at its neck when my arm planted into it. I couldn't retract. It was like it was made of tar. The body then flipped sideways over my arm, melted, and re-formed behind, before delivering a kick that trapped me into the mass coating the door. I struggled like a fly caught in a web as the demon contorted horribly.

Meanwhile, Fern blocked the stranger's attack as she evaluated her identity. No rumors or information that the 5X had seemed to indicate who she was or where she came from. The assassin's leg swept over Fern, followed by a lightning blast that smacked into a vine she'd summoned as a shield. Fern leaped onto it, shooting her pollen spores as their energies collided. With a gesture of her arms, a vine-fist slammed her opponent up into the air.

"Kat!" she cried as the electric woman advanced.

"Just a sec!"

"You need not worry about those two," the creature hissed as I transformed, freeing myself off the wall before tackling it. It lay flat and then released a kick with both feet that sent me the other direction. I flashed back to human as it stood above me, pressing its thick ooze arms into my shoulders, making me fall to my knees. The entity's oozing eyeballs glowed a bright orange. Pain ripped through my skin and spirit. Blood started to drip from my mouth as my skin paled. My body was locked,

and my nerves numb. The mask's mouth stretched open, ready to devour me like in the nightmare.

For a split second, Settris' face appeared in my mind. Luckily, the pistol I dropped was in reach. I snatched it, pressed the barrel against its neck and pulled the trigger. The impact exploded the figure. In mild shock, I wiped its remnants, now mixed with tears, off my face before standing and turning toward the door. Apparently, the plasma was acidic and had eaten it away. We must have been too attentive to our fight to notice.

The assassin kicked a tired Fern my way.

"Fern, are you alright?" I asked, assisting her.

"I'm fine."

"You are persistent."

"Persistence gets you killed," the woman replied, taking a stance with her sparking claws.

"Then maybe you should show some," I said, reloading my guns.

"I won't die again!" she snapped. "I'll zap you both to ashes."

Fern brought her hands together and unleashed dozens of thorny vines at our opponent, who shriveled them to dust. While Fern distracted her, I lunged from behind, thrusted my pistols into her back, and fired. She stumbled forward, then faced me, cracking her neck. Black ooze trickled out one side of her mouth.

"The same thing happened to Modos," I informed. "Only, she changed and—"

"This isn't a good time!" My comrade reminded as more lightning bolts traced around us. Fern tossed a handful of sleep spores that shrank and entered her nostrils. Then I pinned her shoulders and knocked her out the rest of the way with my fist.

"You were saying?" Fern began, continuing our conversation. I inspected our attacker's facial orifices.

"That…thing, in there," I pointed over to the medical room. "It was made of some black stuff. We need to make sure she isn't the same way."

"Well, there is only one way to truly find that out."

"And what's that?"

"We should test this substance. Maybe it's related to the samples Jak'al and Cyclone retrieved back at the mountain."

"That's a great idea, but where do we start?" I questioned. "We're not in Apex anymore and we don't have a lab."

"Yes, but Tourniquet does. Remember? That's exactly where those came from."

"But remember? Only Princess Quazar and Settris could have opened that door."

"Then we find another route," she said. "We lure Tourniquet's guards away from his laboratory at the mountain where he experimented on Candice Luda, and make sure we have ample time to study the samples for a match."

We looked down to a centipede crawling out the fallen woman's ear and down her face. I stepped on it and ground it with the toe of my boot. I was officially sick of those.

***

Upon retrieving our samples from Modos and the electric woman, Fern and I returned to our quarters to relay our idea to the guys, who were more than eager to participate. Thankfully, we retraced our steps from another hidden path leading to the dungeon that we used as a back entrance we had discovered when half of my team was searching for BlackByrd. I also remembered the lab from my dream, wondering if the other room was real and how I found it. Could it have been Settris, and if so, how did she?

"No guards," Jared whispered softly.

"For now," Jak'al murmured, carrying the unconscious assassin who was being constantly induced with Fern's sleep spores.

"Actually, there are a few in the east corridor. We will head the opposite direction, and if they get too close, Fern can tranquilize them easily," I blurted out before rubbing my head. The other four stared at me. "What?"

Jak'al sniffed the air, then his eyes opened widely. "She's right," he growled in astonishment. "How did I miss that?"

"It seems Tourniquet is using some sort of fume. He knew we were coming. We must proceed cautiously."

"Not to sound rude, Kat," Fern started. "But how do *you* know that?"

"I-I-" I stuttered. "I don't know. Maybe the dream?"

"Vivid dream," Cyclone stated.

"Vivid, but helpful. Stations everyone," Jared ordered, taking flight. Jak'al dropped the woman on the examination table while Fern followed. Cyclone and I stepped into the adjacent corridor to keep watch as he tapped my shoulder.

"Is everything alright?" he asked. "What was that back there?"

"That dream," I said. "It's important, but I don't know why. Maybe that place I saw does exist."

"Do you think it could be Settris?"

KAT

"I don't know but—what do you want?" I snapped. Cyclone gave me a confused expression as someone exited their hiding spot around the corner. Then Cyclone knew who I was speaking to.

"How did you know it was me?" *his* frail voice hissed. "Are you like her too?"

"In more ways than you could ever know." I turned around. "Enrage."

His flesh was corroded in claw and blast marks, bruises despite his pitch-color. Two crutches steadied his crooked gait, and his tattoos seemed much dimmer than usual. The same could be said for the bloodlust in his vision. Bandages were wrapped tightly around his limbs, torso, and neck. I guess I hadn't realized the physical turmoil he had endured during the elimination round, but was that enough to satiate my own despair? In all my hatred, I couldn't help feeling sorry for him.

"Look, I apologized, but I'll do it again just to make it clear. I'm sorry—for everything."

"Let me make something clear to you," I began. "You will never understand the kind of love we had for each other with anyone in your life. You are a coward who took everything from me."

"I already know that kind of love—"

"No, you don't!" I yelled. "You killed Keisha; now Connie?"

"I never meant for any of this to happen!" he cried out. "She was a victim of circumstance."

"A victim of circumstance?" Cyclone yelled. "She was more than that! She was a cousin, a friend, a teammate!"

"A circumstance I didn't cause!" he yelled in defense. "Tourniquet sickens me just as much as he sickens you. I'm tired—of all this! It doesn't make any difference how many times or in what ways I say it, because you'll never accept—*I'm* sorry."

We stared at him as he fell, clawing the ground.

"*I'm* sorry. Me. I'm a screw up, useless. A piece of filth!" he spat. "I did it—and there's nothing I can do to bring them back!" Cyclone and I turned to each other. "I don't deserve your forgiveness!"

"Anton," I murmured under my breath.

"I don't deserve your respect!" his voice cracked.

He was the kind of person who could fight hours on end, yet speaking even proved a challenge for him. My heart housed itself into a tightening chamber, constricted by the very snake who created the futile contests. This was Tourniquet's doing. All of it. Connie wasn't the only victim of circumstance. We all were; and it took me too long to notice. We were all in this together, like it or not, forced to combat each other in competitions that had not yet reached their conclusions.

"Tourniquet did this to me. Cursed me with these abilities, and told me about your cousin. I had no idea. But during her last moments, she sacrificed herself. To keep you," he turned to Cyclone. "And the remaining from perishing."

I teared up, my throat throbbed with sobs until I registered what he said. "Wait," I said, stifling a sniff. "Told you about her?" His eyes shrank. "What do you mean?" He shivered as he stood. "Y-you-you knew?" His eyes shifted anxiously. "You knew this would happen! How did you know?"

Cyclone stopped me from advancing as the rest of my team exchanged uncomfortable glances within the opposite room. Enrage shuddered as he cried, steam rolling off his marks.

"Tourniquet came to me," he explained. "My father was in *New Hope*. He said he could be healed if I did him a favor."

"And what was that?" Cyclone demanded, holding me still.

"Unfortunately," he said, "he told me to bring Connie to the island. He knew she believed this was the only way to repay him for informing her about Hurricane. Then he would provide me the opportune moment to strike, thus taking her life. He didn't mention she had family. I thought that was the humane part."

"Tourniquet is anything but humane."

"Which is what I now know, and why he needs to be stopped at all costs. I have to go." He hobbled down the hallway as my knees gave out again, tears stealing my vision again. Cyclone embraced me, rocking me as Fern came up.

"We've found it."

***

"Cyclone mentioned that the green substance was supplied to Tourniquet by Hurricane and Fever." Jak'al began. "Originally, we were unable to find a match—until now."

"Upon seeing that twice," Jared explained. "I was reminded about Fantasmo back in Apex." Fantasmo emerged from the same underground cult as some of our other usual suspects, L.I.E., Little Institute for Evil.

"The formula also revealed particles of lightessence like Fantasmo's ectomateria, or materializing ectoplasm. It allows his ghostly abilities to operate," Fern explained.

"But Fantasmo is half-ghost and half-human," Cyclone replied. "You're not implying that she's a ghost, are you?"

"Not exactly. But she's not human either."

"In fact, her molecular structure is decreasing at an exponential rate," Jak'al said. "She can hardly even materialize."

"But her powers were completely different from Fantasmo's," I spoke. "And she did mention something about not wanting to die again."

"Which brings us to the black plasma," Jared said. "Fern and Jak'al found that the green plasma acted as a base for the other. The black formula is a dependent of the independent green."

"You can't have one," I whispered, relaying events of late in my mind. I stared at my reflection through one of the containers housing the same green liquid my team was studying. "Without the other."

"The chemical properties of the black are also found in the green, but we discovered one variable that completely separates it from the other."

"Phantomessence," I said unwillingly. My team turned to me. "Don't ask me how I know, I just do."

"Actually, no. We aren't yet fully aware of the missing variable. We just know that one exists."

"No, this stuff is *called* phantomessence," I clarified. "That's what I meant."

"All we know is that a different component was discovered in the black."

"Not to mention that Jexter was discovered in the black," I said, shuddering. "In my dream, and again with Modos. She," I motioned to our unconscious little powerplant, "only had the centipede, but I'm sure they're connected, and that he's the missing link."

"Which means we need to find and interrogate him next," Jared answered.

"Looking forward to another long-winded chat?" Fern teased at him.

"Anything that gives us the answers we need."

"And about the dying remark?" Cyclone asked.

"Not entirely human, and dying again with a failing molecular structure," I stated. "Is there a chance she could be a clone?"

"But of whom?" Fern asked. We all looked at her funny. "I mean, none of us has seen this woman, right? And with all the notes we took, not even the slightest hint."

"True," Jak'al said. "Maybe she fell to the contests before we arrived?"

"What are you up to, Tourniquet?" I asked, accidentally pressing my hand onto a hidden panel on a nearby machine. We turned as the ground shook violently. The wall before us opened, emitting several rays of light as it split down the middle.

This time my mind wasn't playing tricks on me. Were those visions coming from Settris; and what was she trying to tell me? Was her death the herald of these strange new powers? I wasn't sure of anything right now, other than heading into the room from my dream. I led the way. We stepped into it and then down the flimsy, grated staircase. The next room was enormous, much unlike the previous in every way. Heaps of scrap metal lay in several spots. I looked up as something hanging along the walls grabbed my attention.

"Guys, you need to come see this," I cried before a clanging noise charged from behind.

"Stop right there!"

Name: Korax AKA Subject 57-960

Weapons: Koimi-Missiles-weapons advanced with a rare comet extract

Powers: Code Download- can download and upload throughout numerous vessels

Power Type: Cosmictry

CHAPTER SEVENTEEN: KORAX

My mission now commenced; my target was locked with nowhere to run. I aimed my rockets at the youth in front of me and had every intention of effortlessly obliterating them with a simple flick of the wrist.

"You must be one of the machines Garika warned us about," their leader said, stepping forward.

"A machine far more advanced than any human," I answered. "Once BlackByrd ruined me, the Master upgraded my vessel with koimirium." I enjoyed how flawlessly the rare comet extract made my new aerodynamic, devilish armor. Keeping it was an opportunity that would not be wasted. "Now, allow me to demonstrate its value by taking your life."

"That's not going to happen!" he snapped.

"I do not recall addressing you," I pointed with my raptor claws. "Fret not, for I will reunite you with your lost family, Katherine of the 5X."

Her eyes shot open in fear. Her body shuddered and lips trembled anxiously.

CHAPTER SEVENTEEN

"Not if we can help it!" the other human male replied as she stared at him. "We are a team, and we've come too far to be beaten by someone like you!"

"On the contrary, you are dealing with me exactly."

I blasted swarms of my koimi-missiles at the dispersing group. The leader took to the air, blasting icy spheres toward me. He evaded the humming energy stream emitted from my palm, resulting in a smoking crater in the wall behind. My sights locked onto the hybrid creature charging from one side and his comrade from the other. My waist loosened, allowing my torso to spin circularly, beams escaping my palms.

"What fools," I taunted. "If only you were not so human. So tame."

"I'll show you tame!" the beast yelled, tackling me to the ground.

"Remove yourself, Supin!" I said, scanning my databanks for his species. I released more koimi-missiles that flew past him before soaring into his back. He went forward as I rolled to the top of my back, grabbed him with the metal talons of my feet, and threw him on my opposite side.

I flipped around to receive a pillar of wind that made my torso bend backward. My jets activated, enabling me to deliver a precise headbutt to the stormy male as soon as he appeared. I performed a handstand and left the young man with two red beams emitting from my feet that blazed into his flesh. Katherine formed into a panther and swiped her claws as I slid under her and kicked upward. She flashed human again and shot at me while in the air. A few of her bullets planted into my suit while I flipped, missing the others. She landed and rolled to her feet.

"You want to fight me! Go ahead!" Her arm flew past me.

"I prefer to present the master with a human head, if you don't mind."

"I do mind," she retorted angrily. "It's *my* head!"

I shot more koimi-missiles and countered her. Soon after, pollen spores from the other female struck me many times. I grabbed her arms as she defended herself, then I drove her toward the wall before ramming her into it. A beam from my left foot drew a burning line into the wall as she dropped to her right, twisted in the air sideways, and threw her right heel into my face. I stumbled as wire-thin vines pulled me flat against the floor.

"Futile," I said, arching my back into the vines and modifying my systems for war. My body spasmed and fell as they stared. The Krow Specters and Cyborg Centurions along the walls leaped off their hooks as I downloaded into each of them individually. The master's impressive software enabled fluid movement of teleporting mid-fight into any other mechanical body while leaving the former an empty casing.

My code became a blue mist encompassing the area as my programs downloaded in and out of the machines fighting the team. Their leader grabbed a robot's arm and flung it to its back. He then flew into the air and dove down, pummeling its face before realizing that I had entered the one behind him. My arms placed him in a vice-grip, cracking his back. After landing in another vessel, I shot bullets from the wrist compartments, just to be intercepted by the Supin again. His fists pounded the scrap as I attacked from another machine. They attacked in vain. I could feel nothing.

Once an opening appeared, I returned to my body and rearranged its system settings. Instead of koimi-missiles shooting out of my wrist compartments, panels slid out of them, unleashing jets powerful enough to tear through the plant girl's vines.

"Kat, move!" the plant girl cried, guarding her comrade as I flew at them. She delivered a burning spore into my systems' sights. Shrapnel shot out of my crushed face. My raptor claws yanked her hair as she leapt onto my back. We flew. I typed a code in my systems which rapidly sent us into a line of portals while her teammates screamed after her.

We teleported inside one of the main rooms while others traveled to the next arena and crashed through a window overhead, into a new portal.

"Koimi-missiles, offline," my system blared.

We shot through each of them as I thrashed, trying to remove the young woman. In a short time, her face became the same shade as the plants she fought with.

"Radial beacons, offline."

I managed to steer us away from a mountain and into the next portal.

"Phantomessence grid, offline."

What a pitiful alternative. Or so we were bound to discover.

***

The portal reopened, spitting me onto an uneven horizon of what felt like oddly shaped pieces of metal. I slipped heavily and repetitively until I managed to brace myself. I scanned the premises through a damaged gaze, then lost it completely. A disturbing call of a distant creature caught my attention as something slithered amongst the scraps.

"Who's there?" I inquired. No answer. Suddenly, the entity emerged and shrieked as a blast of warm energy made it retreat. I turned to the direction of the heat signature, sensing another's presence. "Who are you?"

"My name is Fe—" it was a human female. The sound of vines and scraping thorns weaving between metal appeared. "You may call me Rose." Her voice became a muffled echo. "I am an Angel of Anarchy, like you, Korax."

"How do you know my name?"

She paused in thought. "Many have spoken of you."

"Good, I presume," I stated. "My valor of attack on Felinis and Locust must have exceeded my reputation."

"Indeed," she replied, her armor clanging with her movements. "And who were they again?"

"The rebels," I responded. "You have not forgotten about our former allies, have you?"

"I was recently inducted."

"Then recite our pledge," I tested. "If you can." I heard the electronic beeping of a device.

"I forever serve the one who brings peace to the world through difference. Justice will rise from his ashes; fear and pride shall be his horse."

"Affirmative. Where are we?" I asked, changing the subject.

"The Knight's Graveyard in the Depths," she responded. The cemetery was used in the Days of Reyes. Any past knight, honorable or treacherous, was tossed out like trash. No burial. Left in the Depths. Surely it consisted of past contenders as well. Due to the innumerable bodies, solid land became a distant memory.

"That creature must have come from the Arakna Pit. They tend to play in the sea of bodies. We are close." I started crawling along the shaky armor of forgotten and decayed warriors as she followed.

"Where do you think you're going?"

"Back to the master for repairs."

"Tourniquet ordered me here for training in balance. He programmed your portal to arrive so you could take me back," she said. Was she telling the truth?

"Then why is my portal dispatcher damaged?" I asked. "I'm beginning to think you are the plant girl."

"What authority have you to question me?" she yelled. "I care not for your idle technology, nor is it of my regard that the master failed to create it to be more efficient. You fail to follow his demands, and you can indulge in reporting your folly to him all by yourself, now am I understood?"

"Affirmative!" I spoke.

"Excellent," she replied. "Now I believe it best to head toward the Arakna Pit. It seems the plateau reaches its highest point there."

"Yes," I answered. "If we remain in the Knight's Graveyard, then we may unintentionally join it."

"Your vision is damaged," she reminded. "You can't make it on your own."

"You are correct. I will require assistance."

***

KORAX

Rose and I had been walking for quite a long time, but the exact time remained unknown. Every now and then a beeping noise was emitted from the device strapped to her wrist. When I questioned her about it, she merely informed it would sound for potential threats. She was reserved and quite keen on our surroundings. However, when she spoke, I was reminded of the plant girl from the laboratory. She professed her identity was otherwise; therefore, I had every reason to place my trust in her. Didn't I?

"You said Tourniquet gave you a new suit?" she began, initiating a conversation.

"Correction, a repaired one," I replied. "Repaired with an alloy of koimirium and phantomessence, both of which were supplied by Hurricane and Fever from the future. Once I destroy Katherine of the 5X, he will allow me to keep the upgraded vessel."

"And if you fail?" she hissed with a hint of concern.

"For that, I know not, for I have never have." My memory sparked. "When he ordered me to attack those who rebelled, I did. When he ordered me to attack the target he supplied, I did."

"But you haven't destroyed her yet," Rose said. "Behind every success awaits the ravaging jaws of failure."

"Are you one of Felinis' conspirators?" I said, trying to reactivate my weapons system.

"Why exactly did they rebel?" she questioned, testing.

"Felinis, the master's high servant, had a team employed only with ensuring all the master's plans were carried out. The experiments, the phantomessence, and machines, such as I. However, they despised the master's attack upon the Inigmus C.O.R.E., for reasons that remain unknown."

"Why did Tourniquet attack them?"

"When *the master*," I corrected her, "Sought contenders for the competitions, he brought some from the Inigmus C.O.R.E., so they dispatched a squadron heading toward Eka's Island. To allow the contests to progress, he created cybernetic vessels to distract the Tah'leet Soldiers. Those cybernetic bodies are fueled by—"

"Their citizens," Rose realized fearfully, her armor clanged louder than before. "Those robots—are—walking prisons."

"The master is punishing the Inigmus C.O.R.E. by forcing the Tah'leet Soldiers to attack their own home for disrupting the contests. Additional machines were other participants of the master's contests."

"Then," she said rather hesitantly, "I can see why they would ludicrously dishonor their master. Such punishment wouldn't be needed if they hadn't interfered."

"Affirmative," I agreed. "That is what makes me superior. Unlike the master's machines, I require no body for mobility."

"I see. We have arrived." Her voice echoed at the mouth of the cave.

"We need not traverse the cave's entirety," I began. "A near exit will lead us out of the Depths."

She stepped to the wall to investigate. "Any idea about these?" Immediately after her words, the device she referred to sprayed her directly. She coughed harshly. "We need to hurry! Something's crawling out of the walls!"

My weapons systems still malfunctioned. "Calm yourself!" I ordered, sensing the mist and absorbing it in my circuitry. "If danger lurked, your device would sound. This is a man-made hallucinogenic gas."

"Hallucinogenic gas?" Rose asked. "What for?"

"I am unsure, but we must depart before someone arrives."

Her alarm beeped as she dived in front of me, blocking an oncoming blast from our new foe with a tool I could only assume was a sword. "They already have." She stood. "Rust."

"Traitor!" I cried, attempting to grab his neck. "Animal informed us of how you tried to recruit him to your deceit!"

"Tourniquet is my master, and I will carry out his commands," he professed.

"Perform no pretense with me," I demanded.

"I have none," Rust stated. "I forever serve the one who brings peace to the world through difference. Justice will rise from his ashes; fear and pride shall be his horse."

"Blasphemer!" I jabbed my fingers into his gut as my knee met his skull. I patiently waited for him to fall, but instead, his face stretched irregularly as Rose let out a familiar scream. "That scream!"

A strange tendril wrapped around me. It felt like a million bug legs crawling atop my metal coat as it pulled me in. I activated my jets as they sputtered and smoked. Still malfunctioning.

"Rose, some assistance would prove most sufficient!"

Her saber sliced the tendril, freeing me. "Why do I always find centipedes?" she asked.

I saved her statement into my memory banks. The tendril waved about, horrendously spewing phantomessence everywhere and bathing us in its coarse blackness. Rust's spine twisted without warning. His vertebras lengthened into extraordinarily complex fingers connected to a masked figure reaching out from within the plasma.

"Phantomessence grid, online. Radial beacons, online. Koimi-missiles, online."

"Why, thank you, Rust. That was quite rejuvenating." My wrist compartments repositioned onto my shoulders as my koimi-missiles splattered his distorting form across the walls of the Arakna Pit. Rose sighed tiredly.

"What was that about? Did he know we were here?"

"Unlikely," I replied. "You mentioned you had seen this previously?"

"I only know that this is linked to something similar to a black version of our jester friend."

"Jexter, yes." I confirmed. "But he lacks motive with us."

"So you agree?" I nodded. "That it is Jexter? Who does he have motive with?"

"Find the master." I ordered my systems while successfully summoning a portal.

"That will save us some time!" Rose exclaimed excitedly. "Now all you need is your sight."

"Yes, unfortunately, I believe our path ends here," I said. "You have been asking a lot of interesting questions for someone who supposedly knows the master. I do not require vision to see past your lie."

***

Ocean waves crashed against the cliff underneath an outdoor arena where two men fought. The armored man formed into a pit wolf and sank his teeth into his opponent. The hooded one teleported through a black cloud before kicking him. Upon his recovery, the armored one stuck his spear into the ground, spun around it, and unleashed a fluid combination of strikes. The audience roared. While in the air, the hooded one morphed into a crow and shot through his rival's torso.

The now-bloody male re-formed into human, taking a knee along with his victory. He wiped a spot of phantomessence off his face. The armored one gripped his staff bitterly as a female aided him.

"It's okay," she said, rubbing the medicinal root onto the cloth. "You did your best."

"AGH! It burns!" he winced.

Moments later, a portal in the air spat Rose and I out again. Bystanders ran as we crashed, leaving patches of fire where we landed. I pushed off the ground and tried to face Rose.

"Fern!" It was the group from the laboratory.

"You lied to me!" I yelled, pointing with my talon, but still unable to see fully. "Why did you refuse to provide your true identity?"

"You brought me there yourself," Fern said. "And no one ever threatens my friends."

"Threatens?" the master began, snapping his fingers and restoring my vision. "He was simply following my orders. Now, who would like to explain this situation to me?"

Fern masked her voice behind a helmet and had interwoven vines fastening ancient armor to her body from the Knight's Graveyard. I knew not to trust her. She hinted not of her plant manipulation; instead, she chose to wield a sword to further her illusion that she must have dropped when we teleported last.

"Our battle in the laboratory intensified, and she intervened, forcing me to attack her rather than my target," I began. "When I transported us elsewhere, I presumed she had vanished, and that a fellow Angel of Anarchy appeared."

"And does your target not stand before you now?" the master inquired.

"A new feud has risen. Hasn't it, *Rose?*" I asked as she stepped forward.

"You refuse to end your target?" the master questioned.

"Fern, don't!" the 5X leader warned.

"It's fine," she said solemnly. "This won't be long. I tricked him once. Now I get to do it again."

"You are not the only clever one." Her eyes shrank as I released the hallucinogenic gas I held captive from the cave wall. "I could not see what existed. Now, you can see what does not."

While she fumbled, my wrist flicked, replacing my raptor claws with machetes. I struck her way as a thick vine shielded her. She used the last of her dampening strength to keep it upright. Unfortunately, she could not predict that she would ultimately be weighed down by her own armor. I pushed against her abilities with my jets. In seconds, I flew through the plant and sent a beam burning down her back. She stood paralytic, too hurt to even scream. Small tear droplets sat in the corner of her eyes. She gasped as her friends kneeled to catch her.

"Get her to the infirmary—now!" the leader cried before glaring at me. "She helped you! Have you no heart?"

KORAX

"Now," I said back, "isn't that a silly question to ask a machine?" I utilized the power of koimirium and flew off the scene.

Name: Gaako
Weapons: Electric Staff
Powers: Shapeshifting, Invisibility
Power Type: Elemental

CHAPTER EIGHTEEN: GAAKO

H e's never pulled anything like that before!" Garika complained regarding BlackByrd's final blow. "What's his problem?"

"I don't know." I winced as she tended to my wounds in the infirmary before the doors swung open. Medics rushed a stretcher holding a wounded Fern toward us as the rest of the 5X followed. "What happened, who did this?" I panicked, running to Jared and pulling a strained chest muscle.

"A robot," he growled, "named Korax. The same one Garika had fought before." Garika covered her mouth fearfully as he tried to remain strong.

"Wait," Garika said, peering over to Kat. "Where's Settris?"

"Didn't you hear?" she muttered. "She died. They called it an 'Elimination Round'."

"What? No!" she exclaimed.

"Why are you so surprised?" Kat asked solemnly. "That's what they do here. But you two already knew that."

"We weren't there, we didn't know!" I said.

CHAPTER EIGHTEEN

"Let me guess," Jak'al began. "Both of you were out, luring more people to their deaths? Does this one come with a vacation?"

"It's not like that!" I yelled. "You don't understand."

"I *don't* understand, Gaako!" Jak'al snapped. "What could possibly be worth killing your own friends for? We were comrades in arms—The Extended-X. You indirectly killed Lance and Amethyst by bringing them here. And if we hadn't washed up—"

"We thought you were dead!"

"And that makes it better?" Kat yelled.

"We didn't know what to do!"

"Save the world, same as always!" Jak'al yelled.

"Or not kill people?" Kat suggested.

"We didn't!" Garika groaned.

"You were supposed to!" Jak'al cried. "According to Tourniquet's plans, you shouldn't have even been reunited!"

I crossed my arms and stepped forward. "And what would you know about Tourniquet's plans?"

"Not enough," he said, crossing his arms. "Care to share?" We stared at each other for a short while. "Who are you to even wield Lance's staff? You're a liar and a thief, just like all of Apex's criminals."

I whipped out the staff and extended it at his face as he backed into the wall, catching the attention of the medical personnel. "How dare you compare those felons to the likes of me!"

"This is a great way to prove your innocence!" Kat snapped.

"Enough!" Jared cried from afar. "We have more important things to deal with right now. We still need to find Jexter, and Fern could end up dead!"

"We're all dead, thanks to you," Jak'al growled at me.

"None of you had any idea of my intentions, or felt what it was like to be away from her for all these years! I was alone."

"You had us," Cyclone said. "Does that mean anything to you?"

"I just wanted to see her again!" I shivered with adrenaline. A wave of silence overcame us until Jak'al spoke.

"Well now you have her. Have a nice life."

"Come on, Gaako, let's get out of here." Garika said, removing me from my old friend. "Let's go." she insisted more pointedly as my old teammates and I entered a seemingly telepathic conversation conducted only by eyesight. Who was bound to look away first? My heart throbbed in my chest as Garika jerked her head back mockingly at them. Some never consider if you have seen another for the last time. Although now was far from it, I still hoped that wasn't my last chance to make things right.

***

Garika and I had returned to our joint quarters as we contemplated the consequences of our recent decisions. I sat straight on the bed, resting my aching back against the headboard—unable to sleep—while she took place beside me.

"Why is everyone treating us like this?" Garika started.

"Maybe because we brought them to an island to be slaughtered against their will?" I suggested. "We can't deny it anymore. They have every reason to hate us."

"We did our part!" she cried out. "Is it our fault that Tourniquet came to us? That Settris died and Fern got hurt? No! We followed his orders, and got what we wanted."

"You say that, but you seemed pretty upset about them. Imagine how the rest of Settris and Kat's family must feel."

"Yeah, you're right," she moaned. "But it could have been anyone. And they're not the only ones with family, we sacrificed a lot too."

"But was it worth it?"

She gritted her teeth and angrily tossed to her side.

"You know what I mean!" I pressed. "*We're* worth it, but what about the friends we've lost? The friends we've killed? Can we forgive ourselves for that?"

Garika faced me. "They were your friends."

"And BlackByrd?" I questioned. "You know he's your target. And Jak'al was right. It doesn't make sense that Tourniquet even allows us to be together, since we didn't actually kill the others."

"Were they meant for us? Maybe we were just supposed to bring them. I don't recall him ordering us to do the deed."

"So technically, we didn't do anything," I inquired. "If they cared enough for themselves, they would have fought back. So are we really guilty? Wait, where exactly did you find BlackByrd?"

"Apex City Asylum," She answered.

"Apex City Asylum?" I repeated. "When exactly?"

"The day we left on the ship." Her tone dissolved as we realized it.

"You mean the day after I left for the island with Lance and Amethyst?" We groaned in unison. "This whole time we were in the same place at some time."

"But completely oblivious."

"I just wish things were different."

"Whatever," she replied dismissively. "This is too much. Right now, we should be resting up. There's no telling what Tourniquet's got planned for tomorrow."

"No matter how we look at it, we screwed up." Tears formed as our sights turned to the other. "I'm sorry I left Archangel."

"I'm sorry I stayed bad," Garika sighed admittedly. "You got a call from the 5X. You were ecstatic, but I couldn't be happy for you."

"Didn't you want some sort of criminal empire?"

"Yeah," she chuckled. "An empire of two—us—king and queen."

"We were foolish then," she readjusted her posture.

"How is this any different?"

I stared off into the ceiling. "Have we really changed from the people we once were?"

"I'm not sure anymore."

"We said we did it for love."

"But no love is like this. We know this isn't love."

"Then it must be hate. The hate of the fools we became again," I said. "We haven't changed—not really. Or everything else would've changed too. Jared and the others took us in, and what did we do?"

CHAPTER EIGHTEEN

"Stole the hope we once gave to people." Garika teared up more. "Well, you gave…more than me."

"Oh, you weren't so bad," I assured her. "You were doing a lot better. I was so proud of you."

She laughed and bit her lip as I continued.

"You lost Felix. No one ever comes back from that. Don't blame yourself. We need a sign."

She faced me once more. "Actually, I did see something. A light near the beach front. It became this woman. With armor and—"

"Hair made of fire," we finished together.

"I saw her."

"I stepped on her. Don't ask."

"Do you know who she is?" Garika asked. "She seemed harmless, yet strong. Like a protector of sorts."

"No, I haven't any idea. Maybe she could be our way out, you know, being a protector and all."

"Do you think Tourniquet would intervene and keep us apart?" Garika asked. "I'm all for leaving, but we need a better plan than just impulse."

"Impulsive decisions are what got us here in the first place," I reminded. "We'll do whatever it takes to survive."

Suddenly an awkward feeling arose in the back of my neck as my hand shot toward it. It was bulging from beneath my skin. I charged to the mirror and turned around. My eyes widened fearfully and I thrashed with every intention of ripping off all my skin if I had to.

"Gaako, what's gotten into you?" Garika yelled.

"I'm trying to figure that out!"

I fell to the floor, pulling at the device, attempting to squeeze my fingers into the tiny gap. I could barely take hold of it. Frantically, I slammed backward into the wall, hoping it would fall out.

"Oh my gosh!" she exclaimed. "What is that?"

"I don't know!"

She briefly examined it, then freaked. "Do I have one?" I checked and nodded.

***

All living Angels of Anarchy sat on either side of an oblong mahogany table decorated with colorful foods. Fruit sat at the base of a bronze cornucopia surrounded by plates displaying diverse meats. Some of the meats were unrecognizable, and an uneasy feeling washed over me upon noticing several elite members were absent. The thought of eating at a time like this made me cringe. The oily eyes of past competitors' portraits lining the red velvety walls stared emptily at us, dreading our impending fates. Some were recognizable political leaders, some celebrities that had supposedly died, others were dressed in themes representing different time periods, like the Victorian era.

"Each of you have been dedicated since the beginning," Tourniquet began, overlooking the hoard from his throne at an end of the table, "and survived this far—a privilege that some competitors will never delight in. Many of you have annihilated your targets and been graciously rewarded. Several of you have yet to do so." He eyed Korax and Garika.

CHAPTER EIGHTEEN

We fight. Like animals in arenas scattered on an island in the middle of nowhere, and are rewarded as long as we make someone else fall face-first into a crypt?

"But those days are behind you," he said, raising a golden red-rubied chalice and taking the first drink before passing it to Princess Quazar. "Renew yourself in celebration, for it could be your last."

We feasted. I didn't want any food; I barely even wanted life. The three-hundred-pound sack of muscle scarfed his down like a ravaging wolf. It was quite disgusting. Princess Quazar's bony hand met his as she silently reminded him to use his manners. Everyone in the room lacked any form of moral conscience—myself included, unfortunately. I noticed Talon didn't consume any of the chalice's contents prior to handing it to me. Although her appearance was that of a lunatic, I sensed a calming presence.

Things are not always as they appear, a woman's voice entered my mind. I stared questioningly at her as her index claw met her lips.

I stared into the liquid housed in the chalice. Was it the blood of dead contestants? My reflection watched me from the red realm, bearing the same disappointed gaze as the dreary paintings. I lost everything to gain what I now have. And what I now have was the reason I lost everything. But I loved Josie, and refused to allow any additional suffering betwixt us. Taking even one sip meant throwing what little I still had away into the abyss which all carnal things are birthed and return. I was more than this. At least I hoped I was.

Tourniquet's dark expression met mine. "Gaako, drink." A second before I could breathe a refute, his fist banged the table. "Drink!"

I threw the chalice. His heavy throne slid as he stood, fuming.

"It's carnal. All of it," I began. "Anything you could possibly offer, and there's always a catch." Garika gasped. I turned to everyone else. "Why do you think you all haven't earned your rewards yet? He's lied to you, yet you continue to serve him. And for what? Power you're going to keep until someone takes something more precious—your life?"

"You say that," Tourniquet answered, "but didn't I give you the woman you fought for?" I felt like a fool. I peered over to Garika, whose jaw was clenched, arms crossed, and our eyes wet from staring so hard.

"Are you trying to get us killed?" she hissed.

"No, I am," Tourniquet said as we turned. "You think I'm going to let that foolish outburst die without you? Now was not the setting to announce this. I had been wondering whether or not to host another elimination round. Now you all have Gaako to thank," he motioned. "As I will be dedicating it to him."

"You did this to us before we got here!" I protested, turning and pointing at the metal trap under the nape of my neck. "Now take these off!"

"Ah, yes…that. At least you know how serious I am."

"Like Hell!" we snapped.

"I'm glad you like Hell," Tourniquet smirked, amused. "I am more than obliged to show you it. As you should all know," he announced. "Many of you have been given abilities with the help of a special chemical capable of housing so many at once. Like you, Gaako is one of many projects. However, a noteworthy difference is that a portion of his new power," he announced as I gaped, "came from my own."

Everyone went livid.

CHAPTER EIGHTEEN

"You ungrateful fool!" the pirate snapped, stabbing his cutlass into the table. "I've lost more upon arriving, but you are given fragments of the Master's own abilities?"

"I would love to have a face—" Jexter whined.

"So I could scream it off?" Garika challenged while Isabelle chuckled mildly.

"QUIET!" Princess Quazar yelled. "Daddy's not done yet."

Reluctantly, the crowd died down.

Tourniquet cleared his throat and continued. "Whoever kills Gaako during the Arakna Pit Elimination Round will receive that exact ability."

"Please, explain your extraction methods then!" I tested, catching him in another secret. "That's how I got my new abilities," I said to all those present. "He's been taking contestants powers, and Man—"

"Power is all I ever wanted," Light yelled. "To be worshipped by millions while my enemies bow before me."

"You are no god," I snapped.

"And you're about to meet yours!"

"Save it for the Elimination Round." Her neck snapped to Tourniquet.

"And who all will be participating?" Chaos asked.

He simply raised his hand, snapping his fingers. Our minds grew foggier and foggier. "You will not look, speak of, or remember any of this. You will sleep, and this will be your dream, which you shall also soon forget."

***

GAAKO

My eyes examined the room, but everything seemed normal. Everything besides the sudden urge to be present at the Arakna Pit. The bed moved as I jumped. I must have forgotten about her.

"Good morning," she groaned, sitting up as I threw my arms around her in an embrace. "My, this is quite the wakeup call." She held me at arm's length as I teared up. "Whoa, what's up? What's the matter?"

"Josie," I clasped her hands. "I don't care about the decisions I've made anymore. If I'm right or wrong, but I know I've spent years of my life trying to make my way back to you. We've lost so much, and made countless, unredeemable mistakes. But we did them together, and never have I ever stopped loving you. Promise me something."

"Yes?"

"Promise me if something happens to me while we're still on the island, that you will leave and save yourself."

"Never!" she spat. "Don't you ever talk like that! We didn't come this far to back down now!"

"Promise me!" I yelled. Her face froze, but I couldn't help it. "I'm not asking, I'm telling you. Neither of us have been heroes, and there's no reason to start now. If anyone deserves to be in these contests, it's us."

She wailed, pulling herself to me.

I continued as she held me, "I hope and pray nothing does, but if we are destined to be judged for the crimes we committed, then so be it."

***

293

CHAPTER EIGHTEEN

Lights perched on tripods, and torches along the cave wall helped bounce its anonymous purple glow throughout the rest of it. The Arakna Pit wasn't a coincidental name. I could do without the occasional sightings of ten-foot long centipedes and spiders the size of cars with neon-glowing eyes. Situated below a statue wearing a dress made of cobwebs were skulls with intertwining bugs. The remnants of the statue's head had several sockets. Was she part spider herself?

Garika and I stepped deeper into the pit, hearing an echo of cheering and applause. Garika's fingers squeezed mine. Our hearts pounded faster as our eyes shifted in the audience's direction. Their fleshless bodies resembled waves of blood as they shrieked in their seats. I started to shake involuntarily as they became normal again. Which was their true form?

An electric haze acting like a mystic pest zapper barricaded the three thrones that Tourniquet, Isabelle, and Princess Quazar sat in. Tourniquet stood, silencing the spectators.

"Welcome to the second Elimination Round," he began. "In this contest, competitors will endure the pit's labyrinth." Tourniquet snapped his fingers. Everyone watched in awe as walls grew, linking to the ceiling. "Many will suffer from a dream-like state caused by a hallucinogenic gas. Ten seconds without moving will cause emissions from the vents. Twenty seconds, death by spinal device. And, like the last round, at least three must die, so I suggest finishing quickly. Also, when one exits the arena, there will be no reentry under any circumstances."

"Who would be dumb enough to go *back* in?" I mumbled as Garika shrugged lightly.

Tourniquet proceeded to summon those competing. "Viper, Korax, Jexter, Isabelle, Blood, Chaos, Light, Garika, and Gaako." All but one were hellbent on killing me.

"God help us," I whispered.

Garika's grip tightened on my hand as we stared into the labyrinth's mouth—the gates of Hell. If I wasn't so terrified, I would've given her a kiss, but something reminded me it could be our last. And I was not ready to say goodbye.

"GO!"

We shot into the maze, cutting corners faster than we could tell what lay behind them. It was impossible to know its exact length, but Garika and I got a superb lead.

"We should make a trap!" I suggested as we ran.

"What did you have in mind?"

"Creating a trap—," we instantly froze, *"—inside a bigger trap?"* Slowly, Garika and I turned to the voice. Our faces distorted in horror.

"Wait, the vents!" I reminded. "Don't fall for it! It's just our imagination!"

"Then how are we both seeing it?" Garika screamed.

"That, and you haven't stopped moving since you entered."

I grew cold, suddenly realizing that not only was the face speaking, but that it was *real*. Its mouth separated and deformed eyes stared hollowly back at us. It must have been the bulging, disfigured face of a tormented giant, given its extraordinary size. It was connected to the wall by a golden base and its reverberating voice was disturbingly alluring. Horrified, I sliced it with my spear.

"AHHHH!" The tip of my weapon spliced open the wall as a mixture of blood and spiders poured out the festering wound, revealing a complex system of gross organs.

CHAPTER EIGHTEEN

"GARIKA, RUN!" She led the way as the wall continued screaming, lifted, and slammed the adjacent opening, making the rest of the labyrinth shake. I fumbled back to my feet and heard her voice up ahead.

"Help!" I passed through the next few corridors, following the voice. "Gaako! Gaako!" I slid, stopping my run and stared forward. "Gaako! Help me! Where are you?" Another face yelled, mimicking Garika's speech pattern.

"The walls—" I choked. "Have eyes."

"And faces," Jexter said, coming my way. I snatched my spear as Garika sounded from behind. Was it actually her, or another wall-face? "And don't they always? Why, I'm practically at home here! Talking to walls, surrounded by yarators, ironically leaving piles of dead bodies in the living room!"

"Not this body!" I advanced and dropped to his side, hitting his face with the opposite end of the spear before flinging him to the wall. I grabbed his shoulders and shoved his head into the mouth of a wall-face as he pushed to safety. He swung his arms, flinging smoke bombs, and thrusted both feet into me while performing a handstand.

He was about to attack again when Garika flipped, slid into his legs, and tripped him. She balanced on her arm kicked backward and backhanded his jaw in her next step.

"AHHHHHHHHHHHHHHHHHHHHHHHHHHHHHHHHH—"

"—AHHHHHHHHHHHHHHHHHHHHHHHHHHHHHHHHH!" the wall finished, using her voice. Jexter stumbled. Garika fell to her knees in bewilderment.

"Garika, let's go!" I kneeled, shaking her out of daze.

"I—I know," she started. "I've just never heard anything mock me. How does it know my voice?"

"That doesn't matter! We need to get out of here—now!"

We left Jexter behind as Isabelle passed him.

"Where do ya' think you're going?" He whipped his tongue around her neck and pulled her to his upward kick. Jexter spun, his foot pinning Isabelle to the wall as she kept her spear between them. Isabelle's visor lowered as energy blazed out, sending him into the grotesque wall before she advanced.

Garika and I trailed the next hall. Another terrifying face awaited us as we reached another dead end. Then a new laughing expression until we headed the correct way.

"You killed me, Gaako!" I heard a muffled Lance say.

"It's just the walls again!" Garika replied, looking paler by the minute. Suddenly, a fanged arrow jabbed into my shoulder from the wall behind. I turned to see Viper stepping out of the fissure as the wall-face screamed. He had just walked through its innards. Did that mean others could have been further ahead?

"How was my impression of your friend?" Viper asked through Lance's body. "You never suspected you would be facing him again, did you? It was your fault that he died, correct?"

"That's none of your business."

"I presume the same could be said of the master's gift?" Light commented, rising out of a shadow. She ran up to Garika, leaving me with Viper. Light threw her leg at Garika as she caught it and flung her around. Light's blades swept against Garika's face and she howled, unleashing a screech louder than the previous.

"AHHHHHHHHHHHHHHHHHHHHHHHHHHHHHHHHH!"

Viper and I covered our ears. Even the faces on the walls looked irritated. Then I turned to an unsuspecting Viper and extended my staff into his chest. The lightning shocked him before he kicked me away. My staff stabbed the ground beside Garika. She pulled it up and used it to block Light's next move. She overpowered Light, shoving her weapons down and kicked her. Light shadow-ported behind Garika, stabbed her feet blades into her shoulders, and flipped her backward. Viper backflipped in midair, shooting toxic arrows into my spinning spear that Garika had just tossed me.

"You betrayed us, Gaako."

I turned to see…Jared? Other random garbled voices entered my head. They increased as soon as the 5X formed around me. Where had everyone else gone?

"We trusted you! If it weren't for you, I'd still be alive!" I questioned Amethyst's sudden appearance, attempting to focus on the real world. "You're not the only one who ever loved!"

I fell victim to her swift kick. Kat—no, Garika—came to my aid, whipping Fern—no, Light—around. Apparently, they were Light's duplicates who had assumed the form of the 5X due to the gas vents. I hadn't noticed their activation. Viper reappeared, summoning a serpent that shielded him and chomped my shoulder.

Jak'al's conjoining fists slammed me against the wall. Blood sprayed from my mouth as Cyclone tossed me to Kat while in her panther form.

"You can't hurt me; you're not real!" My open hand shoved into the nose of the apparition as it became Josie.

"OW!" she cried. I jumped. "We don't have time for playing around!"

"Which do you prefer?" Viper said as we turned. "The gas or my poison?" He asked, morphing into the 5X, readying an arrow.

With an intensifying leap of faith, I extended the spear and its electric tip trailed the length of the flying arrow, splitting it in two. Even from behind his mask, I could tell Viper was gaping. Garika stepped next to him and shrieked. He turned angrily. Before he could stab her with a snake arrow, I leaped, gouging my weapon into his shoulder. His serpent retracted as he convulsed with electricity and fell unconscious.

Garika and I progressed as spiders bled out the walls, making their way to Light. A large, green-eyed one stabbed her palms, keeping her craggy blades from ejecting. Just as it lunged, a unique sword cut through the creature. She looked up as Chaos stepped over her.

"I wouldn't stay there too long if I were you." Her mouth still hung open in shock until he walked away.

Ahead of us, Isabelle pushed Jexter out of the wall, both covered in blood, just before she blasted him backward and took the lead. Immediately after, the air around me morphed into a demon, choking its smoky tentacles around my limbs, cutting off their circulation. My head shook until the monstrosity became Korax.

"Imagine the master's power flowing through my koimirium."

"Funny enough, I can't seem to wrap my head around that." I extended my staff as it pierced his armor. I stood, spinning the lance as Garika took a stance. We ran at him as Korax's arms whirled twice. His right foot snatched Garika and flung her down, then blasted a beam that sent her body into a crevice. He turned to me as both my feet soared into him while I stayed balanced on the spear. Upon landing, I swept it upward, striking from below. I spun the weapon multiple times toward him, hitting the machine in various spots as his body loosened and rotated to dodge.

My next hit allowed Korax to flip over me and shoot his signature koimi-missiles at point blank. I ducked forward and threw my left heel into his face. I threw my staff around his neck, spun him into a headlock, and slammed him over me. Korax's metal neck scraped as it bent. He opened his hand, moments away from launching another beam, when spidery legs escaped the mouth of the wall-face behind.

I distanced myself as Garika peeled out of the crevice. The rest of the bug crawled out of the face and toward Korax. It was followed by countless others. He flailed his arms and attempted to sear them to a crisp, but they disappeared into his circuit boards and between his broken mechanical neck. Who knew machines could fear? His body sparked and twitched as they gnawed his innerworkings, a mixture of phantomessence and koimirium spilling out of his sides. A creature on the ceiling trapped Korax in an almost indestructible webbing. It was a yarator. Much larger than Jexter's. The yarator spun its stinger, impaled, then lifted him, causing his fluids to rain on us.

We ran, panting as we went, down multiple halls and dead ends before stopping to catch our breaths. Garika and I turned upon hearing two low growls. A pair of blood wolves leered at us, their stocky shoulders rocking as they stalked forward. I assumed my pit wolf form and towered over them. They leaped, chomping my arm, before I slammed it to the ground and received a second bite from the other. Garika kicked it away. They rushed back and forth before charging once more. One pinned Garika. She braced herself as it nipped at her neck, drooling and causing burn marks to appear on her bubbling skin. My fangs clamped its spine as it yipped harshly. I flung it beside the other as Blood appeared. He must have been using them to scout the correct path.

I had a feeling you were close, I echoed telepathically.

"I am truly sorry for this," he said through his thick accent. "Chaos and I must leave. This is my final chance for redemption under Kambhu."

"And why are you telling this?" I replied. "We're seeking forgiveness from others as well."

"I shall send them my condolences." His twin sickles curved around my lance as I instantly flashed human. The wolves advanced on Garika. He removed his sickles and spun, kicking me away before morphing into a swirl of blood and reforming behind me, kicking my back. I stopped myself with the staff and then swiped it past him several times. When an opening appeared, I braced my lance between the living walls and flipped, catapulting upward. I faced Blood while airborne and jousted at him as he melted into a puddle of blood. Just prior to landing completely, his hand re-formed, snatching my ankle and slamming me down as he fully re-formed.

"AHHHHHHHHHHHHHHHHHHHHHHHHHHHHHHHH!"

Garika caught one of Blood's sevims in an acidic spiral that revealed an entire blood-stitched skeleton underneath its liquid fur. Once it landed, the bloody bones took a few exhausted steps and slumped into a red mass. The second charged from behind, chomping the now-visible nerves in the bend of Garika's knee. She fell as it toppled her sideways.

"JOSIE!" I screamed as Blood's sickle scraped my side. Chaos entered behind him. I was already so weak from fighting, it was impossible to take them on together. Garika managed to throw the sevim onto its side and push herself away before ending it like its twin. The room shook as the wall-faces laughed. My eyes jolted as more gas filled the area.

"Let us depart, Chaos," Blood insisted. "We needn't further interfere."

"And let Tourniquet's power be squandered by this fool?" He motioned at me with his sword. "He has no idea what he is capable of. Perhaps a reversal spell that can undo all of Tourniquet's madness." The two eyed me like buried treasure. I couldn't help but to agree with their intentions, but it wouldn't start with my death. I snatched Garika's arm like a thief in the night and pulled her over my back while entering my pit wolf form and pushed through the labyrinth. If we reached another dead end, we would soon meet ours.

"Chaos Wind!" Chaos screamed as Blood summoned more sevims trailing behind us. The blood wolves nipped at my heels as I avoided the elemental strike. The faces around us opened, unleashing several medium-sized bugs. Chaos severed more spiders in half, then turned to hear his comrade screaming. "Blood!"

Centipedes coiled around Blood, weighing him to the cave floor. Thankfully, Garika and I made our escape as his sevims retreated. Chaos desperately tried to free him, but he only received bites and poisonous stings. Blood's wounds hindered his abilities.

"We must leave!" Chaos cried as the blood wolves lay down around their master, pouting. "You returned to save us, now save yourself!" Blood's skin was paling the more he was constricted by the bugs. A sevim pressed its head on his chest. "Move! I can slice them!"

"Now…" he choked and stammered. "Listen to yourself. Have faith…save…Mantis. Stop…Tourniquet. We are assassins. This… is…our mission."

We heard the distant mournful howls of his sevims. Garika winced, pulling her bleeding leg. I glanced down to huge drops of blood trailing behind us.

"That's not mine," Garika said. Apparently, the blood was splattered in front of us as well. "That's Isabelle's!" she observed. "She's ahead. We should follow that."

"Stay here," I said, forming human. "Just keep moving so the vents don't activate. I can find the exit, and come back for you."

"Th-that's a good idea," she said. "That'll get us out quicker."

"Yes," I agreed, grabbing her shoulders. "Look. I love you. I will come back."

"I know." She nodded, crying a bit. "It's just a bit hard to stand." She chuckled mildly. I morphed again, running ahead and surveying the halls. Unbeknownst to me, she gradually walked forward, painting the fleshy, taunting walls with her reddened hand. She struggled to stay balanced. A gas vent caught her eye, and her mind. "What?" she cried. "I was moving!"

Unfortunately, even Isabelle had made some wrong turns. Drops from her blood cape had led to several dead ends riddled with more faces. Gas breathed upon my heels. Sweat poured out of my face as my muscles tightened. Each of my turns seemed to be the wrong one.

Wall. Gas vent. Face. Wall. Gas vent. Face. Wall. Gas vent. Face. *Wall. Gas vent. Face. Wall. Gas vent. Face. Wall. Gas vent. Face.*

I screamed, then turned human. Each turn, wrong. Wrong each turn. Turn each wrong? As I continued the suicidal chase of my life, a literal light at the end of the tunnel appeared. Was it truly the beautiful end? Or was I dead? Tears flowed down my cheeks as I raced, heart pounding, lungs pumping hysterically. Though coated in all manner of dirt and fluids, I rejoiced.

CHAPTER EIGHTEEN

"Josie, I've found it! I've found it!" I paused; the end in front of me, and the reason for all my recent turmoil behind. No, I had to save her. I couldn't profess love while living in hate any longer. I felt ashamed for even considering such pointless options. But the light—now before me. It was so tempting. What awaited me? What if the 5X would not forgive me? Immediately, the opening jolted, narrowing. I left. To retrieve Garika.

She continued stumbling down the path I had trodden. Her hand pressed the wall long enough to gain a breath. Two seconds later a vent misted her, sending her into a hacking cough.

"I have to keep going…for him," she told herself. More mist. "I can't let him see me like this, or he'll never let me live it down."

"I have to keep going…for her," I told myself. The faces laughed. "She needs me. And I need her."

She examined the walls. Now they were all faces with no part of the wall visible. Even the ceiling. Her foot slipped hard into a mouth growing on the floor. She blankly pulled her leg out of it while the others blew more hallucinogens on her.

"Garika! Josie!" Her back straightened automatically like she became possessed.

"There you are!" I cried, running to her as she held out her hand. "We need to hurry! The exit is closing!"

"He is here," she turned back to me.

I trembled. Her eyes were glazed, lost in an entirely different world. She was completely unconscious of all that was happening around her. I was the only real thing in her sights.

"Garika!" I pleaded. "Stop goofing off and let's go! We're running out of time!"

"There, he calls again," she said, drawing a line in the air.

"Yes, I'm right here!" I shouted.

"Felix," she said, turning to walk away. "My dear brother."

"What? No...come back! It's the walls again!" I yelled.

Although her back faced me, I could tell she was smiling. "Felix! How I've missed you!"

"JOSIE!" I begged, coughing as a gas vent went off in my face. "WE'RE SO CLOSE!" I refused to see the labyrinth's end without her. With my remaining strength, I yanked her off the ground and charged toward the exit.

"FELIX!" she cried, reaching out to a figment of her imagination.

The exit jolted again. Closing by the second. I must have been stronger than I thought to carry the weight of Garika and myself, and strangely feel lighter than air. The pass was still open by a sliver. We passed through the opening and carelessly rolled across the safe zone.

"We-we did it." I breathed heavily, turning to Garika. "Josie, we're safe..." My jaw dropped. I knew it felt too perfect. Now I understood why everything felt so much lighter. Her body lay in front of me before dissolving into particles of dust. Disappearing from my grasp. Evaporating from my life. All this time—*she* was my hallucination.

"Felix!" I heard her exclaim happily from somewhere inside the maze. I felt like a fool. Of course, Tourniquet disallowed re-entry. He set this up. All by his own volition. We were both tricked. In the same way we had tricked everybody else.

"Go on with Felix," I mumbled. "Any fate is better than mine." The maze opening I peered through shut as she screamed her last.

"AHHHHHHHHHHHHHHHHHHHHHHHHHHHHHHHHHHHHH!"

Name: Cyclone
Weapons: None
Powers: Wind Manipulation, Flying
Power Type: Elemental

CHAPTER NINETEEN: CYCLONE

We floated around the infirmary, hoping Fern would jump awake any minute so we could race to her side and be first to assist. Clearly, Jared would've won. He sat on the edge of the bed, staring like a madman into her eyelids. He was acting so protective, so much that he refused to let us see her. It gave us the impression that her temporary coma-like state was somehow our fault. Jared seemed unaware of how he treated us. Jak'al refused to remain indoors, so he stood outside, muttering prayers.

I couldn't sit still any longer. Sitting still too long made me fall asleep. Sleeping reminded me of the darkness; the darkness I would eventually become. After losing Fever, Hurricane must have returned to the future, but he still invaded my dreams. He would chase me through darkened miles of woods canopied by an even longer dominating tornadic sky. Upon reaching an opening I would look up and scream as his soul forged with mine, my winds affecting the real world.

"NO!" Gusts sent stuff that had been hanging on the walls crashing on the floor, earning me several glares from the medical staff. Sweat came off my brow as my nerves quaked. I stormed out of there. No pun intended.

"Where are you going?" Jak'al asked as he and Kat walked toward me.

"I know we haven't found Jexter, but Korax did this to her, and needs to pay! And neither of you are going to stop me."

"Which is why we're coming with you," Kat stated. I contemplated that. "You know what Jared said about traveling alone."

"Fine." No doubt they were more persistent than me, so I saw no need in arguing with them.

***

The secret room where we met Korax was our only lead, so we took the path in the woods leading to the dungeon entrance. Though we left in the evening, it still felt as though we were being watched, and not just from the lost souls of the haunted woods. I turned back every now and then to ensure the ghost was clear—I mean, the coast was clear. No one was on our trail. That was until leaves rustled from an upper limb. A woman wearing a white battle corset and matching sharp-heeled boots leaped off it, landing in front of us.

"Shall we dance, my darlings?" Craggy blades slid out of the sides of her wrists.

"We have no reason to fight you, Light," I started, remembering her name from our notes. "So what's the big idea?"

"A little birdie told me that new competitors had been stalking me." Knowing this world, she probably meant that literally. She continued. "While I'm flattered, you should know that anyone who invades my territory will be hunted—and it will be enjoyed."

"Don't get too excited." I clenched my fists. "You're one of several." Her limber body flipped into a white mist before she reappeared out of my shadow. She spun fast and horizontally sliced the tip of my eyelashes with her foot blade. Her next one swept my cheekbone. I yelped, stumbling back and shoved twin gusts before she could strike next.

She planted her feet blades into the forest floor as her torso bent back. Kat shot at her, but before she knew it, Light kicked her sideways into a tree. Kat ducked as Light backflipped, her feet blades slicing the air in front of her. Jak'al grabbed her as soon as she stood upright, tossed her slender body into the air, and sent her flying into a tree. With vengeance in her eyes, her knives advanced. She cut his furry chest as Kat's panther appeared out of nowhere.

"Now things are getting interesting," Light muttered.

Kat lunged, her tail smacking the woman in white. Light turned toward me and cartwheeled. I was dazed; blanketed with even more cuts and bruises than when we started. I qucikly found myself facing up. Her heel stabbed the ground around me several times before I rolled to my feet, forcing more aerial spheres at her. Light charged and sliced through the wind. She balanced on her right palm blade as I placed her in a lock. Her left foot thrusted upward, and would have nearly stabbed my head if I hadn't moved. She completed her flip and cartwheel-kicked me. Her move proved advantageous for me. I landed on my hands and utilized my wind to fly over and stomp her from the air.

She vanished through the mist again. Kat turned, alerting us, and shot the woman out of the tree branch she was perched on. I foolishly flew onto the thick branch. At every hit, she moved faster and faster until she became a pure white blur. She was forcing me to keep up with her movements. My arms were weakening from blocking her. A single blink would mean the death of me.

"I can't do this much longer!" I called with quaking muscles.

"What's wrong?" Light taunted, barely breaking a sweat. "Am I too much for you?"

Chunks of bark flew off the tree as Jak'al viciously charged up it. I had never seen him so engulfed with rage. Without warning, his claws pierced her neck as if he was still climbing the tree. My jaw dropped.

She screamed, writhing to escape, and unable to phase through the shadows. Her eyes insanely trailed into mine as she forced her side wrist blade toward him. Jak'al clamped his teeth viciously into her neck. She groaned. Her struggling ceased. His gaze reflected the stare of eyes resembling craterless moons. I was frozen. He arched his back, taking to all fours, and growled heavily. Jak'al nudged Light's body to the ground before joining her, dragging her further into the woods and mutilating the very ground he treaded.

My skin crawled. Blood cold, yet rushing to my head. Heart begging to jump out of my chest and run away. Shock filled my nerves. Fear overcame me.

"Jak'al!" Kat yelled, grazing her necklace and chasing him.

"Kat, wait!" I called after her, except she didn't stop. My shaking hand pulled up my commu-tracker. "Jared," I said, still stunned. "Jared."

Luckily, he answered. "What is it?"

"Remember, Jak'al in Apex—when Jak'al—met us?" Before he was civilized, Jak'al was savagely attacking our city, deeming humans as threats. During our investigation, however, we discovered he was being tracked by a wicked space witch by whom he was previously incarcerated. Had he not changed, we would've bagged him like any other criminal. But he was a refugee, not a reprobate. Until now.

"Yeah." Jared's tone raised nervously.

"He relapsed…and…and Kat bolted."

"On my way."

***

Thanks to the commu-tracker signal, Jared was there in minutes. I was still shaken up, still trying to wrap my head around everything I just witnessed. To think we were teammates—friends—and to watch him kill someone. She probably would've killed us, but I doubted that anyone, no matter how bad, deserved death.

"She's gone. They're both gone!" I wept chokingly. "I-I-I can't do this anymore!"

"You can and you will! You are one of the bravest people I know."

"How? I'm weak! And the biggest person who tells me that is me!"

"From the future!"

"Not just the future!"

"Look!" He gripped my shoulders and shook me, trapping me with a determined glare. "This is the most dangerous situation we've ever faced. We could all use a hero right now. No one said you had to do this on your own. That's why we're here. I wouldn't have recruited you if I thought you weren't capable. I trust that judgement even today. And maybe if the time comes, you will have to stand up and take my place." I couldn't believe my ears. Did Light give me a concussion?

"I could never take your place," I retorted.

"That's what you think," he replied. "I know you better than you think I do." I was stunned. At everything. What had happened before all this, what happened just before this, and now this! I had to be trapped. In an excruciatingly long, realistic, nightmare.

"Let's get Kat."

"And Jak'al," Jared added as we turned toward a faint glow. Jared's determination grew as he threw an icy sphere at it. The tiny flame expanded into the woman I had seen at the beachfront. She turned to run as I sent a controlled whirlwind around her as she collapsed, fires fizzling from oxygen loss.

"Who are you, and why have we been seeing you at random?" Jared asked her. She refused to speak.

"I'm not letting you out until you give us some answers," I warned, narrowing the eye of my small storm.

"Very well," she panted through a formal accent. "I am Deena, an angel of the Lord. I am your guide through the contests."

"You've been doing an amazing job!" Jared yelled. "Showing up, then disappearing time and time again. Not to mention you attacking me directly."

"I was forced to fight," she explained. "I assumed Talon's form to infiltrate the contests in the hopes of ending them once and for all."

"If you really are a heavenly creature, then why hasn't Tourniquet been stopped already?" I asked.

"I have tried to keep my distance so you all would figure everything out on your own." She sighed, standing, her fiery wings rekindling. "I am not permitted to tell you everything, only that no one has been able to best the beast thus far. None are destined to do so either. Only one. The truth will be revealed in due time."

"How exactly have you helped us before?" I asked.

"I led you where Tourniquet obtained the supplies for his experiments, and to your friend."

"Our friend who betrayed us," Jared spat. "Are you sure you're an angel of the Lord? Because nothing you're saying makes any sense."

"Is that how you feel?" She moved to reveal a lowly Gaako. "She came to me saying how we needed to work together. To get out of here."

"Interesting company you've got there."

"Judge accordingly," Deena stated. "Your comrade acted out in desperation. He acknowledges his errors and seeks mercy from those he trespassed against. The same mercy you showed me when you believed I was only a threat."

"We still haven't made up our mind on that," he stated.

"Look," Gaako changed the subject. "I left Garika to pursue justice, and ultimately wondered if I had made the right choice, but as time changed, so did I. While our team kept me occupied, Lance and Amethyst reminded me of the love Garika and I once shared and how I craved to have that again." He teared up. "I hoped to persuade her to the side of good, not lose myself once more."

"That justifies nothing!" I spat. "Do you realize both of them are dead because of your recklessness? Because you were jealous?"

"I know!" Gaako screamed. "I know! I endangered all of us—and now Garika is dead." Jared and mine's jaws dropped. "Which is why I came." He raised the staff and activated the current pointed as his throat. "To say goodbye."

"NO!" I tackled him as the spear skidded across the forest floor. "We will give you mercy, but we will also give you justice!" I yelled, pinning his wrists. "When we arrive in Apex again, you will serve time for your crimes. After that, we'll discuss your further relations with our team."

His matted hair glued to his sweaty complexion, indicating not even he predicted what his actions would entail.

"It's good to be back." He smiled gratefully as we clasped hands, helping him to his feet.

"For now," I said.

"This is only temporary," Jared reminded

"You shall not regret this," Deena said as the three of us turned to her. She hovered, fire glowing brighter by the second. "I must go. We will meet another time, but I am always closer than you think." She evaporated into a collection of sparks before our investigation commenced.

**

Jared, Gaako, and I updated each other on our knowledge of current events while stepping into the dungeon. Unfortunately, we had seen no sign of Light's corpse, or the other two.

"How can we be sure they headed here?" Gaako asked.

"Any other ideas?" Both were silent. Idealess. "This was the last place we mentioned. If they're not here, then maybe there will be more evidence along the way."

"Like that?" Jared pointed. The whole hallway darkened. Black slime dripped from the ceiling and into a thickening mass along the floor. Even the walls were coated in the horrific material. The only bare spots were two pairs of footprints. I pulled my goggles over my eyes and kneeled, examining them.

"Definitely phantomessence. Not that I needed these to figure that out," I observed. "Jak'al's path continues, however, Kat's boot impressions start just over there."

"That means she just became human there, but no indication of conflict," Gaako said. "Did she even try to stop him?"

"She was behind him, so these could've appeared at a later time."

"Not according to the depth," Gaako said, kneeling beside me. "Considering the rate of which the phantomessence above has been dropping in these spots, these prints are minutes fresh."

I looked up to Jared. "What does that mean?"

He cradled his chin thoughtfully. "They walked in. Together."

"No," I denied. "I refuse to believe they had any connection to all this. They have been on our side the entire time."

"No one's deciding anything yet," Jared said. "All we know is that Light's body was nowhere on the blood path, and that Jak'al and Kat could have come here simultaneously."

I sighed as we continued. We met an adjacent wall leading into to the examination table and robotic room.

CHAPTER NINETEEN

Jared pointed. "Guards were on the opposite side last time. Gaako, secure the bottom. Cyclone, take the top. I'm going to search for that secret room."

"Alright." Gaako unstrapped the metal rod off his back and rolled, turning invisible. It was amazing seeing—or not seeing—him like this. Just as he was about to stealthily knock a guard out, bullets rained down, unveiling his presence. He spun the sparking spear as the lights died. Panicked screams emitted from their groups as gunfire lit the area along with sounds of an angered beast. Then the racket dissipated. The three of us were blinded by the lights. All the guards were either dead or unconscious. Given their appearance, it was very hard to tell.

"No need." Kat stepped down the spiral walkway. "We've taken care of them for you." None of us could believe the sight. She and Jak'al were covered in blood and spots of the same putrid, black substance from the dungeon's hall.

"Don't worry," Jak'al interrupted, holding his opened hands up in surrender. "I don't know what happened back there, but she did deserve it."

"No, she didn't," I replied lowly with a swelling pain in my chest.

"Then why didn't you stop me?" I was quiet.

"Just forget about all that, Cyclone," Kat wrapped her arms around me. I immediately jerked away, looking her up and down. She examined herself casually as if she'd forgotten. "Oh! It's probably just blood from a guard," Then she hugged me again. "Nothing to worry about."

But I had everything in the world to worry about, especially when it came to who I could trust. Who else's blood was on their hands?

THE ENDGAME

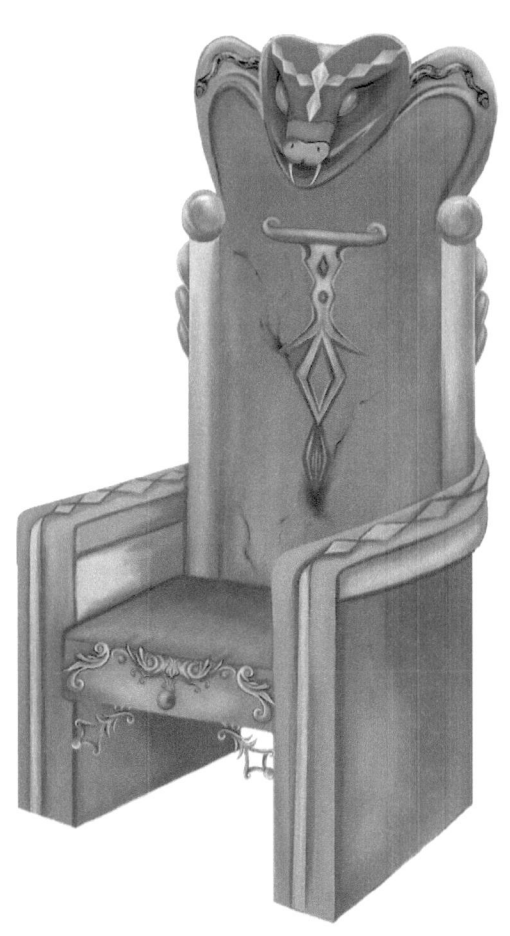

Name: Fern

Weapons: None

Powers: Plant Manipulation, Pollen Spores-comes in heat and sleep variations

Power Type: Elemental

CHAPTER TWENTY: FERN

W hat was I to do? Even my diary mocked me. I could neither focus nor sit upright long enough to write a single sentence. Each time my body slumped into the shadows, the perfect ray of light would disappear. My body paid the price during my epic feud with Korax. After all, he was strong enough to send me to the infirmary. How discouraging. Even on the verge of losing self-control, I was still unable to defeat him.

The infirmary doors swung open as fast as I shut my diary before laying it on the nightstand. Whether it was done out of respect or fear, none could tell, but all medical staff present dropped their current activities to bow to Tourniquet as he strolled down the white hall. My heartbeat matched each step he took until he settled himself at the end of my bed.

"How are you feeling?"

"Fine," I replied, emotionless. His eyes glanced at the nightstand which my diary rested.

"Do you mind?" he asked with mild curiosity. My tongue stuck to the roof of my mouth, but a telekinetic burst robbed me of freewill and I handed him the book. Then a strange pressure pinned me against the bed.

"Amidst the clear of a dark forest," he started, reading out loud. "I beheld a hexagonal tower stretching into the Heavens, covered in bulging eyes." I wanted to protest, but the invisible force pressing my chest hindered me from doing so. "Each side of the tower had climbing clusters of a hundred and eleven eyes. No spot of the tower was left uncovered by the horrific growth. Momentarily, the dust of the earth became a murder of crows that soon circulated the tower, inching closer and closer until each creature had pierced their intended eye."

Medical workers exchanged uneasy glances. Tourniquet closed the leather book and set it against my leg. Although I was covered by several blankets, the touch of the book was cold enough to make me readjust my posture once the pressure had vanished. My breath also became visible.

"That was beautiful," Tourniquet breathed dreamily.

"That was a nightmare," I replied.

"And a lovely read, Fern." All the medics were still bowed to him as he stood and departed whence he came. "But don't worry," he turned back. "You'll have plenty to record soon."

His words sank into me like the jagged teeth of a pit wolf as he left me lost and confused.

***

The sun shined from the glossy windows, gently warming my face. Birds chirped as I peeked, then leaped straight up. Stretching out over the entire floor was a ruby-colored carpet, and mounted to the ceiling was a diamond chandelier that made it seem as if the sun were in the room. The sight was blinding, but equally breathtaking. I felt the gentle caress of satin sheets against my skin.

"I-is this…" My mind became hysterical with all the possible situations that I could've been tangled in right now, "Tourniquet's room?"

"Beautiful, isn't it?" I jumped at the sound of Tourniquet's bellow. He stood on the opposite side of the room, staring outside one of the tall windows wearing white dress pants and buttoning on a fancy, matching long-sleeved shirt. "I brought you here." He turned and suddenly it felt as if everything was exactly how I wanted it to be. Everything was perfect, but a voice in my head screamed otherwise.

"Are you alright?" Jared asked me with his own voice as I stared dumbfounded. "You looked like you've seen a ghost."

"Yeah, no…I'm fine," I sputtered hesitantly, rubbing my aching head. "For a moment, I thought I was still at the infirmary." I laughed, blushing slightly. "I am *here* right?"

"Of course, you are!"

I was thrilled, but something was off. "Where are the others?"

He looked at me funny. "Others?" he responded as if he'd forgotten.

"Yeah, Jak'al, Kat, Cyclone…"

"Oh, them!" Jared never forgot about his own team. "They're fine. They'll be here soon enough." Slowly, my nerves lightened.

"So what is this place?" I retorted.

"Look for yourself," he smiled eagerly.

I got out of the bed and discovered an extravagant white gown draped about me that matched the chandelier and bore an additional thin red embroidery. How it had been put on me, I didn't care. All that mattered is that Jared and I were together. I flew to the window and looked down upon the blinding white sands on the beaches out front.

It was such a beautiful day—and I couldn't run outside fast enough. I was rather impressed that such a place existed on the island after everything that had transpired. I ran hurriedly down the soft carpeted halls just to have my sole renewed with the soothing touch of my next step. I continued running gleefully until reaching an area that acted as both a sky bridge and a veranda. My hand grazed the polished golden rails trailing endlessly toward the ocean. I walked past several openings along the walls and reached one at the center of the high bridge.

My eyes scaled across the white sand as I wondered how to get down. Then, as if on command, three spheres of water lifted from the ocean and hovered at my feet. They were so clear! In an instant, they shifted and flattened into discs. I stepped one foot onto the first panel and it, surprisingly, remained afloat. The watery panel held my weight! It was amazing! Jared gently poked from behind.

"Where are *you* going?" he asked playfully as I laughed.

"I'm going down!"

"That's where you're wrong!" he said before lifting me up.

"No! You'll drop me!"

He stepped forward and the water seeped between his toes. He took another step as the aquatic panels took turns playing the role of stairs. Once on the ground, we watched them morph back into spheres and land back into the water with a humorous plop. Without notice, Jared tackled me into the sands as I let out an unsuspecting yelp.

Grains of sand splotched our once-spotless clothing as we rolled on top of each other across the beach. We laughed wholeheartedly and eventually stopped, entranced by each other's eyes. His mocked the beauty of the neighboring calm blue-green sea; mine, he imagined as a blazing emerald forest. Waves crashed softly behind us until he finally spoke.

"Why did you run off like that?" Jared said as his breathing slowed.

"Running off? I was exploring!"

"With you off exploring without me," he whispered, inching closer. "Then how could I explore you?" A chill ran up my spine. "I want to get lost in you. Fern; you are a journey worth all eternity."

It proved a rather short day. I was unaware of how much time we spent together, but the sun was nigh setting. Perhaps we had fallen asleep, but then again, my dreams had already come true.

***

As for the others…

"Kat? Jak'al?" Cyclone asked. "Where did you go?"

"That doesn't matter, only that we're together now," Kat replied.

"What happened to Light?" Jared asked.

"We're not sure," Jak'al said.

"According to Cyclone, you dragged her away."

"Why would I do that?"

"Can we get back to finding Korax?" Kat insisted.

"But we haven't found Jexter yet," Jared reminded. "He's the one from your dream."

CHAPTER TWENTY

"Yes, but it was Cyclone's idea to search for the cyborg," Kat replied. "And what better place than to trace him than where he found him before?"

"So do you remember where you found the switch at?" Gaako asked her. She stepped over to examine enormous boxes of machinery until her hand flicked back.

"Is this it?" she pointed.

"I'm not sure," he replied, leaning on his staff. "You're the one who found it."

"Oh yeah," she replied peculiarly. "You're right."

***

We remained outside a few extra minutes before returning to the castle's main indoor courtyard which was even more extravagant than all the other rooms combined. In the middle was a fountain with a stone maiden pouring water over herself from an archaic-looking pitcher. The liquid flowing down her shoulders was made to mimic hair. I further examined it as familiar faces poured in the room from adjacent halls.

"I think we're due for a role call," Jared suggested. "I'm Jared, and this is Fern. We're from the 5X."

"Gaako addressed me when you trespassed in the dungeon," said the tigress woman walking in beside an amber-suited assassin.

"And you fought alongside me, fool."

"And you attacked Korax and I, Rust!" I exclaimed.

"I did nothing of the sort," he denied. "All I have seen of you two was the day we fought Talon and Lance."

"You excreted phantomessence."

"How do you know about that?" the tigress woman questioned.

"Modos and that electric woman," I pointed out.

"Luda?" Tourniquet's son asked hopefully, entering from the other side.

"Unfortunately, BlackByrd, it wasn't. This one had golden claws."

"Sounds like Tesla," the hybrid creature deduced. "Another of the master's experiments who supposedly ended up dead."

"Apparently not dead enough. She and Modos attacked Kat and I while at the infirmary," I said. "Which led to our investigation of the black plasma, which is also related to the green found in the mountain. After researching them, we realized she could very easily be a duplicate. If that's your case, Rust, then you could have been here."

"I have been, for quite some time now," he answered. "However, none of us have been able to unmask the true origin of this land."

"Felinis and Rust were here before me," BlackByrd said before turning to Jared and me. "You arrived last. And that," he pointed to the fountain. "Is Hira Conte'. The 'lovely goddess' the Brothers of Legend both loved."

"When we have time," I said, glancing at the statuette then to him. "You should tell that story in its entirety."

"Actually, it might prove useful now," Felinis said as BlackByrd shifted his stand. "Perhaps that clue could explain where we are and why we seem to be the only ones here."

"Very well," BlackByrd said, releasing a heavy sigh. "In the beginning, good and evil were mere illusions, yet dark and light were quite prevalent." Amidst the fountain, his smoke portrayed the scenes. "God created two brothers whose responsibility were to keep the balance between dark and light. Iro, the Brother of Light guarded the daytime; ensuring flowers blossomed as they did, that the birds sang, and sun gave its pleasant light. Eka, the Brother of Darkness, guarded the nighttime; closing the flowers and replacing the birds with bats and other nocturnal fauna illuminated by the moon's glow."

"Seeing they were lonesome, having only each other," Rust spoke, "God promised them wives if they fully mastered their duties. Hira Conte' was given to Iro once he discovered wisdom and patience. But instead of gaining his, Eka fornicated with his brother's beloved while Iro was away. Iro furiously used his sword to split the earth into the continents we have today, while Eka forged an enchanted mask and vanished into the sea. Thus, fear and rage entered the world."

"Since Hira Conte' was the first woman given life, and to later die in a matter of years from a terrible disease, God judged the men with immortality," finished Felinis. "Or so legend states."

"That's the same Eka the island is named for," Rust informed.

"And in whose honor this year's contests were done," Felinis added.

"This year's contests?" I asked. "Is this not the first?"

"No. There have been many more."

"And to whom were they dedicated?"

"Sometimes past victors."

"You mean people who won, yet failed to save his home planet?" I asked. "Is that why he's summoned more people? Because they kept failing?"

She remained suspiciously silent as if she intended to keep that a secret.

"Is something wrong?" I pressed.

"What was the purpose of the past victors you mentioned?" BlackByrd asked in an interrogating manner. "Unless you're saying they fought for the same reasons as everyone else is now, something's missing. Something only you know."

"Yes, tell us more about this home world of his," Jared tested.

"Tourniquet's home world," she started again, "he didn't tell me much about it."

"And here I assumed you two were close," Rust muttered.

"M-maybe," she paused, surveying the premises. "We're in it."

"If we were," said Jared, "how come we're just seeing it now?"

"More importantly," the assassin spoke, "how did we get here?"

"I arrived on Captain Red Blood's ship with Garika and a few others," BlackByrd answered.

"I meant how did we get to this place—"

"His ship was destroyed," I confirmed.

"By me," Felinis and I admitted simultaneously. We stared at each other.

"That's how *we* got here," I said, still looking at Felinis. "We crashed and washed up on the island. What were you talking about?"

"Tourniquet ordered me to destroy the new vessel he forged him."

"So…he lost two ships?" Jared asked, amusedly.

"Yes. Tourniquet wanted absolutely no contact with the outside world. Only the Tah'leet Soldiers' technology was able to penetrate his barriers and reach their Inigmus C.O.R.E."

"Chaos spoke to me of rebellion in which you participated," the assassin told her. "You, he, and Mantis turned against the master upon discovering the truth of him attacking the C.O.R.E. But why?"

CHAPTER TWENTY

"It would cause an idle war," she answered. "At first we believed he launched his assault due the denial of the Android Factor Venture, a program relieving human soldiers of their positions so machines would guard their cities—but it was all a cover. In actuality, it was because of them coming to the island after receiving distress signals. In my eyes, they were but innocents who were not at all involved with the competitions."

"Then what are your morals exactly?" Jared confronted. "Weren't they all innocents? Aren't we all innocents? Did you earnestly support his decisions? Evidently, you've always stood behind him during years of contests, so why the change of heart? Was it the princess?"

She looked embarrassed. "Tourniquet placed her value far above mine after I served him for so long. She was the final factor in my enlightenment. And, I admit, he was powerful and I, afraid. Afraid of what would become of me and the last of my allies after he killed Mantis. You changed as well," she said to Rust. "You were a loyal dog to the master also, and had it not been for our growing distrust, Chaos would've never spoken to you."

"In other words, you wanted my help to bring down Tourniquet," he inferred as she nodded. "I never served him or anyone else. My respect demands to be earned."

"You hailed from the same guild as Chaos. He considered you trustworthy, unlike the red assassin who left Mantis to die long ago. It's a shame we lost him again."

"He never died," Jared smirked. We all faced him.

"Do you jest? What exactly possessed you to say that?" Rust growled between gritted teeth.

The rest of the 5X walked into the room. The cybernetic bodies were hooked back up, hanging here and there on the walls. They seemed to pulse an eerie power. Something big was about to occur. Cyclone pulled on his goggles and surveyed the area.

"Hey, Jared," he called.

"Yeah?"

"Back when we brought Sparkarella here, what happened to her body?" They all grew surprised expressions as a blue lightning bolt shocked his arm.

"That's not my name, *estupido cabra de viento,*" she began.

"Was that your name?"

"Shut it!" she said, gaining on them. "It's Tesla! The last person you will ever see. It took you so long to notice the most obvious things, yet you still lack the most important details." She grabbed the handles to her electric claw-daggers as more lightning charged. Cyclone and Jared readied two spheres of power as Gaako raised his staff. Jak'al and Kat stepped beside Tesla, then faced the others, readying their weapons and sneering.

"So this is how it ends?" Gaako mumbled.

"Guess so," Jak'al growled, extending his claws.

"Kat?" Cyclone asked weakly as the barrels of her guns pointed at his forehead. "I don't understand." Suddenly he recalled the phantomessence covered in their footprints.

Instantly, Kat and Jak'al burst into the room and stopped dead in their tracks, staring at...Jak'al and Kat?

***

CHAPTER TWENTY

Jared's gaze shifted amongst us.

"Care to explain?" Felinis asked. "Mantis was killed by the master, forcing our hand, and you carelessly admit otherwise."

"Yeah, we've only heard rumors," I explained. "We've never actually seen him before."

"Tourniquet and Princess Quazar just *arrested* Mantis," he clarified before collapsing into a violent cough.

"Jared!" I cried, assisting him.

"For...their..." he breathed. "Experiments."

"It doesn't make any sense!" I yelled. "What are you talking about? You shouldn't know that!"

He kept coughing harder and harder. "You...fool!" I jumped at his words. "Don't tell me you forgot," he coughed more as his voice rose a few octaves. His spine ripped out of his back, stretching into black centipedes that scurried across his body. A similar substance seeped from his pores. "About me!" His neck snapped my way. "I heard you wanted to spend some quality time together! How 'bout a hug darlin'?"

***

"They're not who they say they are, Cyclone!" one of the Kats said. He turned to the other one who had black ooze running down her face.

"She's lying!" That was totally believable.

"Jak'al and I left to search for Jexter while you were asleep, hoping we could tie him to the phantomessence."

"Unbeknownst to us," Jak'al spoke, "You left with our clones. When they went savage, you called Jared for backup, and he inadvertently left Fern unattended."

"We came back as soon as we could and she was missing," Kat stated.

"What?" Jared cried frantically. "We have to find her!"

"Wait, how do you know they went savage?" Gaako questioned.

"We saw the devastation on our way here. I know my handiwork, even if it's not actually mine," he answered as his clone snarled. "Can we trust that you had nothing to do with this, Gaako?"

"Yes," he whispered.

"Glad to have you back," Jak'al stated proudly, yet stern. They turned to the clones.

***

The demon laughed hysterically. It was Jexter. But we still didn't know how exactly. BlackByrd's leg stuck to the ghoul's tar-like neck. He tried to pull away, but proved unsuccessful. None of our projectiles seemed to work either.

"I-I can't escape!" he exclaimed frightfully.

Felinis and I charged at it, but it had already consumed him.

"BlackByrd!" I cried. Before I knew it, the same happened to Felinis.

"Fern!" she yelled. "I'm stuck—" a centipede tendril covered her mouth before mercilessly yanking her off her feet as she was swallowed by the darkness.

"No!" I turned to Rust, who attempted to free himself using his amber-ice. More tendrils latched to us, slowly pulling us into the same fate. Rust disappeared. My heart fluttered heavily as breath escaped me just as I corroded along with them.

Name: Princess Quazar
Weapons: None
Powers: Quasar Orbs, Blue Nebula Rays, Backfire Portals, Flying
Power Type: Cosmictry

CHAPTER TWENTY-ONE: PRINCESS QUAZAR

Commotion filled our secret room. I'm surprised the 5X could stumble upon the hidden vector. All were entangled with fighting, until relentless screams from above caught their attention.

"What the heck?" Gaako said, staring up to see our captives shaking violently in their restraints. They were strapped to metal slats connected to a concaved ceiling that kept them from seeing each other. The 5X leader, Jared, dashed underneath the curve of the ceiling and to his screaming friend.

"I thought I lost you!" he cried, freeing the redhead.

"I thought so too!" she shouted. "Jared, look out!"

I plowed into him, spinning in circles, and rammed him into a robot hanging on the wall. He exited my grasp as I turned, buzzing both of us to the ground. I dropped him flat on his back then buzzed away, landing in a kneel as my wings closed. I stepped forward and yelped at the harlequin landing in front of me.

"I feel so much better now!" he cried, inching closer to my face. "Oh please, oh please, oh please, won't you give me some more black ooze?" I snatched his mask out of his hands and shoved it back where it belonged.

"So he was a part of your plan?" Jared hissed, his comrades working him to his feet.

"He was the only available candidate for the phantomessence process to work." Then I realized what I had just said. "Oops! You weren't supposed to know that! Just forget I said anything, okay?"

"Tell us everything, now!" he demanded hatefully.

"Not only was he a candidate," Daddy entered the room on the opposite end with several other Angels of Anarchy behind him. Captain Red Blood, Enrage, Isabelle, and Chaos. Felinis gasped upon seeing Chaos, wondering why he stood with them instead of with her. Probably. "He was a volunteer," I squealed and hovered to them. I hugged Daddy's neck and kissed his cheek, popping my foot. "How ever did you find the place?"

"I sensed an odd presence," Kat started. "When Garika and I arrived, searching for BlackByrd before you and I fought."

I peered back at her.

"How lovely it is to see you, Settris," Daddy remarked.

"Wait," I stopped. "How and when did *this* happen?"

"It is on a supernatural level, my Dear. You wouldn't understand."

"I was getting too close to the truth. Same as all of you," she told the ones previously restrained to the ceiling. "We knew almost as much as he did, so he silenced us by being taken or death." Enrage looked away. Dra-ma! "I had to ensure Kat and her team carried out what I intended to look into. But something got in the way of my message."

"That would be me!" Jexter exclaimed annoyingly. "I was the only disciple capable of surviving the black ooze experiments!"

"Call it what it is. Phantomessence," Settris answered through Kat. "Ironically, you gave yourself away." Jexter's smile faded for a minute. "Your visitation to Kat during the night linked the phantomessence to dreams, ultimately prompting the 5X's research. And for that, we give you our sincerest thanks."

"In fact," Rust told Jexter. "I recall seeing a bug in my cabin directly after receiving a dream in which you were present."

"Yes, the centipedes," Kat said as Settris' demeanor vanished. "They must have used those to hack our dreams."

"Precisely! We were just playing with our new ooze from Hurricane and Fever that enabled us to invade your dreams and hack into your minds," I explained as some grazed their heads, feeling the upmost level of violation.

"They promised us more untampered green phantomessence if we proved Cyclone had arrived at the island," Daddy said. "I had Garika bring them to the beach front."

"Untampered green?" Jared asked. "There was a variable that had a color-changing side effect."

I snapped and wiggled my finger at Viper, who brought Looney into the room, restrained by the wrists.

"Candice!" BlackByrd cried.

"What caused the color change, you ask?" I turned to Jared, waltzing to Looney and grabbing her fluffy, silk shoulder pads. "The powers of other contestants!" I knocked her off the upper walkway as BlackByrd rushed to catch her. I began listing them off. "First, we used the phantomessence, to then hack your dreams, in order to survey who had the best powers, create even stronger competitors, and then leave clones in their wake!" I had a full hand!

"And why would you do that?" Jared asked.

"We needed to see who had the best abilities to test the capabilities of our newly discovered black goo!" I said. "And some people happened to be grateful for the gifts we gave them. Right, Enrage?" We all turned to him. His eyes full of regret. "How much stronger did we make you? Or you, Gaako?"

"Don't you speak to me like that!" the Australian snapped.

"I'm only telling the truth," I shrugged innocently. "You did our bidding, and got what you wanted."

"But to what end? I lost what you gave!"

"Garika's dead?" BlackByrd asked. Gaako nodded and then turned back to me.

"Not to mention, we still had to join the competitions like everybody else!"

"Duh!" I giggled. "Did you honestly think you wouldn't have to work for it? Honestly, you boys were the perfect lab rats to test the safety of someone holding that much power."

"You're evil!" Kat scolded. "Using them as puppets!"

"Lab rats. Puppets. As in test subjects. Tourniquet mentioned your prowess to me after our fight. The fight starting all of this nonsense." Felinis thought aloud before gaping at me, astonished. "You tested others first to ensure they could survive the process, thus paving the way for Princess Quazar to gain abilities also!"

"That is none of your business! What happens between me and Daddy stays between me and Daddy," I scoffed, feeling insulted. "Besides, it'll be a while before they completely adapt to me anyways."

"So, you admit it!" Felinis pointed with her claw.

"I also used Princess Quazar's powers for additional projects. In return, she was granted with twice as much." Daddy smiled.

"But why did everyone else's activate sooner?" Gaako asked.

"Because Daddy gave me the most," I sneered. "And you should be so jealous! After all, that makes me his strongest creation!"

"Not at the moment," he taunted with a challenge.

"What happened to the people you drained?" the giant puppy said. "Did you rob them of their only chance to fight back?"

"They lived," Daddy explained. "Most of the time. I didn't relieve all their abilities. Just the amount I needed."

"And the clones?"

"See that!" I pointed to the mess of the ruined doppelgangers already melted. "The phantomessence clones were temporary, prompting Daddy to create the robotic vessels that he later used on the C.O.R.E."

"And the clones were made to cover victims of your conspiracies, like Tesla here," Gaako said. "None of us witnessed her death, yet she reeks of phantomessence, and she's been competing in a few other contests herself. So to anyone on the outside, she never really died."

"Absolutely. Imagine the irony if she were to win!"

"Don't you think someone would've eventually found out?" Kat asked.

"They seldom do," Tourniquet commented.

"That means you and I," Gaako began, turning to BlackByrd, "never actually fought. You were here, weren't you?"

"Yes," he said, still tending to Looney Luda. "They took me when I was with Candice. We've never crossed paths. What was that strange place anyways?"

"Daddy made that pretty little realm to extract you all at the same time." I laughed.

"Additionally, the clones," Fern said, motioning to the melted masses of her friends, "Must have indicated they were next. They would replace them while the real ones had their powers extracted. But if we were already in that process, where's our clones?"

"We had a change of plans, but it looked like everything worked out for the best!" I explained. "Although we meant to capture them, Jak'al and Kat stupidly left you. The clones then lured Cyclone, who stupidly left you. Forcing him to call Jared, who stupidly left you. And so, stupid you was left alone. We just took you instead!"

"Hold on," Gaako continued with a glint of hopefulness in his voice. "Does all this clone stuff mean some of our friends are still alive?"

"You killed them all on your own." I killed his glint. Can't have any of that nonsense going around!

"You're leaving something out!" Jared caught on.

"Hmm?" I hummed.

"You captured super-powered individuals and gave their skills to others. But you haven't yet mentioned the exact process. How did that happen?"

"Why don't we just show you?" I asked, pressing a switch. The room shook a bit as a glass chamber raised and latched in place. "Our secret weapon," I sneered. The prisoner's limbs were locked, and the untampered green phantomessence filled the basin of the containment.

"Mantis?" Felinis and Chaos cried out. From their expressions, it looked like their whole world had ended, but it hadn't—at least not yet.

Upon hearing his name, his eyes shot open like a wild animal's. They were small. Full of insanity. Delicious.

"Blood was right!" Chaos cried. "I didn't believe him at first, but he claimed the witch's hourglass held the truth. It was Blood's dying wish for me to find you!"

"And I couldn't have done a better job, without your help!" Jexter giggled, bowing toward Mantis as though he'd just finished some grand performance.

"How did I help?" Mantis hissed groggily.

"I was talking to the extraction chamber, Peanut!"

"Locust used to have hair and huge muscles," I cut in. "A real ladies' man. But when he fell trying to save Felinis from Korax, we injected the tampered black phantomessence to assist his robotic mobility, forming Mantis."

"You mean he used to be human?" Jared asked.

"Used to be," Mantis groaned. "Yes."

"But upon discovering his rebellion, I decided to take those powers back. He was a simple prototype after all," Daddy finished.

"A prototype of what? The Cyborg Centurions and Krow Specters?" Felinis deduced. "Which I can only assume are Tah'leets forced to attack their own Inigmus C.O.R.E. solely for wanting to retrieve their captured citizens."

"Yes sir-ee!" The jester explained with dramatic gestures. "Tourniquet arrived at their departments as a spokesperson for change, showcasing Mantis, when he was actually pointing a gun to their face!" He gestured a finger gun to his own cranium. "He knew they would immediately say no, but that cover story simply masked the attack! And to top it all off, he did it in disguise so they would never find him!"

"Korax also confirmed that to me during our conversation," Fern told Felinis. "Some are soldiers. Others are additional competitors, as well as the powered-phantomessence itself. Korax was far advanced because nothing controlled him other than the ooze itself, encased in a robotic vessel. With the koimirium and phantomessence combined, Tourniquet created artificial life."

"Artificial life is still dead; and it's too bad our evidence died in the Arakna Pit," Gaako told Fern. "You were all at the infirmary. There's no way you could've known."

"Actually, we came here looking for him. Good thing too, otherwise, we couldn't have saved you." Said Cyclone before he stopped. "Wait, does that mean the Tah'leet Soldiers were attacking their own homes?" We nodded. "Why didn't they stop?"

"They couldn't." Daddy paused before snapping his fingers and saying. "Observe." This sent Looney into a sudden fit of rage. She pushed BlackByrd away and yanked out her electric crescent daggers, ready to fight him on a whim.

"You brainwashed them," the wind boy breathed.

"Which begs the question..." an invisible voice rang out. A small flame appeared and morphed into an angel that floated in the middle of the room. "A question that remains unanswered. The contests were originally designed for the victor to save your home world, Tourniquet?"

"Hot Stuff! Have you come for your aforementioned hug? You're centuries late though," Jexter laughed, reaching out like a child.

She ignored him, unsheathed her sword, and pointed it at Daddy. "I am Deena, an angel of the Lord. The one has come to smite you."

"He's already smitten," I yelled, flipping my pink hair, "with me!"

"Home world?" Jexter asked, turning to Daddy. "You don't have a home world!"

"Reyes is my home world, fool," Tourniquet snapped at him.

"A lie," Deena stated. "We've been present on Reyes the entire time. Centuries later—as the harlequin observed. Only the kingdom has passed."

"Jexter," Jared addressed. "Didn't you also mention during the kingdom days that a man promised you eternal life?"

"Yes, that was Eka—"

"Like the name of the island," Kat interrupted.

"No," Deena spoke. "The island is Reyes."

"Can you all shut up so I can get back to my story?" Kat made a face as he continued. "Eka forged a mask to hide from his brother, and then he disappeared into the sea. But when he resurfaced, Eka built a kingdom reigning at a distance."

"I thought you said there was a king," Jared replied.

"Even kings have hidden rulers, Giggles, now listen up. Afterward, Eka brought thousands from all around to compete in brutal competitions, and then he renamed himself."

"How does any of this relate to us killing each other?" Fern started up again. "And how do we fit into this?"

"None of you do. He does." Daddy said, eyes blazing at Jared. "Had I known our relation, I would've lured you here like everyone else, but in a cruel and convenient twist of fate, the five of you were well on your way. Centuries upon centuries of bloodlust has fed my purpose: to extinguish the very fires of good my twin could ever conjure. He stole my bride from me. She belonged to me."

"According to the legend, Iro didn't take Hira Conte' from you," Jared replied. "You took her from him, Eka, Brother of Darkness!"

"Listen once, all of you." Daddy roared as some stared at him in awe. I did too! "I am Eka. After claiming sanctuary in Reyes, I renamed it and myself, seeking to end Iro's lineage of good by creating the contests. I lured people from the mainlands, hoping their heroism proved that they were his final descendant. When I realized reliving the past wasn't enough, I decided that the future was my last resort. Hurricane and Fever introduced the untampered green formula that I forged competitors' abilities into, thus creating black phantomessence. Experiments were performed on participants of the target program to ensure Princess Quazar's safety. Furthermore, Jexter allowed us to discover the dream hacking effect—the centipedes—that entered your minds, evaluating your traits. If we liked them, we took them and left clones to hinder suspicion. At that point, I focused on punishing the Inigmus C.O.R.E. with machines. All the while, all of you fought for the glorious reward of your heart's desire and to save a planet that never existed. But you—Jared—are the last of that bloodline. You are Iro's final direct descendant."

Jared turned to Deena, who returned a subtle nod.

"Now it makes sense," He said. "For centuries you failed to follow what you promised yourself so long ago, killing countless innocents in the process!" He screamed in realization. "You made the contests to get back at your brother for the sin you committed! And your grudge will not be satiated today!"

"And behold, here you stand before me," Tourniquet replied. "I assure you. This will be worth the wait!"

His pointed sword flew toward Jared, who dashed away just in time.

"I was disappointed to see you weren't dead during my big reveal," I told Mantis. "Time to take the last of those powers back!" I buzzed toward his containment as he screamed.

"Don't you dare do this!"

"I'm doin' this for you, sweetie!" I told Daddy, who was watching.

Then Chaos stood in front of me and wouldn't budge. I questioned his action and was about to slap him, when he caught my wrist and headbutted me.

"OW!" I stumbled, nearly falling off the walkway. "Excuse me, who's side are you on?"

"The surviving one," he stated. "Mantis, Felinis, and I are leaving."

"Yeah, that worked out so well for you the last time!" I said sarcastically as I took flight and shoved my heels into his abdomen before knocking him away and forming magenta quasar orbs. "Good thing I did my nails today." I blasted them at the group as the ground exploded in multiple spots. Mantis' screams filled the container as I pressed a switch.

He thrashed just as giant needle-like things stabbed into the same holes they had penetrated so many times earlier. A colored aura flooded the glass imprisonment, mixing with the darkening ooze below. Phantomessence!

"We've got to get him out of there, now!" the puppy exclaimed to his team over my orbs raining down on them.

"Sick 'em, Jexter!" I demanded.

"No one's going anywhere!" Jexter sneered while Isabelle hurriedly blocked Jak'al's path. Felinis stepped by his side.

"I've about had enough of you two," she said. Isabelle's spear thrusted at her. A metal coating immediately covered Felinis while the spear's tip sparked off her. Then she blasted magma into Isabelle's shield, which just barely missed Jexter as he flipped toward Jak'al, kicking wildly.

Chaos stood back up. Instantly, his back curved as he grabbed his head coated in a telepathic cloud, screaming. Music to my ears.

"If you choose not to fight for me, then I will *make* you fight for me," Daddy said before turning to our real allies. "The same goes for the lot of you. GO!" Viper rushed to his twin, Rust, while Tesla exchanged blows between Kat and Fern. Cyclone took to Captain Red Blood, and Gaako fought Enrage, leaving BlackByrd with Looney Luda. Twenty of us total. They all looked like they would tear each other to bits like little chew toys. The thought of the carnage made me lick my lips. How exhilarating!

"Resist, Chaos!" Deena ordered, hovering his way.

"I-I can't!" he said, shaking his giant saber. "C-C-Chaos Wind!" She flew backward, but the gusts proved too much for her and sent her crashing into some of the robotic bodies on the walls.

I smiled as Jared flew at me from behind, giant beams blasting out of his eyes and obliterating chunks of the wall and robots. I grunted and lifted off the walkway, throwing numerous quasar orbs at him. He sped forward, pinning me against the wall. What fun! I forced him away with a swift heel jab to the stomach. The side of my hand chopped the back of his neck. His elbow whirled upward as he used my body to bulldoze a crevice in the wall. I was dazed for two seconds when he moved over me and blasted red hot beams into my torso, making it sizzle and pop. My body flew heavily toward the ground before I caught flight and buzzed upside down over the other fights.

I leveled my flight path then stopped buzzing long enough to slice a "V" shape in the air, sending a pair of huge rays engulfing the area around him, all while swerving to miss his incoming attack. I faced forward, buzzing around the robotic vessels still hanging up. My energized nails grazed more suits as I flew past them, sending dismembered mechanic limbs smacking Jared's face. Then I released sonic waves of nebula rays at him. He tried to dodge them, but the bright pink energy zapped through his body, making him spiral out of the air. I chuckled evilly, but he managed to freeze a portion of my shoulder blade with white frost. I shrieked, my vocal chords vibrating hysterically before smacking into the floor. I buzzed to my feet, then inspected a chip of my upper right wing to see it flaking off!

Jared wiped blood off his smirk as my eyes bored into the very depths of his soul!

"Now," I whispered. "I really am going to kill you!"

I buzzed his way, my orbs forming into flaming spheres while I threw them into his next steps. While in the air, I spun my left calf into his face and used my other foot to trap his neck between my heels. He flew to his feet as I kept my arms to my side, burning spheres as I spun toward him. I hovered into a cartwheel, aimed my back toward the ceiling, and sent several rapid kicks into his torso. Then I buzzed behind him and repeated the move on his back. Finally, I faced him and blasted nebula rays that caused his body to skid across the floor.

"Leave him to me," Daddy said, returning to fight Jared. What a doll!

"Alright!" I smiled, turning to a yell. It was the plant girl. Maybe she wanted to go back to the infirmary. Her fist headed toward me, caging a pollen spore to amplify her pulverizing punch. I lunged to dodge, spun backward, and made her fumble by sweeping her legs with my heel. My next stinger heel came down, missing her by inches as she rolled backward onto her feet and took a stance.

"Can't you tell Tourniquet's just using you?" she asked.

"We all have a part to play!"

"And clearly your priorities lie elsewhere," she commented, provoking me to attack. I buzzed toward her as her wrist flew an inch past my nose. I dodged in the nick of time. I planted my hand for balance as an actual plant coiled around my wrist. My mouth dropped open as another root caught my opposite ankle, locking me in an uncomfortable, twisted position. She jumped and landed a foot into me as I collapsed, groaning heavily. With a motion of her hands, the roots dragged me along the floor and threw me into the air. I flipped, then shot quasar orbs at her, but they disappeared into larger vines. Fury filled me as I flew at her, only to be swatted down by an overgrown plant she just summoned.

"You couldn't fight without those, can you?" I taunted, referring to her plants while wiping dirt off my arms and face. We tried to ignore the pain, but knew it was impossible. Both of us grew weaker and tiresome. We couldn't keep it up forever, could we?

"Jealous you couldn't take them the first time? Or that you're losing?"

"I don't have time for this!" I backhanded her just before entering a hover after smacking the other side of her face. Symmetry! I fluidly rolled sideways into her while in the air before my legs slammed her. I launched off her arched back and blasted her. "You were saying?"

CHAPTER TWENTY-ONE

Fern's eyes flashed a bright green as thousands of plants burst through the laboratory floor at once. A shadow overcame my expression as the vines increased in height. I took to the air long enough to escape her flying vegetation. Her pollen spores blazed at me as I caught them in a backfire portal. They reappeared behind her, scorching her back before I shot blue energized nebula rays at her, but her cunning roots restrained my limbs. I writhed to escape. She lifted me higher into the air as I zapped two quasar orbs at her. They exploded on impact, but that didn't faze her. Her hair whipped around and body floated in the air. How did she suddenly obtain aerial powers?

Suddenly, all manner of flora burst through the walls of the quaking laboratory. All the other battles stopped as everyone set their sights to Fern, who was slowly becoming encased in a cocoon—supported by her own pillar of greenery. The roots at the base slithered deep underneath our steps, yet still caused the floor to buckle open. Ivy climbed up the walls and vines coiled through the machines that hadn't fallen during Jared and mine's flight.

The head of her spreading plant growth stretched into the upper walkway before mercilessly plowing through the mountain peak itself. The twisted walkway was only one of many falling objects prompting everyone to take cover. Hopefully some would be squished like flies!

In a matter of seconds I flew up to survey the land. More roots snaked through the battlefields and even to other neighboring islands. The blood hearth where Modos had summoned Isabelle at the Hanara Amphitheatre was buried under the massive greenery. It coated the already-corroded castle ruins and limited the air supply of the any living organisms that could have been inside the beach caves. The weeds trailed off into the ocean water, through sleeping quarters, and coiled up the courtyard fountain. The same green blanketed the naturally leafy areas like the woods and Library of Plants. The island was covered in the biggest jungle I'd ever seen.

Daddy let out a whole-hearted chuckle. I got goosebumps as our eyes met. I knew what would happen next. I was forced to remind myself that his ultimate plan was already in the works. I glanced to the shattered glass chamber to see Mantis crawling weakly along the rupturing floor. I knew trusting my lover was my only option, but my heart kept choking at the very thought of it. Could I take a risk like that or not? Suddenly I looked down to even more goosebumps!

Name: Tourniquet
Weapons: ???
Powers: ???
Power Type: ???

CHAPTER TWENTY-TWO: TOURNIQUET

S ince the beginning, my eyes have witnessed the truth of the world. Purposeless, loveless, and lifeless. I was quite aware of all the chaos my existence erupted. How could I not be proud of my doings? I have feared but once in my life, but was never ashamed or even held the slightest hint of remorse. Though my sins were many, I regretted nothing. If not, then I would have stopped by now, wouldn't I? Nothing is bigger than me. Nothing is stronger than me. I am perfection incarnate—and my plan was just beginning.

The bursting stalk stretching from the middle of the laboratory left little room inside, forcing everyone to fight on the mountain's exterior. As soon as we stood, Jared and I stared at each other for a while.

"Spawn of my beloved brother, Iro," I mocked. "You are his most valuable treasure. But how is it you were not aware of your true identity?"

An otherworldly fury overcame him. Shadows covered Jared's face as his eyes cut at me. His chest and shoulders heaved as his heart pounded furiously. Sweat rolling off his complexion as his blood boiled. And we've barely even fought.

"That's none of your concern."

"I can't help but find it interesting," I smirked. "In fact, none of you discovered that until now. How disappointing. After all of my wiles, nothing seemed to bring you here. But fate had another plan, didn't she?

He just gritted his teeth, deeper shadows etched into his face.

"No matter." While gripping my golden sword with my left hand, I raised it, then glided my right palm down the length of its flat side. "Soon all of you will join the darkness that submits to my dominion." I shot forward, jousting with all my might as he dodged. With his head still down, his right arm automatically knocked my left. His head angled upward ever so slightly revealing a pair of burning red eyes. "That's nothing new." My eyes ignited flames too.

He ignored me, our eyes red with fire as I parried his charging attack. He blasted combinations of his hot and cold abilities, as I swatted them away. Once I proved too slow and received a giant heat blast to the face as he hovered, then pummeled me until my blade slashed his chest. He exclaimed in pain as something caught his attention.

"FERN!" Jared cried.

"Ah, yes," I taunted. "How could we forget about our precious flower?" His ally floated stories above the room we previously fought, entranced by her own abilities. Her canopy of vines grew more, forming a sanctuary for her body, which was already inside a plant-forged cocoon. Jared broke into flight as I snatched his cape. It tightened around his neck as his body stopped in midair. I smirked and threw him to my opposite side.

He landed in a hover and sent beams at me from his eyes, which I deflected. They exploded into the surrounding mountain, forming several smoking craters beneath our steps.

"This fight is between us," I barked, "and escape is not an option! I have waited my entire life for this, and you will see it through! Your death demands it!"

"Don't I get a say in this?"

I pointed my saber at him and rushed, a wind behind me. I swung, but he blocked as sparks flew off his wrist guards. He stepped backward, doing all in his power not to slip and lose balance. But that wouldn't stop me. I was not a devotee of mercy.

"You're implying, after all these years, that I was Iro's only descendant?" he insisted.

"The only one to reach the island, yes!" My saber cut his chest once again and I kicked him to his back. I raised the sword over my head, readying to deliver the final blow. "And the only one needed to fall at my hand!" It soared downward, but he moved. My sword stabbed deep in the mountain as he hovered and spun, kicking the side of my face. I stumbled, but was caught in a series of cold jabs. Then I summoned a greenish aura coating my own fist and plowed his chest above his heart. Immediately, his heartbeat slowed. His adrenaline sluggishly disappeared and became my own.

"What?" He muttered as his heart and body betrayed itself. He fell feebly at my side. I chuckled, lifted my leg, and stomped his back, sending him back inside the mountain everyone previously fought on, continuing our deadly battle.

Smoke billowed off Jared's body as he fell toward the laboratory's floor. While above him, I flung my sword. It spun elliptically, passed him, and I caught it after reappearing behind him from a pillar of smoke. I thrusted both feet into him, kicking him upward, and then reappeared at his side before kicking him outside the mountain wall. He shook off his daze and tackled me, plowing beside the hole I had knocked him through. He flew me toward the opposite mountain wall while ignoring my heavy punches to his shoulders and back. I thrusted my fist at his heart, stealing his adrenaline again, and wrapped my thick arms around his neck. Then I shoved his head into the wall. While still strangling him, Jared managed to bend his neck and back awkwardly, allowing him to kick off the wall for thrust, dragging me down toward the floor with him and leaving a red-and-blue aerial streak trailing behind.

Finally, I released Jared and flew around the giant stalk erupting from the floor. My sword cut its side harshly as I turned, preparing for his oncoming attack. Just as I suspected, Jared appeared into my line of sight as he slammed into my outstretched arm. The impact spun me. He gained momentum at the base of the regenerating stalk, leaving a colored streak spiraling up it before shooting into me, sending us back outside.

The other battles also intensified. I could feast off all their pain for decades. Pain is quite a delicacy, however, an acidic one. The more you delight in someone else's pain, the more it consumes—ultimately leaving one empty and unfulfilled. At least until the desire grows to cause more pain. Or until I place that similar thought of bloodlust into someone else.

**

Still under my influence, Chaos placed the recently appeared angel, Deena, in a headlock. She headbutted him and used her flaming hair to cook his face behind his helmet. He stumbled, but managed to stop her fire sword with his own weapon. They pushed them together and switched places, then rushed to each other.

"Live to your reputation, not your name, Chaos," Deena began. "Resist your master's commands and devise your own." Chaos struck her sword as she kneeled, whipping hers around, protecting herself from the hit. The impact made her slide back as dust flew beneath her boots. "You believed your actions were of no avail, but your cohorts await before your very eyes."

"Tourniquet…" Chaos struggled. "Is too…strong. His grasp on my soul…is too much!" A spark off Deena's hair was sliced by his Chaos Sword as she sidestepped. Her flaming wings flared through him multiple times as she spun. She gripped his wrist with her right hand and yanked him forward. Deena slammed her left elbow into his left skull shoulder pad, breaking it while dislocating his shoulder. Her glowing palm met the forehead of his helmet as both of their eyes glowed while she purged him of my hold.

"Your mind and body are healed. Now hasten yourself!" she cried. "Lead the way as I heal your comrade."

Gaako's spear sliced upward, then sideways past Enrage's face. He ran, shooting short spurts of energy out of his fingertips while Gaako spun his weapon, blocking all but the final two. He gritted his teeth and straightened his stance. Enrage roared and summoned a pair of rapidly spinning blood sabers that struck the lance various times, forcing Gaako to defend himself. Sparks flew off their weaponry before Enrage's blood sabers sliced the wind above Gaako's head. Gaako thrusted backward while steadied on his spear, flipping away from the attacks. He landed on a knee, rolled to Enrage's blind spot, placed him in a lock, and reextended his spear against his neck.

CHAPTER TWENTY-TWO

Enrage clasped the staff and sent red marks up it, scorching Gaako's palms. Instantly, he dropped it, and Enrage knocked it farther away. When he turned, he surveyed the vacant air, realizing his rival had gone invisible. He turned to the automatically raising spear and stretched a mark across the ground. Gaako reappeared while launching himself forward in an aerial kick. Enrage's mark lifted, shifting into a blazing wall that burned Gaako. He rolled, stifling the flames, and stood, glaring at Enrage.

They stared, then charged. Gaako stabbed the mountain and hurled pieces of it at Enrage, who obliterated them with his beams before leaping off the last one and flying toward him. Enrage kicked off Gaako's staff, rolled in the air, and wrapped hot beams around his neck before slamming him down. Enrage stomped Gaako's face as it bled delightfully. The tightening beams singed Gaako's neck as it coiled one end of the lance, disappearing the length of Enrage's arm. He restrained energy igniting his other fingertip, readying his final shot. However, Gaako refused to release the spear, the remnant of his dear friend, and reminder that he deserved this.

"Do it!" he consented weakly. "Nothing's waiting for me out there."

"What are you talking about?" Enrage yelled, the Australian's words reminding him of his own target, Settris.

"I don't want to live another second knowing what I did. To everyone." He explained, peering through bloodshot eyes. "You'd be doing me a favor. You don't even have to feel bad about it! I've caused so much loss already."

His beams retracted into the markings of his pitch-colored arms. "Then I refuse to continue, with your loss. It seems we have much more pressing matters." He motioned to my dear

Quazar speeding at Mantis, who was being healed by Deena. Chaos stepped in front of her once more.

"Not again!" she cursed.

"Tourniquet's reign is over," Enrage told Gaako.

"Now we fight for redemption," he responded, standing.

"Agreed," he said. "That is all that remains."

With their weapons ready, they charged past the other battles, avoiding intersecting attacks, to Princess Quazar. Chaos knocked her backward as she turned to duck both sides of Gaako's lance. She backflipped and smacked Enrage's wrists away to avoid his blood sabers. She fell to her side, slid her feet between his, and rolled, sending her heel into the top of his sharp-boned head. She flew straight up while spinning her body and sent quasar orbs at the men. When she landed at a distance she was unsuspectingly rammed by Chaos.

"Attack a girl while she's down," she complained, covered in dust and sweat. "Sure! You're chivalrous!" She hovered and stood, hailing reinforcements. Captain Red Blood and Tesla's fight moved as they answered her call.

"The area isn't safe for him! We need to move!" Deena ordered Gaako and Enrage, regarding Mantis.

"Go on!" Cyclone answered, running up with Katherine beside him. "We've got this."

"Redemption, right?" Gaako reminded a worrisome Enrage. Both assisted Deena and Mantis to a safer location, that is, assuming one remained. Chaos prepared his weapon. Cyclone brought his hands back, forming gusts. Katherine's guns whirled in her grasp as she reloaded them. Princess Quazar's orbs burned brightly. Captain Red Blood tossed his ruby-encrusted cutlass. Tesla charged electricity from her daggers. All six advanced, switching fight partners every few seconds, moving fluidly to the next.

Katherine's string of bullets soared to Princess Quazar as she moved. Cyclone used his winds to redirect them until Captain Red Blood stomped his face. Chaos' sword met the pirate's as he forced it downward and spun, elbowing him. He staggered and looked down to see the double barrels of Katherine's pistol. Her non-lethal bullet smacked his forehead as she flipped, kicking him away, and then flew backward from a blue bolt. More bolts emitting Tesla's daggers whipped the area. Cyclone's tempest allowed him to fly over her and enter a series of hits and blocks.

"I can heal him to an extent," Deena informed the others. "But due to his mechanical persona, I require a more technological substance." After her words, Tesla landed harshly from Cyclone's wind current. Her body started to melt in several spots. Turning to Tesla, she remarked, "You should do perfectly."

Tesla looked at her in confusion as Deena opened her hand, making her melting vessel glow brightly. She screamed as her phantomessence clone slithered through the cracks of Mantis' mechanical body, her lightning sparking as his systems reenergized and hummed to life. Tesla's former allies barely even noticed—or cared—about her abrupt disappearance.

"Rest," Deena ordered Mantis, then turned to her assistants. "We must remain. I require you to defend me while I complete healing his human half." They nodded.

***

Jared and I continued trading blows. Just as he gained the strength to deliver a stronger hit, I would simply relieve him of it and happily deliver it with my own attack. My fist approached his heart as he froze it between his palms with a spiked ice patch. He glared at me, realizing how I managed to utilize his own stamina against him. I pushed Jared down as he broke off a lengthy spike off the ice patch he summoned. My sword whirled overhead, then pulverized his spike and maneuvered around it. I flung Jared into the air, inadvertently allowing him to grip my torso and slam me against the mountain. Upon recovering, I advanced, roaring madly, and chopped the length of his spike until he ran out of weapon. He soared away.

"You must be proud," I taunted. "You've lost most of your friends, and soon you're going to lose the remaining. I presume that makes us equals."

"Shut up!" Jared protested, clearly offended. "I'm nothing like you!"

"That's what they all say."

He amplified the icy shards of his severed spike and sent them flying. I stabbed my sword into the mountain, bracing myself as several penetrated my armor. Before I could evaluate his next attack, he tackled me into the air, threw me back down, and stomped the bare mountain as I teleported. The dust settled as Jared looked around. My saber landed behind him and I punched him in the air and caught his throat.

"You act like you've lost so much," Jared struggled, his legs twitching. "Pretending you're the victim, when you did all the taking yourself!"

I chuckled until tears formed. "One day you will understand. You will watch the world corrode before your eyes along with everyone you've ever known," I analyzed his features, and reflected on our duel thus far. "Actually, perhaps we are nothing alike." His eyes burned red with hate. "Ah, was it something I said?"

CHAPTER TWENTY-TWO

Without warning, we sped to the skies, leaving a ring of dust below. He flipped, kicking me. Once I stopped, my arm circled the air, summoning pieces of the crumbled laboratory mass below. With an upward thrust of my hand the whole room shook even more. Ground wires of computers and pipes hidden underneath the floor were ripped from their roots and soared to Jared along with the darkness of looming clouds encompassing us. His beams lit up the sky, desecrating the rubble masked in darkness as I suddenly appeared in front of him. The tip of my sword penetrated the side of his lower abdomen, and he screamed horribly.

***

Meanwhile, cradled in her fortress of plants, Fern flinched, turning slightly to the direction of our echoing battle.

***

With my saber protruding out of him, I kicked Jared across the blackening sky then re-formed, digging it up his side and leaving a repulsive gash. Lightning struck between us. Jared avoided it, distancing himself, and winced as he used his heat vision to melt his own skin and glue the wound shut. I directed more pillars of dark energy his way before throwing my saber and plunging it between his eyes—or so I hoped. Unfortunately, he moved just in time. My adrenaline-draining punch soared at him as he flew behind, bending my arm up the length of my back, then ramming his elbow into it. He then faced me, delivering quick frozen punches to my head until finally blasting me out of the sky.

TOURNIQUET

He watched as I collapsed through the mountain, falling at the base of the stalk once more. Then Jared turned his sights toward Fern and valiantly dashed to her aid. I stood, cracking my heavy bones under the weight of my armor, then concocted a brilliant idea while studying the large plant specimen.

***

On the mountain's surface, Rust's amber-ice missed a dodging Viper, who shot a fanged arrow into his knee. Rust winced, reaching for it, as Viper yanked himself forward using the connected soul link and flipped, kicking him into the air.

"Serpent Soul!" he beckoned his signature serpent spirit. Its fangs pierced Rust and shoved him to the mountain. After it evaporated, Viper shot more arrows at Rust from above. He froze them in the air and caught Viper's leg.

"After all we've endured, you still believe Tourniquet's word over mine?" Rust began as Viper lifted his other leg and knocked him sideways to the ground.

"I don't believe him *over* you." He landed as his serpent soul reappeared, slithering behind an unsuspecting Rust. "I only believed him and *never* you." The snake lunged, coiling Rust's body, snapping at him.

"I regret," Rust said, keeping the creature at bay. "Saving you as I did. Putting your life before mine oftentimes, including when Jahil Kambhu ordered your execution! I'm thankful we no longer look nothing alike. Now I get to kill you twice!" His eyes glowed the same shade as the aura flowing around his body. "Rust Tiger!"

Currents of aura morphed into a massive tiger, towering over Viper's snake. It stomped the snake's body, hindering its escape, and clamped its razor teeth into the neck, mercilessly tearing it apart. The apparition disintegrated as Viper grabbed his burning heart. The tiger trotted toward Viper as he panicked, aiming a fist full of arrows. Rust ran up the tail of his familiar and leaped off his head, both of them roaring as the surrounding air manifested into his hammer, which pulverized his twin's throbbing chest. The mountain shuddered, exploding from the immense pressure their abilities offered.

Rust breathed heavily, sweat coating his brow. "Face it, brother," he said, as the tiger nudged for attention. "All you have fought for is moot. You may return to my side when you have forfeited that lie."

***

Felinis and Jak'al were in perfect synchronization as they fought Isabelle and Jexter. Felinis delivered a swift claw smack to Isabelle's shield before Jexter jumped off of it and landed both feet into Jak'al. His legs wrapped around the jackal-man's broad shoulders and he rode him down until cartwheeling away.

"You should leave this traitor for us to tear apart, piece by piece, whisker by whisker!" Jexter hissed, referring to Felinis.

"Trying it will leave you a bloody mess!" Jak'al snarled. The harlequin gasped, pressing his hands to his chest dramatically.

"You affronted me! Nobody affronts me!" His fist landed into a handstand as his legs spun, kicking toward the creature, who punched him beside Isabelle. "You know, we should fight together more often," he suggested, making conversation with her.

"Oh, we will," Isabelle commented, sending her spear at my former high servant. Felinis disarmed her, swept her leg under Isabelle's, then shot a dripping stream of magma. Her shield took most of the impact while her spear rebirthed from her blood cape. She charged into the air and spun vertically above the magma as her visor sent blazing beams at Felinis, obliterating the mountain. Upon landing on the shaking ground, the tigress creature's fists plowed into Isabelle along with her knee after grabbing the spear again. Isabelle stuck the spear in the bend of Felinis' knee and knocked her to her back.

Felinis yanked Isabelle into a kick, flipping to her feet, and unleashed a magma stream trailing her steps. Jexter threw off his mask as his tongue flopped out of his mouth and snatched Felinis' wrists, aiming her magma at Jak'al. Upon recovering, Jak'al ran up to them. Felinis spun sideways in the air to avoid Isabelle's spear again, earning more beams from her visor. Felinis landed, ducking backward while Jexter balanced on her throat to leap at Jak'al.

***

Their fight progressed while my son simultaneously struggled against the young woman I stole from him. He wished not to fight her, but I gave him no choice. Instead, he attempted to speak her to sanity. How cute. But his words made no difference. She was gone. She was mine.

Luda's crescent-shaped daggers clashed with BlackByrd's magic. She smiled evilly, attacking uncontrollably and showing no sign of resistance.

"Candice," he continued, restraining her wrists. "This isn't like you!" She kicked his stomach. BlackByrd then shielded his path with dark pillars that she weaved through, cutting them fiercely. Her midnight hair followed each of her movements until a force field manifested, stopping her. She banged against it, screaming in frustration.

CHAPTER TWENTY-TWO

If it wasn't for my magnificent mind-wiping ability, then she would have sooner exposed the truth of my origins, being from earth rather than the home planet everyone believed they were fighting for. In return for her discovery, I relieved her of speech. Luda understood the world, but now she had to relearn how to communicate in it. At the moment, her survival instincts were her prime motivation. In her eyes, my son was a threat. In mine, he was neither threat nor son.

Her forehead pressed the edge of the force field once she stopped slicing it. She panted heavily.

"I'm sorry," BlackByrd said, releasing the barrier. "But I won't fight you. We've lost enough already." Her body whipped around and her dagger pierced his ankle. He fell, and her boot slammed his face. She pinned him to the ground, pounded his face and chest, before stabbing his sides and electrocuting him. BlackByrd winced until finally pulling her head into his, knocking her unconscious.

***

Jared flew up the growing vegetation, hoping his friend was alright despite the circumstances. Atop the stalk, she awaited, centered in her temple of green. This time there were no devices attached from Hurricane and Fever. Fern had lost control without any amplification, and clearly stronger than she ever was. Would all the plantation disappear upon her death? I was excited to test that theory. Once he leveled himself to the head of the stalk, my saber plunged through its floor. Jared gaped at me, realizing I had traversed the stalk's entirety to reach the top for what I anticipated would be my final attack. Jared's eyes were empty of the fire that used to emblazon them along with all manner of hope.

TOURNIQUET

I leaped out of the leafy fortress and flew toward Jared, my cape billowing like a flag proclaiming victory. More lightning engulfed our aerial match, illuminating the black clouds as my saber raised, coiling the bolt itself into my grasp. I threw my saber point-first into the ground as the immense bolt burned the palms of my hands, reddening them severely. Jared stared at me, flying backward toward the rest of our mountainous battlefield. It was the perfect spot to defeat this pathetic human and destroy Iro's bloodline once and for all! I persevered against the lightning's voltage, roaring over the thunderous claps, and forced my arms to swing the bolt. Jared altered his flight trajectory to evade the lightning trailing spastically in multiple directions until zapping his right eye and plowing him into a growing crater.

I re-formed at my saber, unleashing the bolt and blinding everyone. When our vision returned, they gasped, seeing Jared's body convulsing profoundly. He combated the sensation and eventually stood upright, body smoldering. He looked up at me. The right side of his face bleeding, scorched, and skin puckering from the shock. His hand opened, emitting a soothing gust of ice that covered it with a white layer of frost.

The fire in my eyes burned even brighter than earlier as I growled and gritted my teeth. Oh, how hard I gritted my teeth as they unsheathed from the gums of my mouth, raining down in front of me. Princess Quazar stepped forward, staring with concern. Every battle ceased.

"You think you can stop *me*?" I yelled over the thunder rolling overhead, stretching across the entire sky. My knuckles dislocated from the rest of my widening hands as I fell to my knees. My muscles and sinews swelled and sewed into a greater form. "Do you not consider the depths of time which I have been exposed to? That I have witnessed firsthand?" My limbs shuddered, regenerating the size of logs. My human skull shifted upward, breaking out of its barrier of skin and hair to become a crown surrounded by horns. "I am of a race far superior than yours, both cursed and privileged with overseeing the conception of reality as you know it. I have channeled the darkness I was charged to serve—and now, I have become it."

My insignificant human vessel had fully transformed into a horned, fire-eyed, armored alpha pit wolf. Beneath my tattered cape was a golden barbed tail extending from the rest of my black body and matching my lengthened claws. I thrusted forward, and howled. Anyone who heard it—friend and foe—their remaining energy disappeared and entered mine. All had braced themselves and tried to ignore it, but they could not.

"Jared!" Deena cried, reaching out to him. "Take my hand!"

"NO!" I roared, rushing up to them. But it was too late. The angel was the key to his access of a portion of my brother's powers. She had been waiting patiently on the island in secrecy, waiting for that specific person—just as I had, but for entirely different reasons. Her own flames started to dim. To think that this boy arrived on accident, and now he gained a segment of a millennia's worth of powers with a mere clasping of hands? It could not be happening. It should not be happening. A stroke of fear caressed my conscious. I immediately disregarded it, forcing it away. I have feared but once in my life, and there was no reason to revive that emotion.

Fortunately, Jared's body was still broken. It wouldn't be long until I completed that breaking process. He faced me. Beacons of light shone, consecutively growing at his sides like rays of angelic wings.

"The power of my brother. First family. First foe," my voice echoed across our battlefield. "How long it's been. I will think of him while killing you." I was inspired with my lust for carnage. We flew.

Streaks of white and gold from Jared's laser-like lights painted the sky behind him. Parts of the mountain lay ruined beneath my steps due to my massive claws. I dropped my sword, catching the handle between my teeth, and charged by his side. He stumbled involuntarily, grabbing for the bleeding hit. My claws scraped the mountain, readying to rush past his opposite side when he dodged. I stabbed my saber in the ground and proceeded to slice my golden claws at him, salivating horridly.

When an opening appeared, Jared flipped, kicking me into the air, and burning me with a whirring light connected to his leg. Apparently, Iro's shining lights flowed with each of his movements. Then I discovered they had also replaced his elemental abilities. Instead of heat vision, a golden blast emitted. Had he lost control in the same manner as his partner? Though Iro's power was currently housed inside him, I would ensure it would be short-lived.

I reappeared on the ground behind Jared, retrieved my sword, and swung viciously. His laser wings shielded him as my barbed tail pierced his shoulder. He grimaced painfully, kicking the empty air, as I lifted him and leaped, pulling my knee into his head. My saber plunged downward as he flew to the side, stood upright, and sent a golden beam from his palms, making smoke roll off the mountain. I grunted, rolling along the ground, and caught my sword in my mouth again before running up to him. I punched his chin, sending him upward, and sliced my saber circularly as he landed against it, receiving several cuts. I moved, then flashed human long enough to deliver a few more hits before spinning my cape, reassuming my alpha pit-wolf form and trotting away.

CHAPTER TWENTY-TWO

Jared charged, stopping directly in front of me before spinning vertically, his hysterically beaming lights leaving smoldering gashes in my flesh. Bits of blackened armor clanged onto the ground. With both arms in front of him, Jared plowed into me, flying merely inches over the mountain. I rolled him under me and dug a trench with his body while pressing his shoulders. We landed, crashing along the surface and gaining a great distance from the other.

***

The weak Deena still sadly attempted to heal Mantis. She had foolishly exhausted herself when transferring Iro's powers to Jared. How she had obtained it, I was unaware. Gaako and Enrage stood by protecting her, yet they could hardly protect themselves when my Angels of Anarchy finally regained some of their strength. Jexter and Isabelle forced themselves to their feet, glaring at Felinis and Jak'al. Rust sat on his knees, panting in front of the unconscious Viper, as BlackByrd did the same over Luda. Cyclone, Katherine, and Chaos prepared against Captain Red Blood and Princess Quazar, who stared at our extensive battle.

***

We charged. He dodged under my right swiping claw and shot my chest with a beam before punching my chin upward. My jaws chomped his wrist. I flung him to the opposite side and stomped him. He flipped to his feet. My saber aimed at Jared's throat as I rushed. He moved, burning me with more lights. This continued—endlessly, it seemed. Fighting from air to ground, then leaving gigantic trails of crumbled mountain in our wake.

It was a miracle that any of it remained. Finally, I re-formed human and concocted another brilliant idea. I rushed straight up into the air, summoning the surrounding darkness. The shadows of objects retracted, slithering into the sky and forming a colossal cloud around me. The skies ravaged like never before, other clouds assumed the shape of famished wolves. I was above Jared. In every way. Momentarily, Iro's lights would be snuffed out. I laughed over the darkening scene, the power enhancing my forces beyond their limits and to the peak of their abilities.

"Choose, descendant of Iro," I tested. I motioned to Fern trapped in the stalk, then to everyone remaining below, fighting for their lives. I opened my hand, creating a diamond forged from the souls of slain enemies. I was reminded of how many as it grew in size before compacting to the stature of a miniature coin. "Death Diamond."

I peered down at him before my eyes shrank. His were open. Locked on me as he evaded my attack. Neither filled with grief, nor anger. Not rage. N-n-not f-f-fear. Light. Light. Light, light, light, light, light! He looked just like him! My twin! My enemy! My greatest rival!

"I am Tourniquet," I said, raising higher before my worthy adversary. "I am Eka. Brother of Darkness." I intended to show him—let him feel everything. All would perish. All would fall. His world will would become mine as the lights in his eyes— the lights of my brother's—disappear. Forever. *"You will know my legacy!"*

He continued. With all his light—I mean—might! His body glowing. *His* body burning. *His* body stopping in front of mine. With his feet together, pointing straight down, he opened his arms wide, unleashing Iro's light in one overwhelming move. Instantly, they exploded, sending huge shockwaves across the land and purging the darkness. A beam protruded from the heavens, scorching my body and plunged me into a deep crater.

"Daddy!" my pink-haired princess screamed, hovering to me. Jared landed heavily beside me, vision blurry and stumbling. He stepped over me and pulled my neck closer. My laugh was cut short by coughing.

"What's so funny?" He barked with his fist pulled back.

"You—" I began. "Chose wisely." He dropped me as I continued chuckling. "Iro's light may have suppressed my darkness, but you—" I coughed. "Looked away." His eyes widened. Immediately, his neck whipped around to everyone behind him. Jared growled at me, then flew toward the Death Diamond heading straight at everyone on the mountain as Princess Quazar stepped beside me.

"MOVE!" Jared screamed desperately, tears streaming off his face. Ah, yes. That was the look I was waiting for. His friends were frozen, clinging to one another, awaiting their inevitable end.

All of them were injured to some degree. Hurt. Physically and mentally. I prepared the situation of the competitions for everyone. And there was no escape except through death itself. A fate many others had already encountered. A reality that made my heart pulse with excitement, knowing I brought these people here. Or that I planned to for centuries. I proudly claimed responsibility for all their losses. I was held liable for every teardrop, every droplet of blood. For watching their glimpses of hope flutter away in the ashes of misery which they belonged, engulfed by despair. I was the one who gripped their hearts, wrenching them, ever so slowly until just the right moment to yank it through their ribs and laugh as the debris of their worlds collapsed around them.

Jared pressed himself. But he was too slow. Enrage pushed through the group as they gaped at him. As soon as he stood in front, he screamed, opening his arms as my power collided with his. Fool.

Then I realized what he was doing. I took his humanity and created a demon that unleashed rage. Now he channeled the demonic side to become a human that absorbed it. He betrayed his own abilities—the abilities I placed inside him. His device did not keep him a monster; it disguised him as a human. The human I stole. What inside him could possibly compete against me? How did he obtain this newly found strength?

The blackness peeled off his body as he returned to his original skin tone, the red marks flaring like the sun as he absorbed the impact. Sweat covered his shaking form as he turned to Jared.

"GET FERN," he yelled. "THE IMPACT! IT'S YOUR ONLY CHANCE!" Jared followed his order and immediately directed himself to her a second time. Enrage kept my power at bay while Princess Quazar kept me company, spectating from the side.

"Fern!" Jared's voice cracked as his boots firmly pressed the floor of roots and leaves, landing into the head of the stalk. He was secretly praying I would not reappear for an additional surprise attack. Her hair wisped inside the semi-transparent cocoon as a green mist filled the air. Aside from her plants, she seemed dead, lacking any sign of awareness of what befell around her. Jared lowered his guard as a vine cracked his face, making it sting. Another snatched his ankle, nearly causing him to slip out of the plant mass.

"Fern! If you can hear me, please…stop!"

A heat spore blasted him back as his fingers dug between the roots. Jared persevered, crawling to her as thorny vines wrapped his limbs and neck. When he finally reached the edge of the girl's growing cocoon, Jared pulled himself up, cautiously trying to keep the vines enclosed in his grasp as his muscles strained against his own dead weight.

"We're the 5X!" Jared reminded, voice quaking from the thorns. "We're not leaving without you. *I'm* not leaving without you." His hand grazed her containment. "Now come out of there and fight! I know you can!" The vines tightened, dragging him backward as his eyes became bloodshot. His arms flailed, tearing them as twice as many replaced them. "All this time, you could never fully control your powers. But there's nothing stopping you now," he pleaded, bringing himself closer, determined to save her. His blood flow was becoming hindered by the vines. *"FIGHT!"*

His words flowed through her being. Her sight returned to normalcy.

"Jared?" Fern asked tearfully. "Jared?"

"Yes, I'm here," he answered. "I always was." Her plant cell released her as she heaved forward, dropping to Jared's feet as the vines shriveled. She sobbed heavily as he kneeled, brushing her hair out of her face. The pair locked their sights at one another as her arms flung around him as he embraced her back. A perfect smile shone at her, attached to a dusty, brutalized complexion including a wounded eye, gashes, and dust. They pushed their dry, parched lips into each other.

***

A flash of green filled the sky, creating shockwaves on the island, even rippling the mountain and ocean. Jared and Fern exited the stalk as the impact of my power surged through

Enrage. My diamond vanished inside him. His arms flopped inanimately. Sweat dripped off his brow. Enrage fell. Katherine's eyes widened in fear. Her head threw back and she unleashed a gut-wrenching scream. But nothing came out. Or maybe it did. Maybe the deafening roar of events suppressed it. The man she once hated now laid his head in her lap. Her tears fell to his face. Why was she crying? I chuckled at my dear Enrage who had earned his fate. Did he really believe he could escape? Turning back was no option. He entrusted me to save his father if he successfully killed his assigned target—Katherine's cousin. With magic, I liberated his father from sickness. With magic, I replaced that sickness with a broken heart. A self-made outcast who became a cursed murderer. I was simply relieving my makeshift demon from his wretched anguish and indulging in their pain.

"Why?" Katherine asked weakly.

"Settris would have done the same," Enrage muttered. "She taught me so much; more than I could ever know. And what it means," he turned to Cyclone. "To lay one's life down—for their friends."

"Don't say that!" Cyclone spat. "We can save you!" They couldn't save him. "Where's Deena?" They looked frantically to the fiery angel who had all but died out. She couldn't save him. "Somebody!" But all were too weak. None could save him. His decision had been made. Thanks to me.

"God can," Enrage said.

"What?" Katherine asked.

"I know Settris believed in Him," he continued. "There's no coming out of this for me. The hit would have killed us all—and it now burns inside me. Let me go. Let me die. It's the only way I can be with her in peace, forever."

"No, stay with us!" Cyclone protested. "You're too close to the end."

"Much closer than you think."

"You're going to make it off this island alive! Along with the rest of us!"

"Thank you. Both of you. But we all know that's a lie. Tell me…" Enrage breathed. "Does Jesus love me? Does Jesus really care?"

Their hearts fell. They were at a momentary loss for words. Taken aback by his statement. But his eyes, beaming with solemnity. No. I took his humanity. I stole his dignity! His soul was mine! Mine for the taking! I refused to leave the world alone. I lived for the extermination of hopes and dreams. He would not escape my grasp!

"Of course he does," a manifesting figment said. They turned to a glowing, transparent Settris.

"Connie?" Kat asked with tears, the pair hugged as the light shone.

"No!" I cried from afar. "I'm stronger than you! You will not take more from me!"

"The choice is not yours, Eka," Settris responded. "It is his. You have put this young man through enough hell. Now he chooses to overcome it, thus overcoming you and all your malevolent forces. You may have been the Brother of Darkness, but he has called upon a force far greater than any to take him home. The true Light of the World."

"I am not against his soul's salvation," Katherine exclaimed, turning to Enrage. "But I can't just sit here and watch you die!"

"That was not your earlier concern!" I shouted.

374

"That was before we spoke!" she yelled. "I don't understand, and maybe I'm not meant to. You did all for your father. Connie did all for me, and I know how much I would do for her. Tourniquet blackmailed you, as well as everyone else. I wish circumstances were different. I truly am sorry."

"Our time grows short," Settris mentioned as Katherine turned.

"You will leave us again?"

"Unfortunately, yes. But you already knew that," Settris sighed, grabbing her dear cousin's hand. "You also know, that we will always be together. We have so much family waiting on the other side, and Anton and I will be waiting for you. All of you," she informed the 5X. "Well, will we?" she turned to Enrage.

"Yes," he replied. "I don't want this life. I refuse to be in Tourniquet's control. Another friend encouraged that we now fight for redemption," He turned to Gaako, who shed tears. "I want exactly that. I want Jesus Christ."

"There's no turning back," Settris reminded, raising a brow.

"I wouldn't have it any other way," Enrage said.

"Me either," she smiled. "All have sinned and come short of God's glory. Salvation is but a prayer away. The prayer of a repentant heart wanting to change. Do you wish to change, to believe, sweet Anton?"

"This path is far greater than where I've been." He sighed heavily as the poisons ran through him. "I have sinned. A lot. I don't want to remember. What I've done—what I've seen. I may not be bigger than my mistakes, but You are, Lord." Apparently, he had already begun praying. Although forgiveness was something I never offered. "You gave all, for others and for me. Your Son, Jesus Christ, portrayed that love on the cross. I always heard about it, but never quite understood. But now I know. You don't care about my past. Only my future. I don't want to die. I don't want to go to Hell. I can't imagine anything worse than what we've been through. God, my hope is in You. Save me, Lord. Change my heart and take my soul. You are the only way. I want to come home. I commit my soul to You, Jesus Christ."

Tears ran down everyone's face. They shook. Some hopeful. Some confused. This was the reality they faced. Perhaps death was not the end. Perhaps...I...was...wrong. Where had all the fallen souls departed? Were they not all under my grasp? Were they not all doomed as my prisoners? Of the island? Like me?

Throughout life, people endlessly search for something. Would salvation satiate that curious passion? I hoped they would search for the end. Of everything. A distressing end to all, especially regarding the island. I thought myself as the deliverer of torment. To constantly take one's life, including the optimism of another's. To drain and decrease the emotions my brother well endued to the world. The light. The light was my goal—my enemy, and thing I wanted to destroy. Any part of Iro's legacy.

"Forgive me," Enrage told everyone. "I wish we had more time." For the first time his tears failed to burn his skin. "It feels so good...to cry. To be freed from this monster." He laughed in praise as a feeling of rest rang through him. He had been purged of all worry. Cleansed from all anxiousness. "Please, don't be upset with me. I'm sorry for everything I put you through. The things I never did. The things I left incomplete." He fell to his knees and screamed as everyone cried even more. *"I'M SORRY!"*

Due to silence, one could hear the tears hitting the ground. The choked stifles. I hated it. They shouldn't cry in hope. They shouldn't cry in joy. They should cry in agony. They should scream in fear. But clearly, my influence had long vanished. It was as if they all had forgotten me.

"For what?" Jared finally asked. Enrage's head twitched upward, looking at him as they smiled. He knew that smile confirmed the serenity between them. Their storm had been silenced. He knew he was truly forgiven. Death has that effect at times. Deena's hand reassuringly caressed Enrage's back once she stepped to him.

"Now is the time," she said, "to escort you into Paradise." Her sword raised, summoning a portal to Heaven. How wretched. I recall seeing it before.

"Dad?" Enrage said, as he ran outside the portal, wrapping his arms around his dear boy. How dare he mock a father's love. Enrage realized his father had died, but all he cared for was that they were reunited in the perfect realm.

"Yes, my son!" he exclaimed, tightening his hug. "Everyone's waiting for you!" Anton's soul faded from his body and formed in front of us before he turned, exchanging final farewells while Settris stepped alongside him, clasping his hand. Soon after, Deena escorted the dead into Heaven as the portal closed behind.

"Carry on, Quazar," I said, gaining my princess' attention. She was still gaping, fascinated by the despicable light. "My will. Take and complete. One day you will know more than I ever have. You remember our conversation."

"Not you too! I'm not ready!" she cried back. "Do you think this is going to be easy for me? How dare you leave me when I need you the most! This is your plan! I don't want you to die! Not now, not *ever*!"

"If I believed otherwise, then I wouldn't have granted you the task."

"How is it all possible?" she asked, referring to death, which slowly increased its grasp on me.

"That boy," I snapped, coughing up blood. "Was from Iro's direct lineage, thus the only with the sole capability of dividing my soul and being, besides my own son."

"I'll kill them both," she hissed.

"As I expected. Make it hurt." I smiled before coughing heavily. She inched closer, about to shed more tears. "Weep not for me, but rather let the world in your reign as it reaches its bitter demise. The time will come when you know what to do. Now take your forces. Proceed to the mainlands."

Princess Quazar lifted her head, surveying the area as her newly appointed Angels of Anarchy stared at her in shock, including the unconscious, now awakening. They knew my plot. Some more than others. They anticipated what was bound to occur; eager to fulfill their roles.

"They'll suspect nothing," I finished.

"Yes," she said, more serious than ever as the wet lines on her face disappeared completely, "Master Tourniquet."

I exhaled, "Farewell…my Princess."

The feeling of death. Dearly granted by my own relative. Not bad. Not bad at all. Or so I thought. Centuries caught up with me in a glimpse. Surely that was not the end. My organs failed. My limbs lost feeling as if each of them were saying goodbye. One by one. An unexpected tint of decay spread across my paling corpse, veins bleeding black, resembling the centipedes of our phantomessence experiments. I was returning to the dust from which I was formed. Lines webbed the roughening, papery skin of my face as it flaked, eventually hollowing itself, collapsing inside my own skull. Fragments of bone and whitened-aged hair scattered amidst my magnificent mind. Now eaten by the same cruel acid of time. The mind conjuring all that transpired on Eka's Island. My island. My home. I felt it. All of it.

"Farewell." Then I died.

Princess Quazar stared in horror before breaking into a devastating wail and throwing herself over my empty armor. I was happy that she remained strong for me. I wished not to see her vexed with loss. I would stay by her side. No matter what. I would ensure her safety. Even in death, I would fight for her.

"F-fall back." She called to the rest of my former group. They knew I was dead. They were gripped with fear, prompting her madness. Princess Quazar's blazing fist soared down, denting my armor. "FALL BACK!"

Viper summoned a new serpent soul to snatch Luda, who slowly returned to consciousness as my son attempted to intervene.

"NO!" BlackByrd yelled as Rust instantaneously yanked him away from the snake's lunge. It slithered around her, then loomed toward its mounting owner. The other Angels of Anarchy followed. All but one.

Isabelle. I was surprised she remained aligned with me the length of the large battle. She knew Jexter killed her while under the impression that I would still grant him eternal life when he failed my first task. Isabelle glared at Princess Quazar as she hovered upward, the snake's head catching underneath her step. Then Princess Quazar eyed Jared. Both groups were forced to retreat. All possible damage had been done…for now.

"So, what does this mean for you?" Felinis asked Isabelle from afar. "You are a worthy adversary and can make a championed ally. It is possible to redeem yourself from Tourniquet's hold."

CHAPTER TWENTY-TWO

"Tell me not what I know, *former* high servant," Isabelle responded. "The master was a trickster whom I will no longer be associated. Neither will your partnership remain."

"Lone wolf then, eh?" Jak'al questioned. "Face it, you have nothing left. Your team is gone. Your master is dead. You're free."

Isabelle turned, beginning to walk away. "That remains to be seen."

Jak'al and Felinis stepped back to the remaining nine. Jared tended to Fern, Cyclone supported a distraught, yet hope-filled Katherine. Gaako walked beside my son who carried their fallen, and rather temporary, friend. The last known brethren assassins, Rust and Chaos, assisted Mantis, who was still adapting to Tesla's electricity.

They traversed cautiously down the side of the mountain opposite from the path that led them to our final battle. None were aware of what awaited them. Perhaps a fate far worse than my competitions? What did they believe remained of the outside world? I had taken everything from them. What could they hope to gain? Their path had led to a collection of Fern's vines floating on the tides, stable enough to cradle their weight.

Although their senses were still numb and mortified by recent events, blinding lights caught their attention. Several covered their eyes in an attempt to examine what new potential threat lay before them. They suffered losses. Their bodies were aching, bones burning, and muscles strained beyond regularity as a dreadful sensation overshadowed the scene. They grimaced as their minds were battered with insecurities. Nothing remained. No trust. No confidence. Not even the slightest care. Not because they were empty. Because they were fearless. If they were destined to be reunited with the dead, they were prepared. Each of them had lost someone. I made sure of that. Each of them had already proven their valor to another. In that was their trust. In that was their confidence. Not so much as in strangers, but in each other.

"Who goes there?" a voice announced through a megaphone. Jared's large group exchanged confused glances as the lights dispersed, revealing many fleets of ships with intricately designed weapons systems and even more hordes of armored reinforcements. They all prepped themselves in case a second battle would ensue. If they were destined to die together, then they would do so fighting together. "We have the island's perimeter surrounded. Come forward with your hands placed in the air. We hail from the Inigmus C.O.R.E."

"You were right, Mantis!" Chaos began rather excitedly. "It is the Tah'leet Soldiers! Here to save their people!"

"Yes, their people," Mantis repeated. "That doesn't include us. Not to mention, they still recognize me as a threat for the master taking me to them."

"No!" he cried. "I will not allow it! Our freedom is merely steps away. We must leave now!"

"We'll resolve that issue as it comes about," Felinis reassured.

"Hold on," Jared started, gaining their attention. "We have no reason to trust them."

"Do you have any better ideas?" BlackByrd mumbled, still holding the lifeless Anton. "It's not like we have much of a choice in the matter."

"Yeah, unless you plan to fly us off one by one, it looks like they're our only chance," Gaako said.

"I'm not saying any of this has been easy," Jared explained. "But doesn't this seem a bit too promising after all we've endured?"

"We just defeated Tourniquet," Fern cut in. "The literal Brother of Darkness himself. If these people pull anything, they're the ones in danger."

"Besides," Rust spoke "You all have gained my respect. I will fight alongside any of you at your behest."

"There's no telling what's out there," Katherine said.

"Don't worry," Jak'al commented. "We're about to find out."

"Anything is better than this," Cyclone remarked. "The future is ours. What do you say, Jared?"

"Let's go."

The group piled onto the flashing boats, careful not to glance a studious eye, to suppress any negative connotation they might receive. Thankfully, all had experienced one of life's finer luxuries—loss. Without it, they could not mature. Inner and outward turmoil would be the motif behind every future decision made between Jared's forces and the Tah'leet Soldiers of the Inigmus C.O.R.E. They all craved peace, yet they actually desired the sweet decadence of loss. Although I was now among the dead, I would do everything to share that feeling. After all, it was my legacy.

***

On the opposite side of the island, thousands of other contenders were ordered into a straight line and brought onto the Tah'leet Soldier's ships. Refugees, and murderers alike. Surely they had some method of separating the wicked from the good. Personally, I hoped they would discover them the hard way. Several were concerned about the number of ships compared to the massive quantity of victims, excluding their own citizens. I do believe this was, by far, the deadliest of past competitions; and for that, I was proud. Fortunately for them, thousands more were likely buried, trapped underneath Fern's growth, be it hidden or dead. Since my beautiful island was too great and perilous, the C.O.R.E. could only attempt rescue all potential survivors. Even in death, I hindered joy for others.

I proved to every single participant of the contests just how difficult I could make their lives. Some believed they had reached the epitome of their despair. They did. That is, until they met me. I removed their earthly possessions. Family members, friends, lovers. Positions of authority, senses of security. No corner was a mystery to me. No shadow lurked without my knowledge of it. Nothing was beyond my reach. My control. Except that one. That simple-minded fool who somehow outsmarted me. Only none of them realized—I had to die.

***

Droplets of blood trailed along the sands, excreting from a billowing liquid cape as the warrior used her spear for balance as grains of sand still entered her visor. The warrior had been walking for hours, nearly scaling the entire island as she had before. She was part of no group. Of that, she was quite certain. Moments later, she reached a familiar opening. A solemn place where a large event occurred several centuries before.

Once she stopped, the sand around her feet shifted behind, stretching and assuming the form of a dark-skinned woman. A witch wearing a black-and-white headpiece decorated with jewels and trinkets. Her dress connected to the ground, allowing her to slide along it rather than step.

"I presume you already know why I'm here," The warrior began.

CHAPTER TWENTY-TWO

The witch replied, "Did you honestly consider I wasn't expecting you?"

"Tell me," the warrior adjusted her visor as their colorless eyes met. The desert wind gently waved her brown hair over her shoulders. "Everything."

Without warning or word, the sorceress raised her hand with palm facing upward as more pillars erupted. They interweaved as the center formed to glass, its entirety catching fire. Past scenes were revealed once the sand swirled from inside.

THE END

ABOUT THE AUTHOR

E ver since childhood, Daniel Allen Dorn dreamed of publishing novels and film-making. The cast introduced in *Rise of Tourniquet* were but a portion of Dorn's vast pool of imaginative characters that had also grown with him.

For more about Daniel Dorn and more sketches of the characters in Rise of Tourniquet, visit riseoftourniquet.com

For more about Rose Pokrywka , visit roseace.com.

www.ingramcontent.com/pod-product-compliance
Lightning Source LLC
Chambersburg PA
CBHW021953120726
47898CB00001BA/160